CLASSIC MONSTERS OF PRE-CODE HORROR COMICS

GHOSTS

EDITED BY STEVE BANES

INTRODUCTION BY JOHN ROZUM

PRODUCED BY CLIZIA GUSSONI

yoe®
BOOKS!

IDW PUBLISHING
SAN DIEGO, CALIFORNIA

Dedicated to my Dad
Stephen John Banes
(August 2nd, 1948 – June 17th, 1973)

And don't miss these two
CLASSIC MONSTERS OF PRE-CODE HORROR COMICS...
and more to come!
Visit YoeBooks.com

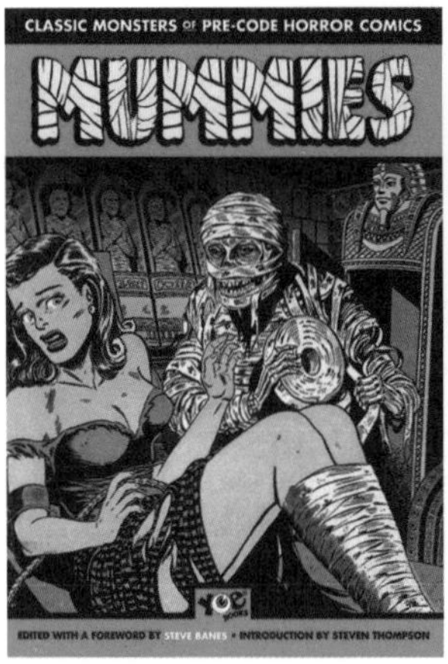
CLASSIC MONSTERS OF PRE-CODE HORROR COMICS
MUMMIES
EDITED WITH A FOREWORD BY STEVE BANES • INTRODUCTION BY STEVEN THOMPSON

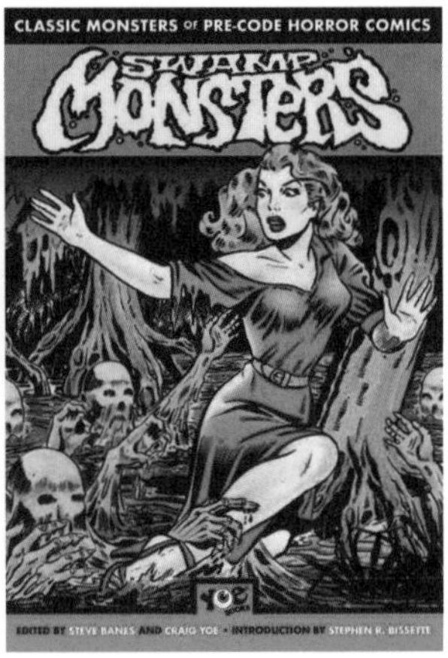
CLASSIC MONSTERS OF PRE-CODE HORROR COMICS
SWAMP MONSTERS
EDITED BY STEVE BANES AND CRAIG YOE • INTRODUCTION BY STEPHEN R. BISSETTE

Steve Banes thanks: Craig 'n Clizia, Mom and Dad, Drazen Kozjan, John Rozum, Mike Howlett, Tommy Stanziola, Thomas O'Brien, Slayla, Pappy, Mr. C, Ben Dickow, Brian Barnes, Donald Brazel and The Record Space, Bryan Reesman, Jim Vadeboncoeur Jr., IDW, CBR, *Famous Monsters*, *Fangoria*, *Rue Morgue*, Rondo Hatton Awards (I never win!), Larry Blamire, all friends and followers of THOIA, and Carol at Crafty Pants Proofing.
For more on grim, grinning GHOSTS, visit a Disney's Haunted Mansion near you!

For more 1950s Pre-Code comic book horrors, visit http://thehorrorsofitall.blogspot.com

Title treatment: Drazen Kozjan.

ISBN: 978-1-68405-549-4
22 21 20 19 1 2 3 4

Yoe Books: Many thanks to Tommy Stanziola.

YoeBooks.com
Craig Yoe & Clizia Gussoni, Chief Executive Officers and Creative Directors • Jeff Trexler, Attorney • Steven Thompson, Publicist

IDW Publishing
Chris Ryall, President, Publisher, & CCO • John Barber, Editor-In-Chief • Cara Morrison, Chief Financial Officer • Matt Ruzicka, Chief Accounting Officer • David Hedgecock, Associate Publisher • Jerry Bennington, VP of New Product Development • Lorelei Bunjes, VP of Digital Services •
Justin Eisinger, Editorial Director, Graphic Novels & Collections • Eric Moss, Senior Director, Licensing and Business Development

Ted Adams and Robbie Robbins, IDW Founders

UNCANNY, SPOOKY, CREEPY TALES

JANUARY

Ghost STORIES

A MACFADDEN PUBLICATION
UNITED STATES 25¢
CANADA 30¢

The Phantom in Armor
"When Ghost Slays Ghost"

"What is a ghost? A tragedy condemned to repeat itself time and again? A moment of pain, perhaps. Something dead which still seems to be alive. An emotion suspended in time. Like a blurred photograph. Like an insect trapped in amber."
—Guillermo Del Toro, Antonio Trashorras, and David Munõz
The Devil's Backbone (2001)

For thousands of years people have believed that a person's spirit exists separately from their body and that upon death, while the body decays, the spirit continues on to some manner of perceived afterlife. This spirit was invisible.

This spirit only became an object of fear when it behaved in an unnatural manner by remaining here in the material world, upsetting the normal order of things. Unlike the spirits that moved on to the afterlife, those that stuck around to strike fear into the living could often be seen in some manner of misty, intangible, physical form; a ghost.

Often thought to be the spirits of deceased people seeking revenge, or trapped on earth for the horrors they committed in their lives, the appearance of a ghost was typically regarded as an omen of death. Perhaps the most famous ghost anchored to the world of the living for his wicked ways is Jacob Marley in Charles Dickens' classic, *A Christmas Carol* (1843). As for ghosts seeking vengeance, we'll get to that.

Dickens' novel was part of a long tradition of telling ghost stories at Christmas. In a culture where ghosts are typically connected with another holiday arriving at the end of October, this may seem a bit odd, but in the dead of winter when darkness prevailed, and all you had were the light of a few candles and a hearth to keep whatever might be lurking in that darkness at bay, it was the perfect way to occupy a cold night while the wind howled outside, and the veil between the living world and the dead seemed most threadbare.

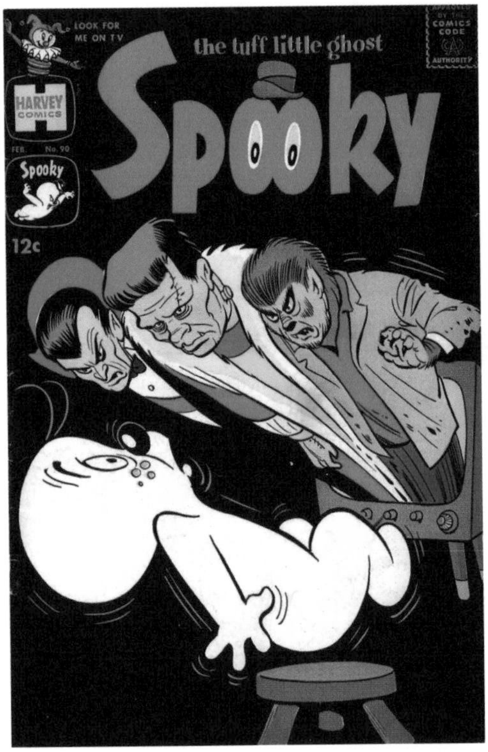
LOOK FOR ME ON TV
the tuff little ghost
Spooky
HARVEY COMICS
FEB. No. 90
Spooky
12c
APPROVED BY THE COMICS CODE AUTHORITY

Ghosts have been a worldwide part of folklore and literature probably since the beginning of storytelling around the fire. Homer alludes to them in both the *Illiad* and the *Odyssey*, but the first real, participating dramatic role performed by a ghost was that of murdered Queen Clytemnestra in *The Eumenides* by Aeschylus written in the 5th century BCE. Her ghost sets the play in motion by pleading with the Furies to rise and revenge her by punishing her son Orestes, who murdered her in the play's prequel.

Typically, if a ghost appeared in a story it was assumed that it was, in fact, the spirit of a dead person. This would change with Shakespeare, who used ghosts in *Hamlet* and *Macbeth* as psychological manifestations meant to showcase and reflect the guilt of the characters who witnessed them, most likely not as actual physical apparitions, but as mental imaginings.

While Horace Walpole invented the gothic tale with his ghost-filled *The Castle of Otranto* back in 1764, the ghost story would reach its height in popularity during the Victorian era, when writers such as Sheridan Le Fanu, M.R. James, Algernon Blackwood, Henry James, and a slew of others would craft some of the finest ghost stories of all time. M.R. James removed the ghost stories from their gothic trappings and historical settings and set them in the contemporary world. This not only made the stories more believable to the reader, but more relatable in the sense that they could more easily imagine such things happening to them.

So what is a ghost? A psychic scar marking the place of a tragic event that happened in the past? A poor soul not realizing that they are dead and should have moved on? A deceased person with unfinished business seeking closure and release? An other-dimensional being entering our world in intangible form? Depending on the needs of the story it could be any of these things.

In the volume you hold, filled with tales culled from obscure horror-themed comic books over half a century old, most of the ghosts fall into the most traditional, and elemental type of fear-inducing ghost; the ghost out for revenge. That revenge comes in many forms, but typically all of those forms are gruesome. There are other types of ghosts too. Like Shakespeare's ghosts, there are specimens that serve as manifestations of a guilty conscience, often happening to also serve as a tool for vengeance. Unlike the ghosts in *A Christmas Carol*, who led Scrooge towards a life-changing revelation, the outcomes

PREVIOUS PAGE *The cover of the January 1928 issue of the pulp magazine,* Ghost Stories, *produced by Macfadden Publications.*

ABOVE Spooky *#90, February 1966, Harvey Comics. Artist unknown.*

RIGHT *The lobby card for the movie* 13 Ghosts *(Columbia, 1960).*

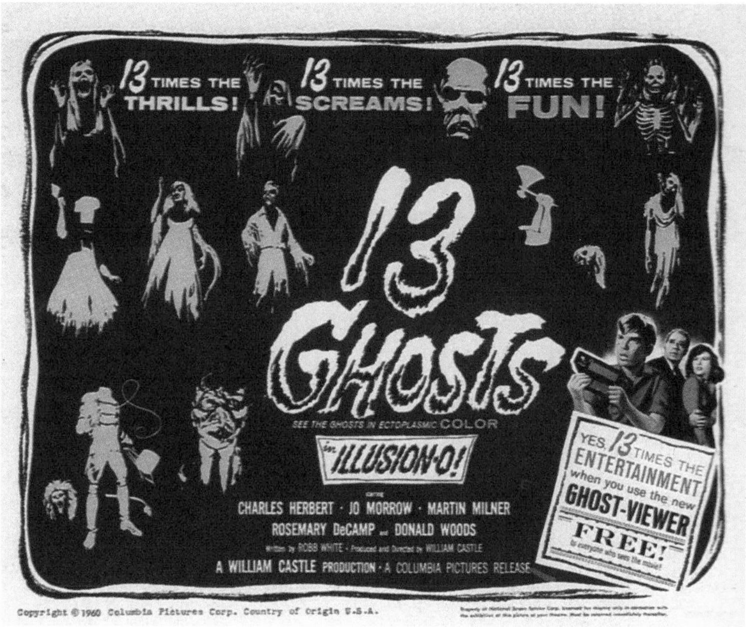
13 TIMES THE THRILLS!
13 TIMES THE SCREAMS!
13 TIMES THE FUN!
13 GHOSTS
SEE THE GHOSTS IN ECTOPLASMIC COLOR
in ILLUSION-O!
CHARLES HERBERT · JO MORROW · MARTIN MILNER
ROSEMARY DeCAMP and DONALD WOODS
A WILLIAM CASTLE PRODUCTION · A COLUMBIA PICTURES RELEASE
YES, 13 TIMES THE ENTERTAINMENT when you use the new GHOST-VIEWER
FREE!
Copyright © 1960 Columbia Pictures Corp. Country of Origin U.S.A.

for the protagonists in these tales tends to be a bit darker.

Unlike most of the ghost stories told in forms of literature not involving panels and word balloons, which tended to concern themselves with the perspective of the living and the effect their encounters with the uncanny had on them, these comic book ghost stories have something unique going on. In most of the stories, the ghost is the central character, and we are given direct insight into their thoughts and feelings, which makes them more human and less other. Being privy to those insights in many cases makes them more horrible than if they appeared as a misty form at the end of a dark hallway.

Ghost stories are perfect for comic book anthologies in the sense that many of these comics featured a host who would introduce the stories. This interaction between host and reader, or storyteller and audience, gives them an aspect much like the members of the Chowder Society in Peter Straub's *Ghost Story* (1979), or the characters in Henry James' *The Turn of the Screw* (1898), who gathered together on cold winter nights to swap tales of ghosts and horrors.

Whether you prefer your ghosts on Christmas or Halloween, one thing is for certain, these stories are best read by candlelight, late at night, with the wind moaning outside and a tree branch tapping at the window.

—John Rozum

John Rozum is a cut paper artist and writer. He is the creator of the critically acclaimed comic book series Xombi *and* Midnight, Mass, *and has also written for* Scooby-Doo, The X-Files, The Hangman, *and* Dexter's Laboratory, *all of which included stories about ghosts. He has also written for* Detective Comics, *various* Superman *titles,* The Powerpuff Girls, *and* The Foundation, *which did not. He is currently developing numerous creator-owned projects in a variety of genres, and yes, ghosts will be involved in some of them. You can find him at http://johnrozum.blogspot.com.*

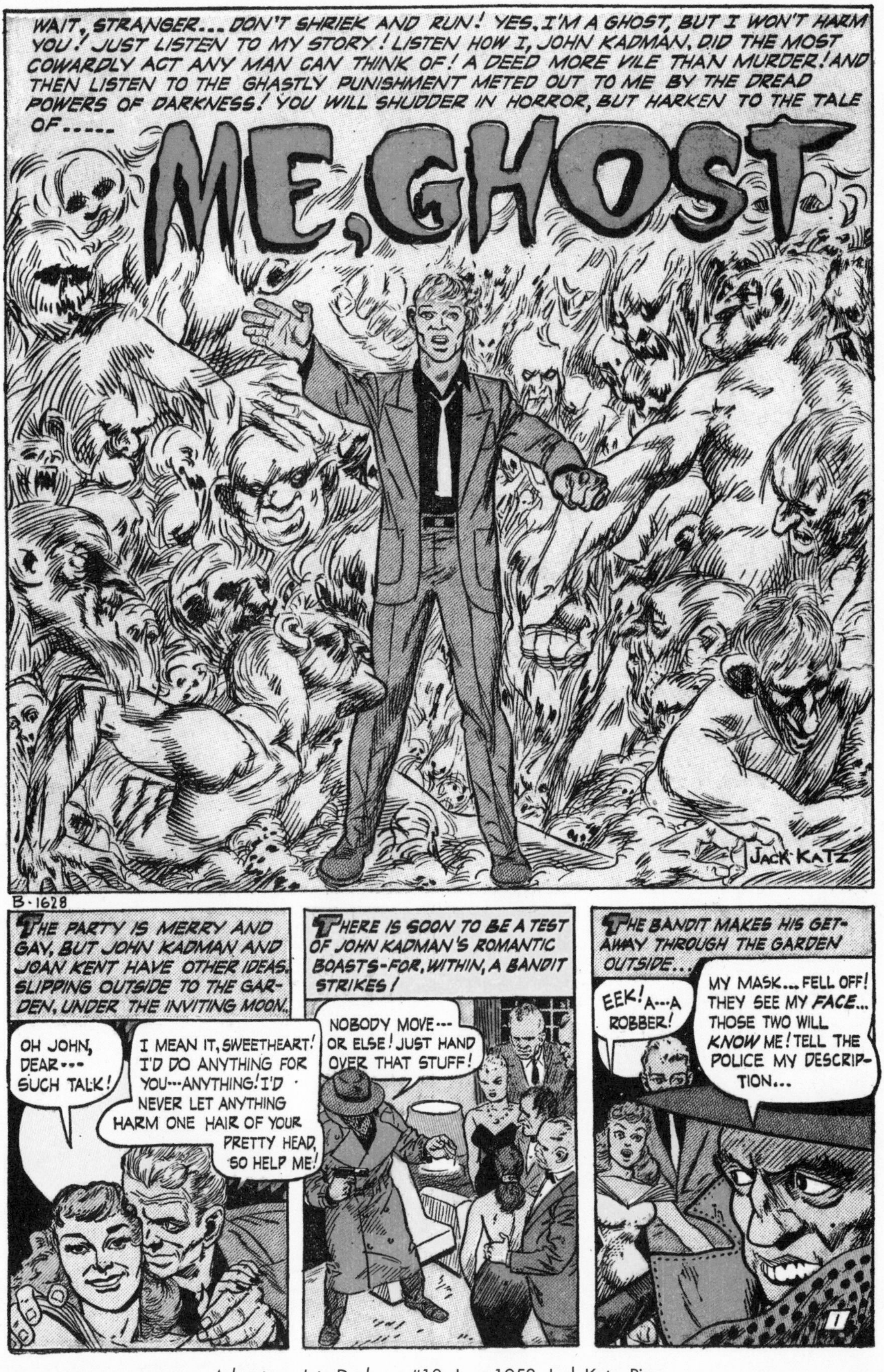
WAIT, STRANGER... DON'T SHRIEK AND RUN! YES, I'M A GHOST, BUT I WON'T HARM YOU! JUST LISTEN TO MY STORY! LISTEN HOW I, JOHN KADMAN, DID THE MOST COWARDLY ACT ANY MAN CAN THINK OF! A DEED MORE VILE THAN MURDER! AND THEN LISTEN TO THE GHASTLY PUNISHMENT METED OUT TO ME BY THE DREAD POWERS OF DARKNESS! YOU WILL SHUDDER IN HORROR, BUT HARKEN TO THE TALE OF.....
ME, GHOST
JACK KATZ
B-1628
THE PARTY IS MERRY AND GAY, BUT JOHN KADMAN AND JOAN KENT HAVE OTHER IDEAS. SLIPPING OUTSIDE TO THE GARDEN, UNDER THE INVITING MOON.
OH JOHN, DEAR--- SUCH TALK!
I MEAN IT, SWEETHEART! I'D DO ANYTHING FOR YOU---ANYTHING! I'D NEVER LET ANYTHING HARM ONE HAIR OF YOUR PRETTY HEAD, SO HELP ME!
THERE IS SOON TO BE A TEST OF JOHN KADMAN'S ROMANTIC BOASTS-FOR, WITHIN, A BANDIT STRIKES!
NOBODY MOVE--- OR ELSE! JUST HAND OVER THAT STUFF!
THE BANDIT MAKES HIS GETAWAY THROUGH THE GARDEN OUTSIDE...
EEK! A---A ROBBER!
MY MASK... FELL OFF! THEY SEE MY FACE... THOSE TWO WILL KNOW ME! TELL THE POLICE MY DESCRIPTION...
1

Adventures Into Darkness #10, June 1953. Jack Katz. Pines.

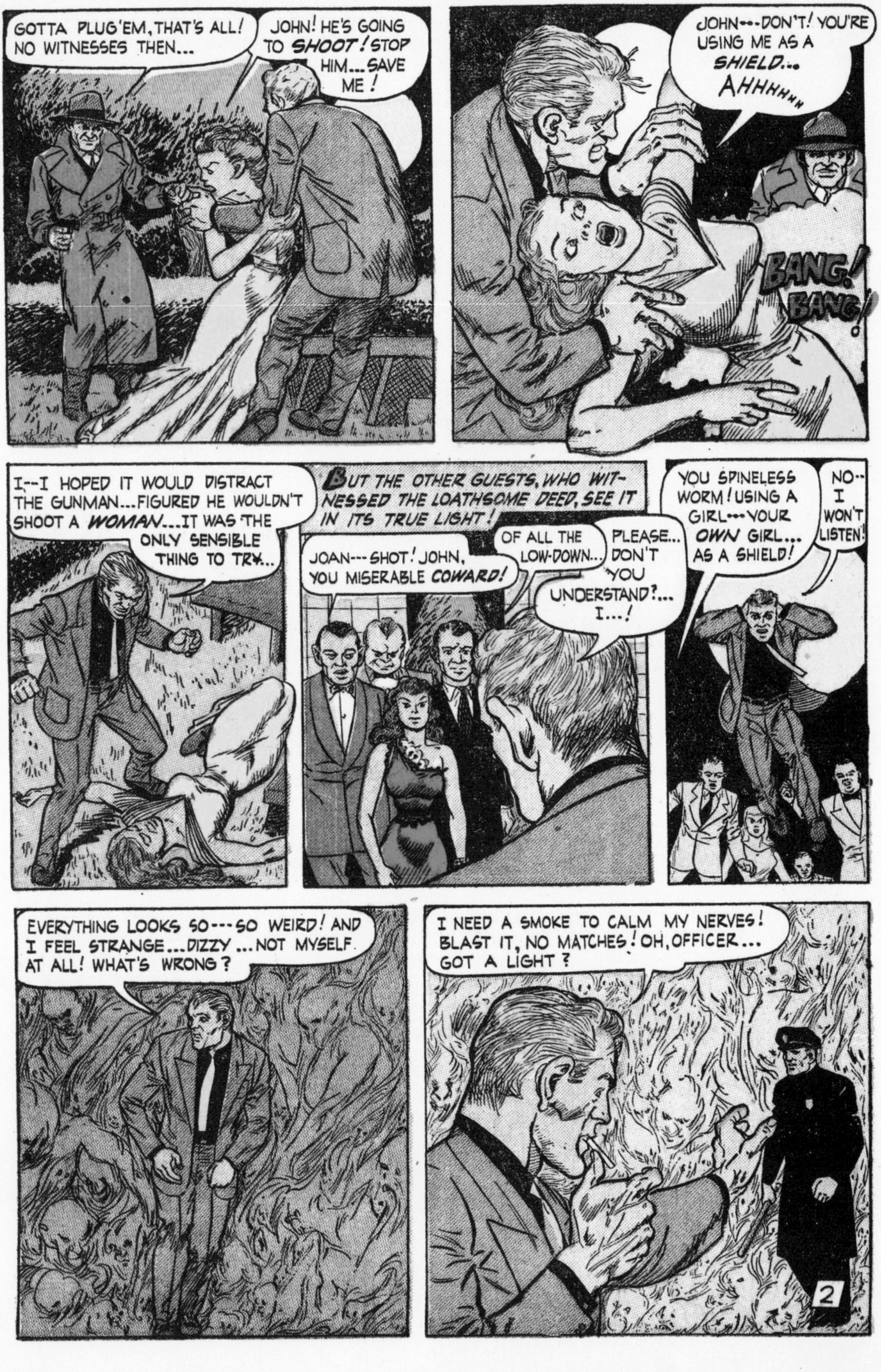
GOTTA PLUG 'EM, THAT'S ALL! NO WITNESSES THEN...
JOHN! HE'S GOING TO SHOOT! STOP HIM... SAVE ME!
JOHN---DON'T! YOU'RE USING ME AS A SHIELD... AHHHHHH
BANG! BANG!
I--I HOPED IT WOULD DISTRACT THE GUNMAN...FIGURED HE WOULDN'T SHOOT A WOMAN...IT WAS THE ONLY SENSIBLE THING TO TRY...
BUT THE OTHER GUESTS, WHO WITNESSED THE LOATHSOME DEED, SEE IT IN ITS TRUE LIGHT!
JOAN---SHOT! JOHN, YOU MISERABLE COWARD!
OF ALL THE LOW-DOWN...
PLEASE... DON'T YOU UNDERSTAND?... I...!
YOU SPINELESS WORM! USING A GIRL---YOUR OWN GIRL... AS A SHIELD!
NO-- I WON'T LISTEN!
EVERYTHING LOOKS SO---SO WEIRD! AND I FEEL STRANGE...DIZZY ...NOT MYSELF AT ALL! WHAT'S WRONG?
I NEED A SMOKE TO CALM MY NERVES! BLAST IT, NO MATCHES! OH, OFFICER... GOT A LIGHT?
2

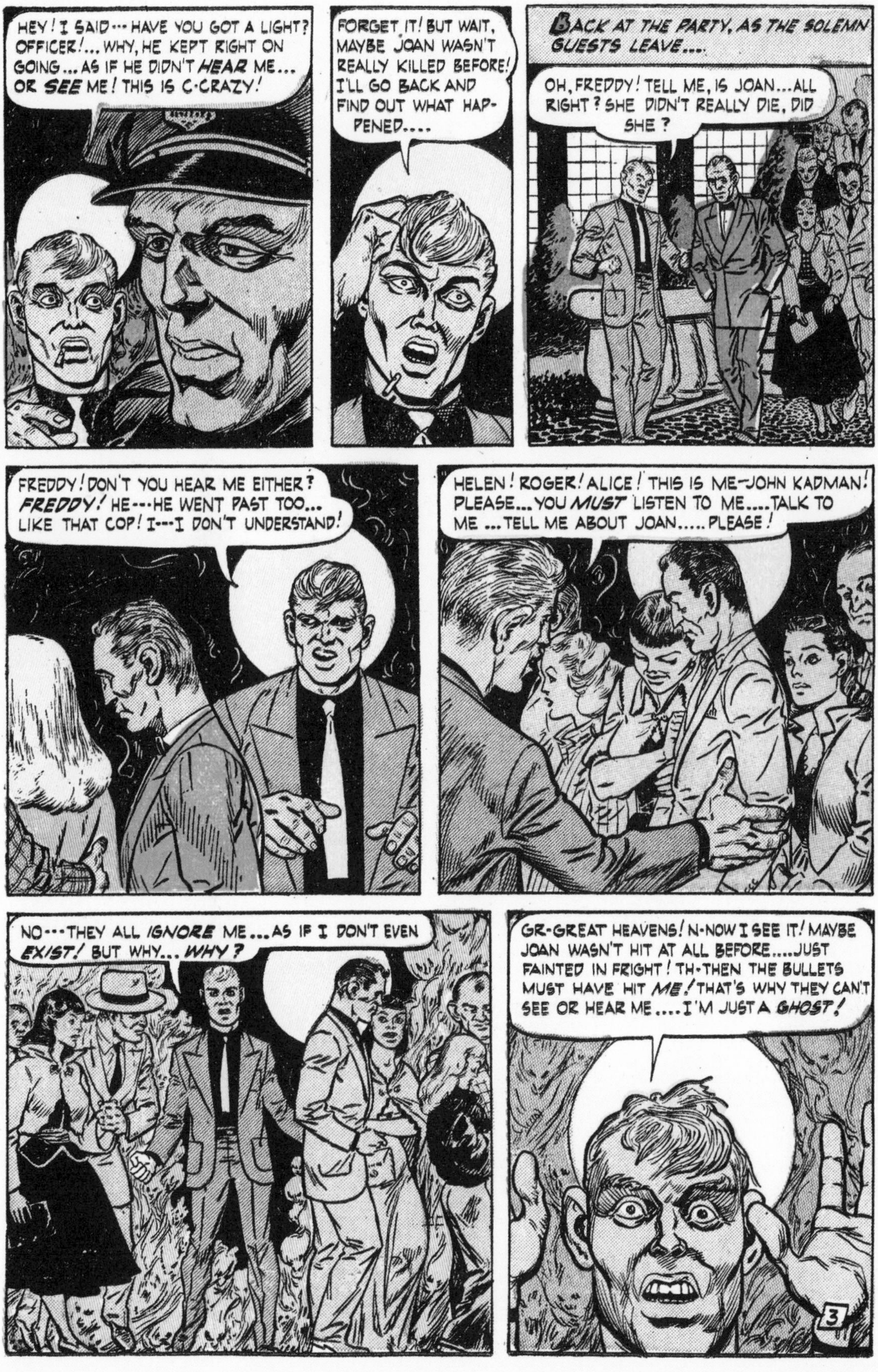
HEY! I SAID--- HAVE YOU GOT A LIGHT? OFFICER!... WHY, HE KEPT RIGHT ON GOING... AS IF HE DIDN'T HEAR ME... OR SEE ME! THIS IS C-CRAZY!
FORGET IT! BUT WAIT, MAYBE JOAN WASN'T REALLY KILLED BEFORE! I'LL GO BACK AND FIND OUT WHAT HAP-PENED....
BACK AT THE PARTY, AS THE SOLEMN GUESTS LEAVE....
OH, FREDDY! TELL ME, IS JOAN... ALL RIGHT? SHE DIDN'T REALLY DIE, DID SHE?
FREDDY! DON'T YOU HEAR ME EITHER? FREDDY! HE---HE WENT PAST TOO... LIKE THAT COP! I---I DON'T UNDERSTAND!
HELEN! ROGER! ALICE! THIS IS ME—JOHN KADMAN! PLEASE... YOU MUST LISTEN TO ME.... TALK TO ME ... TELL ME ABOUT JOAN..... PLEASE!
NO--- THEY ALL IGNORE ME... AS IF I DON'T EVEN EXIST! BUT WHY... WHY?
GR-GREAT HEAVENS! N-NOW I SEE IT! MAYBE JOAN WASN'T HIT AT ALL BEFORE.... JUST FAINTED IN FRIGHT! TH-THEN THE BULLETS MUST HAVE HIT ME! THAT'S WHY THEY CAN'T SEE OR HEAR ME.... I'M JUST A GHOST!
3

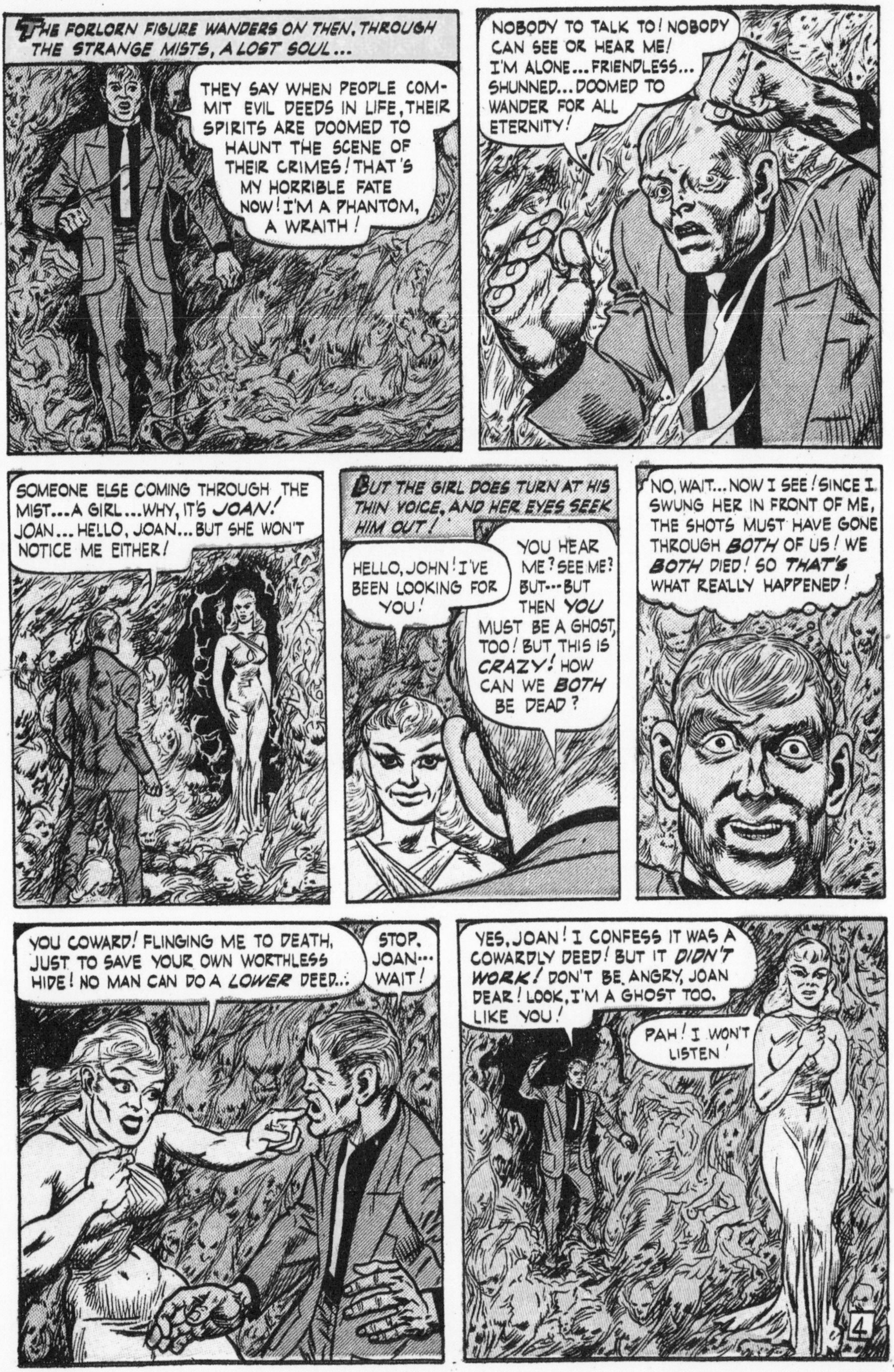
THE FORLORN FIGURE WANDERS ON THEN, THROUGH THE STRANGE MISTS, A LOST SOUL...
THEY SAY WHEN PEOPLE COMMIT EVIL DEEDS IN LIFE, THEIR SPIRITS ARE DOOMED TO HAUNT THE SCENE OF THEIR CRIMES! THAT'S MY HORRIBLE FATE NOW! I'M A PHANTOM, A WRAITH!
NOBODY TO TALK TO! NOBODY CAN SEE OR HEAR ME! I'M ALONE... FRIENDLESS... SHUNNED... DOOMED TO WANDER FOR ALL ETERNITY!
SOMEONE ELSE COMING THROUGH THE MIST... A GIRL... WHY, IT'S JOAN! JOAN... HELLO, JOAN... BUT SHE WON'T NOTICE ME EITHER!
BUT THE GIRL DOES TURN AT HIS THIN VOICE, AND HER EYES SEEK HIM OUT!
HELLO, JOHN! I'VE BEEN LOOKING FOR YOU!
YOU HEAR ME? SEE ME? BUT---BUT THEN YOU MUST BE A GHOST, TOO! BUT THIS IS CRAZY! HOW CAN WE BOTH BE DEAD?
NO, WAIT... NOW I SEE! SINCE I SWUNG HER IN FRONT OF ME, THE SHOTS MUST HAVE GONE THROUGH BOTH OF US! WE BOTH DIED! SO THAT'S WHAT REALLY HAPPENED!
YOU COWARD! FLINGING ME TO DEATH, JUST TO SAVE YOUR OWN WORTHLESS HIDE! NO MAN CAN DO A LOWER DEED...
STOP, JOAN... WAIT!
YES, JOAN! I CONFESS IT WAS A COWARDLY DEED! BUT IT DIDN'T WORK! DON'T BE ANGRY, JOAN DEAR! LOOK, I'M A GHOST TOO, LIKE YOU!
PAH! I WON'T LISTEN!
4

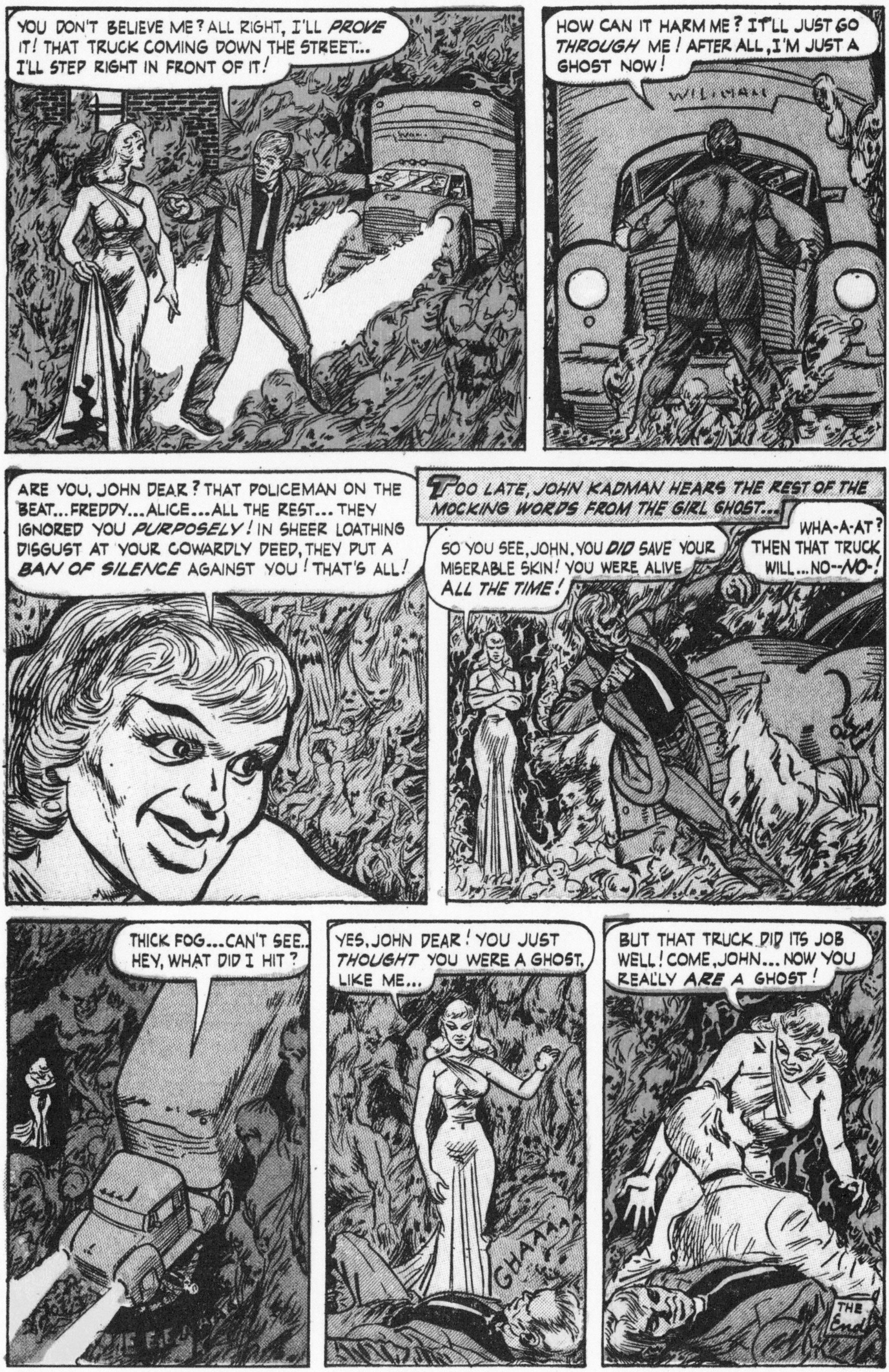
YOU DON'T BELIEVE ME? ALL RIGHT, I'LL PROVE IT! THAT TRUCK COMING DOWN THE STREET... I'LL STEP RIGHT IN FRONT OF IT!
HOW CAN IT HARM ME? IT'LL JUST GO THROUGH ME! AFTER ALL, I'M JUST A GHOST NOW!
ARE YOU, JOHN DEAR? THAT POLICEMAN ON THE BEAT... FREDDY... ALICE... ALL THE REST... THEY IGNORED YOU PURPOSELY! IN SHEER LOATHING DISGUST AT YOUR COWARDLY DEED, THEY PUT A BAN OF SILENCE AGAINST YOU! THAT'S ALL!
TOO LATE, JOHN KADMAN HEARS THE REST OF THE MOCKING WORDS FROM THE GIRL GHOST...
SO YOU SEE, JOHN, YOU DID SAVE YOUR MISERABLE SKIN! YOU WERE ALIVE ALL THE TIME!
WHA-A-AT? THEN THAT TRUCK WILL... NO--NO-!
THICK FOG... CAN'T SEE.. HEY, WHAT DID I HIT?
YES, JOHN DEAR! YOU JUST THOUGHT YOU WERE A GHOST, LIKE ME...
BUT THAT TRUCK DID ITS JOB WELL! COME, JOHN... NOW YOU REALLY ARE A GHOST!
THE End

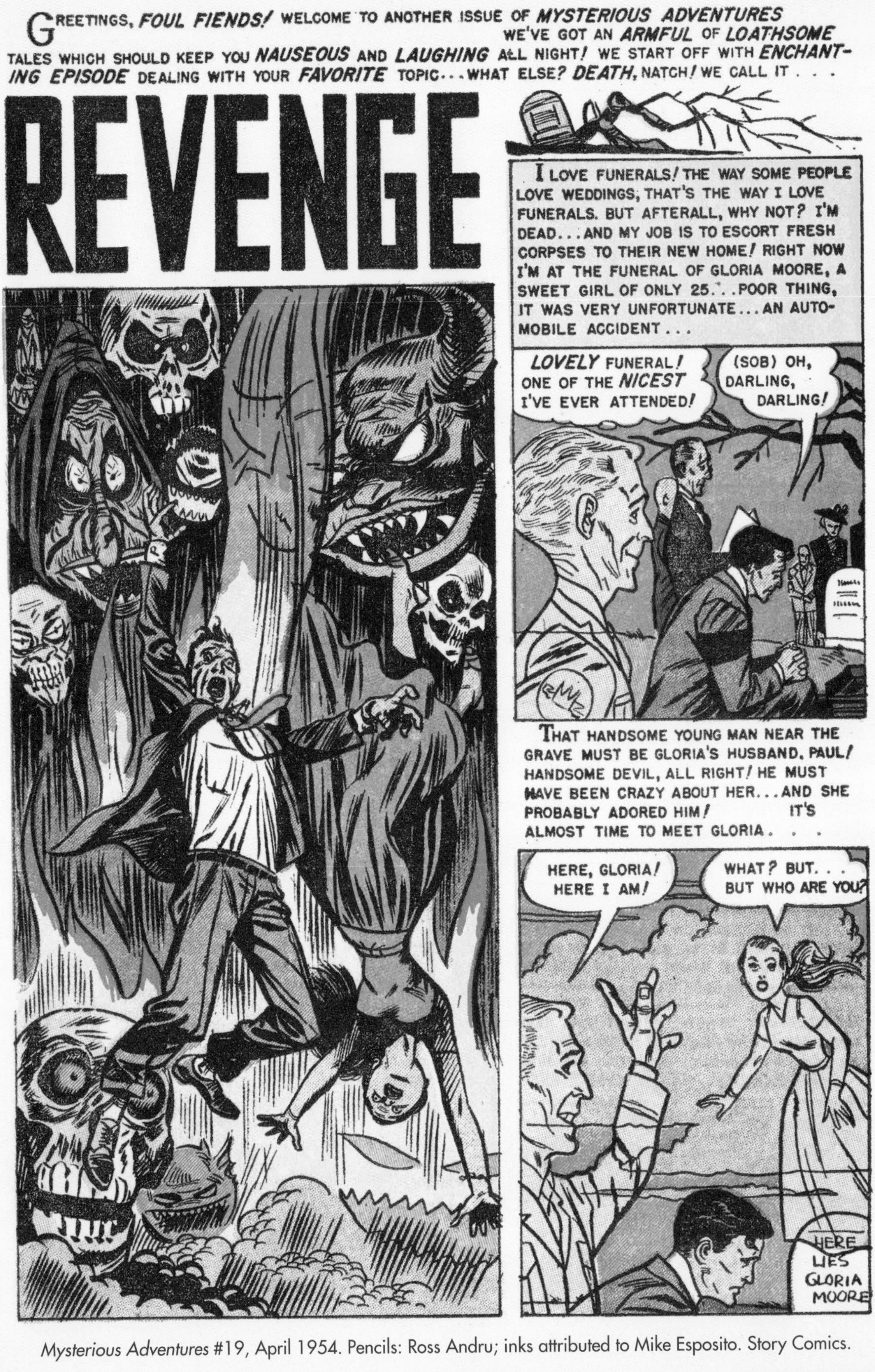
GREETINGS, FOUL FIENDS! WELCOME TO ANOTHER ISSUE OF MYSTERIOUS ADVENTURES WE'VE GOT AN ARMFUL OF LOATHSOME TALES WHICH SHOULD KEEP YOU NAUSEOUS AND LAUGHING ALL NIGHT! WE START OFF WITH ENCHANTING EPISODE DEALING WITH YOUR FAVORITE TOPIC... WHAT ELSE? DEATH, NATCH! WE CALL IT . . .
REVENGE
I LOVE FUNERALS! THE WAY SOME PEOPLE LOVE WEDDINGS, THAT'S THE WAY I LOVE FUNERALS. BUT AFTERALL, WHY NOT? I'M DEAD... AND MY JOB IS TO ESCORT FRESH CORPSES TO THEIR NEW HOME! RIGHT NOW I'M AT THE FUNERAL OF GLORIA MOORE, A SWEET GIRL OF ONLY 25... POOR THING, IT WAS VERY UNFORTUNATE... AN AUTOMOBILE ACCIDENT...
LOVELY FUNERAL! ONE OF THE NICEST I'VE EVER ATTENDED!
(SOB) OH, DARLING, DARLING!
THAT HANDSOME YOUNG MAN NEAR THE GRAVE MUST BE GLORIA'S HUSBAND, PAUL! HANDSOME DEVIL, ALL RIGHT! HE MUST HAVE BEEN CRAZY ABOUT HER... AND SHE PROBABLY ADORED HIM! IT'S ALMOST TIME TO MEET GLORIA . . .
HERE, GLORIA! HERE I AM!
WHAT? BUT... BUT WHO ARE YOU?
HERE LIES GLORIA MOORE

Mysterious Adventures #19, April 1954. Pencils: Ross Andru; inks attributed to Mike Esposito. Story Comics.

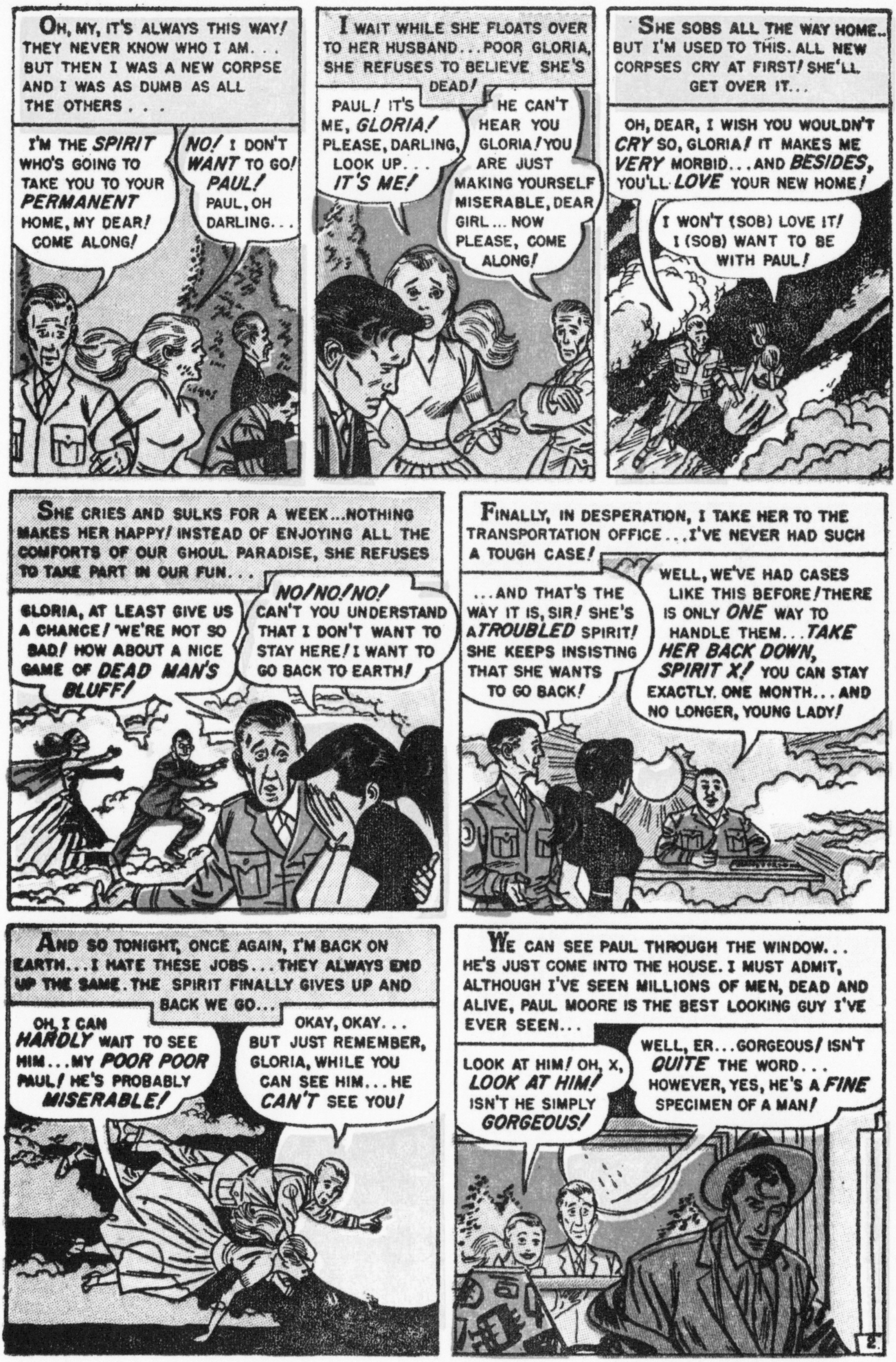
OH, MY, IT'S ALWAYS THIS WAY! THEY NEVER KNOW WHO I AM. . . BUT THEN I WAS A NEW CORPSE AND I WAS AS DUMB AS ALL THE OTHERS . . .
I'M THE SPIRIT WHO'S GOING TO TAKE YOU TO YOUR PERMANENT HOME, MY DEAR! COME ALONG!
NO! I DON'T WANT TO GO! PAUL! PAUL, OH DARLING. . .
I WAIT WHILE SHE FLOATS OVER TO HER HUSBAND . . . POOR GLORIA, SHE REFUSES TO BELIEVE SHE'S DEAD!
PAUL! IT'S ME, GLORIA! PLEASE, DARLING, LOOK UP. . . IT'S ME!
HE CAN'T HEAR YOU GLORIA! YOU ARE JUST MAKING YOURSELF MISERABLE, DEAR GIRL... NOW PLEASE, COME ALONG!
SHE SOBS ALL THE WAY HOME.. BUT I'M USED TO THIS. ALL NEW CORPSES CRY AT FIRST! SHE'LL GET OVER IT...
OH, DEAR, I WISH YOU WOULDN'T CRY SO, GLORIA! IT MAKES ME VERY MORBID... AND BESIDES, YOU'LL LOVE YOUR NEW HOME!
I WON'T (SOB) LOVE IT! I (SOB) WANT TO BE WITH PAUL!
SHE CRIES AND SULKS FOR A WEEK...NOTHING MAKES HER HAPPY! INSTEAD OF ENJOYING ALL THE COMFORTS OF OUR GHOUL PARADISE, SHE REFUSES TO TAKE PART IN OUR FUN. . .
GLORIA, AT LEAST GIVE US A CHANCE! WE'RE NOT SO BAD! HOW ABOUT A NICE GAME OF DEAD MAN'S BLUFF!
NO! NO! NO! CAN'T YOU UNDERSTAND THAT I DON'T WANT TO STAY HERE! I WANT TO GO BACK TO EARTH!
FINALLY, IN DESPERATION, I TAKE HER TO THE TRANSPORTATION OFFICE. . . I'VE NEVER HAD SUCH A TOUGH CASE!
. . . AND THAT'S THE WAY IT IS, SIR! SHE'S A TROUBLED SPIRIT! SHE KEEPS INSISTING THAT SHE WANTS TO GO BACK!
WELL, WE'VE HAD CASES LIKE THIS BEFORE! THERE IS ONLY ONE WAY TO HANDLE THEM... TAKE HER BACK DOWN, SPIRIT X! YOU CAN STAY EXACTLY ONE MONTH. . . AND NO LONGER, YOUNG LADY!
AND SO TONIGHT, ONCE AGAIN, I'M BACK ON EARTH. . . I HATE THESE JOBS. . . THEY ALWAYS END UP THE SAME. THE SPIRIT FINALLY GIVES UP AND BACK WE GO. . .
OH, I CAN HARDLY WAIT TO SEE HIM. . . MY POOR POOR PAUL! HE'S PROBABLY MISERABLE!
OKAY, OKAY. . . BUT JUST REMEMBER, GLORIA, WHILE YOU CAN SEE HIM. . . HE CAN'T SEE YOU!
WE CAN SEE PAUL THROUGH THE WINDOW. . . HE'S JUST COME INTO THE HOUSE. I MUST ADMIT, ALTHOUGH I'VE SEEN MILLIONS OF MEN, DEAD AND ALIVE, PAUL MOORE IS THE BEST LOOKING GUY I'VE EVER SEEN. . .
LOOK AT HIM! OH, X, LOOK AT HIM! ISN'T HE SIMPLY GORGEOUS!
WELL, ER. . . GORGEOUS! ISN'T QUITE THE WORD. . . HOWEVER, YES, HE'S A FINE SPECIMEN OF A MAN!
2

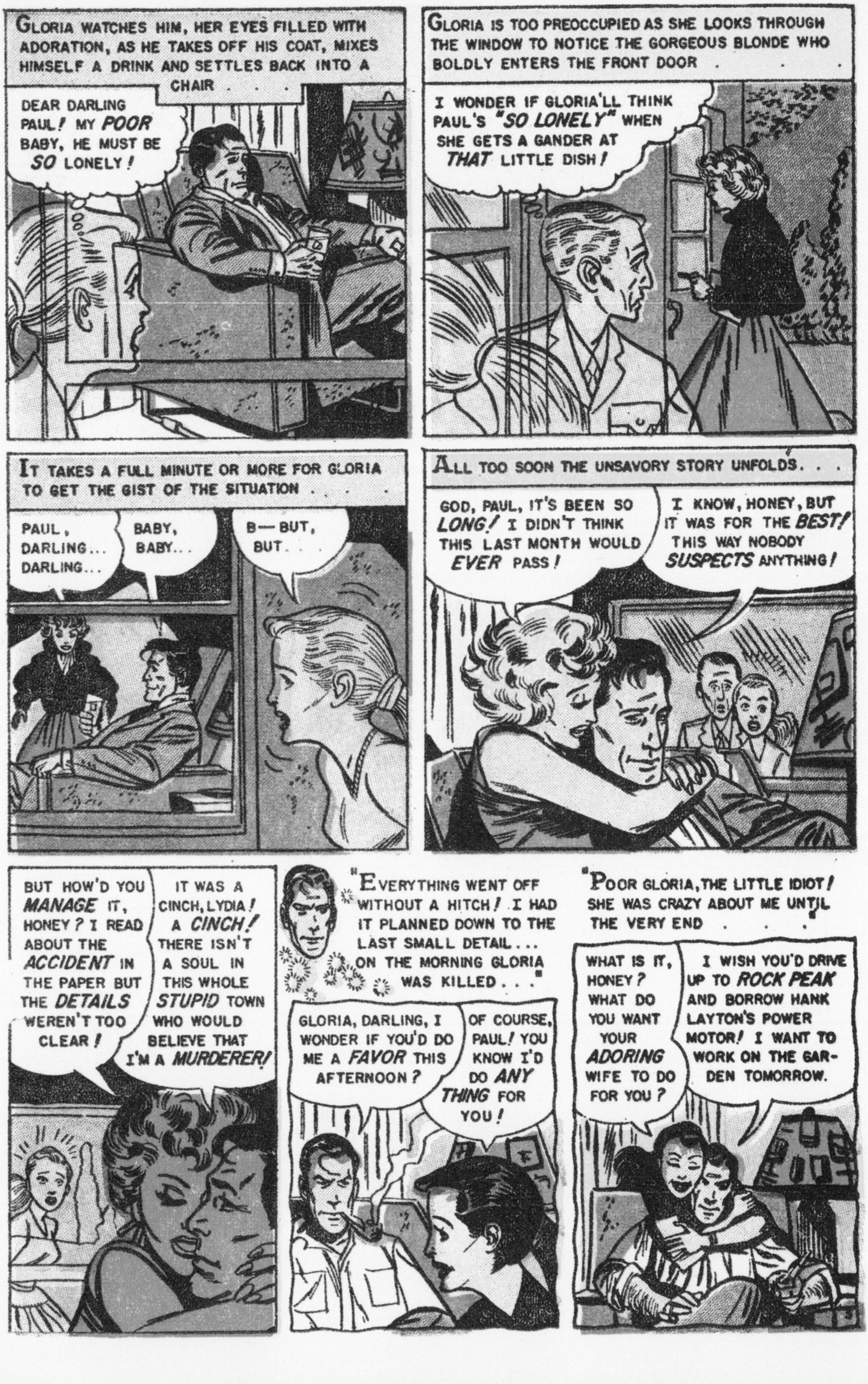
GLORIA WATCHES HIM, HER EYES FILLED WITH ADORATION, AS HE TAKES OFF HIS COAT, MIXES HIMSELF A DRINK AND SETTLES BACK INTO A CHAIR . . .
DEAR DARLING PAUL! MY POOR BABY, HE MUST BE SO LONELY!
GLORIA IS TOO PREOCCUPIED AS SHE LOOKS THROUGH THE WINDOW TO NOTICE THE GORGEOUS BLONDE WHO BOLDLY ENTERS THE FRONT DOOR . . .
I WONDER IF GLORIA'LL THINK PAUL'S "SO LONELY" WHEN SHE GETS A GANDER AT THAT LITTLE DISH!
IT TAKES A FULL MINUTE OR MORE FOR GLORIA TO GET THE GIST OF THE SITUATION . . .
PAUL, DARLING... DARLING...
BABY, BABY...
B—BUT, BUT. . .
ALL TOO SOON THE UNSAVORY STORY UNFOLDS. . .
GOD, PAUL, IT'S BEEN SO LONG! I DIDN'T THINK THIS LAST MONTH WOULD EVER PASS!
I KNOW, HONEY, BUT IT WAS FOR THE BEST! THIS WAY NOBODY SUSPECTS ANYTHING!
BUT HOW'D YOU MANAGE IT, HONEY? I READ ABOUT THE ACCIDENT IN THE PAPER BUT THE DETAILS WEREN'T TOO CLEAR!
IT WAS A CINCH, LYDIA! A CINCH! THERE ISN'T A SOUL IN THIS WHOLE STUPID TOWN WHO WOULD BELIEVE THAT I'M A MURDERER!
"EVERYTHING WENT OFF WITHOUT A HITCH! I HAD IT PLANNED DOWN TO THE LAST SMALL DETAIL... ON THE MORNING GLORIA WAS KILLED . . ."
GLORIA, DARLING, I WONDER IF YOU'D DO ME A FAVOR THIS AFTERNOON?
OF COURSE, PAUL! YOU KNOW I'D DO ANY THING FOR YOU!
"POOR GLORIA, THE LITTLE IDIOT! SHE WAS CRAZY ABOUT ME UNTIL THE VERY END . . ."
WHAT IS IT, HONEY? WHAT DO YOU WANT YOUR ADORING WIFE TO DO FOR YOU?
I WISH YOU'D DRIVE UP TO ROCK PEAK AND BORROW HANK LAYTON'S POWER MOTOR! I WANT TO WORK ON THE GAR-DEN TOMORROW.

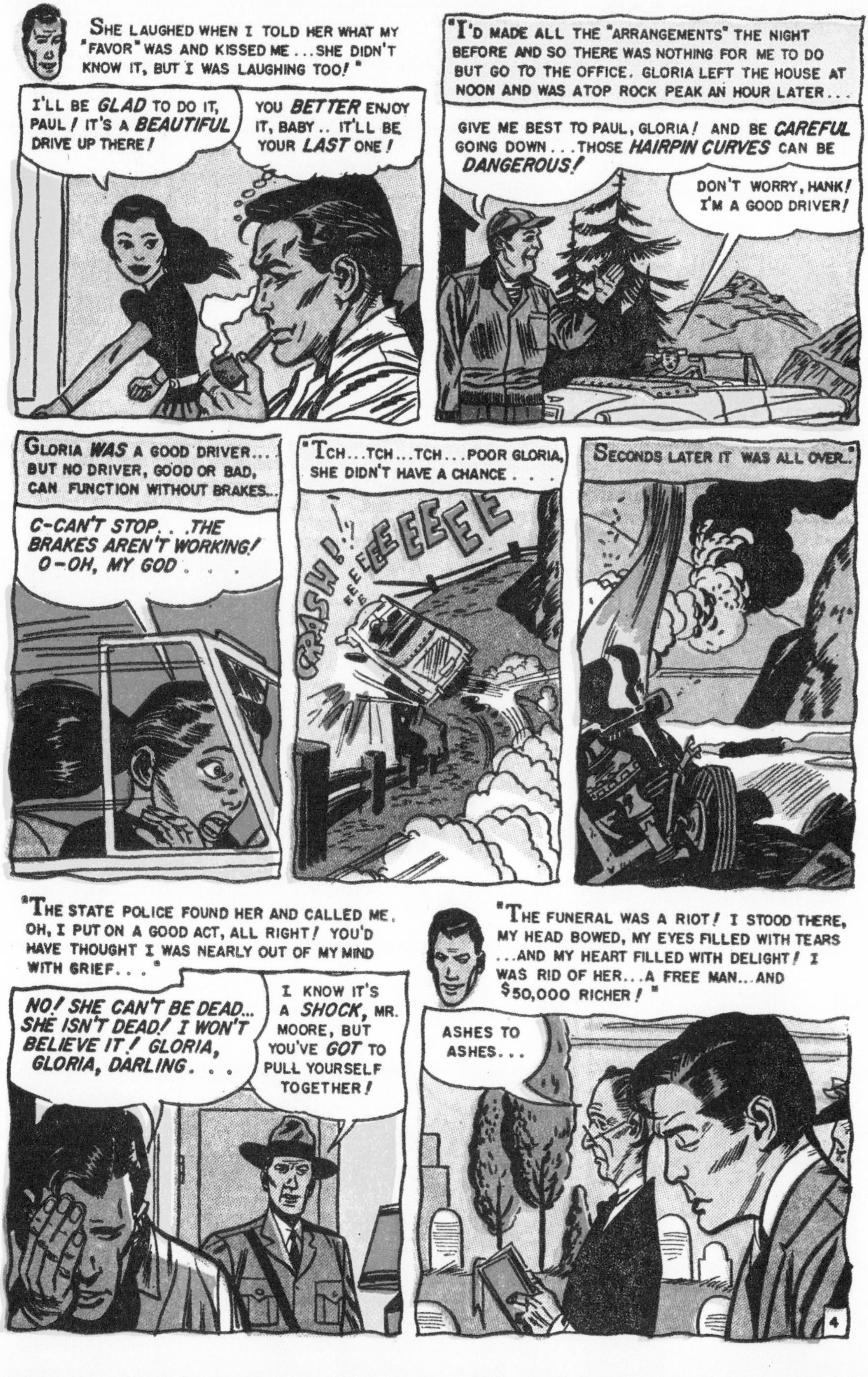
"SHE LAUGHED WHEN I TOLD HER WHAT MY "FAVOR" WAS AND KISSED ME . . . SHE DIDN'T KNOW IT, BUT I WAS LAUGHING TOO!"
I'LL BE GLAD TO DO IT, PAUL! IT'S A BEAUTIFUL DRIVE UP THERE!
YOU BETTER ENJOY IT, BABY .. IT'LL BE YOUR LAST ONE!
"I'D MADE ALL THE "ARRANGEMENTS" THE NIGHT BEFORE AND SO THERE WAS NOTHING FOR ME TO DO BUT GO TO THE OFFICE. GLORIA LEFT THE HOUSE AT NOON AND WAS ATOP ROCK PEAK AN HOUR LATER . . .
GIVE ME BEST TO PAUL, GLORIA! AND BE CAREFUL GOING DOWN . . . THOSE HAIRPIN CURVES CAN BE DANGEROUS!
DON'T WORRY, HANK! I'M A GOOD DRIVER!
GLORIA WAS A GOOD DRIVER . . . BUT NO DRIVER, GOOD OR BAD, CAN FUNCTION WITHOUT BRAKES . . .
C-CAN'T STOP. . .THE BRAKES AREN'T WORKING! O-OH, MY GOD . . .
"TCH . . . TCH . . . TCH . . . POOR GLORIA, SHE DIDN'T HAVE A CHANCE . . .
EEEEEEEEE
CRASH!
SECONDS LATER IT WAS ALL OVER."
"THE STATE POLICE FOUND HER AND CALLED ME. OH, I PUT ON A GOOD ACT, ALL RIGHT! YOU'D HAVE THOUGHT I WAS NEARLY OUT OF MY MIND WITH GRIEF . . ."
NO! SHE CAN'T BE DEAD... SHE ISN'T DEAD! I WON'T BELIEVE IT! GLORIA, GLORIA, DARLING . . .
I KNOW IT'S A SHOCK, MR. MOORE, BUT YOU'VE GOT TO PULL YOURSELF TOGETHER!
"THE FUNERAL WAS A RIOT! I STOOD THERE, MY HEAD BOWED, MY EYES FILLED WITH TEARS . . .AND MY HEART FILLED WITH DELIGHT! I WAS RID OF HER . . . A FREE MAN . . . AND $50,000 RICHER!"
ASHES TO ASHES . . .
4

I CAN HARDLY BEAR TO LOOK AT GLORIA. SHE JUST FLOATS THERE, SHOCKED, CHOKED WITH RAGE AND HORROR.

HE KILLED ME! DID YOU HEAR WHAT HE SAID... HE KILLED ME ...MURDERED ME!

NOW, GLORIA, TRY TO BE CALM! THESE THINGS, UNFORTUNATELY, SOMETIMES HAPPEN, BUT...

BUT THERE IS NO CALMING HER ...SHE'S LIKE A WILD WOMAN ...ER, WILD GHOST.

HE DID IT FOR *HER!* FOR THAT *PEROXIDED CHEAP HUSSY!* OH, I'LL GET *EVEN*... IF IT'S THE LAST THING I DO, *I'LL GET EVEN!*

GLORIA, YOU *SHOULDN'T* TALK THAT WAY. IT'S AGAINST THE *RULES!* I CAN'T *PERMIT* IT!

AN HOUR PASSED... AN HOUR IN WHICH GLORIA HAS YELLED, SOBBED, AND HAD HYSTERICS. NOW I TRY TO CONVINCE HER TO ACCOMPANY ME BACK "HOME".

PLEASE, SPIRIT X, *PLEASE,* DON'T START *THAT* AGAIN! I'M *NOT* GOING BACK! PAUL IS *MINE*... I WON'T LET HIM GO!

GOOD LORD, DON'T TELL ME YOU *STILL* LOVE HIM? HE *MURDERED* YOU!

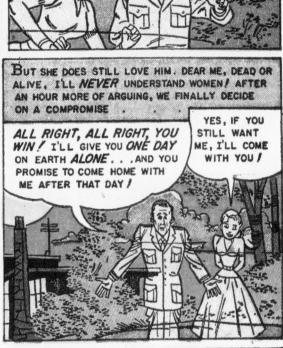

BUT SHE DOES STILL LOVE HIM. DEAR ME, DEAD OR ALIVE, I'LL *NEVER* UNDERSTAND WOMEN! AFTER AN HOUR MORE OF ARGUING, WE FINALLY DECIDE ON A COMPROMISE.

ALL RIGHT, ALL RIGHT, YOU WIN! I'LL GIVE YOU *ONE DAY* ON EARTH *ALONE* ...AND YOU PROMISE TO COME HOME WITH ME AFTER THAT DAY!

YES, IF YOU STILL WANT ME, I'LL COME WITH YOU!

I LEAVE WITH MISGIVINGS... WHAT IS SHE GOING TO DO DURING THOSE 24 HOURS? MY LAST GLIMPSE OF HER IS AS SHE FLOATS SILENTLY BACK TO THE WINDOW.

I DON'T *LIKE* THIS MESS... DON'T LIKE IT ONE BIT! THAT LOOK IN HER EYE...

BUT, HONEY, I DON'T UNDERSTAND. WHAT *HAPPENED* TO THE BRAKES? WHY DIDN'T THEY WORK?

THEY DIDN'T WORK BECAUSE THE NIGHT BEFORE I MADE A TINY *PUNCTURE* IN THE BRAKE DRUM BY THE TIME POOR GLORIA HIT THE DOWNGRADE, ALL THE BRAKE FLUID HAS SEEPED OUT! *SIMPLE,* EH, DARLING?

PAUL, DARLING, YOU'RE SO CLEVER! AND DON'T FORGET, YOU PROMISED BABY SHE COULD HAVE A NEW *MINK!*

DON'T WORRY, BABY, I HAVEN'T FORGOTTEN! AS FOR POPPA, THAT INSURANCE I TOOK OUT ON GLORIA IS GOING TO FURNISH A BIG NEW *CADILLAC*... PLUS DOUGH TO BURN!

5

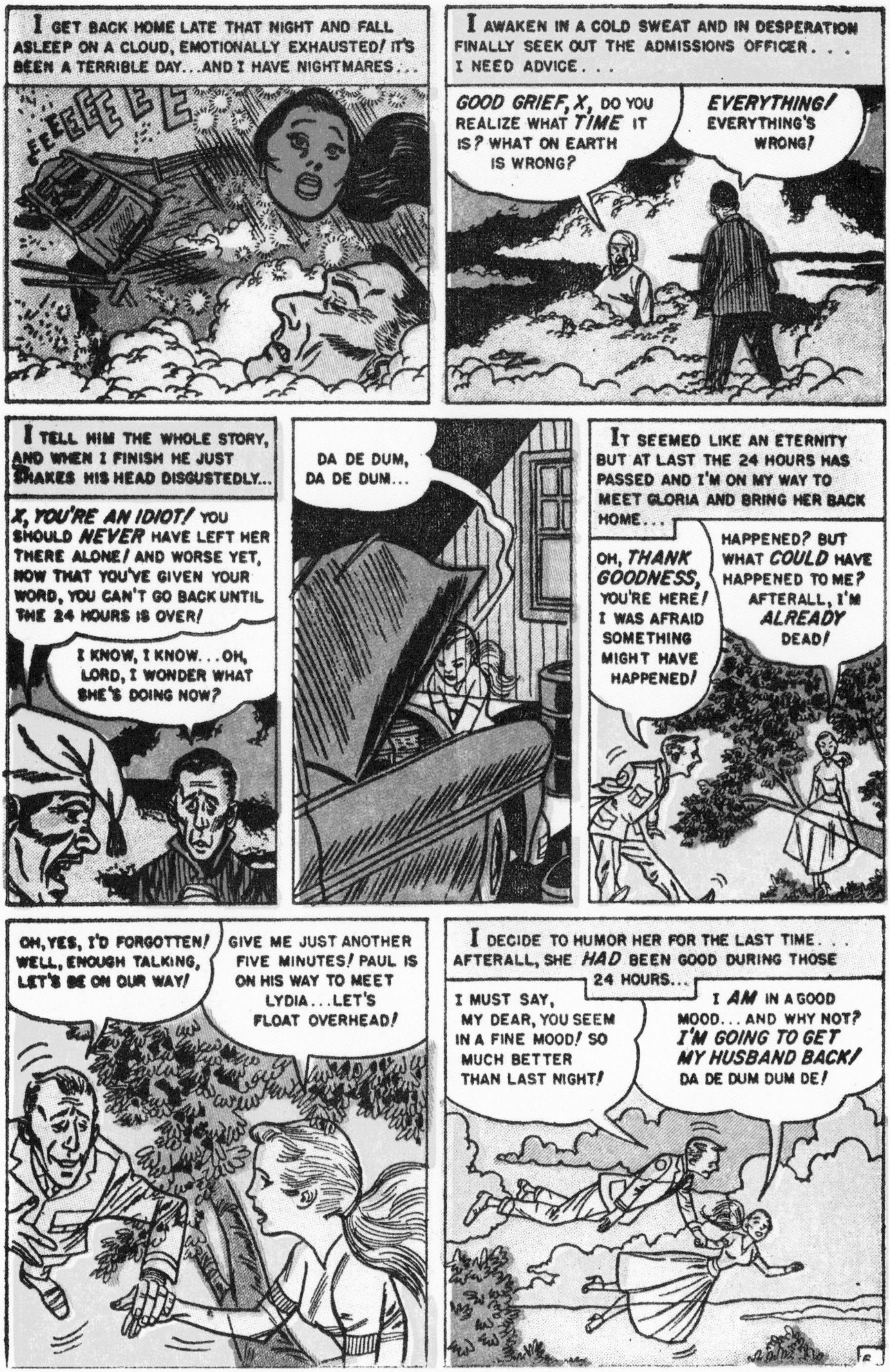
I GET BACK HOME LATE THAT NIGHT AND FALL ASLEEP ON A CLOUD, EMOTIONALLY EXHAUSTED! IT'S BEEN A TERRIBLE DAY...AND I HAVE NIGHTMARES...
EEEEEEEEE
I AWAKEN IN A COLD SWEAT AND IN DESPERATION FINALLY SEEK OUT THE ADMISSIONS OFFICER . . . I NEED ADVICE . . .
GOOD GRIEF, X, DO YOU REALIZE WHAT TIME IT IS? WHAT ON EARTH IS WRONG?
EVERYTHING! EVERYTHING'S WRONG!
I TELL HIM THE WHOLE STORY, AND WHEN I FINISH HE JUST SHAKES HIS HEAD DISGUSTEDLY...
X, YOU'RE AN IDIOT! YOU SHOULD NEVER HAVE LEFT HER THERE ALONE! AND WORSE YET, NOW THAT YOU'VE GIVEN YOUR WORD, YOU CAN'T GO BACK UNTIL THE 24 HOURS IS OVER!
I KNOW, I KNOW...OH, LORD, I WONDER WHAT SHE'S DOING NOW?
DA DE DUM, DA DE DUM...
IT SEEMED LIKE AN ETERNITY BUT AT LAST THE 24 HOURS HAS PASSED AND I'M ON MY WAY TO MEET GLORIA AND BRING HER BACK HOME...
OH, THANK GOODNESS, YOU'RE HERE! I WAS AFRAID SOMETHING MIGHT HAVE HAPPENED!
HAPPENED? BUT WHAT COULD HAVE HAPPENED TO ME? AFTERALL, I'M ALREADY DEAD!
OH, YES, I'D FORGOTTEN! WELL, ENOUGH TALKING, LET'S BE ON OUR WAY!
GIVE ME JUST ANOTHER FIVE MINUTES! PAUL IS ON HIS WAY TO MEET LYDIA...LET'S FLOAT OVERHEAD!
I DECIDE TO HUMOR HER FOR THE LAST TIME. . . AFTERALL, SHE HAD BEEN GOOD DURING THOSE 24 HOURS...
I MUST SAY, MY DEAR, YOU SEEM IN A FINE MOOD! SO MUCH BETTER THAN LAST NIGHT!
I AM IN A GOOD MOOD... AND WHY NOT? I'M GOING TO GET MY HUSBAND BACK! DA DE DUM DUM DE!

GOING TO GET YOUR HUSBAND BACK? B-BUT... BUT... OH, NO! NO! YOU'VE... YOU'VE...

THAT'S RIGHT, X, OLD BOY, I'VE FIXED THE BRAKES!

H-HEY, THE BRAKES! I CAN'T STOP... I...

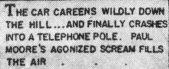

THE CAR CAREENS WILDLY DOWN THE HILL... AND FINALLY CRASHES INTO A TELEPHONE POLE. PAUL MOORE'S AGONIZED SCREAM FILLS THE AIR.

YAAAAGH!

CRASH!

PAUL IS DEAD AND IT IS ONLY SECONDS LATER WHEN HIS SPIRIT ARISES FROM THE MANGLED METAL...

GLORIA! W-WHAT ARE YOU DOING HERE? WHERE AM I?

HELLO, DARLING! DON'T LOOK SO SURPRISED, YOU'LL GET USED TO IT AFTER A WHILE! WE'RE DEAD!

OH, MY, WHAT'LL I DO? WHAT'LL I DO!

I CAN'T TAKE YOU WITH ME NOW! YOU'RE A MURDERER! YOU'RE BOTH MURDERERS!

FOR AN INSTANT, I'M UTTERLY BEWILDERED. NEITHER ONE OF THEM BELONGS IN GHOUL HEAVEN... BUT WHAT WILL I DO WITH THEM? THEN A VOICE ANSWERS MY QUESTION.

DON'T WORRY, X, I'VE COME FOR THEM! THEY'RE MINE NOW.

NO... NO... NOT THAT!

DON'T FRET, DARLING, IT DOESN'T MATTER! WE'LL BE TOGETHER!

I WATCH AS THE OTHER MESSENGER LEADS THEM DOWNWARD... DOWNWARD... WELL, AT LEAST GLORIA'S HAPPY! SHE'S GOT PAUL BACK JUST LIKE SHE SAID SHE WOULD...

PAUL, DARLING, DARLING! YOU'RE MINE AGAIN! MINE!

GET AWAY FROM ME, GLORIA! LEAVE ME ALONE!

SORRY, BUB, YOU'LL NEVER ESCAPE HER NOW!

TCH, TCH, TCH... AND SHE WAS SUCH A NICE GIRL!

WELCOME HOME, KIDDIES!

THE END

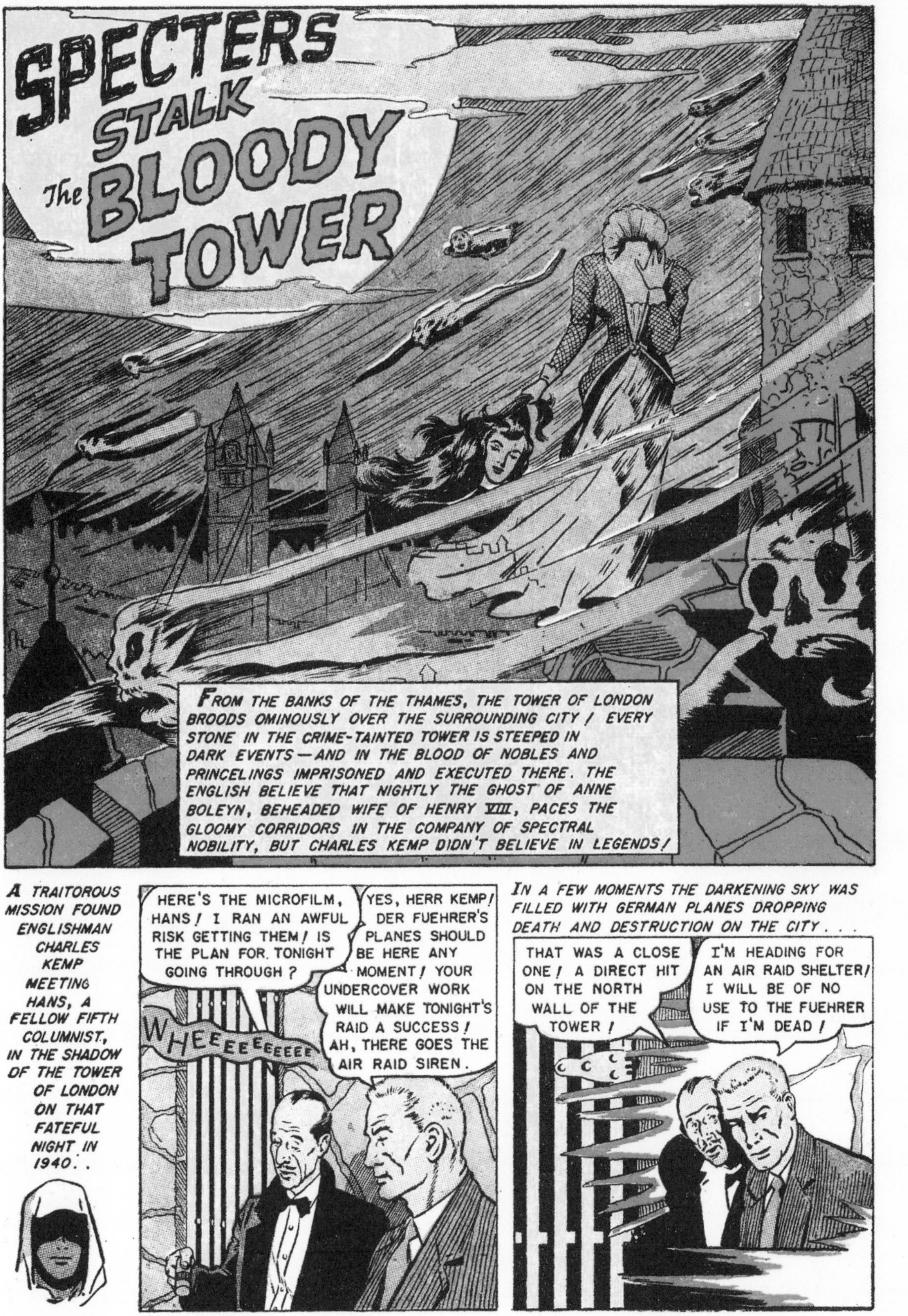
SPECTERS STALK The BLOODY TOWER
FROM THE BANKS OF THE THAMES, THE TOWER OF LONDON BROODS OMINOUSLY OVER THE SURROUNDING CITY! EVERY STONE IN THE CRIME-TAINTED TOWER IS STEEPED IN DARK EVENTS—AND IN THE BLOOD OF NOBLES AND PRINCELINGS IMPRISONED AND EXECUTED THERE. THE ENGLISH BELIEVE THAT NIGHTLY THE GHOST OF ANNE BOLEYN, BEHEADED WIFE OF HENRY VIII, PACES THE GLOOMY CORRIDORS IN THE COMPANY OF SPECTRAL NOBILITY, BUT CHARLES KEMP DIDN'T BELIEVE IN LEGENDS!
A TRAITOROUS MISSION FOUND ENGLISHMAN CHARLES KEMP MEETING HANS, A FELLOW FIFTH COLUMNIST, IN THE SHADOW OF THE TOWER OF LONDON ON THAT FATEFUL NIGHT IN 1940. .
HERE'S THE MICROFILM, HANS! I RAN AN AWFUL RISK GETTING THEM! IS THE PLAN FOR TONIGHT GOING THROUGH?
YES, HERR KEMP! DER FUEHRER'S PLANES SHOULD BE HERE ANY MOMENT! YOUR UNDERCOVER WORK WILL MAKE TONIGHT'S RAID A SUCCESS! AH, THERE GOES THE AIR RAID SIREN.
WHEEEEEEEEEE
IN A FEW MOMENTS THE DARKENING SKY WAS FILLED WITH GERMAN PLANES DROPPING DEATH AND DESTRUCTION ON THE CITY . . .
THAT WAS A CLOSE ONE! A DIRECT HIT ON THE NORTH WALL OF THE TOWER!
I'M HEADING FOR AN AIR RAID SHELTER! I WILL BE OF NO USE TO THE FUEHRER IF I'M DEAD!

The Hand of Fate #16, February 1953. Artist unknown. Ace Magazines.

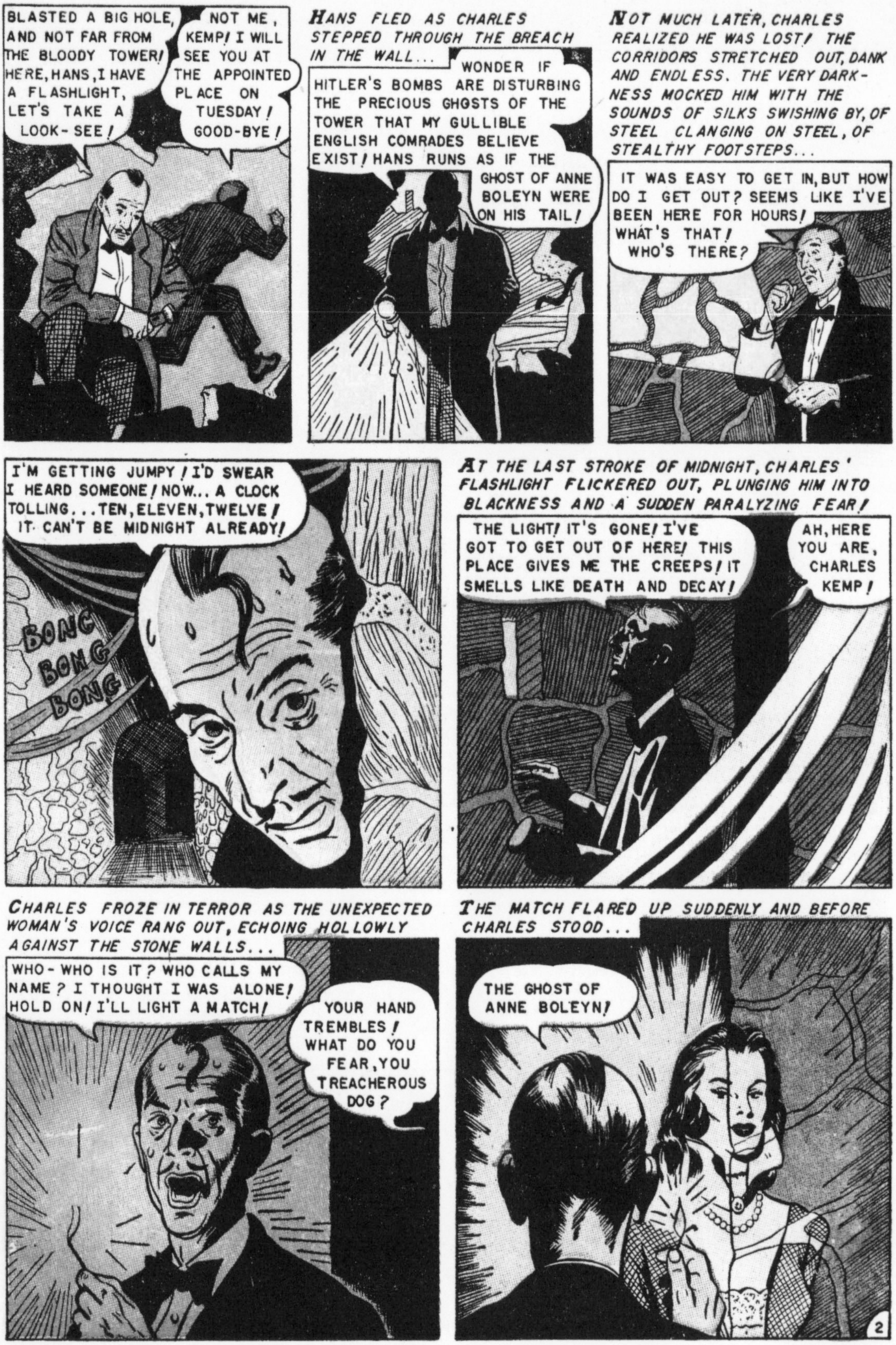
BLASTED A BIG HOLE, AND NOT FAR FROM THE BLOODY TOWER! HERE, HANS, I HAVE A FLASHLIGHT, LET'S TAKE A LOOK-SEE!
NOT ME, KEMP! I WILL SEE YOU AT THE APPOINTED PLACE ON TUESDAY! GOOD-BYE!
HANS FLED AS CHARLES STEPPED THROUGH THE BREACH IN THE WALL...
WONDER IF HITLER'S BOMBS ARE DISTURBING THE PRECIOUS GHOSTS OF THE TOWER THAT MY GULLIBLE ENGLISH COMRADES BELIEVE EXIST! HANS RUNS AS IF THE GHOST OF ANNE BOLEYN WERE ON HIS TAIL!
NOT MUCH LATER, CHARLES REALIZED HE WAS LOST! THE CORRIDORS STRETCHED OUT, DANK AND ENDLESS. THE VERY DARKNESS MOCKED HIM WITH THE SOUNDS OF SILKS SWISHING BY, OF STEEL CLANGING ON STEEL, OF STEALTHY FOOTSTEPS...
IT WAS EASY TO GET IN, BUT HOW DO I GET OUT? SEEMS LIKE I'VE BEEN HERE FOR HOURS! WHAT'S THAT! WHO'S THERE?
I'M GETTING JUMPY! I'D SWEAR I HEARD SOMEONE! NOW... A CLOCK TOLLING... TEN, ELEVEN, TWELVE! IT CAN'T BE MIDNIGHT ALREADY!
BONG BONG BONG
AT THE LAST STROKE OF MIDNIGHT, CHARLES' FLASHLIGHT FLICKERED OUT, PLUNGING HIM INTO BLACKNESS AND A SUDDEN PARALYZING FEAR!
THE LIGHT! IT'S GONE! I'VE GOT TO GET OUT OF HERE! THIS PLACE GIVES ME THE CREEPS! IT SMELLS LIKE DEATH AND DECAY!
AH, HERE YOU ARE, CHARLES KEMP!
CHARLES FROZE IN TERROR AS THE UNEXPECTED WOMAN'S VOICE RANG OUT, ECHOING HOLLOWLY AGAINST THE STONE WALLS...
WHO-WHO IS IT? WHO CALLS MY NAME? I THOUGHT I WAS ALONE! HOLD ON! I'LL LIGHT A MATCH!
YOUR HAND TREMBLES! WHAT DO YOU FEAR, YOU TREACHEROUS DOG?
THE MATCH FLARED UP SUDDENLY AND BEFORE CHARLES STOOD...
THE GHOST OF ANNE BOLEYN!
2

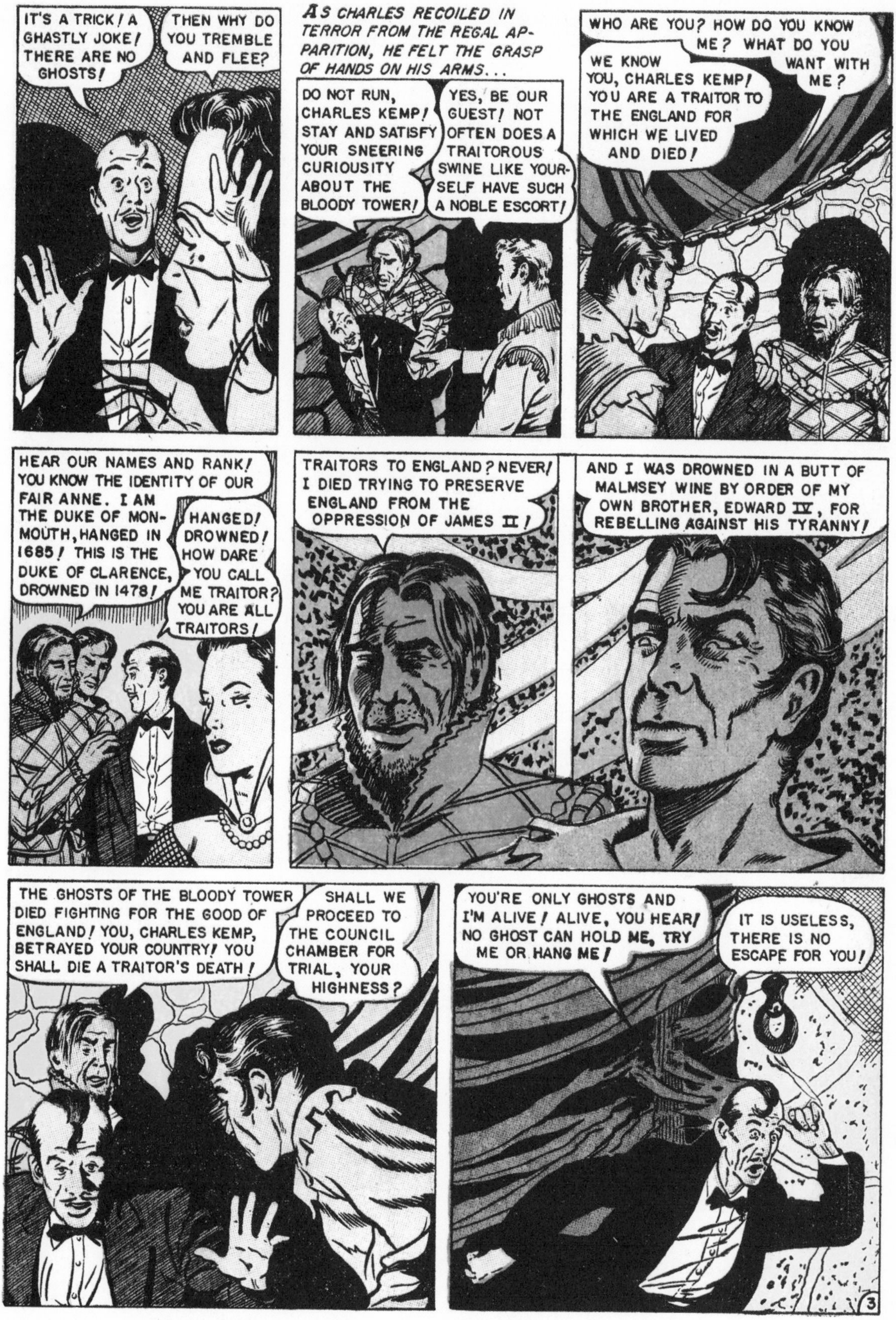
IT'S A TRICK! A GHASTLY JOKE! THERE ARE NO GHOSTS!
THEN WHY DO YOU TREMBLE AND FLEE?
AS CHARLES RECOILED IN TERROR FROM THE REGAL APPARITION, HE FELT THE GRASP OF HANDS ON HIS ARMS...
DO NOT RUN, CHARLES KEMP! STAY AND SATISFY YOUR SNEERING CURIOUSITY ABOUT THE BLOODY TOWER!
YES, BE OUR GUEST! NOT OFTEN DOES A TRAITOROUS SWINE LIKE YOURSELF HAVE SUCH A NOBLE ESCORT!
WHO ARE YOU? HOW DO YOU KNOW ME? WHAT DO YOU WANT WITH ME?
WE KNOW YOU, CHARLES KEMP! YOU ARE A TRAITOR TO THE ENGLAND FOR WHICH WE LIVED AND DIED!
HEAR OUR NAMES AND RANK! YOU KNOW THE IDENTITY OF OUR FAIR ANNE. I AM THE DUKE OF MONMOUTH, HANGED IN 1685! THIS IS THE DUKE OF CLARENCE, DROWNED IN 1478!
HANGED! DROWNED! HOW DARE YOU CALL ME TRAITOR? YOU ARE ALL TRAITORS!
TRAITORS TO ENGLAND? NEVER! I DIED TRYING TO PRESERVE ENGLAND FROM THE OPPRESSION OF JAMES II!
AND I WAS DROWNED IN A BUTT OF MALMSEY WINE BY ORDER OF MY OWN BROTHER, EDWARD IV, FOR REBELLING AGAINST HIS TYRANNY!
THE GHOSTS OF THE BLOODY TOWER DIED FIGHTING FOR THE GOOD OF ENGLAND! YOU, CHARLES KEMP, BETRAYED YOUR COUNTRY! YOU SHALL DIE A TRAITOR'S DEATH!
SHALL WE PROCEED TO THE COUNCIL CHAMBER FOR TRIAL, YOUR HIGHNESS?
YOU'RE ONLY GHOSTS AND I'M ALIVE! ALIVE, YOU HEAR! NO GHOST CAN HOLD ME, TRY ME OR HANG ME!
IT IS USELESS, THERE IS NO ESCAPE FOR YOU!
3

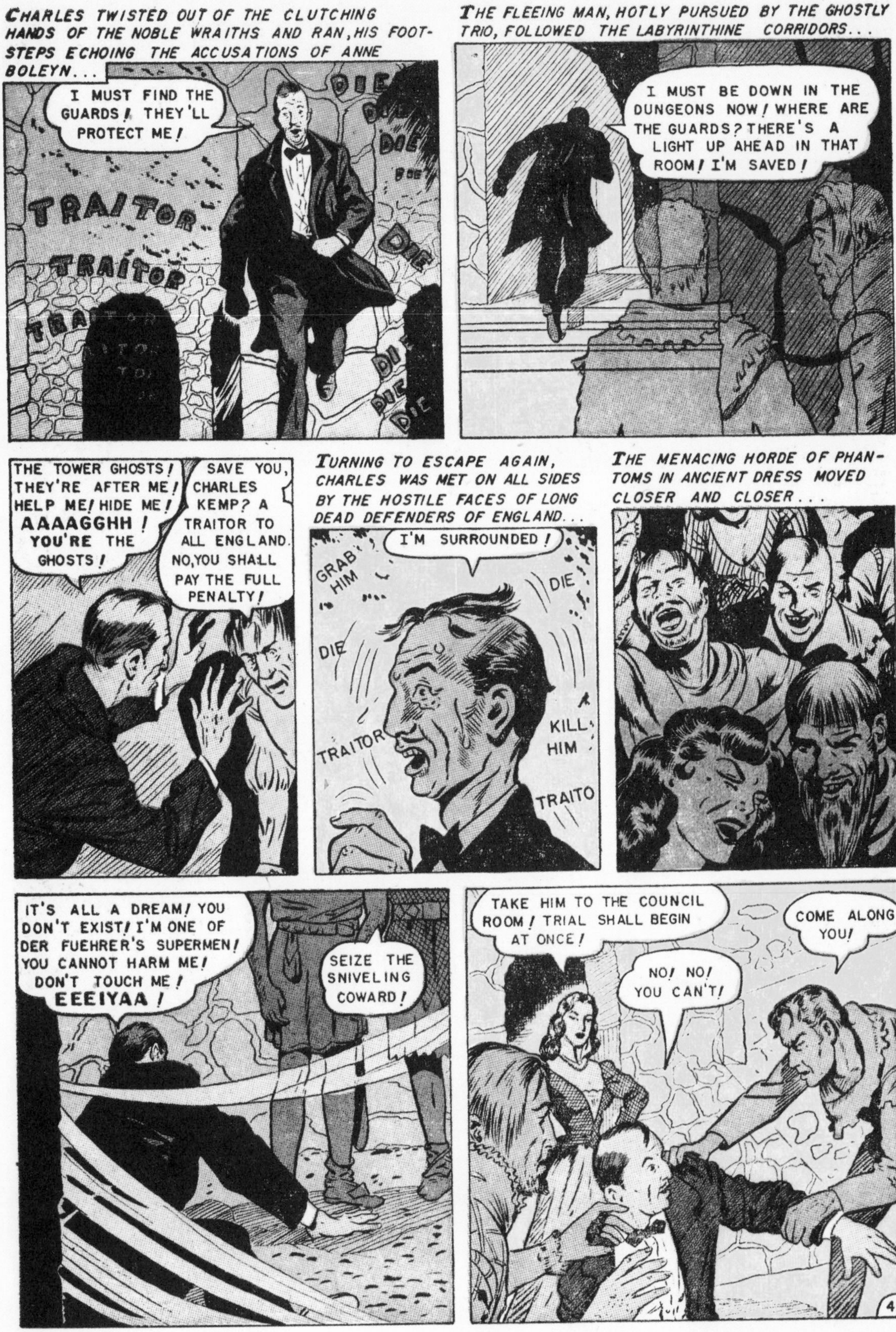
CHARLES TWISTED OUT OF THE CLUTCHING HANDS OF THE NOBLE WRAITHS AND RAN, HIS FOOT-STEPS ECHOING THE ACCUSATIONS OF ANNE BOLEYN...
I MUST FIND THE GUARDS! THEY'LL PROTECT ME!
TRAITOR
TRAITOR
DIE
DIE
THE FLEEING MAN, HOTLY PURSUED BY THE GHOSTLY TRIO, FOLLOWED THE LABYRINTHINE CORRIDORS...
I MUST BE DOWN IN THE DUNGEONS NOW! WHERE ARE THE GUARDS? THERE'S A LIGHT UP AHEAD IN THAT ROOM! I'M SAVED!
THE TOWER GHOSTS! THEY'RE AFTER ME! HELP ME! HIDE ME! AAAAGGHH! YOU'RE THE GHOSTS!
SAVE YOU, CHARLES KEMP? A TRAITOR TO ALL ENGLAND. NO, YOU SHALL PAY THE FULL PENALTY!
TURNING TO ESCAPE AGAIN, CHARLES WAS MET ON ALL SIDES BY THE HOSTILE FACES OF LONG DEAD DEFENDERS OF ENGLAND...
I'M SURROUNDED!
GRAB HIM
DIE
DIE
TRAITOR
KILL HIM
TRAITO
THE MENACING HORDE OF PHAN-TOMS IN ANCIENT DRESS MOVED CLOSER AND CLOSER...
IT'S ALL A DREAM! YOU DON'T EXIST! I'M ONE OF DER FUEHRER'S SUPERMEN! YOU CANNOT HARM ME! DON'T TOUCH ME! EEEIYAA!
SEIZE THE SNIVELING COWARD!
TAKE HIM TO THE COUNCIL ROOM! TRIAL SHALL BEGIN AT ONCE!
COME ALONG YOU!
NO! NO! YOU CAN'T!
4

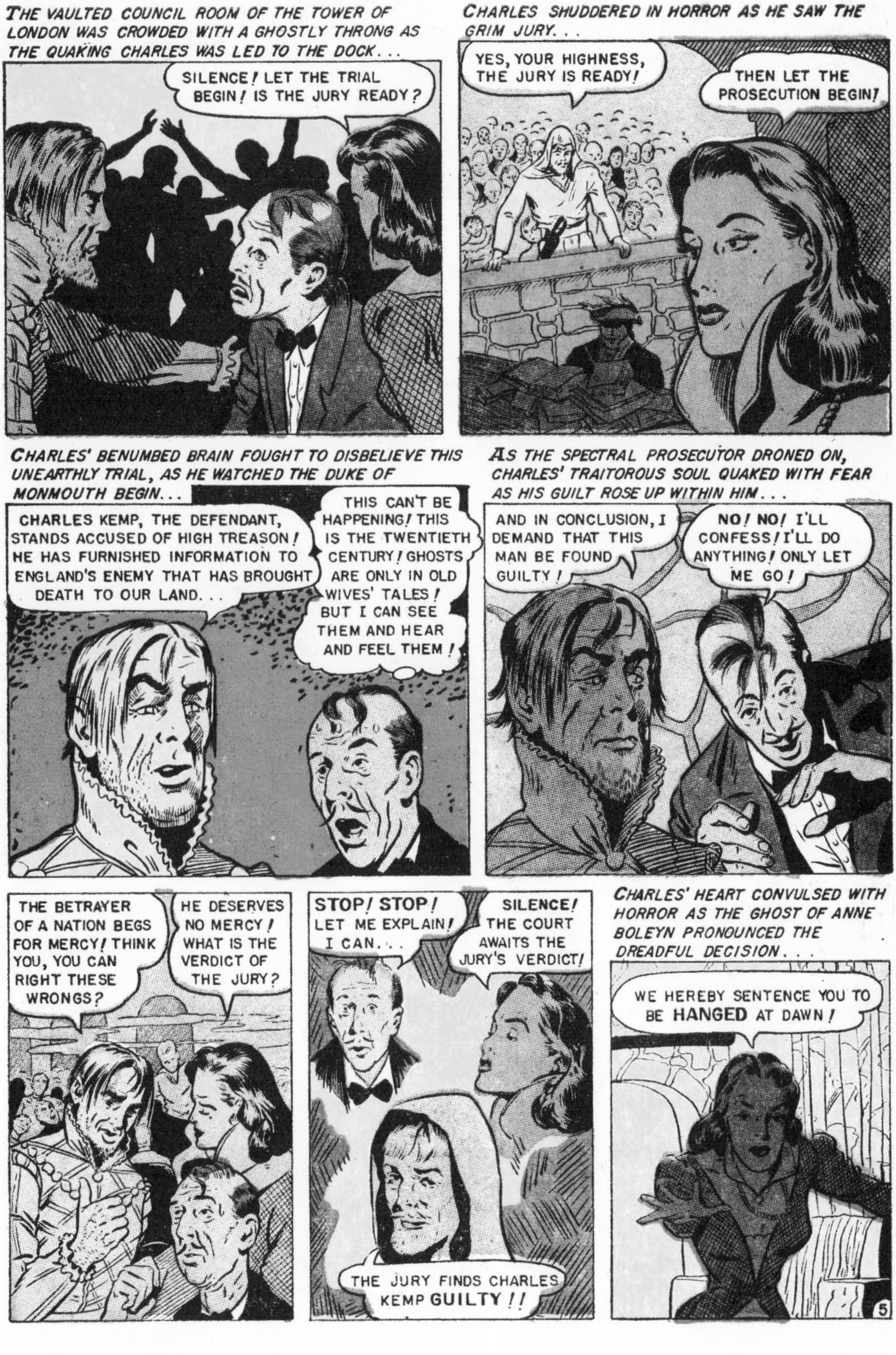
THE VAULTED COUNCIL ROOM OF THE TOWER OF LONDON WAS CROWDED WITH A GHOSTLY THRONG AS THE QUAKING CHARLES WAS LED TO THE DOCK...
SILENCE! LET THE TRIAL BEGIN! IS THE JURY READY?
CHARLES SHUDDERED IN HORROR AS HE SAW THE GRIM JURY...
YES, YOUR HIGHNESS, THE JURY IS READY!
THEN LET THE PROSECUTION BEGIN!
CHARLES' BENUMBED BRAIN FOUGHT TO DISBELIEVE THIS UNEARTHLY TRIAL, AS HE WATCHED THE DUKE OF MONMOUTH BEGIN...
CHARLES KEMP, THE DEFENDANT, STANDS ACCUSED OF HIGH TREASON! HE HAS FURNISHED INFORMATION TO ENGLAND'S ENEMY THAT HAS BROUGHT DEATH TO OUR LAND...
THIS CAN'T BE HAPPENING! THIS IS THE TWENTIETH CENTURY! GHOSTS ARE ONLY IN OLD WIVES' TALES! BUT I CAN SEE THEM AND HEAR AND FEEL THEM!
AS THE SPECTRAL PROSECUTOR DRONED ON, CHARLES' TRAITOROUS SOUL QUAKED WITH FEAR AS HIS GUILT ROSE UP WITHIN HIM...
AND IN CONCLUSION, I DEMAND THAT THIS MAN BE FOUND GUILTY!
NO! NO! I'LL CONFESS! I'LL DO ANYTHING! ONLY LET ME GO!
THE BETRAYER OF A NATION BEGS FOR MERCY! THINK YOU, YOU CAN RIGHT THESE WRONGS?
HE DESERVES NO MERCY! WHAT IS THE VERDICT OF THE JURY?
STOP! STOP! LET ME EXPLAIN! I CAN...
SILENCE! THE COURT AWAITS THE JURY'S VERDICT!
THE JURY FINDS CHARLES KEMP GUILTY!!
CHARLES' HEART CONVULSED WITH HORROR AS THE GHOST OF ANNE BOLEYN PRONOUNCED THE DREADFUL DECISION...
WE HEREBY SENTENCE YOU TO BE HANGED AT DAWN!
5

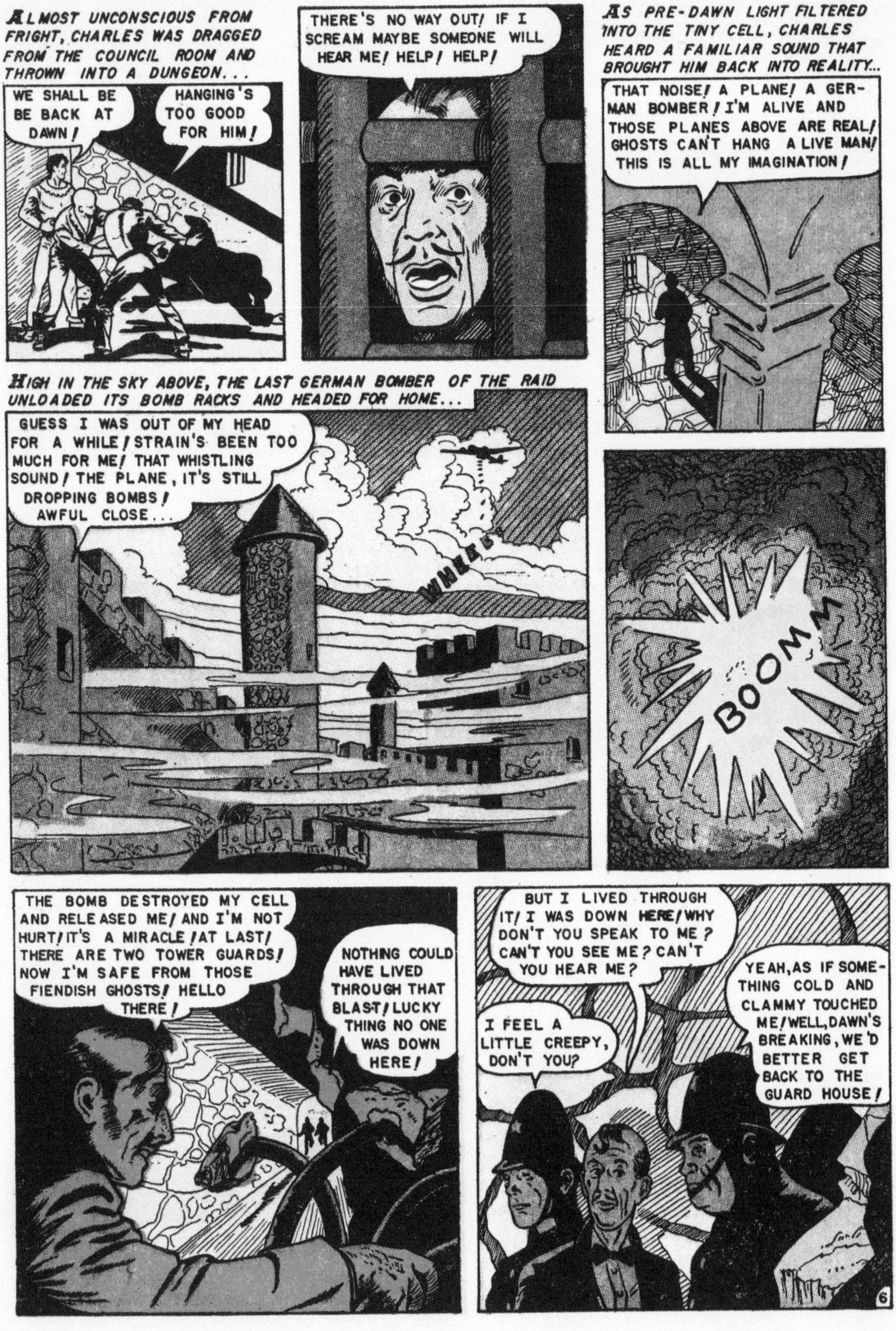
ALMOST UNCONSCIOUS FROM FRIGHT, CHARLES WAS DRAGGED FROM THE COUNCIL ROOM AND THROWN INTO A DUNGEON...
WE SHALL BE BE BACK AT DAWN!
HANGING'S TOO GOOD FOR HIM!
THERE'S NO WAY OUT! IF I SCREAM MAYBE SOMEONE WILL HEAR ME! HELP! HELP!
AS PRE-DAWN LIGHT FILTERED INTO THE TINY CELL, CHARLES HEARD A FAMILIAR SOUND THAT BROUGHT HIM BACK INTO REALITY...
THAT NOISE! A PLANE! A GERMAN BOMBER! I'M ALIVE AND THOSE PLANES ABOVE ARE REAL! GHOSTS CAN'T HANG A LIVE MAN! THIS IS ALL MY IMAGINATION!
HIGH IN THE SKY ABOVE, THE LAST GERMAN BOMBER OF THE RAID UNLOADED ITS BOMB RACKS AND HEADED FOR HOME...
GUESS I WAS OUT OF MY HEAD FOR A WHILE! STRAIN'S BEEN TOO MUCH FOR ME! THAT WHISTLING SOUND! THE PLANE, IT'S STILL DROPPING BOMBS! AWFUL CLOSE...
BOOMM
THE BOMB DESTROYED MY CELL AND RELEASED ME! AND I'M NOT HURT! IT'S A MIRACLE! AT LAST! THERE ARE TWO TOWER GUARDS! NOW I'M SAFE FROM THOSE FIENDISH GHOSTS! HELLO THERE!
NOTHING COULD HAVE LIVED THROUGH THAT BLAST! LUCKY THING NO ONE WAS DOWN HERE!
BUT I LIVED THROUGH IT! I WAS DOWN HERE! WHY DON'T YOU SPEAK TO ME? CAN'T YOU SEE ME? CAN'T YOU HEAR ME?
I FEEL A LITTLE CREEPY, DON'T YOU?
YEAH, AS IF SOMETHING COLD AND CLAMMY TOUCHED ME! WELL, DAWN'S BREAKING, WE'D BETTER GET BACK TO THE GUARD HOUSE!
6

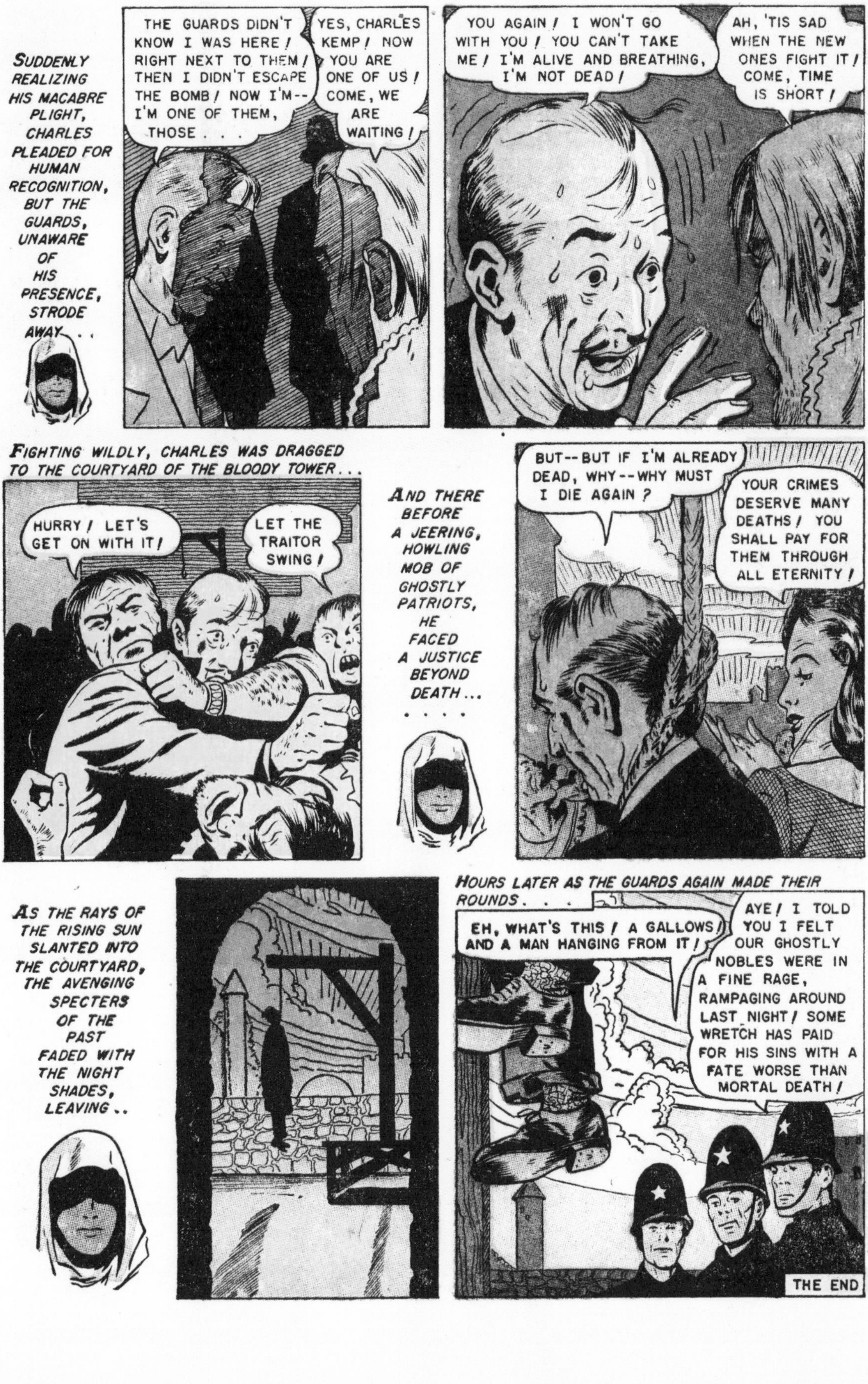
SUDDENLY REALIZING HIS MACABRE PLIGHT, CHARLES PLEADED FOR HUMAN RECOGNITION, BUT THE GUARDS, UNAWARE OF HIS PRESENCE, STRODE AWAY . . .
THE GUARDS DIDN'T KNOW I WAS HERE! RIGHT NEXT TO THEM! THEN I DIDN'T ESCAPE THE BOMB! NOW I'M-- I'M ONE OF THEM, THOSE . . .
YES, CHARLES KEMP! NOW YOU ARE ONE OF US! COME, WE ARE WAITING!
YOU AGAIN! I WON'T GO WITH YOU! YOU CAN'T TAKE ME! I'M ALIVE AND BREATHING, I'M NOT DEAD!
AH, 'TIS SAD WHEN THE NEW ONES FIGHT IT! COME, TIME IS SHORT!
FIGHTING WILDLY, CHARLES WAS DRAGGED TO THE COURTYARD OF THE BLOODY TOWER . . .
HURRY! LET'S GET ON WITH IT!
LET THE TRAITOR SWING!
AND THERE BEFORE A JEERING, HOWLING MOB OF GHOSTLY PATRIOTS, HE FACED A JUSTICE BEYOND DEATH . . . .
BUT--BUT IF I'M ALREADY DEAD, WHY--WHY MUST I DIE AGAIN?
YOUR CRIMES DESERVE MANY DEATHS! YOU SHALL PAY FOR THEM THROUGH ALL ETERNITY!
AS THE RAYS OF THE RISING SUN SLANTED INTO THE COURTYARD, THE AVENGING SPECTERS OF THE PAST FADED WITH THE NIGHT SHADES, LEAVING ..
HOURS LATER AS THE GUARDS AGAIN MADE THEIR ROUNDS . . .
EH, WHAT'S THIS! A GALLOWS! AND A MAN HANGING FROM IT!
AYE! I TOLD YOU I FELT OUR GHOSTLY NOBLES WERE IN A FINE RAGE, RAMPAGING AROUND LAST NIGHT! SOME WRETCH HAS PAID FOR HIS SINS WITH A FATE WORSE THAN MORTAL DEATH!
THE END

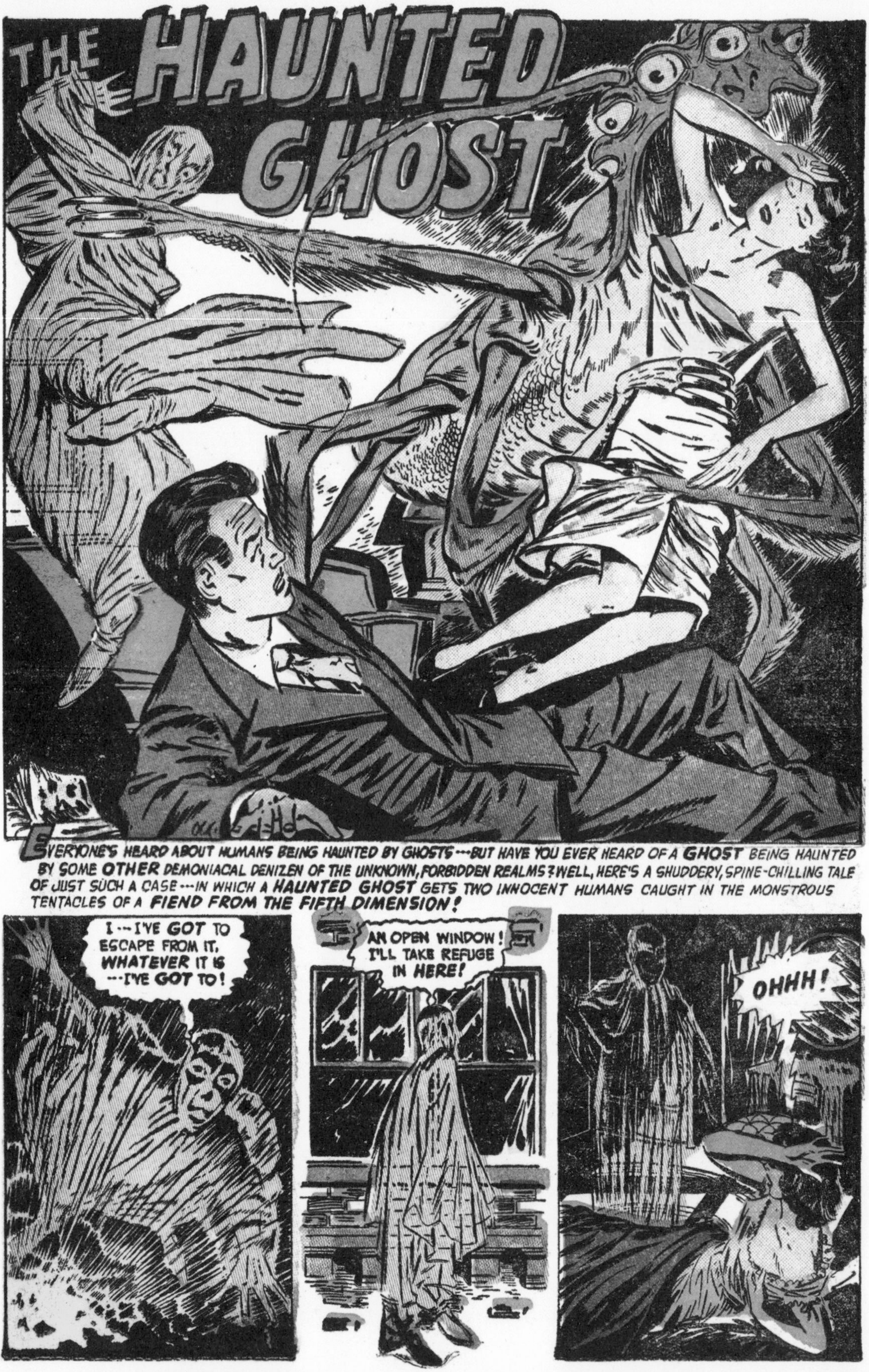
THE HAUNTED GHOST
EVERYONE'S HEARD ABOUT HUMANS BEING HAUNTED BY GHOSTS---BUT HAVE YOU EVER HEARD OF A GHOST BEING HAUNTED BY SOME OTHER DEMONIACAL DENIZEN OF THE UNKNOWN, FORBIDDEN REALMS? WELL, HERE'S A SHUDDERY, SPINE-CHILLING TALE OF JUST SUCH A CASE---IN WHICH A HAUNTED GHOST GETS TWO INNOCENT HUMANS CAUGHT IN THE MONSTROUS TENTACLES OF A FIEND FROM THE FIFTH DIMENSION!
I---I'VE GOT TO ESCAPE FROM IT, WHATEVER IT IS---I'VE GOT TO!
AN OPEN WINDOW! I'LL TAKE REFUGE IN HERE!
OHHH!

Adventures Into The Unknown #26, December 1951. King Ward. ACG.

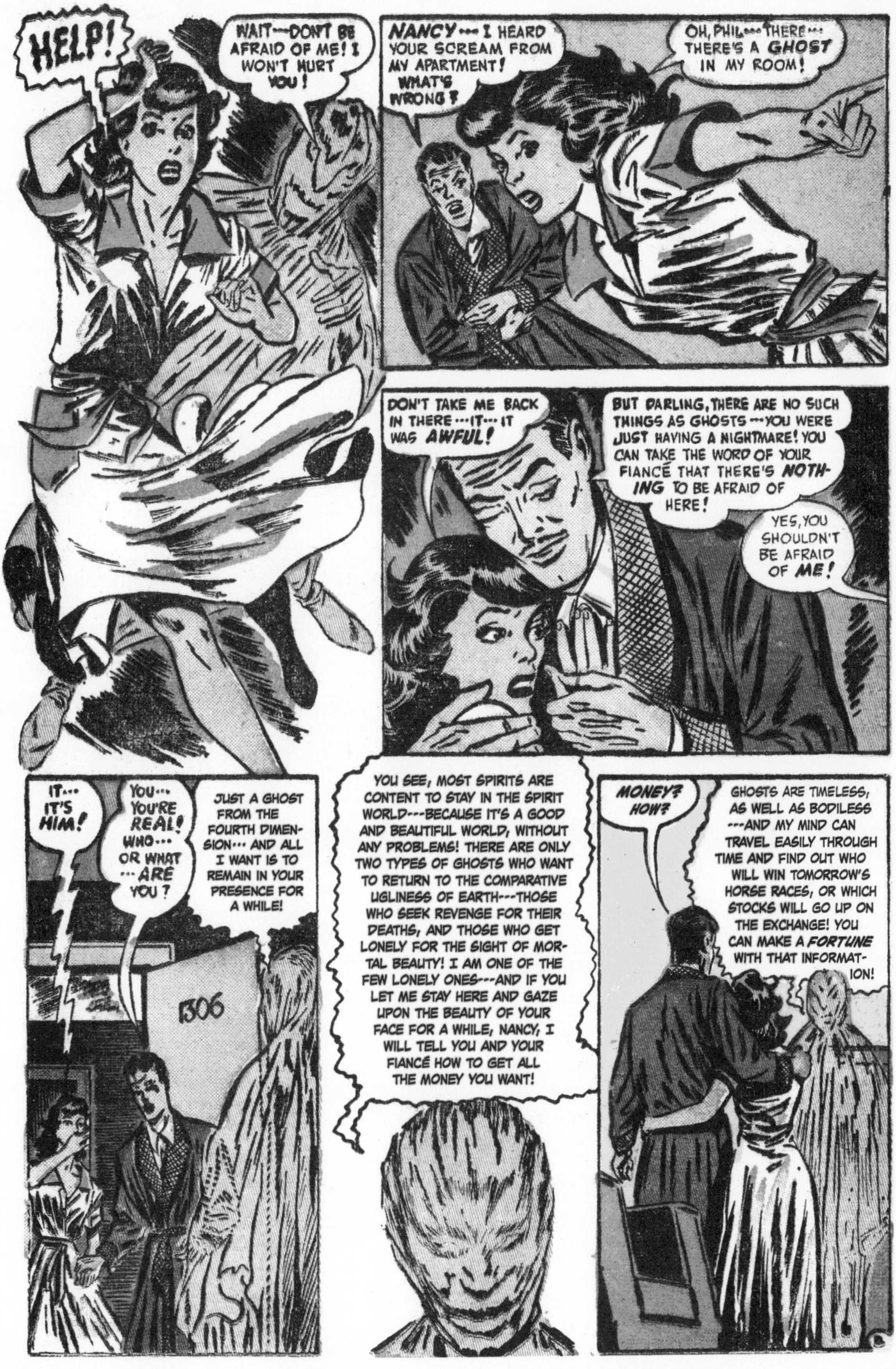

HELP!
WAIT---DON'T BE AFRAID OF ME! I WON'T HURT YOU!
NANCY--- I HEARD YOUR SCREAM FROM MY APARTMENT! WHAT'S WRONG?
OH, PHIL--- THERE--- THERE'S A GHOST IN MY ROOM!
DON'T TAKE ME BACK IN THERE---IT--- IT WAS AWFUL!
BUT DARLING, THERE ARE NO SUCH THINGS AS GHOSTS---YOU WERE JUST HAVING A NIGHTMARE! YOU CAN TAKE THE WORD OF YOUR FIANCÉ THAT THERE'S NOTHING TO BE AFRAID OF HERE!
YES, YOU SHOULDN'T BE AFRAID OF ME!
IT--- IT'S HIM!
YOU--- YOU'RE REAL! WHO--- OR WHAT---ARE YOU?
JUST A GHOST FROM THE FOURTH DIMENSION--- AND ALL I WANT IS TO REMAIN IN YOUR PRESENCE FOR A WHILE!
1306
YOU SEE, MOST SPIRITS ARE CONTENT TO STAY IN THE SPIRIT WORLD---BECAUSE IT'S A GOOD AND BEAUTIFUL WORLD, WITHOUT ANY PROBLEMS! THERE ARE ONLY TWO TYPES OF GHOSTS WHO WANT TO RETURN TO THE COMPARATIVE UGLINESS OF EARTH---THOSE WHO SEEK REVENGE FOR THEIR DEATHS, AND THOSE WHO GET LONELY FOR THE SIGHT OF MORTAL BEAUTY! I AM ONE OF THE FEW LONELY ONES---AND IF YOU LET ME STAY HERE AND GAZE UPON THE BEAUTY OF YOUR FACE FOR A WHILE, NANCY, I WILL TELL YOU AND YOUR FIANCÉ HOW TO GET ALL THE MONEY YOU WANT!
MONEY? HOW?
GHOSTS ARE TIMELESS, AS WELL AS BODILESS---AND MY MIND CAN TRAVEL EASILY THROUGH TIME AND FIND OUT WHO WILL WIN TOMORROW'S HORSE RACES, OR WHICH STOCKS WILL GO UP ON THE EXCHANGE! YOU CAN MAKE A FORTUNE WITH THAT INFORMATION!

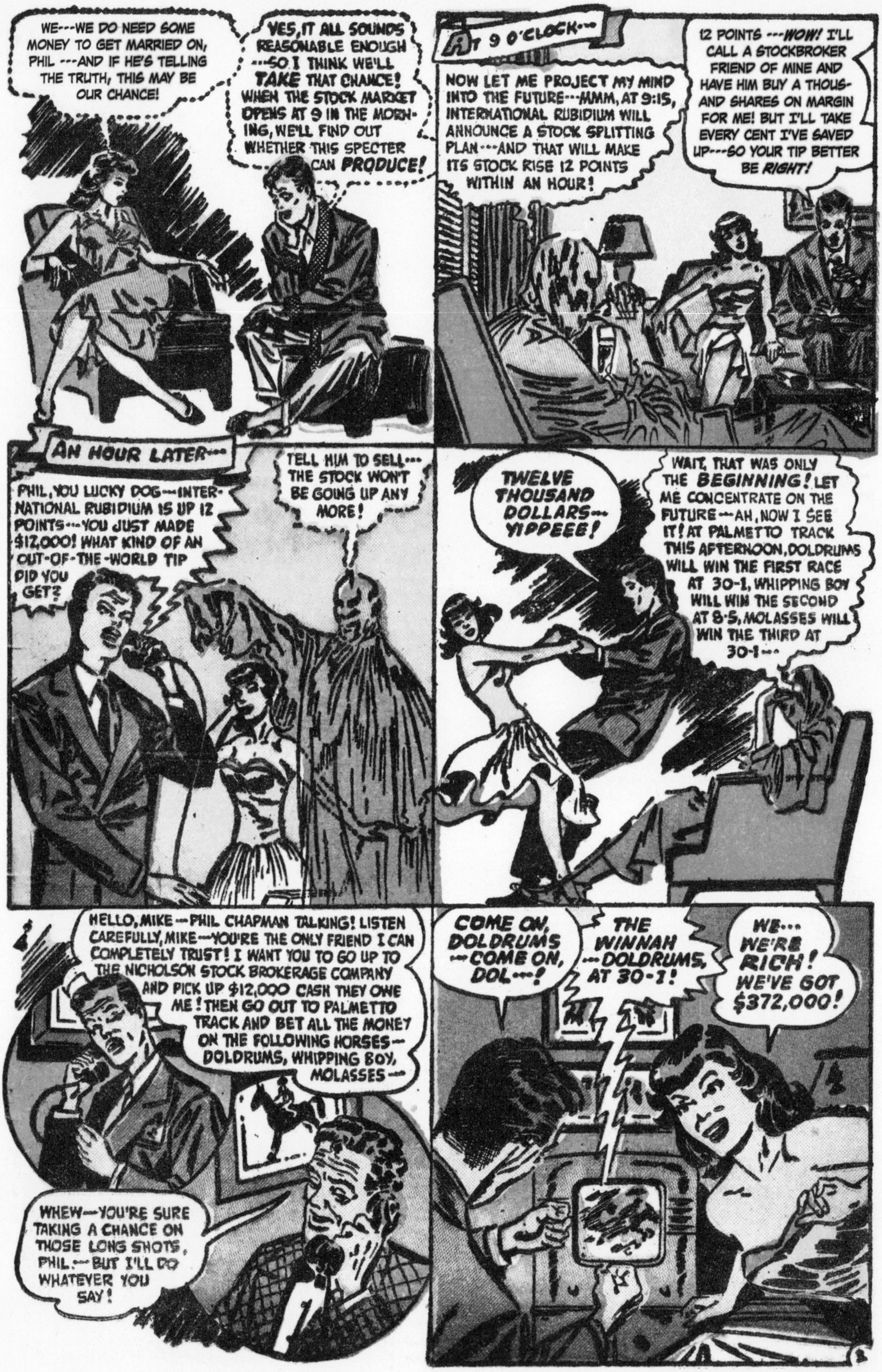

WE---WE DO NEED SOME MONEY TO GET MARRIED ON, PHIL ---AND IF HE'S TELLING THE TRUTH, THIS MAY BE OUR CHANCE!
YES, IT ALL SOUNDS REASONABLE ENOUGH ---SO I THINK WE'LL TAKE THAT CHANCE! WHEN THE STOCK MARKET OPENS AT 9 IN THE MORNING, WE'LL FIND OUT WHETHER THIS SPECTER CAN PRODUCE!
AT 9 O'CLOCK---
NOW LET ME PROJECT MY MIND INTO THE FUTURE---MMM, AT 9:15, INTERNATIONAL RUBIDIUM WILL ANNOUNCE A STOCK SPLITTING PLAN---AND THAT WILL MAKE ITS STOCK RISE 12 POINTS WITHIN AN HOUR!
12 POINTS ---WOW! I'LL CALL A STOCKBROKER FRIEND OF MINE AND HAVE HIM BUY A THOUSAND SHARES ON MARGIN FOR ME! BUT I'LL TAKE EVERY CENT I'VE SAVED UP---SO YOUR TIP BETTER BE RIGHT!
AN HOUR LATER---
PHIL, YOU LUCKY DOG---INTERNATIONAL RUBIDIUM IS UP 12 POINTS---YOU JUST MADE $12,000! WHAT KIND OF AN OUT-OF-THE-WORLD TIP DID YOU GET?
TELL HIM TO SELL--- THE STOCK WON'T BE GOING UP ANY MORE!
TWELVE THOUSAND DOLLARS--- YIPPEEE!
WAIT, THAT WAS ONLY THE BEGINNING! LET ME CONCENTRATE ON THE FUTURE---AH, NOW I SEE IT! AT PALMETTO TRACK THIS AFTERNOON, DOLDRUMS WILL WIN THE FIRST RACE AT 30-1, WHIPPING BOY WILL WIN THE SECOND AT 8-5, MOLASSES WILL WIN THE THIRD AT 30-1---
HELLO, MIKE---PHIL CHAPMAN TALKING! LISTEN CAREFULLY, MIKE---YOU'RE THE ONLY FRIEND I CAN COMPLETELY TRUST! I WANT YOU TO GO UP TO THE NICHOLSON STOCK BROKERAGE COMPANY AND PICK UP $12,000 CASH THEY OWE ME! THEN GO OUT TO PALMETTO TRACK AND BET ALL THE MONEY ON THE FOLLOWING HORSES--DOLDRUMS, WHIPPING BOY, MOLASSES--
WHEW---YOU'RE SURE TAKING A CHANCE ON THOSE LONG SHOTS, PHIL.--BUT I'LL DO WHATEVER YOU SAY!
COME ON, DOLDRUMS ---COME ON, DOL---!
THE WINNAH ---DOLDRUMS, AT 30-1!
WE--- WE'RE RICH! WE'VE GOT $372,000!

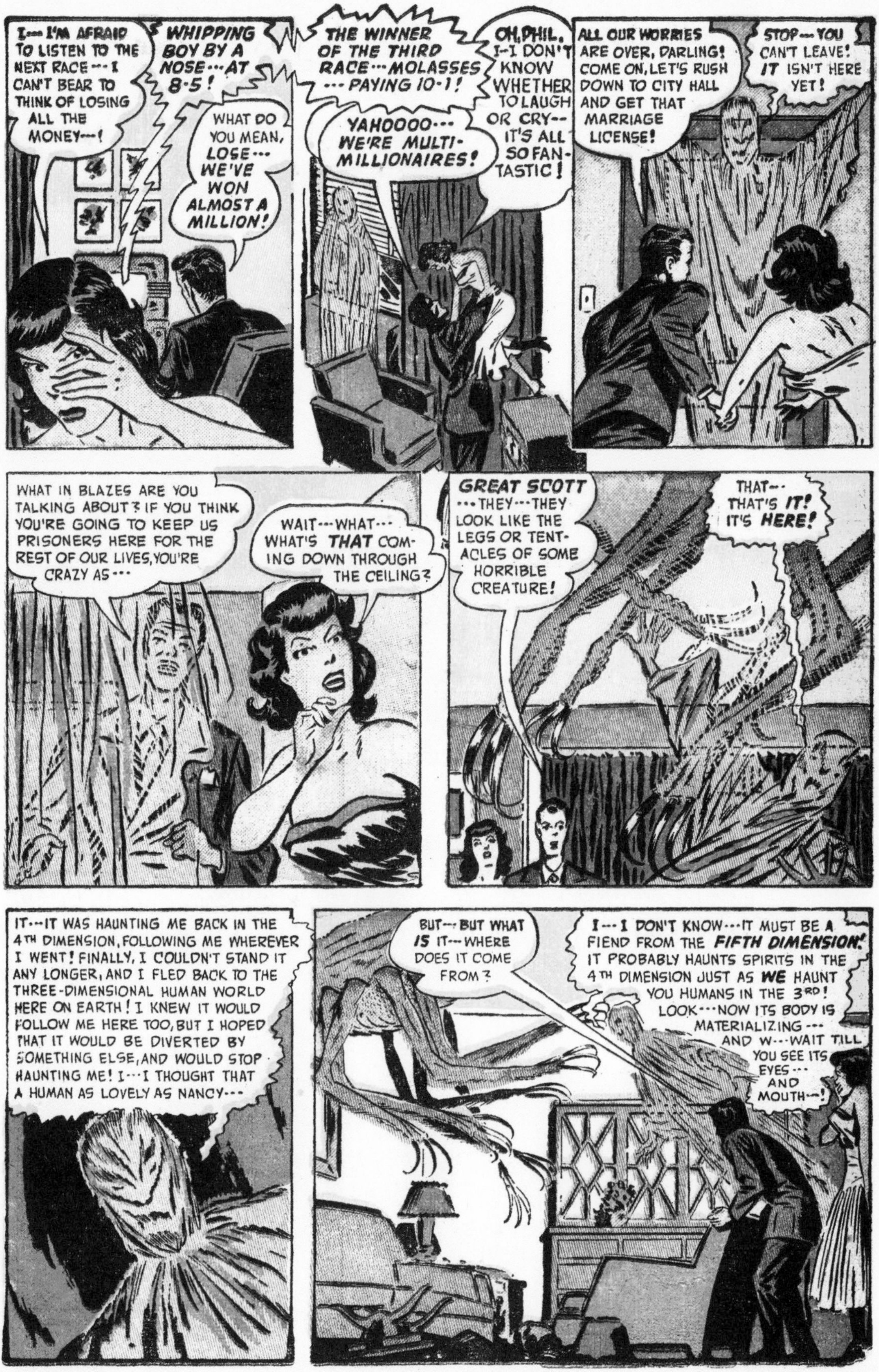

I--- I'M AFRAID TO LISTEN TO THE NEXT RACE --- I CAN'T BEAR TO THINK OF LOSING ALL THE MONEY---!
WHIPPING BOY BY A NOSE --- AT 8-5!
WHAT DO YOU MEAN, LOSE --- WE'VE WON ALMOST A MILLION!
THE WINNER OF THE THIRD RACE --- MOLASSES --- PAYING 10-1!
YAHOOOO--- WE'RE MULTI-MILLIONAIRES!
OH, PHIL, I-I DON'T KNOW WHETHER TO LAUGH OR CRY-- IT'S ALL SO FANTASTIC!
ALL OUR WORRIES ARE OVER, DARLING! COME ON, LET'S RUSH DOWN TO CITY HALL AND GET THAT MARRIAGE LICENSE!
STOP--- YOU CAN'T LEAVE! IT ISN'T HERE YET!
WHAT IN BLAZES ARE YOU TALKING ABOUT? IF YOU THINK YOU'RE GOING TO KEEP US PRISONERS HERE FOR THE REST OF OUR LIVES, YOU'RE CRAZY AS ---
WAIT --- WHAT --- WHAT'S THAT COMING DOWN THROUGH THE CEILING?
GREAT SCOTT --- THEY --- THEY LOOK LIKE THE LEGS OR TENTACLES OF SOME HORRIBLE CREATURE!
THAT-- THAT'S IT! IT'S HERE!
IT --- IT WAS HAUNTING ME BACK IN THE 4TH DIMENSION, FOLLOWING ME WHEREVER I WENT! FINALLY, I COULDN'T STAND IT ANY LONGER, AND I FLED BACK TO THE THREE-DIMENSIONAL HUMAN WORLD HERE ON EARTH! I KNEW IT WOULD FOLLOW ME HERE TOO, BUT I HOPED THAT IT WOULD BE DIVERTED BY SOMETHING ELSE, AND WOULD STOP HAUNTING ME! I --- I THOUGHT THAT A HUMAN AS LOVELY AS NANCY---
BUT --- BUT WHAT IS IT --- WHERE DOES IT COME FROM?
I --- I DON'T KNOW --- IT MUST BE A FIEND FROM THE FIFTH DIMENSION! IT PROBABLY HAUNTS SPIRITS IN THE 4TH DIMENSION JUST AS WE HAUNT YOU HUMANS IN THE 3RD! LOOK --- NOW ITS BODY IS MATERIALIZING --- AND W --- WAIT TILL YOU SEE ITS EYES --- AND MOUTH--!

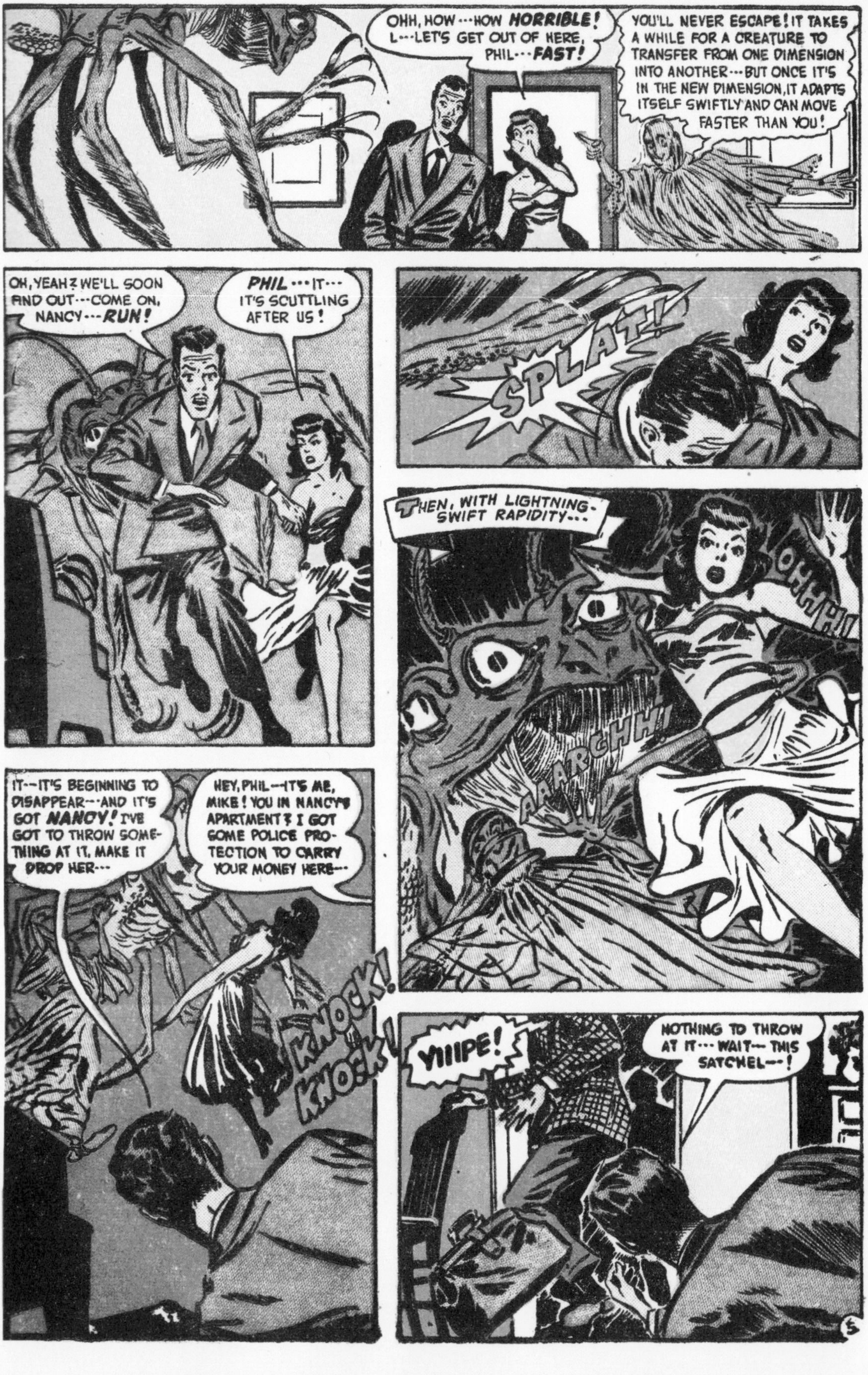
OHH, HOW ···HOW HORRIBLE! L···LET'S GET OUT OF HERE, PHIL··· FAST!
YOU'LL NEVER ESCAPE! IT TAKES A WHILE FOR A CREATURE TO TRANSFER FROM ONE DIMENSION INTO ANOTHER···BUT ONCE IT'S IN THE NEW DIMENSION, IT ADAPTS ITSELF SWIFTLY AND CAN MOVE FASTER THAN YOU!
OH, YEAH? WE'LL SOON FIND OUT···COME ON, NANCY···RUN!
PHIL···IT··· IT'S SCUTTLING AFTER US!
SPLAT!
THEN, WITH LIGHTNING-SWIFT RAPIDITY···
OHHH!
AAARGHH!
IT--IT'S BEGINNING TO DISAPPEAR---AND IT'S GOT NANCY! I'VE GOT TO THROW SOMETHING AT IT, MAKE IT DROP HER---
HEY, PHIL---IT'S ME, MIKE! YOU IN NANCY'S APARTMENT? I GOT SOME POLICE PROTECTION TO CARRY YOUR MONEY HERE---
KNOCK! KNOCK!
YIIIPE!
NOTHING TO THROW AT IT··· WAIT--- THIS SATCHEL---!
5

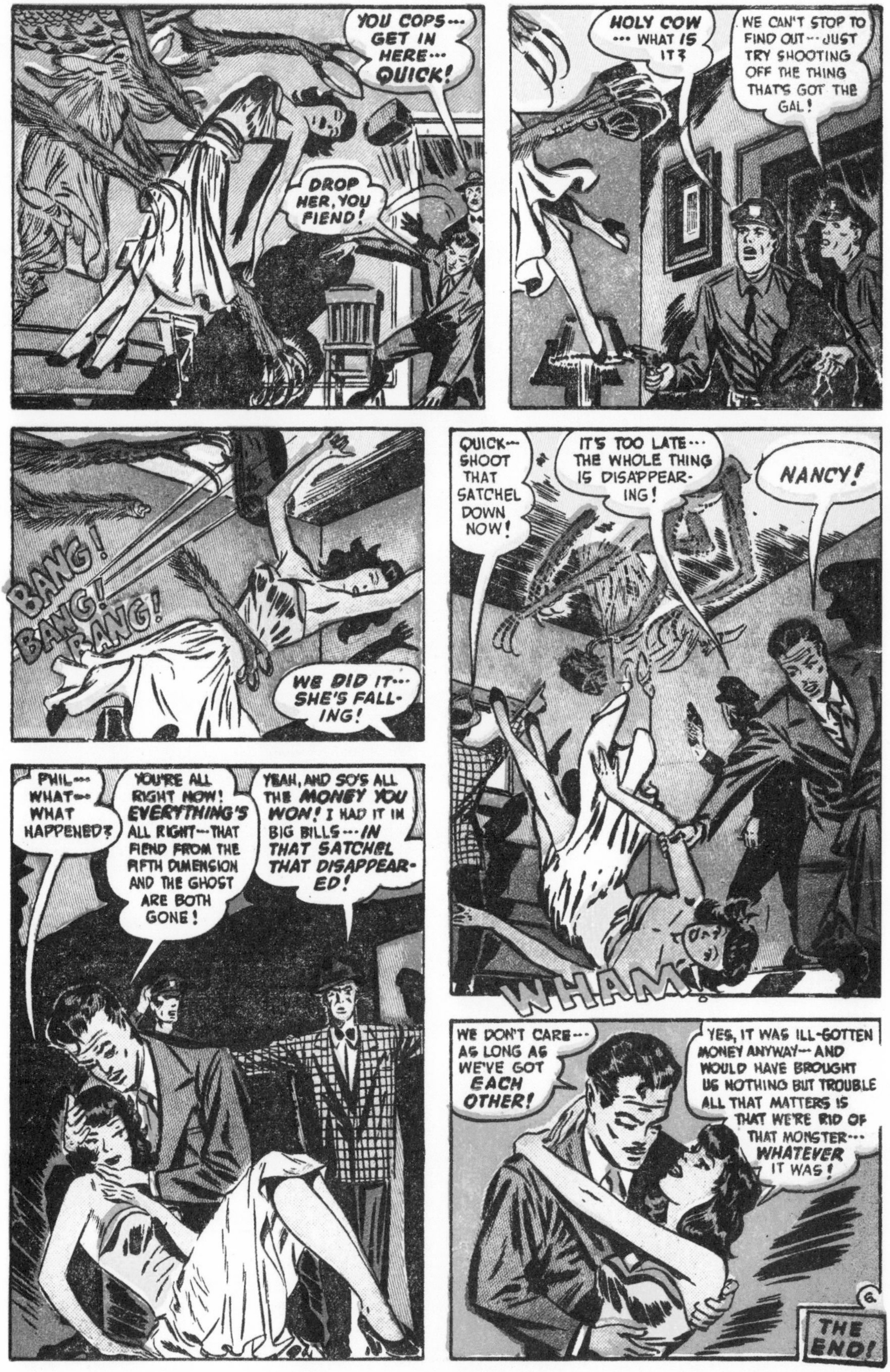
YOU COPS--- GET IN HERE--- QUICK!
DROP HER, YOU FIEND!
HOLY COW --- WHAT IS IT?
WE CAN'T STOP TO FIND OUT--- JUST TRY SHOOTING OFF THE THING THAT'S GOT THE GAL!
BANG! BANG! BANG!
WE DID IT--- SHE'S FALLING!
QUICK--- SHOOT THAT SATCHEL DOWN NOW!
IT'S TOO LATE--- THE WHOLE THING IS DISAPPEARING!
NANCY!
WHAM!
PHIL--- WHAT--- WHAT HAPPENED?
YOU'RE ALL RIGHT NOW! EVERYTHING'S ALL RIGHT---THAT FIEND FROM THE FIFTH DIMENSION AND THE GHOST ARE BOTH GONE!
YEAH, AND SO'S ALL THE MONEY YOU WON! I HAD IT IN BIG BILLS---IN THAT SATCHEL THAT DISAPPEARED!
WE DON'T CARE--- AS LONG AS WE'VE GOT EACH OTHER!
YES, IT WAS ILL-GOTTEN MONEY ANYWAY--- AND WOULD HAVE BROUGHT US NOTHING BUT TROUBLE ALL THAT MATTERS IS THAT WE'RE RID OF THAT MONSTER--- WHATEVER IT WAS!
6
THE END!

JURY of the UNDEAD

A MONSTER IN HUMAN FORM THEY CALLED HIM! A CRUEL AND SADISTIC MAN WHO USED HIS POWERS FOR HIS OWN EVIL PLEASURE IN THE SUFFERING OF OTHERS! BUT THERE IS A THING CALLED RETRIBUTION, AND THE REVENGE OF THE FATES CAN BE MORE TERRIBLE THAN THAT PLANNED BY MERE MAN! SO BACK THEY CAME, THE VENGEFUL CORPSES, TO BRING UNDREAMED OF TERROR TO *THE HANGING JUDGE!*

JUDGE TOBIAS PENTON IS ABOUT TO PRONOUNCE SENTENCE ON SOME POOR DEVIL...

BRING THE PRISONER BEFORE THE BAR! I AM, ER, READY TO SENTENCE HIM!

HASN'T A CHANCE!

POOR GUY!

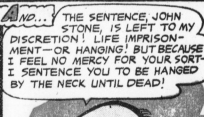

AND... THE SENTENCE, JOHN STONE, IS LEFT TO MY DISCRETION! LIFE IMPRISONMENT—OR HANGING! BUT BECAUSE I FEEL NO MERCY FOR YOUR SORT—I SENTENCE YOU TO BE HANGED BY THE NECK UNTIL DEAD!

Journey Into Fear #14, July 1953. Iger Shop. Superior.

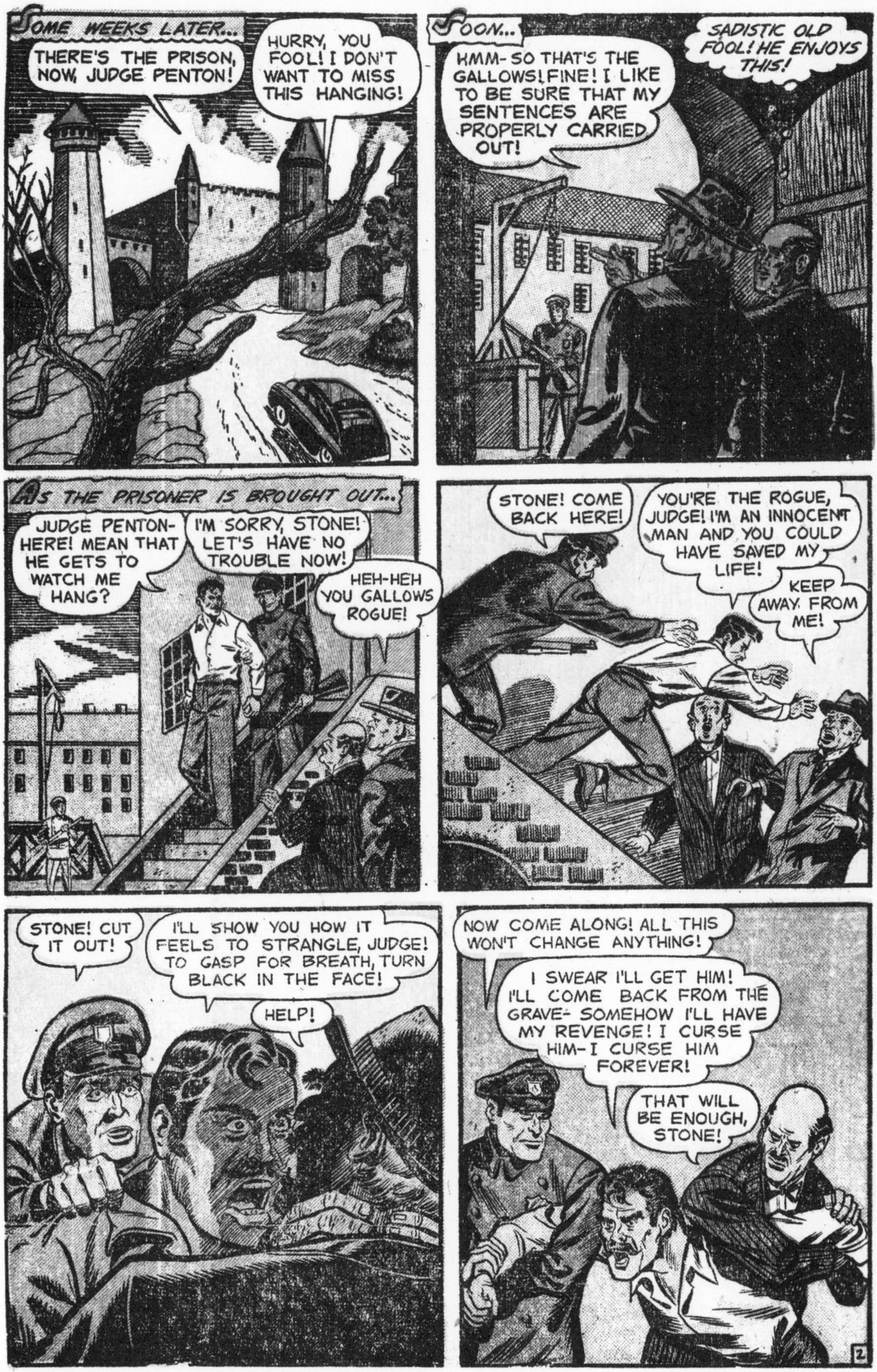
SOME WEEKS LATER...
THERE'S THE PRISON, NOW, JUDGE PENTON!
HURRY, YOU FOOL! I DON'T WANT TO MISS THIS HANGING!
SOON...
HMM- SO THAT'S THE GALLOWS! FINE! I LIKE TO BE SURE THAT MY SENTENCES ARE PROPERLY CARRIED OUT!
SADISTIC OLD FOOL! HE ENJOYS THIS!
AS THE PRISONER IS BROUGHT OUT...
JUDGE PENTON-HERE! MEAN THAT HE GETS TO WATCH ME HANG?
I'M SORRY, STONE! LET'S HAVE NO TROUBLE NOW!
HEH-HEH YOU GALLOWS ROGUE!
STONE! COME BACK HERE!
YOU'RE THE ROGUE, JUDGE! I'M AN INNOCENT MAN AND YOU COULD HAVE SAVED MY LIFE!
KEEP AWAY FROM ME!
STONE! CUT IT OUT!
I'LL SHOW YOU HOW IT FEELS TO STRANGLE, JUDGE! TO GASP FOR BREATH, TURN BLACK IN THE FACE!
HELP!
NOW COME ALONG! ALL THIS WON'T CHANGE ANYTHING!
I SWEAR I'LL GET HIM! I'LL COME BACK FROM THE GRAVE- SOMEHOW I'LL HAVE MY REVENGE! I CURSE HIM- I CURSE HIM FOREVER!
THAT WILL BE ENOUGH, STONE!
2

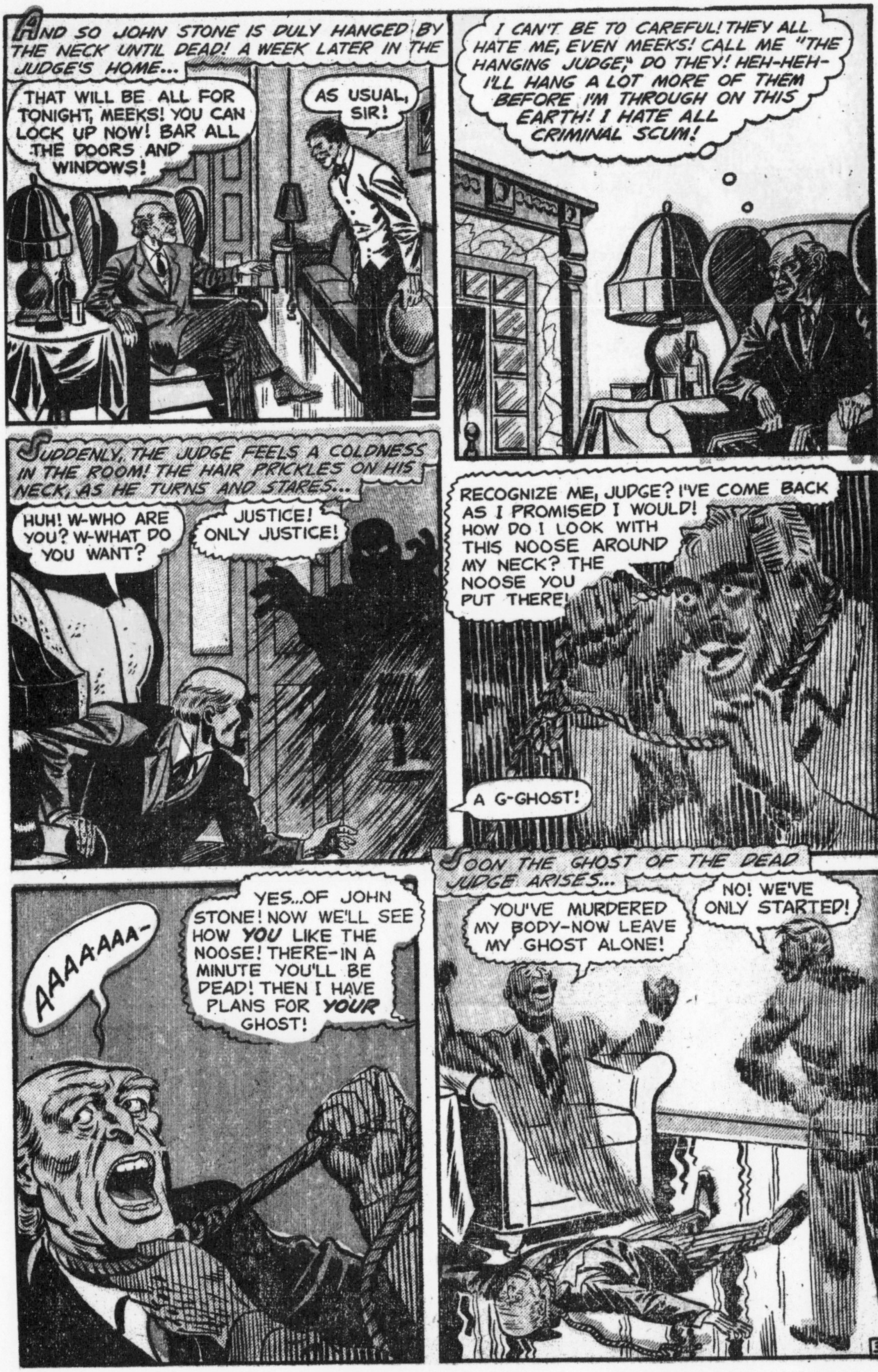
AND SO JOHN STONE IS DULY HANGED BY THE NECK UNTIL DEAD! A WEEK LATER IN THE JUDGE'S HOME...
THAT WILL BE ALL FOR TONIGHT, MEEKS! YOU CAN LOCK UP NOW! BAR ALL THE DOORS AND WINDOWS!
AS USUAL, SIR!
I CAN'T BE TO CAREFUL! THEY ALL HATE ME, EVEN MEEKS! CALL ME "THE HANGING JUDGE," DO THEY! HEH-HEH-I'LL HANG A LOT MORE OF THEM BEFORE I'M THROUGH ON THIS EARTH! I HATE ALL CRIMINAL SCUM!
SUDDENLY, THE JUDGE FEELS A COLDNESS IN THE ROOM! THE HAIR PRICKLES ON HIS NECK, AS HE TURNS AND STARES...
HUH! W-WHO ARE YOU? W-WHAT DO YOU WANT?
JUSTICE! ONLY JUSTICE!
RECOGNIZE ME, JUDGE? I'VE COME BACK AS I PROMISED I WOULD! HOW DO I LOOK WITH THIS NOOSE AROUND MY NECK? THE NOOSE YOU PUT THERE!
A G-GHOST!
AAAAAAA-
YES...OF JOHN STONE! NOW WE'LL SEE HOW YOU LIKE THE NOOSE! THERE-IN A MINUTE YOU'LL BE DEAD! THEN I HAVE PLANS FOR YOUR GHOST!
SOON THE GHOST OF THE DEAD JUDGE ARISES...
YOU'VE MURDERED MY BODY-NOW LEAVE MY GHOST ALONE!
NO! WE'VE ONLY STARTED!
3

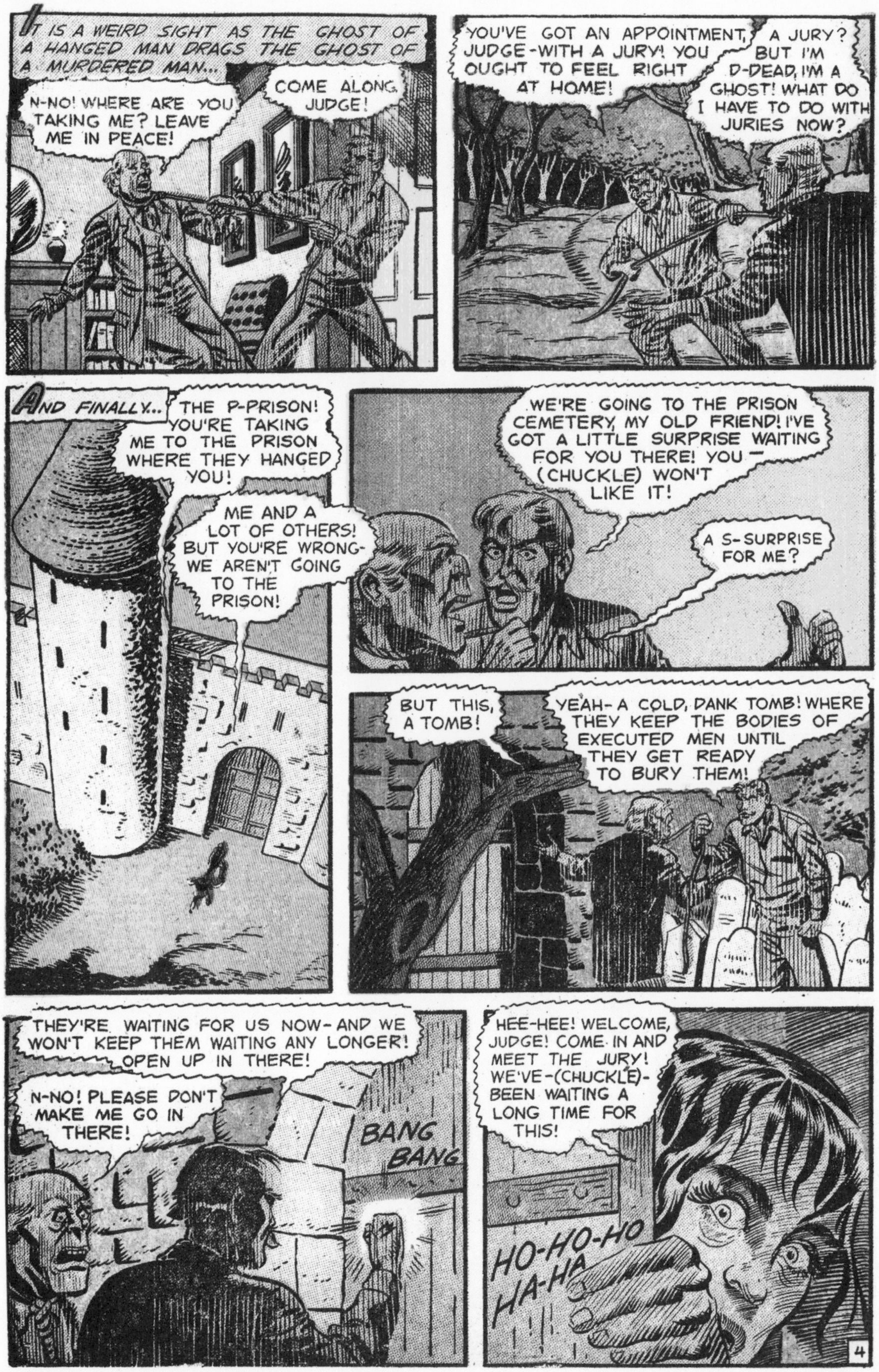
IT IS A WEIRD SIGHT AS THE GHOST OF A HANGED MAN DRAGS THE GHOST OF A MURDERED MAN...
N-NO! WHERE ARE YOU TAKING ME? LEAVE ME IN PEACE!
COME ALONG, JUDGE!
YOU'VE GOT AN APPOINTMENT, JUDGE-WITH A JURY! YOU OUGHT TO FEEL RIGHT AT HOME!
A JURY? BUT I'M D-DEAD, I'M A GHOST! WHAT DO I HAVE TO DO WITH JURIES NOW?
AND FINALLY...
THE P-PRISON! YOU'RE TAKING ME TO THE PRISON WHERE THEY HANGED YOU!
ME AND A LOT OF OTHERS! BUT YOU'RE WRONG-WE AREN'T GOING TO THE PRISON!
WE'RE GOING TO THE PRISON CEMETERY, MY OLD FRIEND! I'VE GOT A LITTLE SURPRISE WAITING FOR YOU THERE! YOU— (CHUCKLE) WON'T LIKE IT!
A S-SURPRISE FOR ME?
BUT THIS, A TOMB!
YEAH- A COLD, DANK TOMB! WHERE THEY KEEP THE BODIES OF EXECUTED MEN UNTIL THEY GET READY TO BURY THEM!
THEY'RE WAITING FOR US NOW- AND WE WON'T KEEP THEM WAITING ANY LONGER! OPEN UP IN THERE!
N-NO! PLEASE DON'T MAKE ME GO IN THERE!
BANG BANG
HEE-HEE! WELCOME, JUDGE! COME IN AND MEET THE JURY! WE'VE-(CHUCKLE)- BEEN WAITING A LONG TIME FOR THIS!
HO-HO-HO HA-HA
4

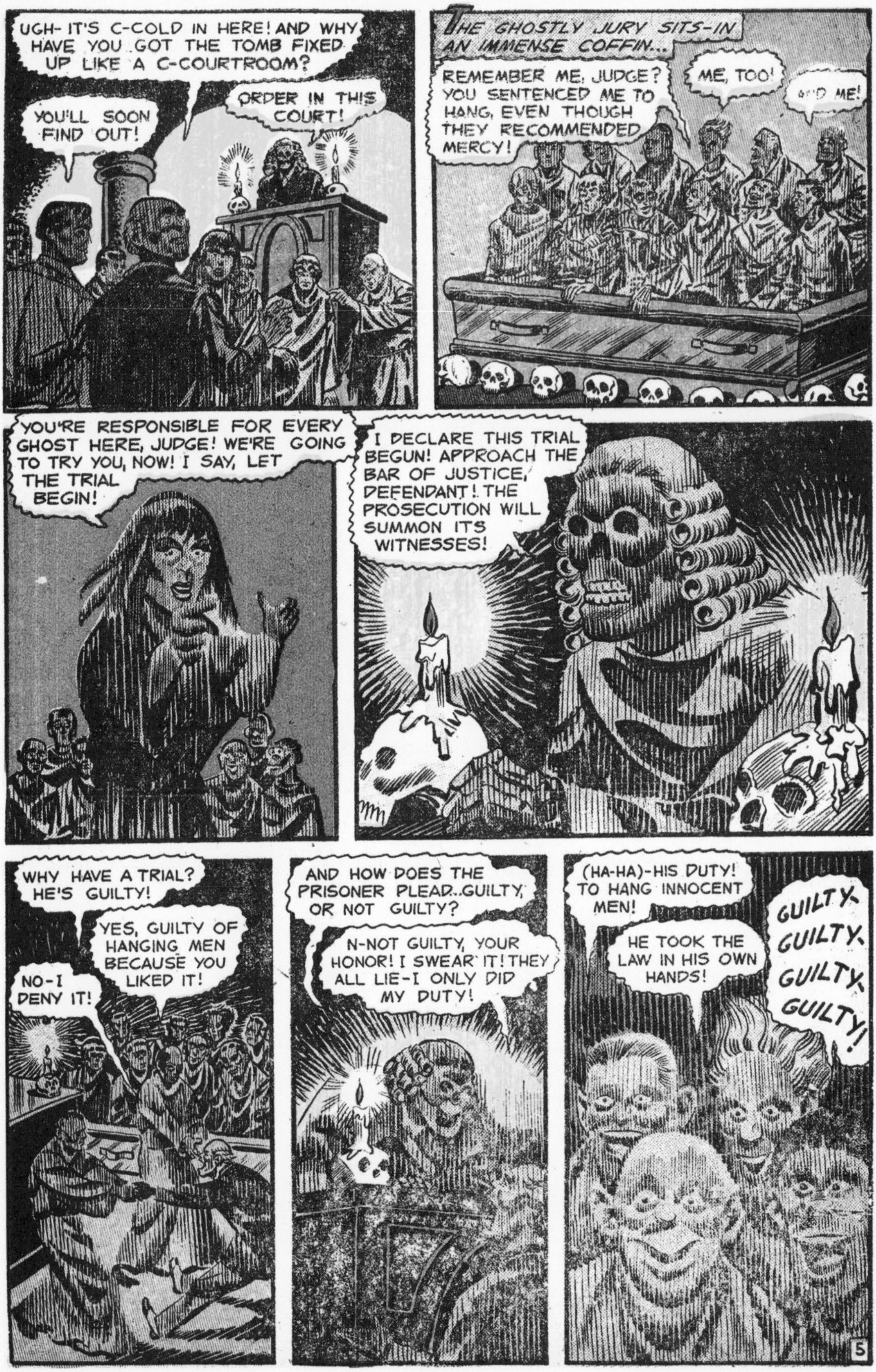
UGH- IT'S C-COLD IN HERE! AND WHY HAVE YOU GOT THE TOMB FIXED UP LIKE A C-COURTROOM?
YOU'LL SOON FIND OUT!
ORDER IN THIS COURT!
THE GHOSTLY JURY SITS-IN AN IMMENSE COFFIN...
REMEMBER ME, JUDGE? YOU SENTENCED ME TO HANG, EVEN THOUGH THEY RECOMMENDED MERCY!
ME, TOO!
AND ME!
YOU'RE RESPONSIBLE FOR EVERY GHOST HERE, JUDGE! WE'RE GOING TO TRY YOU, NOW! I SAY, LET THE TRIAL BEGIN!
I DECLARE THIS TRIAL BEGUN! APPROACH THE BAR OF JUSTICE, DEFENDANT! THE PROSECUTION WILL SUMMON ITS WITNESSES!
WHY HAVE A TRIAL? HE'S GUILTY!
YES, GUILTY OF HANGING MEN BECAUSE YOU LIKED IT!
NO-I DENY IT!
AND HOW DOES THE PRISONER PLEAD...GUILTY, OR NOT GUILTY?
N-NOT GUILTY, YOUR HONOR! I SWEAR IT! THEY ALL LIE-I ONLY DID MY DUTY!
(HA-HA)-HIS DUTY! TO HANG INNOCENT MEN!
HE TOOK THE LAW IN HIS OWN HANDS!
GUILTY- GUILTY- GUILTY- GUILTY!
5

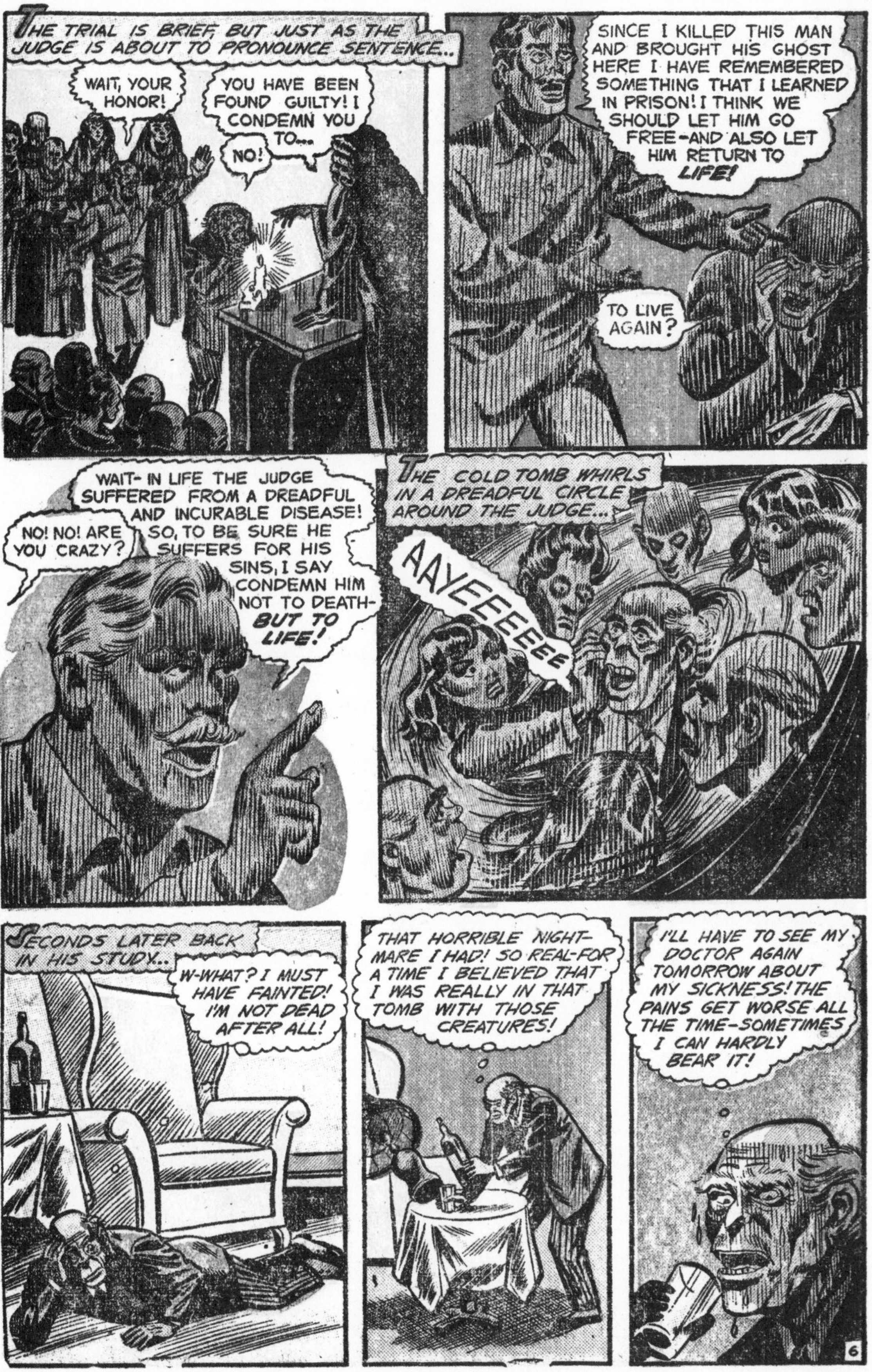
THE TRIAL IS BRIEF, BUT JUST AS THE JUDGE IS ABOUT TO PRONOUNCE SENTENCE...
WAIT, YOUR HONOR!
YOU HAVE BEEN FOUND GUILTY! I CONDEMN YOU TO...
NO!
SINCE I KILLED THIS MAN AND BROUGHT HIS GHOST HERE I HAVE REMEMBERED SOMETHING THAT I LEARNED IN PRISON! I THINK WE SHOULD LET HIM GO FREE-AND ALSO LET HIM RETURN TO LIFE!
TO LIVE AGAIN?
WAIT- IN LIFE THE JUDGE SUFFERED FROM A DREADFUL AND INCURABLE DISEASE! SO, TO BE SURE HE SUFFERS FOR HIS SINS, I SAY CONDEMN HIM NOT TO DEATH- BUT TO LIFE!
NO! NO! ARE YOU CRAZY?
THE COLD TOMB WHIRLS IN A DREADFUL CIRCLE AROUND THE JUDGE...
AAYEEEEEEE
SECONDS LATER BACK IN HIS STUDY...
W-WHAT? I MUST HAVE FAINTED! I'M NOT DEAD AFTER ALL!
THAT HORRIBLE NIGHT-MARE I HAD! SO REAL-FOR A TIME I BELIEVED THAT I WAS REALLY IN THAT TOMB WITH THOSE CREATURES!
I'LL HAVE TO SEE MY DOCTOR AGAIN TOMORROW ABOUT MY SICKNESS! THE PAINS GET WORSE ALL THE TIME-SOMETIMES I CAN HARDLY BEAR IT!
6

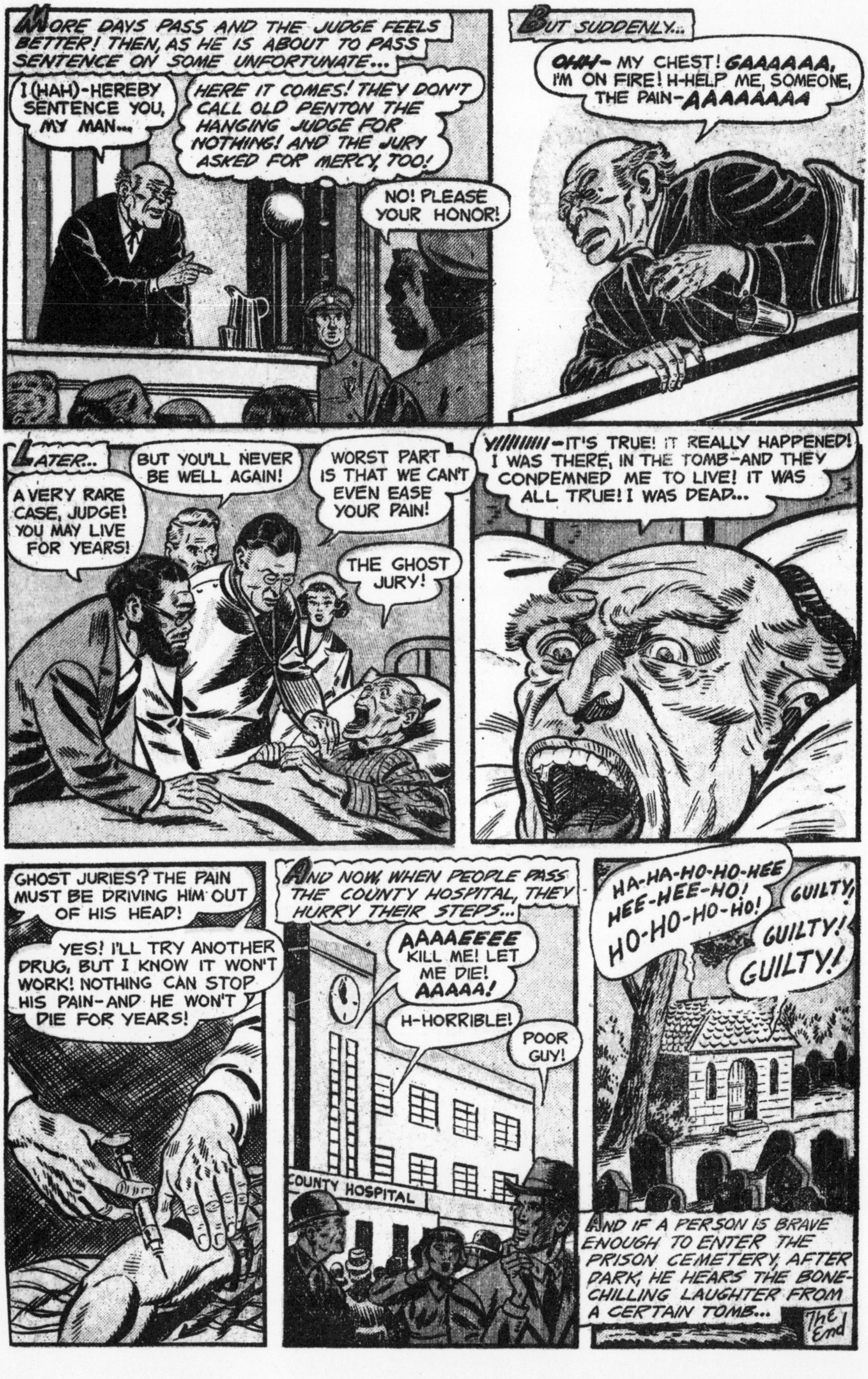
MORE DAYS PASS AND THE JUDGE FEELS BETTER! THEN, AS HE IS ABOUT TO PASS SENTENCE ON SOME UNFORTUNATE...
I (HAH)-HEREBY SENTENCE YOU, MY MAN...
HERE IT COMES! THEY DON'T CALL OLD PENTON THE HANGING JUDGE FOR NOTHING! AND THE JURY ASKED FOR MERCY, TOO!
NO! PLEASE YOUR HONOR!
BUT SUDDENLY...
OHH- MY CHEST! GAAAAAA, I'M ON FIRE! H-HELP ME, SOMEONE, THE PAIN-AAAAAAAA
LATER...
A VERY RARE CASE, JUDGE! YOU MAY LIVE FOR YEARS!
BUT YOU'LL NEVER BE WELL AGAIN!
WORST PART IS THAT WE CAN'T EVEN EASE YOUR PAIN!
THE GHOST JURY!
YIIIIIIIII-IT'S TRUE! IT REALLY HAPPENED! I WAS THERE, IN THE TOMB-AND THEY CONDEMNED ME TO LIVE! IT WAS ALL TRUE! I WAS DEAD...
GHOST JURIES? THE PAIN MUST BE DRIVING HIM OUT OF HIS HEAD!
YES! I'LL TRY ANOTHER DRUG, BUT I KNOW IT WON'T WORK! NOTHING CAN STOP HIS PAIN-AND HE WON'T DIE FOR YEARS!
AND NOW, WHEN PEOPLE PASS THE COUNTY HOSPITAL, THEY HURRY THEIR STEPS...
AAAAEEEE KILL ME! LET ME DIE! AAAAA!
H-HORRIBLE!
POOR GUY!
COUNTY HOSPITAL
HA-HA-HO-HO-HEE HEE-HEE-HO! HO-HO-HO-HO!
GUILTY! GUILTY! GUILTY!
AND IF A PERSON IS BRAVE ENOUGH TO ENTER THE PRISON CEMETERY AFTER DARK, HE HEARS THE BONE-CHILLING LAUGHTER FROM A CERTAIN TOMB...
The End

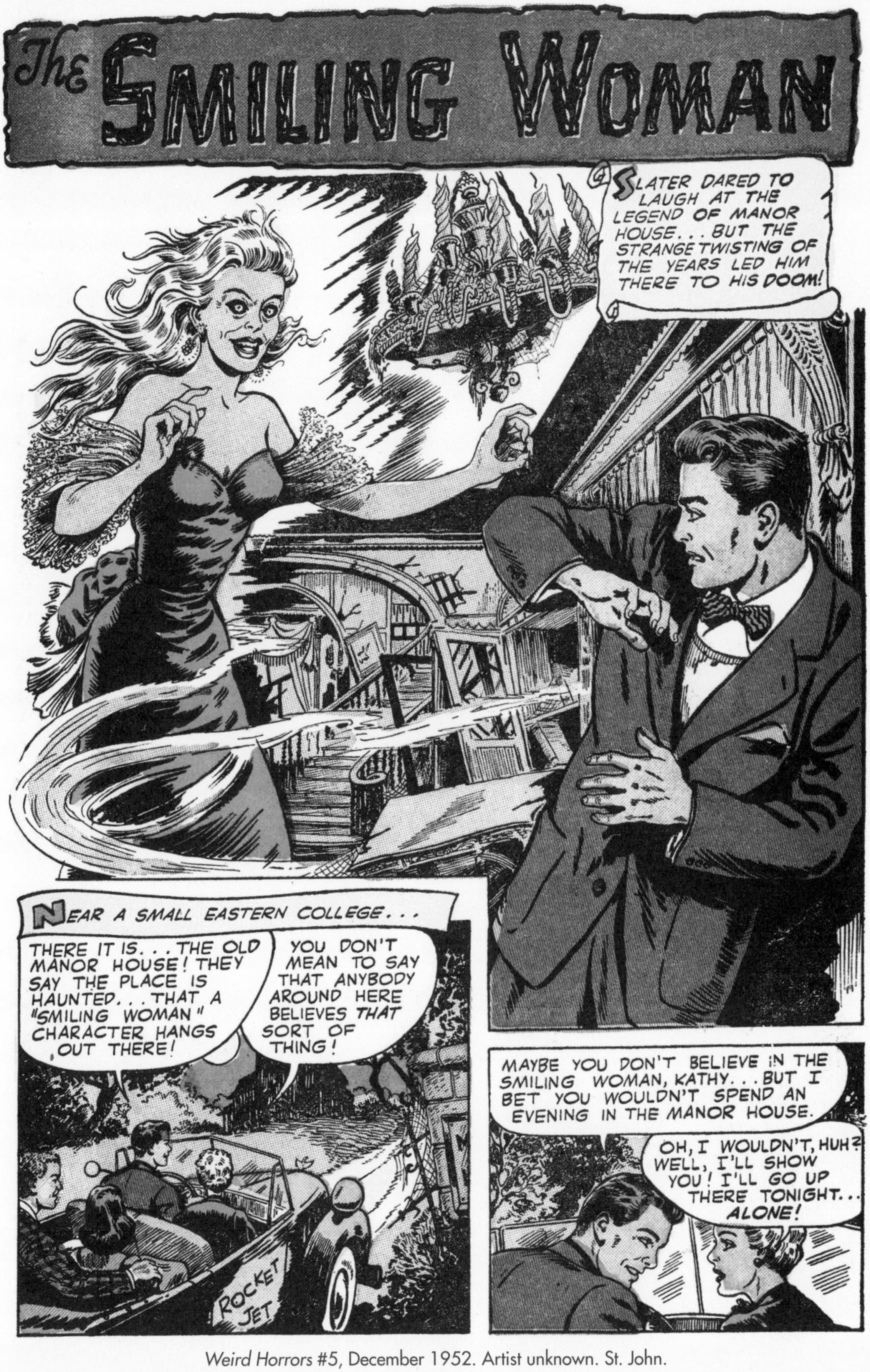
The Smiling Woman
Slater dared to laugh at the legend of Manor House... but the strange twisting of the years led him there to his doom!
Near a small eastern college...
There it is...the old Manor House! They say the place is haunted...that a "Smiling Woman" character hangs out there!
You don't mean to say that anybody around here believes that sort of thing!
Rocket Jet
Maybe you don't believe in the Smiling Woman, Kathy...but I bet you wouldn't spend an evening in the Manor House.
Oh, I wouldn't, huh? Well, I'll show you! I'll go up there tonight... alone!

Weird Horrors #5, December 1952. Artist unknown. St. John.

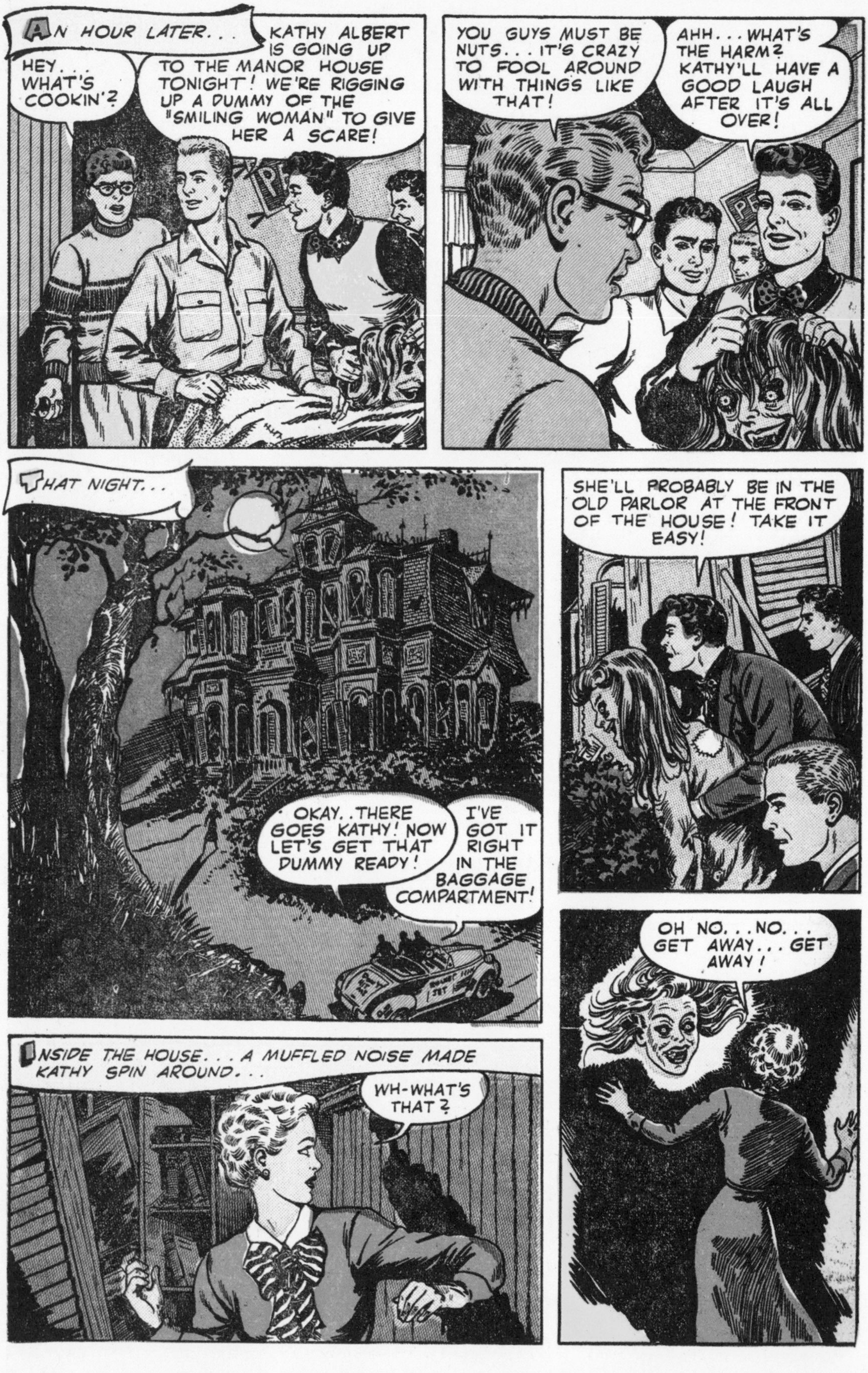
AN HOUR LATER...
HEY... WHAT'S COOKIN'?
KATHY ALBERT IS GOING UP TO THE MANOR HOUSE TONIGHT! WE'RE RIGGING UP A DUMMY OF THE "SMILING WOMAN" TO GIVE HER A SCARE!
YOU GUYS MUST BE NUTS... IT'S CRAZY TO FOOL AROUND WITH THINGS LIKE THAT!
AHH...WHAT'S THE HARM? KATHY'LL HAVE A GOOD LAUGH AFTER IT'S ALL OVER!
THAT NIGHT...
OKAY..THERE GOES KATHY! NOW LET'S GET THAT DUMMY READY!
I'VE GOT IT RIGHT IN THE BAGGAGE COMPARTMENT!
SHE'LL PROBABLY BE IN THE OLD PARLOR AT THE FRONT OF THE HOUSE! TAKE IT EASY!
INSIDE THE HOUSE... A MUFFLED NOISE MADE KATHY SPIN AROUND...
WH-WHAT'S THAT?
OH NO...NO... GET AWAY... GET AWAY!

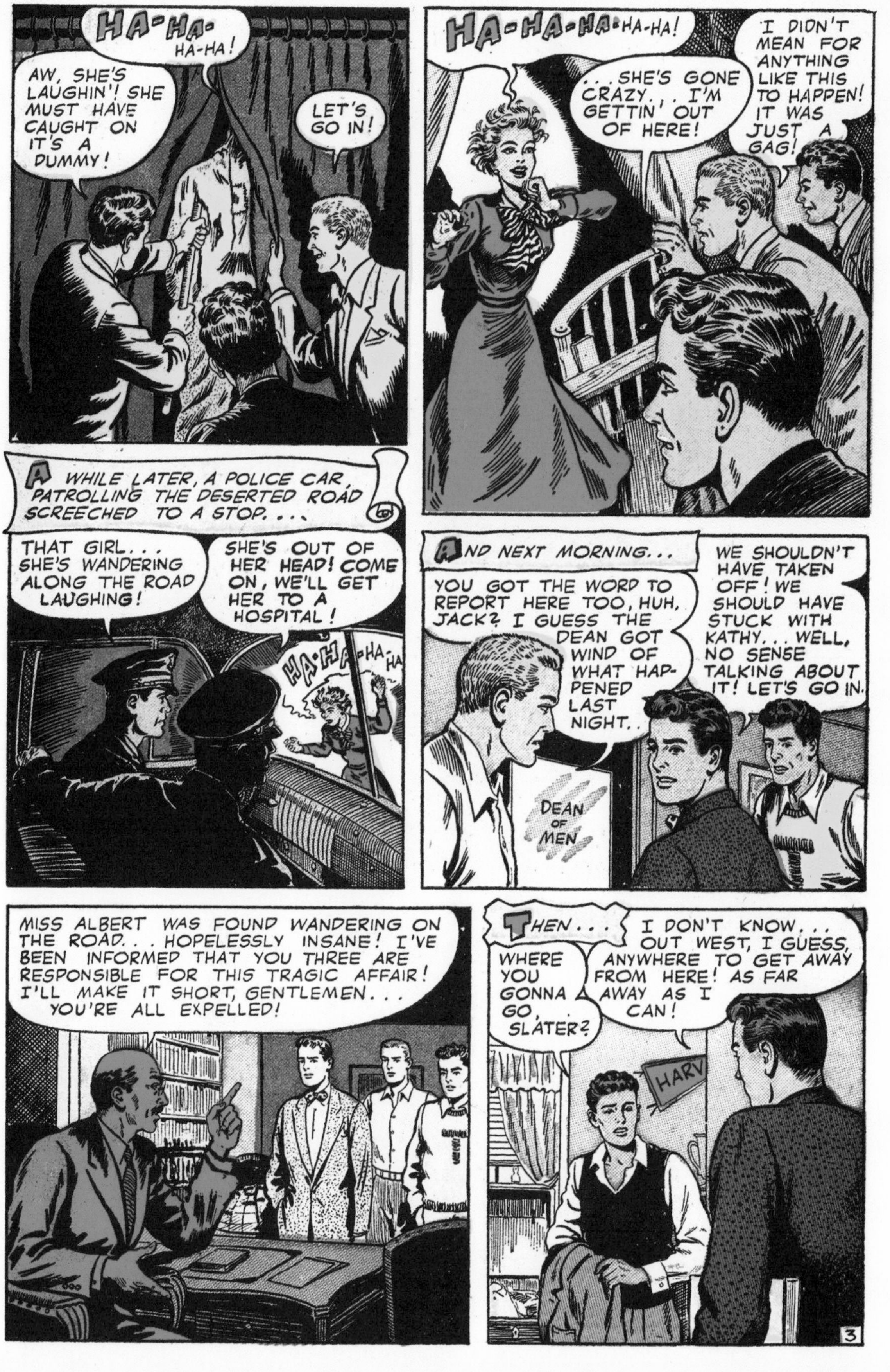
HA-HA-HA-HA!
AW, SHE'S LAUGHIN'! SHE MUST HAVE CAUGHT ON IT'S A DUMMY!
LET'S GO IN!
HA-HA-HA-HA-HA!
...SHE'S GONE CRAZY... I'M GETTIN' OUT OF HERE!
I DIDN'T MEAN FOR ANYTHING LIKE THIS TO HAPPEN! IT WAS JUST A GAG!
A WHILE LATER, A POLICE CAR, PATROLLING THE DESERTED ROAD SCREECHED TO A STOP...
THAT GIRL... SHE'S WANDERING ALONG THE ROAD LAUGHING!
SHE'S OUT OF HER HEAD! COME ON, WE'LL GET HER TO A HOSPITAL!
HA-HA-HA-HA
AND NEXT MORNING...
YOU GOT THE WORD TO REPORT HERE TOO, HUH, JACK? I GUESS THE DEAN GOT WIND OF WHAT HAPPENED LAST NIGHT..
WE SHOULDN'T HAVE TAKEN OFF! WE SHOULD HAVE STUCK WITH KATHY... WELL, NO SENSE TALKING ABOUT IT! LET'S GO IN.
DEAN OF MEN
MISS ALBERT WAS FOUND WANDERING ON THE ROAD... HOPELESSLY INSANE! I'VE BEEN INFORMED THAT YOU THREE ARE RESPONSIBLE FOR THIS TRAGIC AFFAIR! I'LL MAKE IT SHORT, GENTLEMEN... YOU'RE ALL EXPELLED!
THEN...
WHERE YOU GONNA GO, SLATER?
I DON'T KNOW... OUT WEST, I GUESS, ANYWHERE TO GET AWAY FROM HERE! AS FAR AWAY AS I CAN!
HARV
3

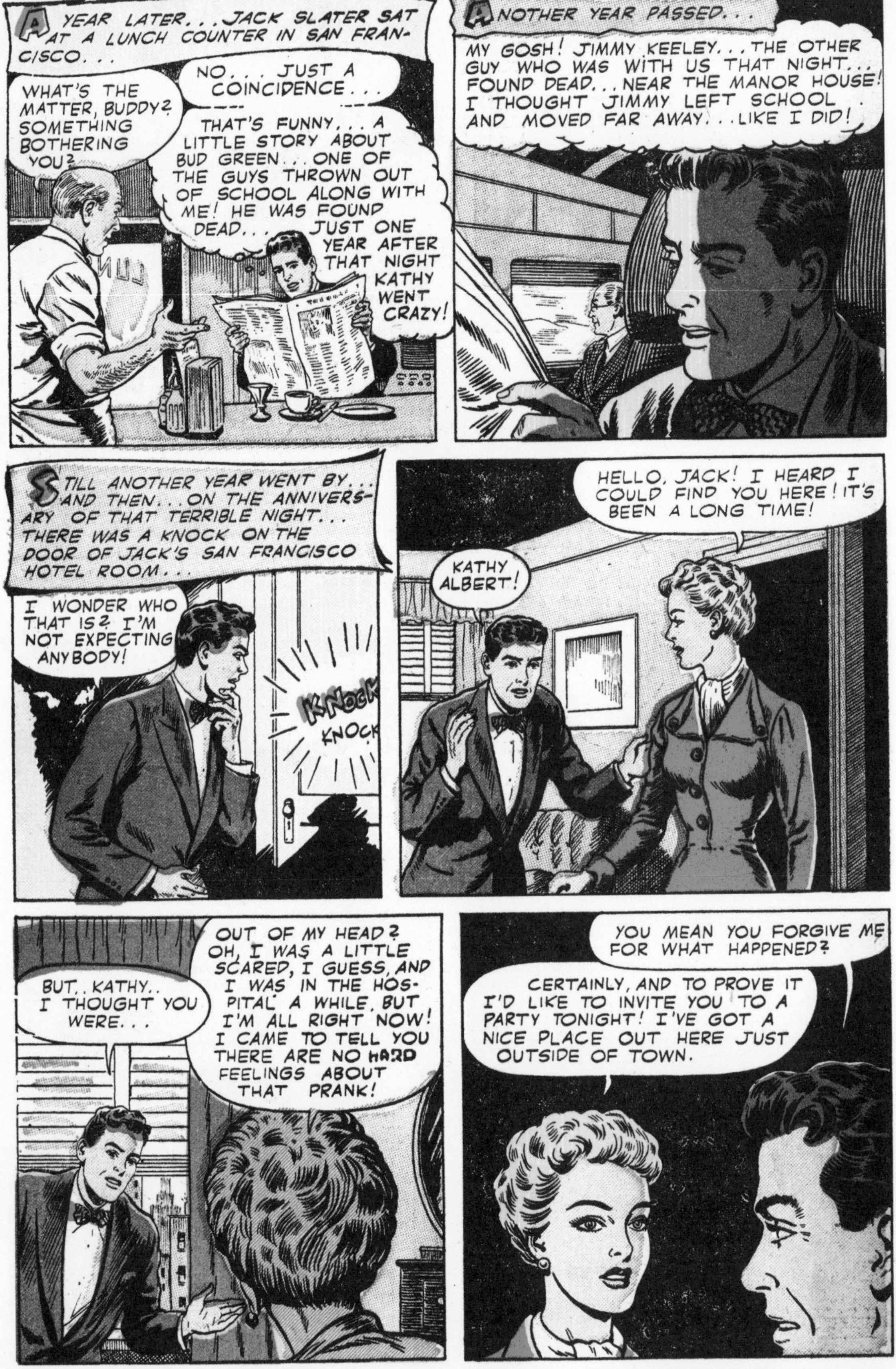
A YEAR LATER... JACK SLATER SAT AT A LUNCH COUNTER IN SAN FRANCISCO...
WHAT'S THE MATTER, BUDDY? SOMETHING BOTHERING YOU?
NO... JUST A COINCIDENCE...
THAT'S FUNNY... A LITTLE STORY ABOUT BUD GREEN... ONE OF THE GUYS THROWN OUT OF SCHOOL ALONG WITH ME! HE WAS FOUND DEAD... JUST ONE YEAR AFTER THAT NIGHT KATHY WENT CRAZY!
ANOTHER YEAR PASSED...
MY GOSH! JIMMY KEELEY... THE OTHER GUY WHO WAS WITH US THAT NIGHT... FOUND DEAD... NEAR THE MANOR HOUSE! I THOUGHT JIMMY LEFT SCHOOL AND MOVED FAR AWAY... LIKE I DID!
STILL ANOTHER YEAR WENT BY... AND THEN... ON THE ANNIVERSARY OF THAT TERRIBLE NIGHT... THERE WAS A KNOCK ON THE DOOR OF JACK'S SAN FRANCISCO HOTEL ROOM...
I WONDER WHO THAT IS? I'M NOT EXPECTING ANYBODY!
KNOCK
KNOCK
HELLO, JACK! I HEARD I COULD FIND YOU HERE! IT'S BEEN A LONG TIME!
KATHY ALBERT!
BUT, KATHY.. I THOUGHT YOU WERE...
OUT OF MY HEAD? OH, I WAS A LITTLE SCARED, I GUESS, AND I WAS IN THE HOSPITAL A WHILE, BUT I'M ALL RIGHT NOW! I CAME TO TELL YOU THERE ARE NO HARD FEELINGS ABOUT THAT PRANK!
YOU MEAN YOU FORGIVE ME FOR WHAT HAPPENED?
CERTAINLY, AND TO PROVE IT I'D LIKE TO INVITE YOU TO A PARTY TONIGHT! I'VE GOT A NICE PLACE OUT HERE JUST OUTSIDE OF TOWN.

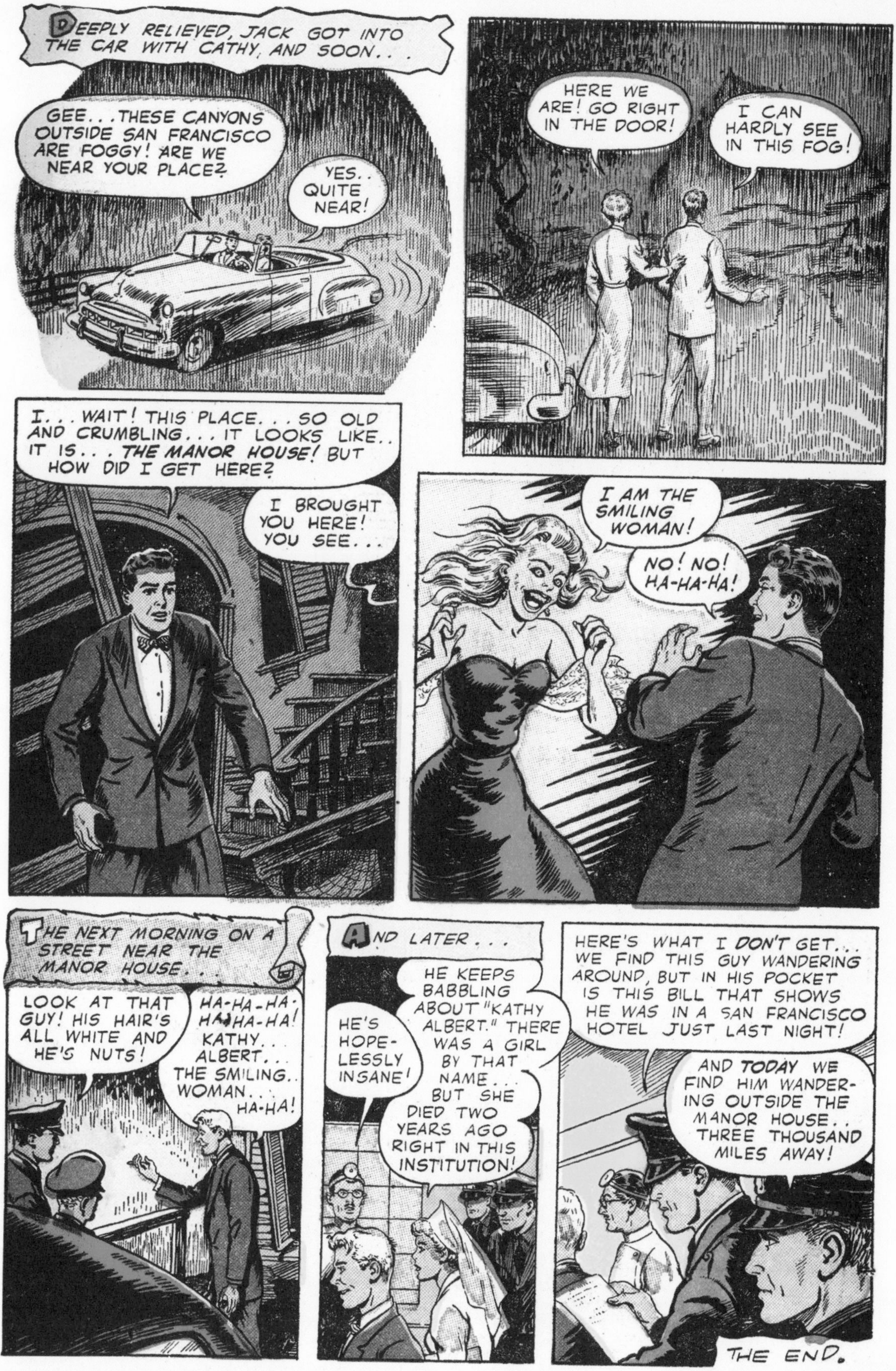
DEEPLY RELIEVED, JACK GOT INTO THE CAR WITH CATHY, AND SOON...
GEE... THESE CANYONS OUTSIDE SAN FRANCISCO ARE FOGGY! ARE WE NEAR YOUR PLACE?
YES.. QUITE NEAR!
HERE WE ARE! GO RIGHT IN THE DOOR!
I CAN HARDLY SEE IN THIS FOG!
I... WAIT! THIS PLACE... SO OLD AND CRUMBLING... IT LOOKS LIKE.. IT IS... THE MANOR HOUSE! BUT HOW DID I GET HERE?
I BROUGHT YOU HERE! YOU SEE...
I AM THE SMILING WOMAN!
NO! NO! HA-HA-HA!
THE NEXT MORNING ON A STREET NEAR THE MANOR HOUSE...
LOOK AT THAT GUY! HIS HAIR'S ALL WHITE AND HE'S NUTS!
HA-HA-HA-HA-HA-HA! KATHY... ALBERT... THE SMILING.. WOMAN... HA-HA!
AND LATER...
HE'S HOPE-LESSLY INSANE!
HE KEEPS BABBLING ABOUT "KATHY ALBERT." THERE WAS A GIRL BY THAT NAME... BUT SHE DIED TWO YEARS AGO RIGHT IN THIS INSTITUTION!
HERE'S WHAT I DON'T GET... WE FIND THIS GUY WANDERING AROUND, BUT IN HIS POCKET IS THIS BILL THAT SHOWS HE WAS IN A SAN FRANCISCO HOTEL JUST LAST NIGHT!
AND TODAY WE FIND HIM WANDER-ING OUTSIDE THE MANOR HOUSE.. THREE THOUSAND MILES AWAY!
THE END.

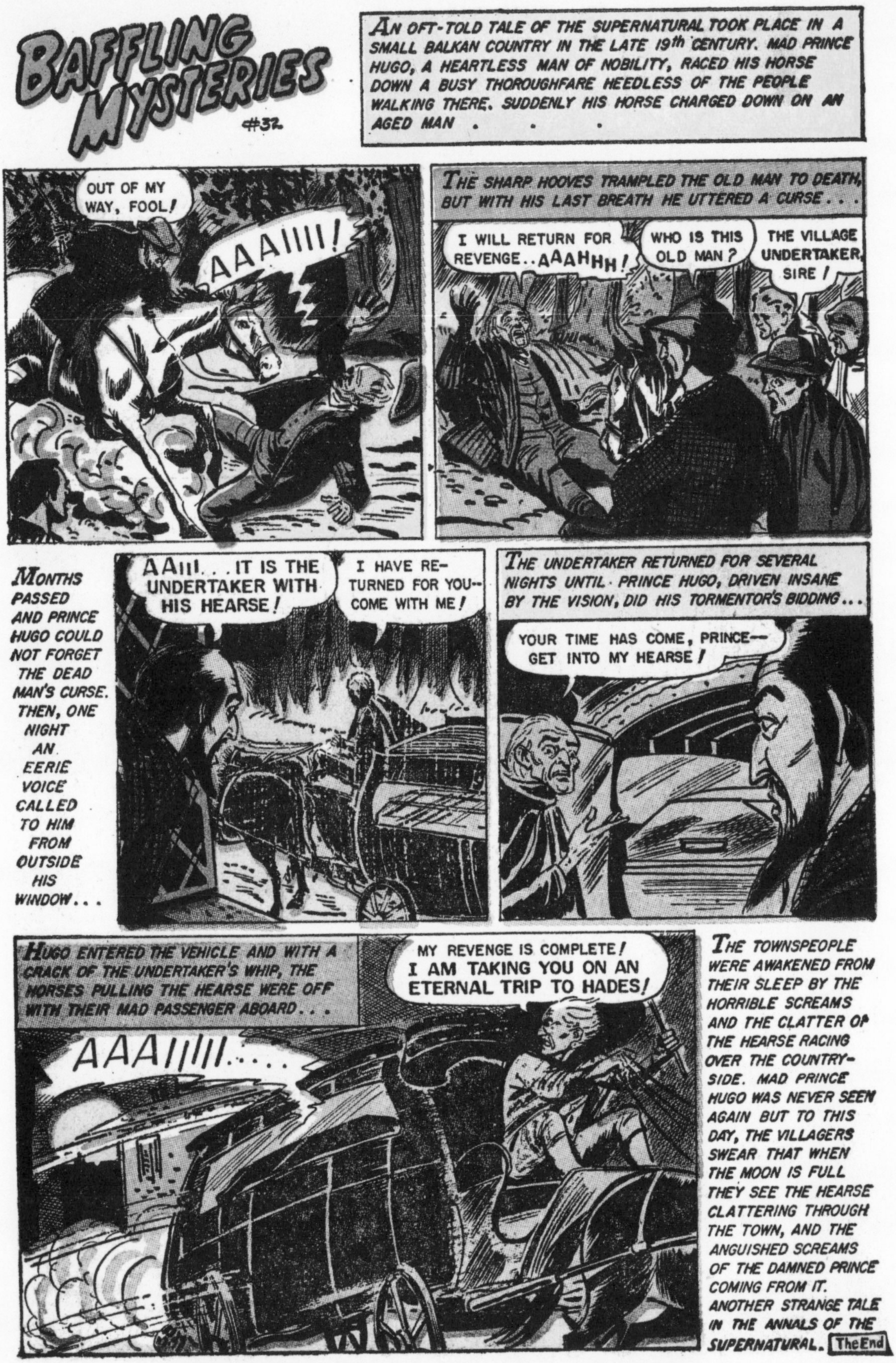
BAFFLING MYSTERIES
#32
AN OFT-TOLD TALE OF THE SUPERNATURAL TOOK PLACE IN A SMALL BALKAN COUNTRY IN THE LATE 19th CENTURY. MAD PRINCE HUGO, A HEARTLESS MAN OF NOBILITY, RACED HIS HORSE DOWN A BUSY THOROUGHFARE HEEDLESS OF THE PEOPLE WALKING THERE. SUDDENLY HIS HORSE CHARGED DOWN ON AN AGED MAN . . .
OUT OF MY WAY, FOOL!
AAAIIII!
THE SHARP HOOVES TRAMPLED THE OLD MAN TO DEATH, BUT WITH HIS LAST BREATH HE UTTERED A CURSE . . .
I WILL RETURN FOR REVENGE.. AAAHHH!
WHO IS THIS OLD MAN?
THE VILLAGE UNDERTAKER, SIRE!
MONTHS PASSED AND PRINCE HUGO COULD NOT FORGET THE DEAD MAN'S CURSE. THEN, ONE NIGHT AN EERIE VOICE CALLED TO HIM FROM OUTSIDE HIS WINDOW . . .
AAIII. . . IT IS THE UNDERTAKER WITH HIS HEARSE!
I HAVE RE-TURNED FOR YOU-- COME WITH ME!
THE UNDERTAKER RETURNED FOR SEVERAL NIGHTS UNTIL PRINCE HUGO, DRIVEN INSANE BY THE VISION, DID HIS TORMENTOR'S BIDDING . . .
YOUR TIME HAS COME, PRINCE-- GET INTO MY HEARSE!
HUGO ENTERED THE VEHICLE AND WITH A CRACK OF THE UNDERTAKER'S WHIP, THE HORSES PULLING THE HEARSE WERE OFF WITH THEIR MAD PASSENGER ABOARD . . .
MY REVENGE IS COMPLETE! I AM TAKING YOU ON AN ETERNAL TRIP TO HADES!
AAAIIIII.....
THE TOWNSPEOPLE WERE AWAKENED FROM THEIR SLEEP BY THE HORRIBLE SCREAMS AND THE CLATTER OF THE HEARSE RACING OVER THE COUNTRY-SIDE. MAD PRINCE HUGO WAS NEVER SEEN AGAIN BUT TO THIS DAY, THE VILLAGERS SWEAR THAT WHEN THE MOON IS FULL THEY SEE THE HEARSE CLATTERING THROUGH THE TOWN, AND THE ANGUISHED SCREAMS OF THE DAMNED PRINCE COMING FROM IT. ANOTHER STRANGE TALE IN THE ANNALS OF THE SUPERNATURAL.
The End

Baffling Mysteries #19, January 1954. Sy Grudko. Ace Magazines.

COVER GALLERY

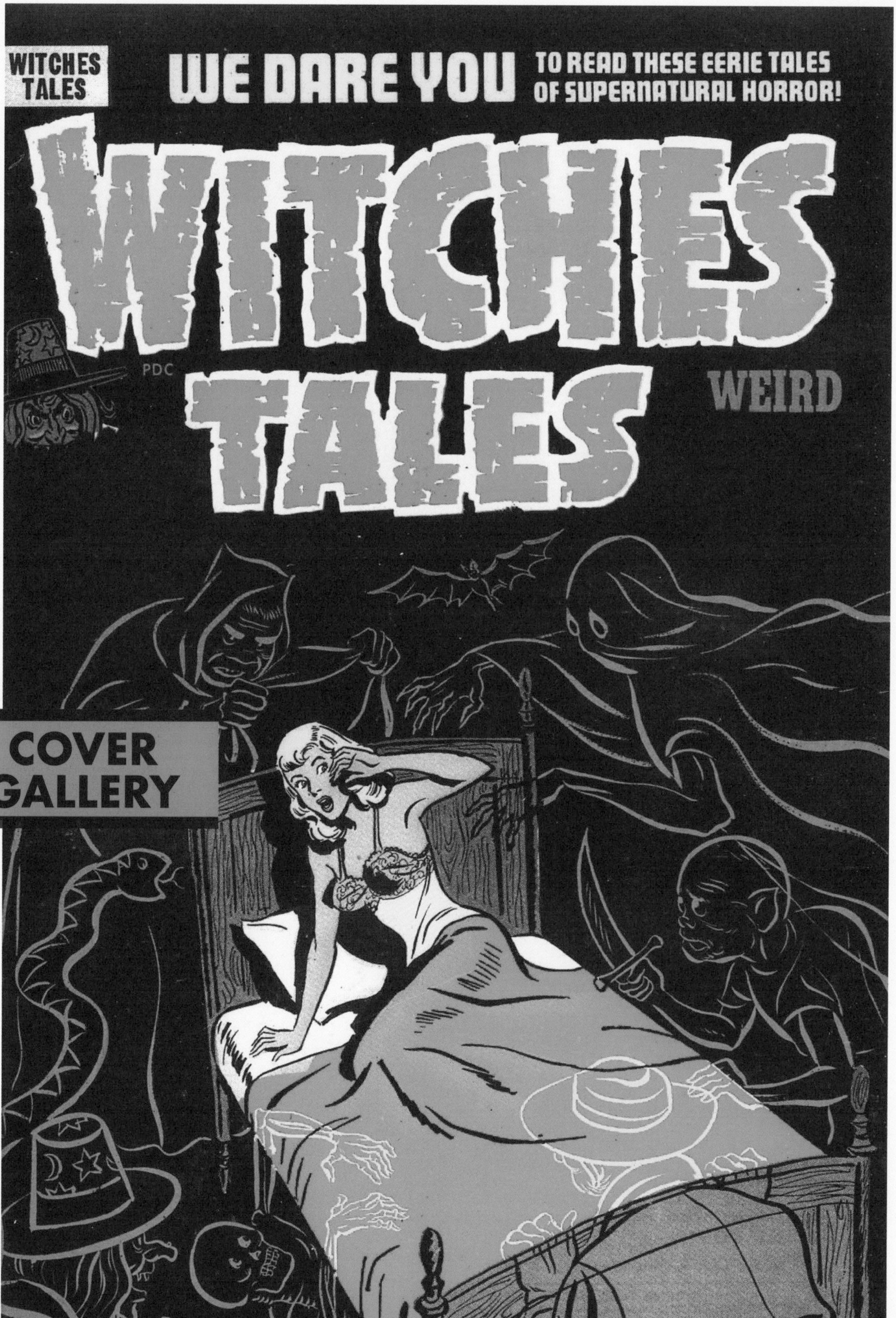
WITCHES TALES
WE DARE YOU TO READ THESE EERIE TALES OF SUPERNATURAL HORROR!
WITCHES TALES
PDC
WEIRD

Witches Tales #2, March 1951. Al Avison. Harvey.

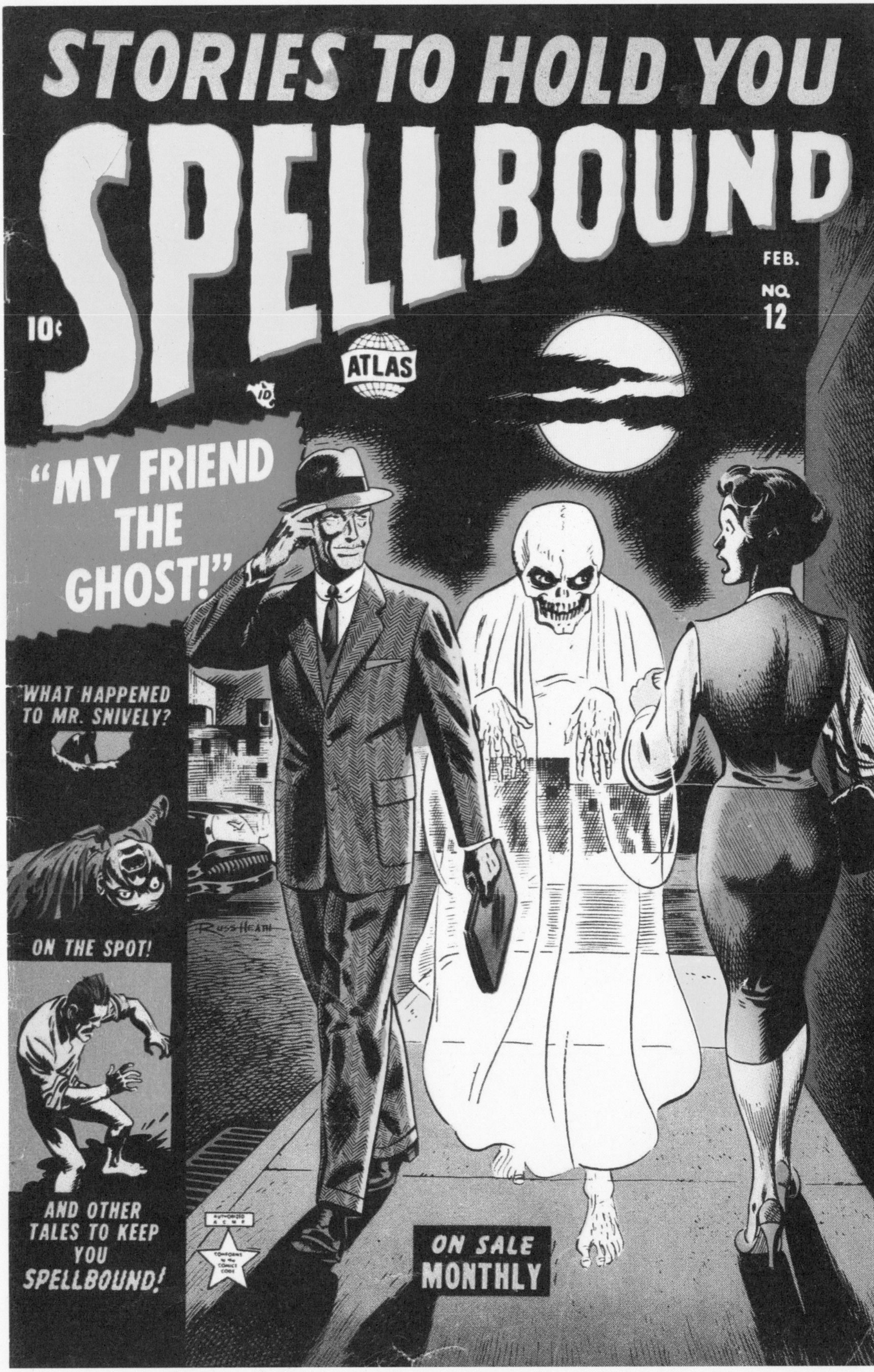
STORIES TO HOLD YOU
SPELLBOUND
10¢
FEB.
NO. 12
ATLAS
"MY FRIEND THE GHOST!"
WHAT HAPPENED TO MR. SNIVELY?
ON THE SPOT!
AND OTHER TALES TO KEEP YOU SPELLBOUND!
ON SALE MONTHLY

Spellbound #12, February 1953. Russ Heath. Atlas.

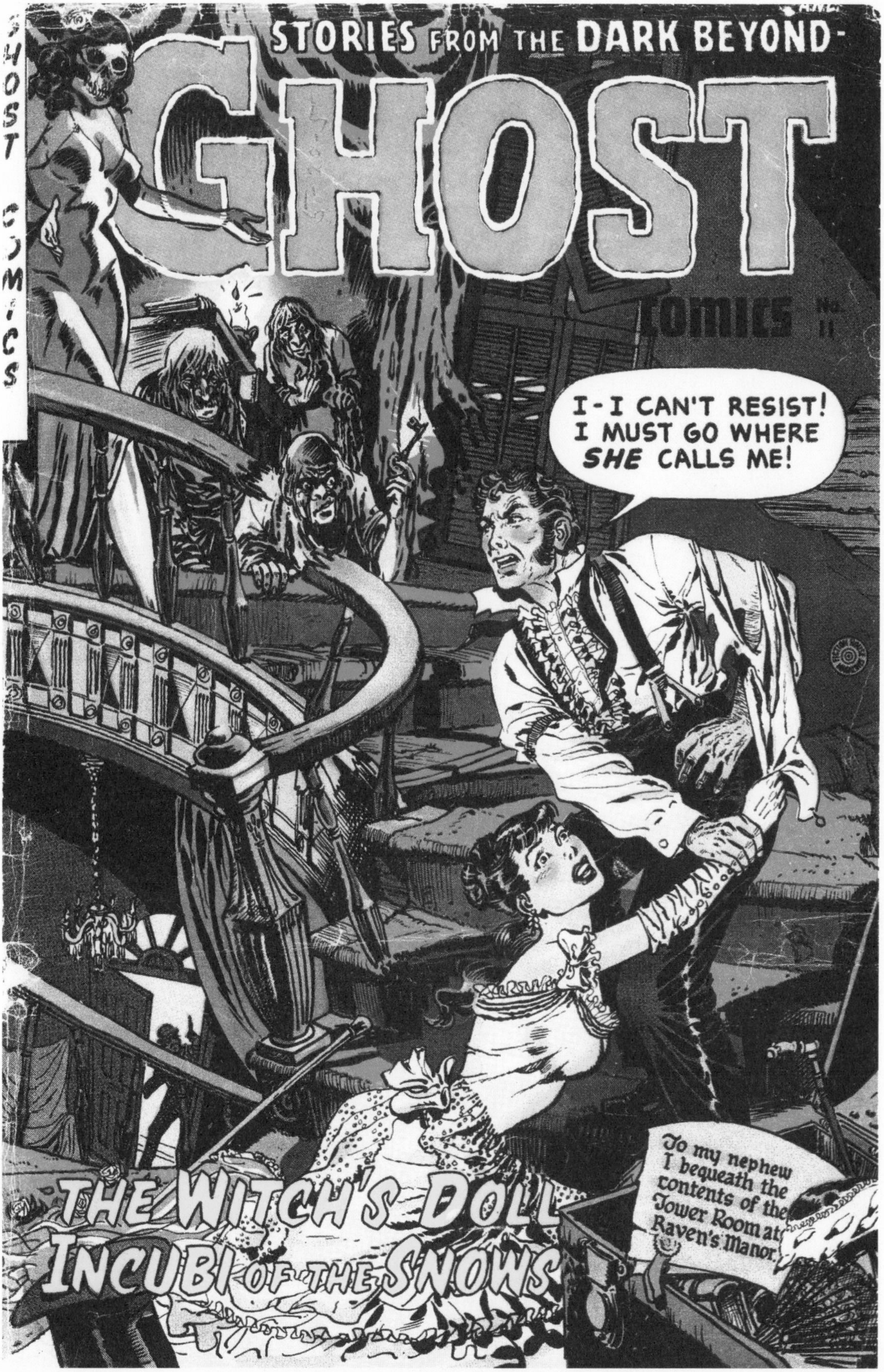
STORIES FROM THE DARK BEYOND-
GHOST
COMICS
No. 11
GHOST COMICS
I-I CAN'T RESIST! I MUST GO WHERE *SHE* CALLS ME!
To my nephew I bequeath the contents of the Tower Room at Raven's Manor.
THE WITCH'S DOLL
INCUBI OF THE SNOWS

Ghost Comics #11, 1954. Maurice Whitman. Fiction House.

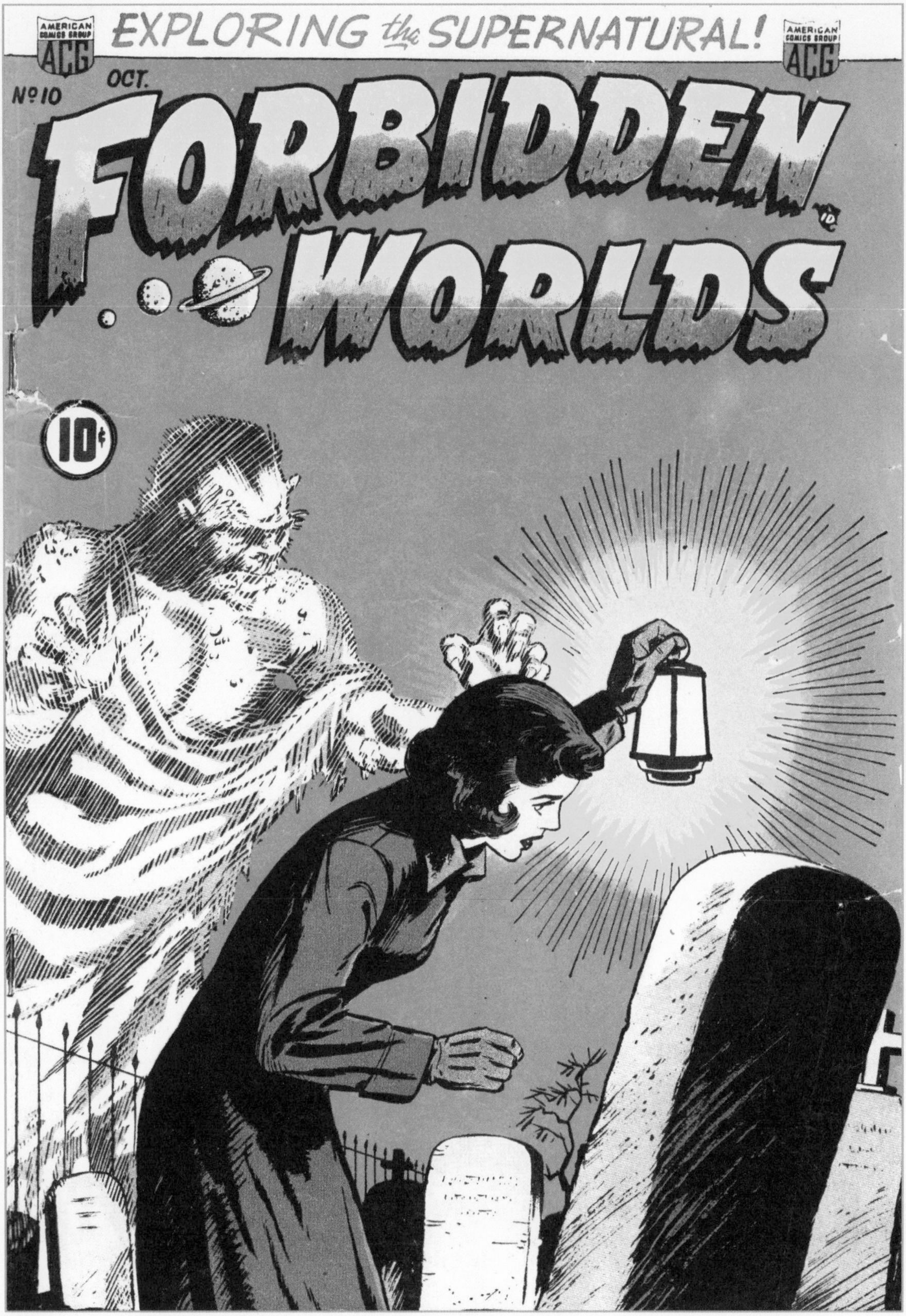
EXPLORING the SUPERNATURAL!
AMERICAN COMICS GROUP ACG
AMERICAN COMICS GROUP ACG
OCT.
No 10
FORBIDDEN WORLDS
10¢

Forbidden Worlds #10, October 1952. Ken Bald. ACG.

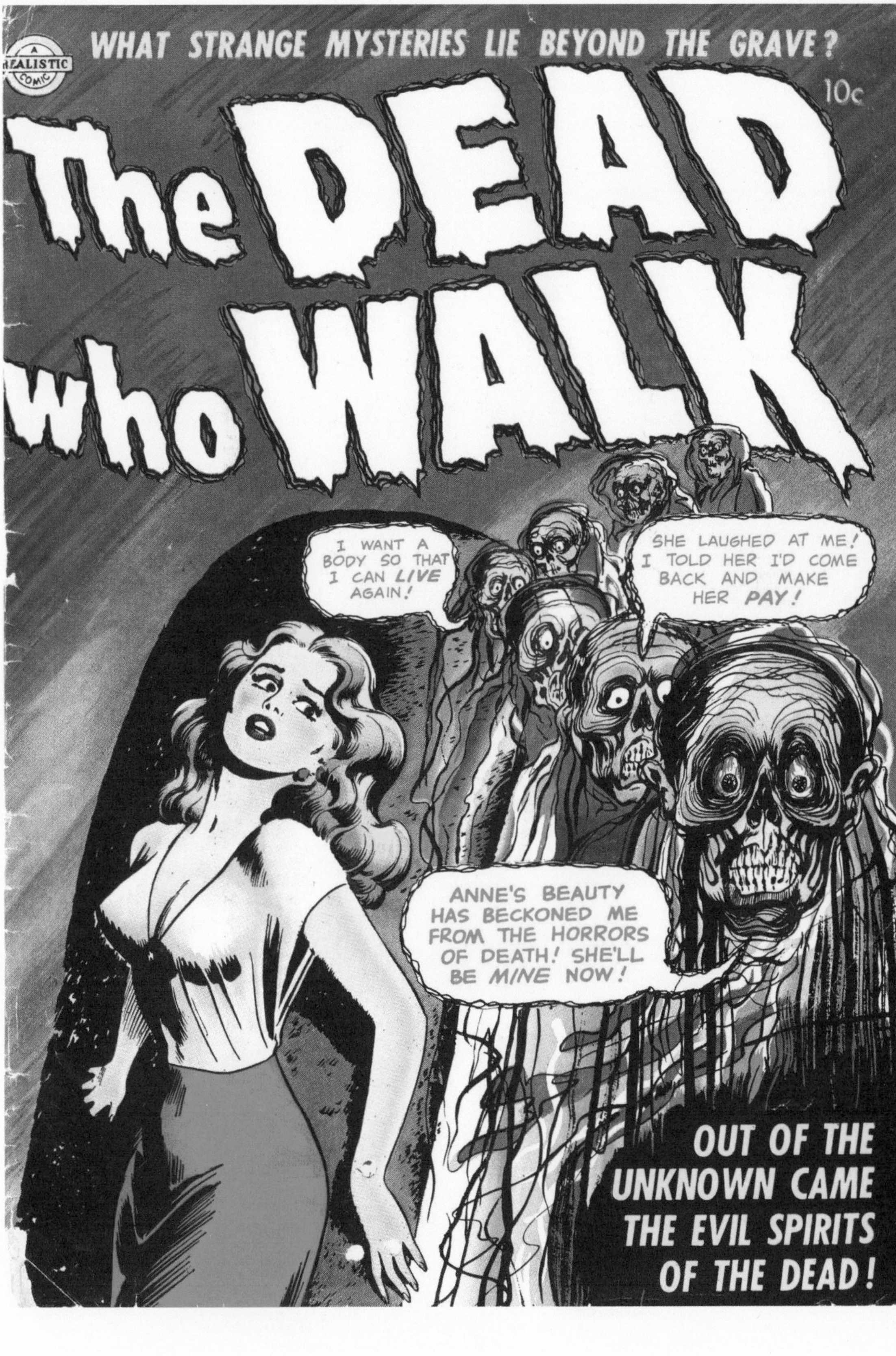
A REALISTIC COMIC
WHAT STRANGE MYSTERIES LIE BEYOND THE GRAVE?
10¢
The DEAD who WALK
I WANT A BODY SO THAT I CAN LIVE AGAIN!
SHE LAUGHED AT ME! I TOLD HER I'D COME BACK AND MAKE HER PAY!
ANNE'S BEAUTY HAS BECKONED ME FROM THE HORRORS OF DEATH! SHE'LL BE MINE NOW!
OUT OF THE UNKNOWN CAME THE EVIL SPIRITS OF THE DEAD!

The Dead Who Walk #24, 1953. Attributed to Tex Blaisdell. Avon.

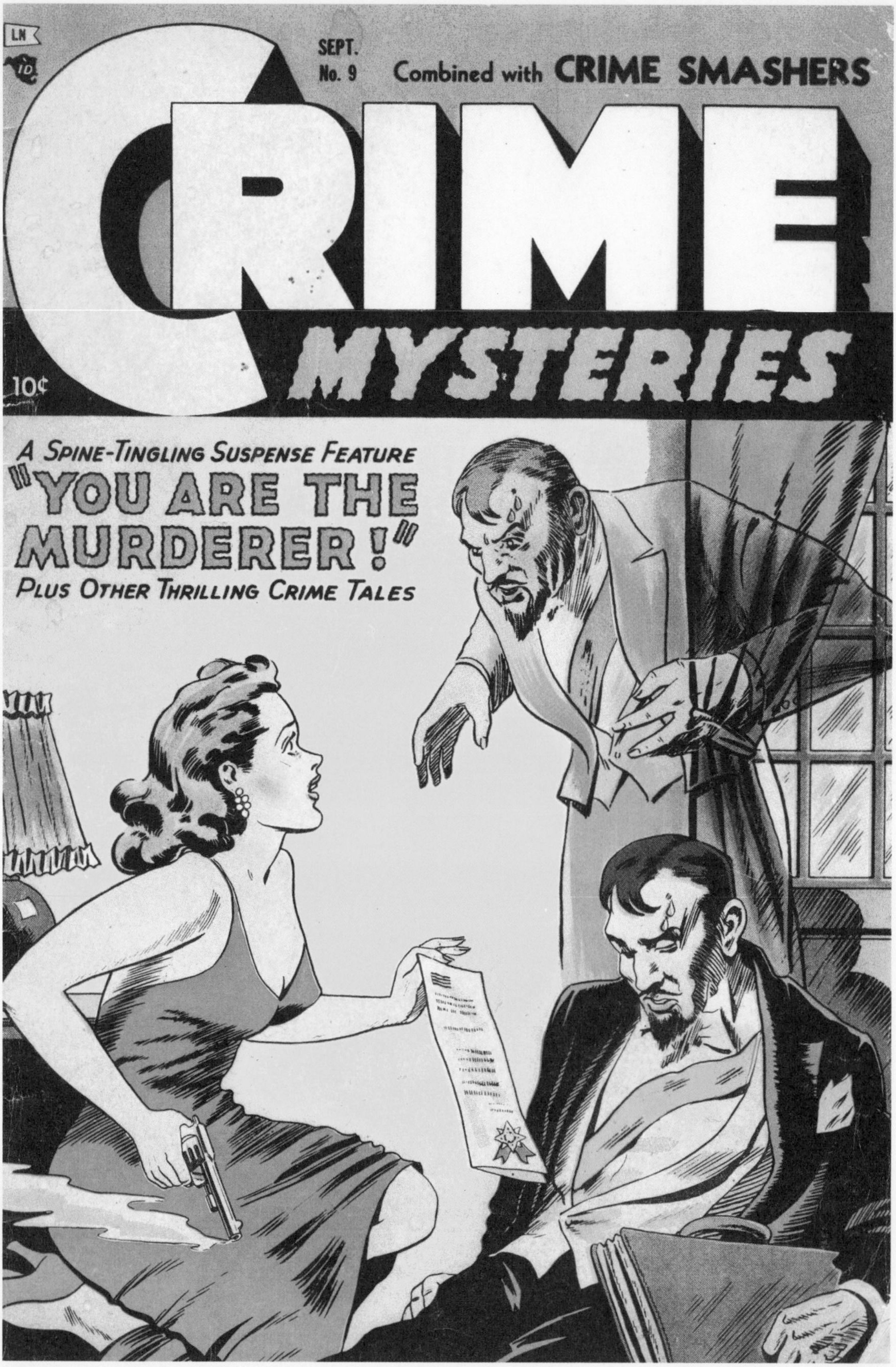
SEPT.
No. 9
Combined with CRIME SMASHERS
CRIME
MYSTERIES
10¢
A SPINE-TINGLING SUSPENSE FEATURE
"YOU ARE THE MURDERER!"
PLUS OTHER THRILLING CRIME TALES

Crime Mysteries #9, September 1953. Artist unknown. Ribage.

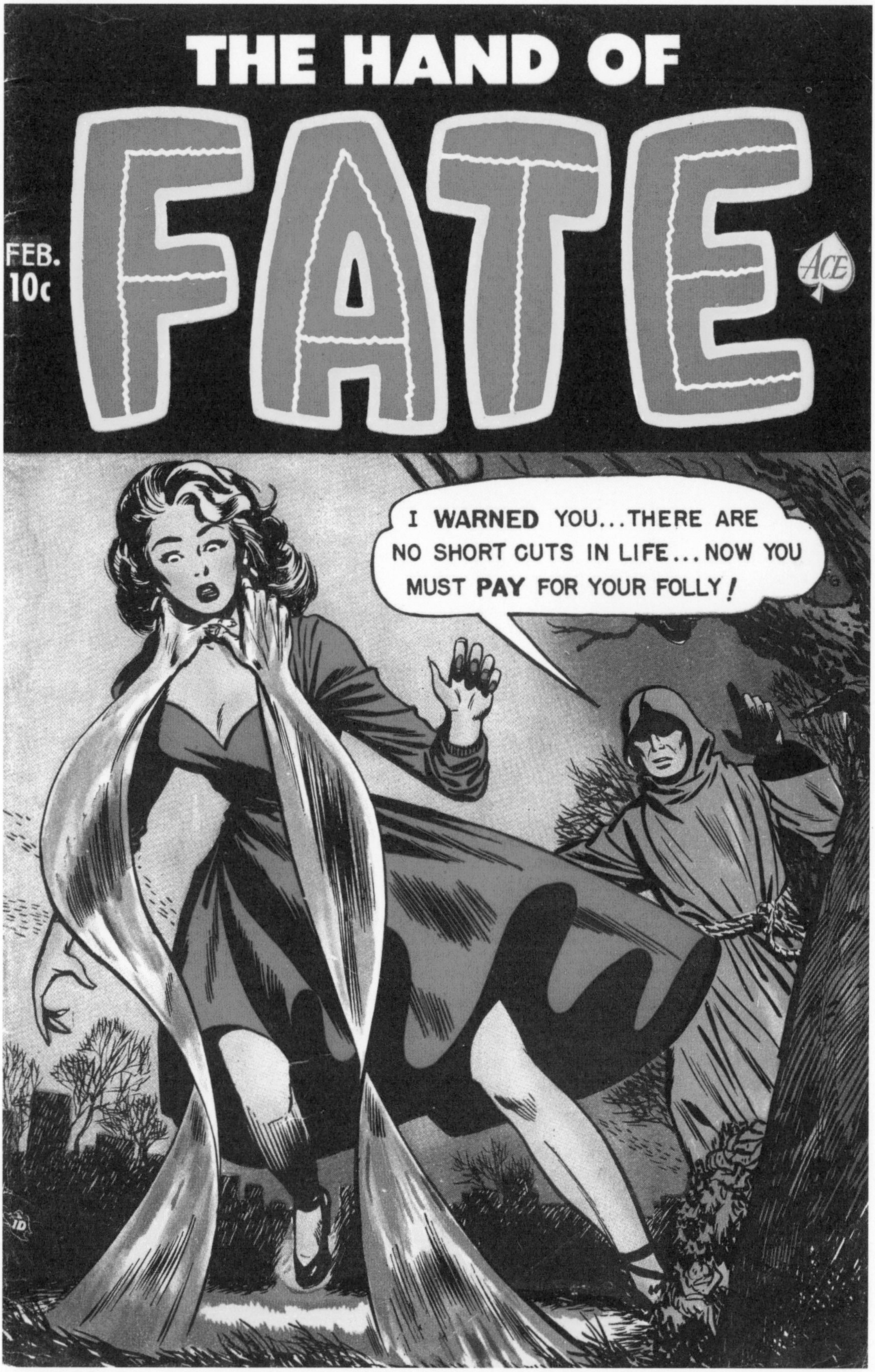
THE HAND OF
FATE
FEB.
10c
ACE
I WARNED YOU...THERE ARE NO SHORT CUTS IN LIFE...NOW YOU MUST PAY FOR YOUR FOLLY!

The Hand of Fate #16, February 1953. Frank Giusto. Ace Magazines.

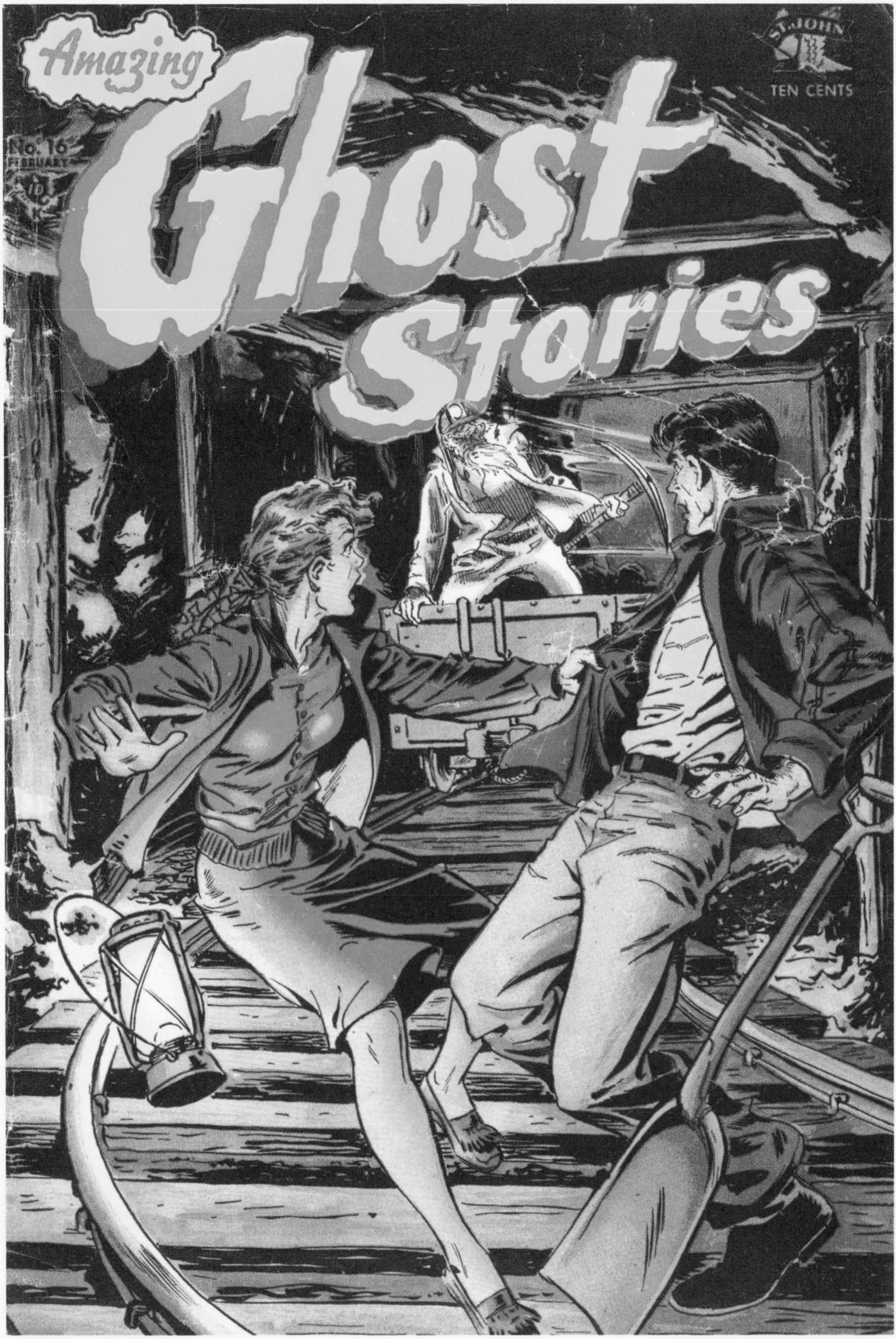
Amazing
Ghost Stories
No. 16
FEBRUARY
ST. JOHN
TEN CENTS

Amazing Ghost Stories #16, February 1955. Matt Baker. St. John.

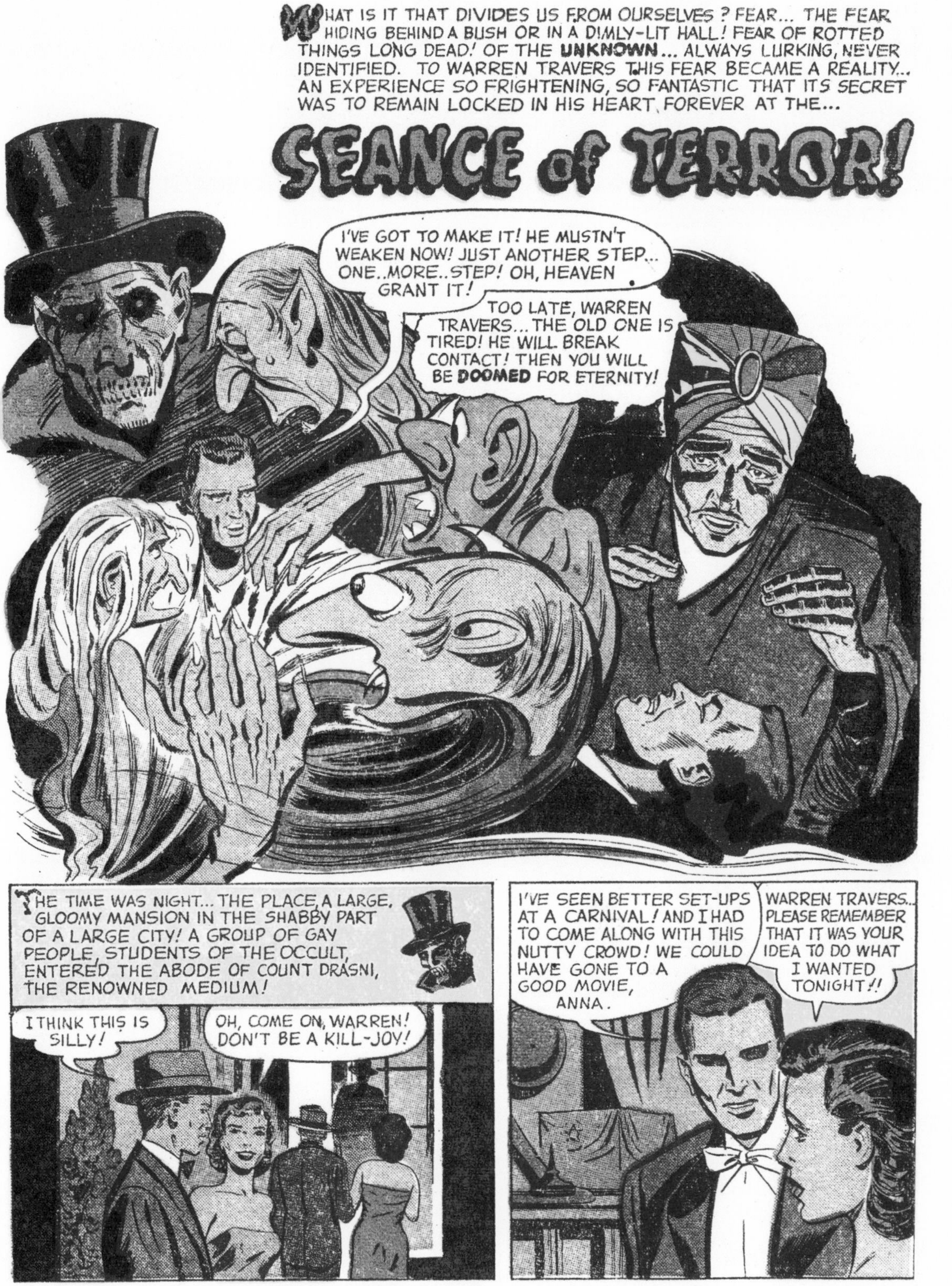
WHAT IS IT THAT DIVIDES US FROM OURSELVES? FEAR... THE FEAR HIDING BEHIND A BUSH OR IN A DIMLY-LIT HALL! FEAR OF ROTTED THINGS LONG DEAD! OF THE UNKNOWN... ALWAYS LURKING, NEVER IDENTIFIED. TO WARREN TRAVERS THIS FEAR BECAME A REALITY... AN EXPERIENCE SO FRIGHTENING, SO FANTASTIC THAT ITS SECRET WAS TO REMAIN LOCKED IN HIS HEART FOREVER AT THE...
SEANCE of TERROR!
I'VE GOT TO MAKE IT! HE MUSTN'T WEAKEN NOW! JUST ANOTHER STEP... ONE..MORE..STEP! OH, HEAVEN GRANT IT!
TOO LATE, WARREN TRAVERS... THE OLD ONE IS TIRED! HE WILL BREAK CONTACT! THEN YOU WILL BE DOOMED FOR ETERNITY!
THE TIME WAS NIGHT... THE PLACE, A LARGE, GLOOMY MANSION IN THE SHABBY PART OF A LARGE CITY! A GROUP OF GAY PEOPLE, STUDENTS OF THE OCCULT, ENTERED THE ABODE OF COUNT DRASNI, THE RENOWNED MEDIUM!
I THINK THIS IS SILLY!
OH, COME ON, WARREN! DON'T BE A KILL-JOY!
I'VE SEEN BETTER SET-UPS AT A CARNIVAL! AND I HAD TO COME ALONG WITH THIS NUTTY CROWD! WE COULD HAVE GONE TO A GOOD MOVIE, ANNA.
WARREN TRAVERS... PLEASE REMEMBER THAT IT WAS YOUR IDEA TO DO WHAT I WANTED TONIGHT!!

This Magazine is Haunted #4, April 1952. Attributed to Edd Ashe. Fawcette.

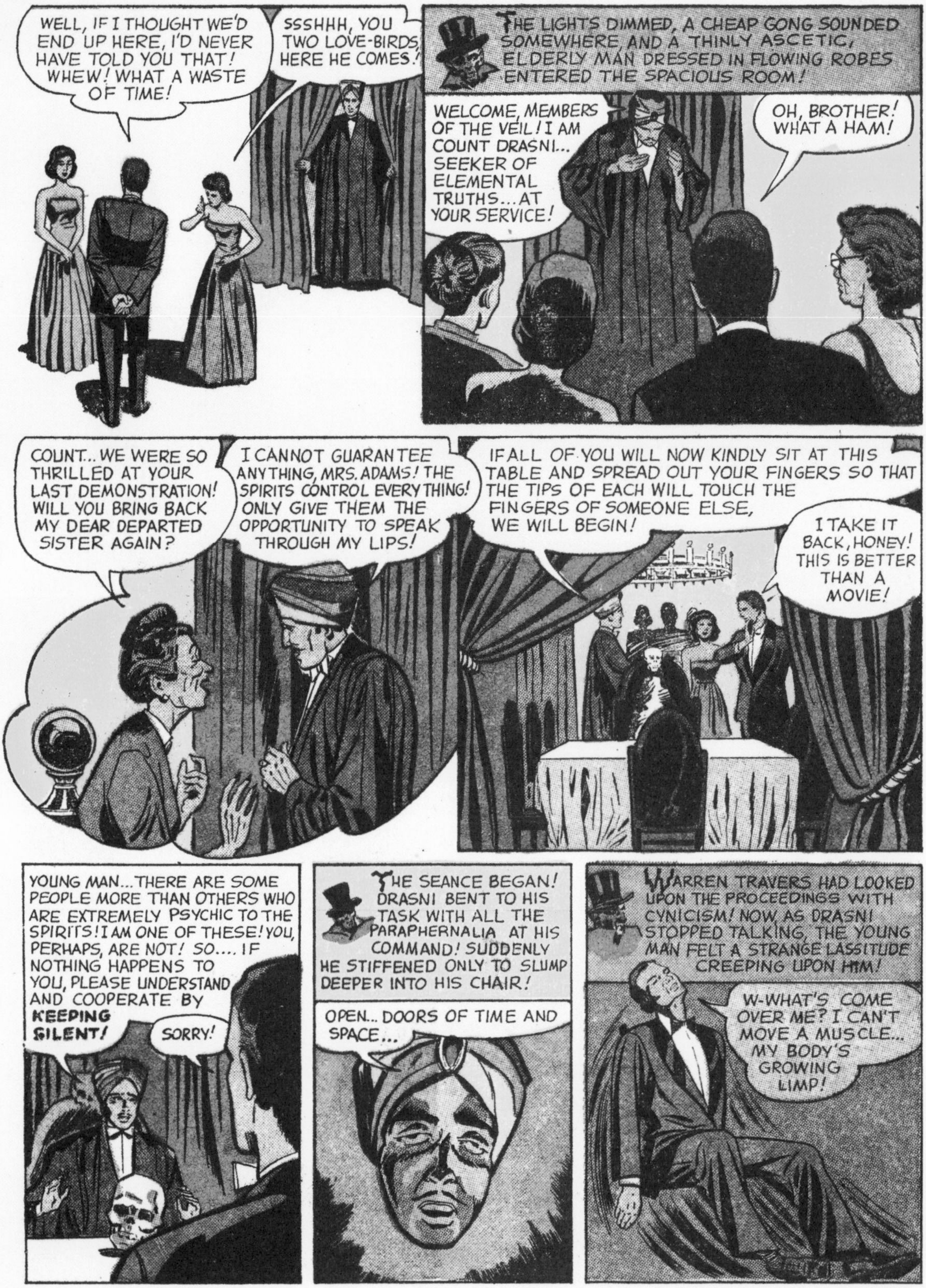

WELL, IF I THOUGHT WE'D END UP HERE, I'D NEVER HAVE TOLD YOU THAT! WHEW! WHAT A WASTE OF TIME!
SSSHHH, YOU TWO LOVE-BIRDS, HERE HE COMES!
THE LIGHTS DIMMED, A CHEAP GONG SOUNDED SOMEWHERE, AND A THINLY ASCETIC, ELDERLY MAN DRESSED IN FLOWING ROBES ENTERED THE SPACIOUS ROOM!
WELCOME, MEMBERS OF THE VEIL! I AM COUNT DRASNI... SEEKER OF ELEMENTAL TRUTHS... AT YOUR SERVICE!
OH, BROTHER! WHAT A HAM!
COUNT... WE WERE SO THRILLED AT YOUR LAST DEMONSTRATION! WILL YOU BRING BACK MY DEAR DEPARTED SISTER AGAIN?
I CANNOT GUARANTEE ANYTHING, MRS. ADAMS! THE SPIRITS CONTROL EVERYTHING! ONLY GIVE THEM THE OPPORTUNITY TO SPEAK THROUGH MY LIPS!
IF ALL OF YOU WILL NOW KINDLY SIT AT THIS TABLE AND SPREAD OUT YOUR FINGERS SO THAT THE TIPS OF EACH WILL TOUCH THE FINGERS OF SOMEONE ELSE, WE WILL BEGIN!
I TAKE IT BACK, HONEY! THIS IS BETTER THAN A MOVIE!
YOUNG MAN... THERE ARE SOME PEOPLE MORE THAN OTHERS WHO ARE EXTREMELY PSYCHIC TO THE SPIRITS! I AM ONE OF THESE! YOU, PERHAPS, ARE NOT! SO.... IF NOTHING HAPPENS TO YOU, PLEASE UNDERSTAND AND COOPERATE BY KEEPING SILENT!
SORRY!
THE SEANCE BEGAN! DRASNI BENT TO HIS TASK WITH ALL THE PARAPHERNALIA AT HIS COMMAND! SUDDENLY HE STIFFENED ONLY TO SLUMP DEEPER INTO HIS CHAIR!
OPEN... DOORS OF TIME AND SPACE...
WARREN TRAVERS HAD LOOKED UPON THE PROCEEDINGS WITH CYNICISM! NOW, AS DRASNI STOPPED TALKING, THE YOUNG MAN FELT A STRANGE LASSITUDE CREEPING UPON HIM!
W-WHAT'S COME OVER ME? I CAN'T MOVE A MUSCLE... MY BODY'S GROWING LIMP!

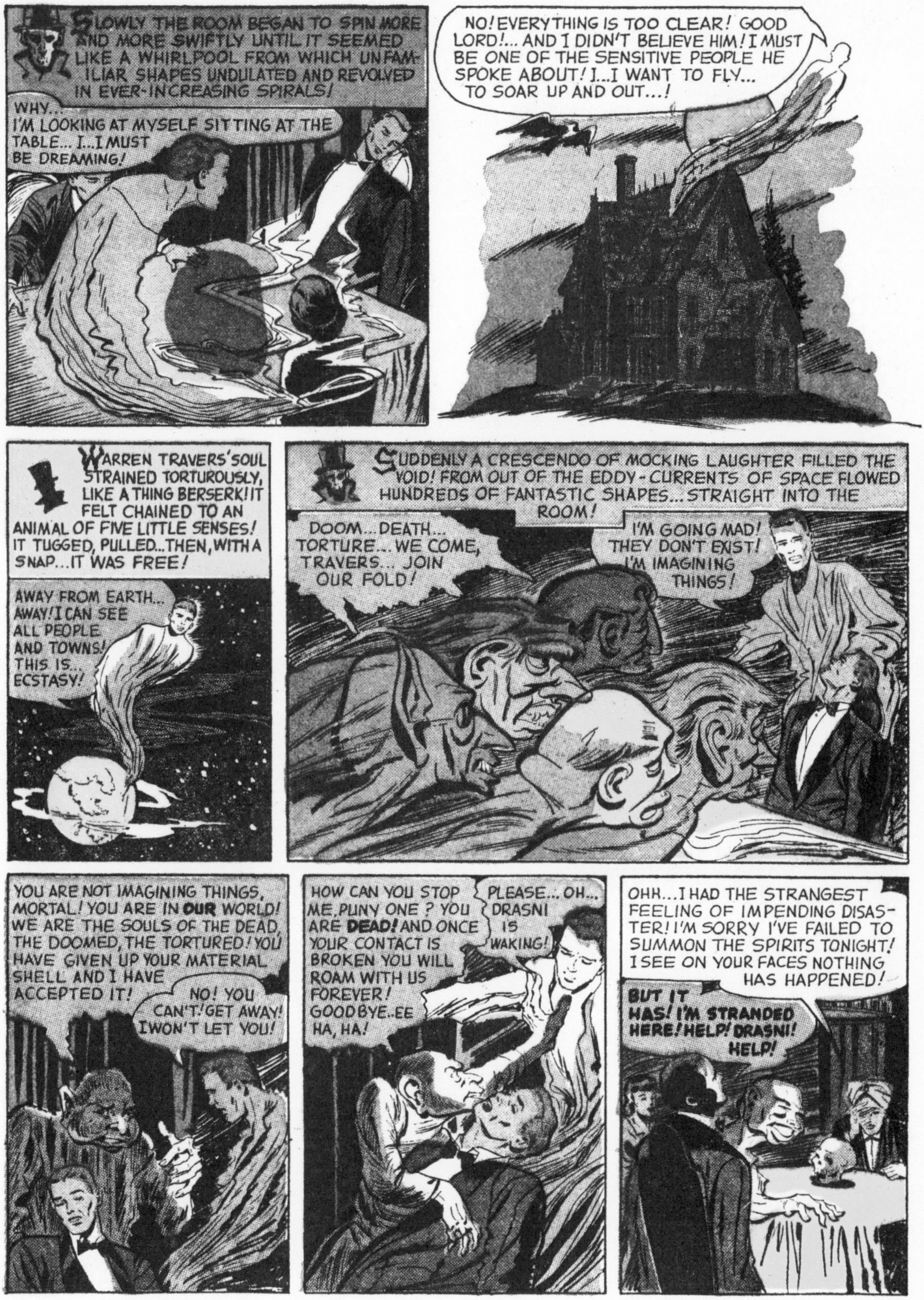
SLOWLY THE ROOM BEGAN TO SPIN MORE AND MORE SWIFTLY UNTIL IT SEEMED LIKE A WHIRLPOOL FROM WHICH UNFAMILIAR SHAPES UNDULATED AND REVOLVED IN EVER-INCREASING SPIRALS!
WHY... I'M LOOKING AT MYSELF SITTING AT THE TABLE... I...I MUST BE DREAMING!
NO! EVERYTHING IS TOO CLEAR! GOOD LORD!... AND I DIDN'T BELIEVE HIM! I MUST BE ONE OF THE SENSITIVE PEOPLE HE SPOKE ABOUT! I...I WANT TO FLY... TO SOAR UP AND OUT...!
WARREN TRAVERS'S SOUL STRAINED TORTUROUSLY, LIKE A THING BERSERK! IT FELT CHAINED TO AN ANIMAL OF FIVE LITTLE SENSES! IT TUGGED, PULLED...THEN, WITH A SNAP...IT WAS FREE!
AWAY FROM EARTH... AWAY! I CAN SEE ALL PEOPLE AND TOWNS! THIS IS... ECSTASY!
SUDDENLY A CRESCENDO OF MOCKING LAUGHTER FILLED THE VOID! FROM OUT OF THE EDDY-CURRENTS OF SPACE FLOWED HUNDREDS OF FANTASTIC SHAPES... STRAIGHT INTO THE ROOM!
DOOM... DEATH... TORTURE... WE COME, TRAVERS... JOIN OUR FOLD!
I'M GOING MAD! THEY DON'T EXIST! I'M IMAGINING THINGS!
YOU ARE NOT IMAGINING THINGS, MORTAL! YOU ARE IN OUR WORLD! WE ARE THE SOULS OF THE DEAD, THE DOOMED, THE TORTURED! YOU HAVE GIVEN UP YOUR MATERIAL SHELL AND I HAVE ACCEPTED IT!
NO! YOU CAN'T! GET AWAY! I WON'T LET YOU!
HOW CAN YOU STOP ME, PUNY ONE? YOU ARE DEAD! AND ONCE YOUR CONTACT IS BROKEN YOU WILL ROAM WITH US FOREVER! GOODBYE..EE HA, HA!
PLEASE... OH... DRASNI IS WAKING!
OHH... I HAD THE STRANGEST FEELING OF IMPENDING DISASTER! I'M SORRY I'VE FAILED TO SUMMON THE SPIRITS TONIGHT! I SEE ON YOUR FACES NOTHING HAS HAPPENED!
BUT IT HAS! I'M STRANDED HERE! HELP! DRASNI! HELP!

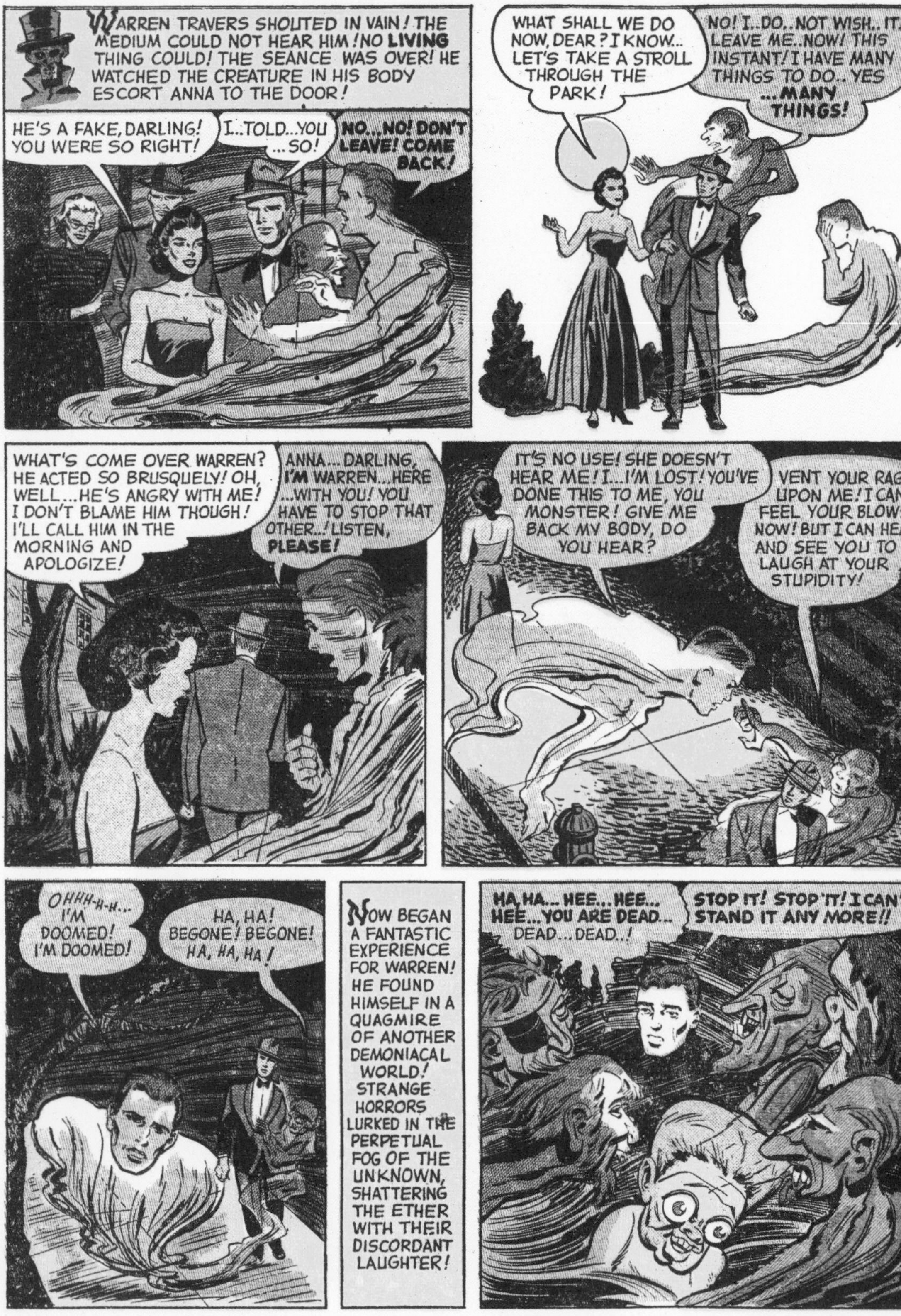

WARREN TRAVERS SHOUTED IN VAIN! THE MEDIUM COULD NOT HEAR HIM! NO LIVING THING COULD! THE SEANCE WAS OVER! HE WATCHED THE CREATURE IN HIS BODY ESCORT ANNA TO THE DOOR!
HE'S A FAKE, DARLING! YOU WERE SO RIGHT!
I...TOLD...YOU ...SO!
NO...NO! DON'T LEAVE! COME BACK!
WHAT SHALL WE DO NOW, DEAR? I KNOW... LET'S TAKE A STROLL THROUGH THE PARK!
NO! I..DO..NOT WISH.. IT! LEAVE ME..NOW! THIS INSTANT! I HAVE MANY THINGS TO DO.. YES ...MANY THINGS!
WHAT'S COME OVER WARREN? HE ACTED SO BRUSQUELY! OH, WELL...HE'S ANGRY WITH ME! I DON'T BLAME HIM THOUGH! I'LL CALL HIM IN THE MORNING AND APOLOGIZE!
ANNA...DARLING, I'M WARREN...HERE ...WITH YOU! YOU HAVE TO STOP THAT OTHER...! LISTEN, PLEASE!
IT'S NO USE! SHE DOESN'T HEAR ME! I...I'M LOST! YOU'VE DONE THIS TO ME, YOU MONSTER! GIVE ME BACK MY BODY, DO YOU HEAR?
VENT YOUR RAGE UPON ME! I CAN'T FEEL YOUR BLOWS NOW! BUT I CAN HEAR AND SEE YOU TO LAUGH AT YOUR STUPIDITY!
OHHH-H-H... I'M DOOMED! I'M DOOMED!
HA, HA! BEGONE! BEGONE! HA, HA, HA!
NOW BEGAN A FANTASTIC EXPERIENCE FOR WARREN! HE FOUND HIMSELF IN A QUAGMIRE OF ANOTHER DEMONIACAL WORLD! STRANGE HORRORS LURKED IN THE PERPETUAL FOG OF THE UNKNOWN, SHATTERING THE ETHER WITH THEIR DISCORDANT LAUGHTER!
HA, HA... HEE...HEE... HEE...YOU ARE DEAD... DEAD...DEAD..!
STOP IT! STOP IT! I CAN'T STAND IT ANY MORE!!

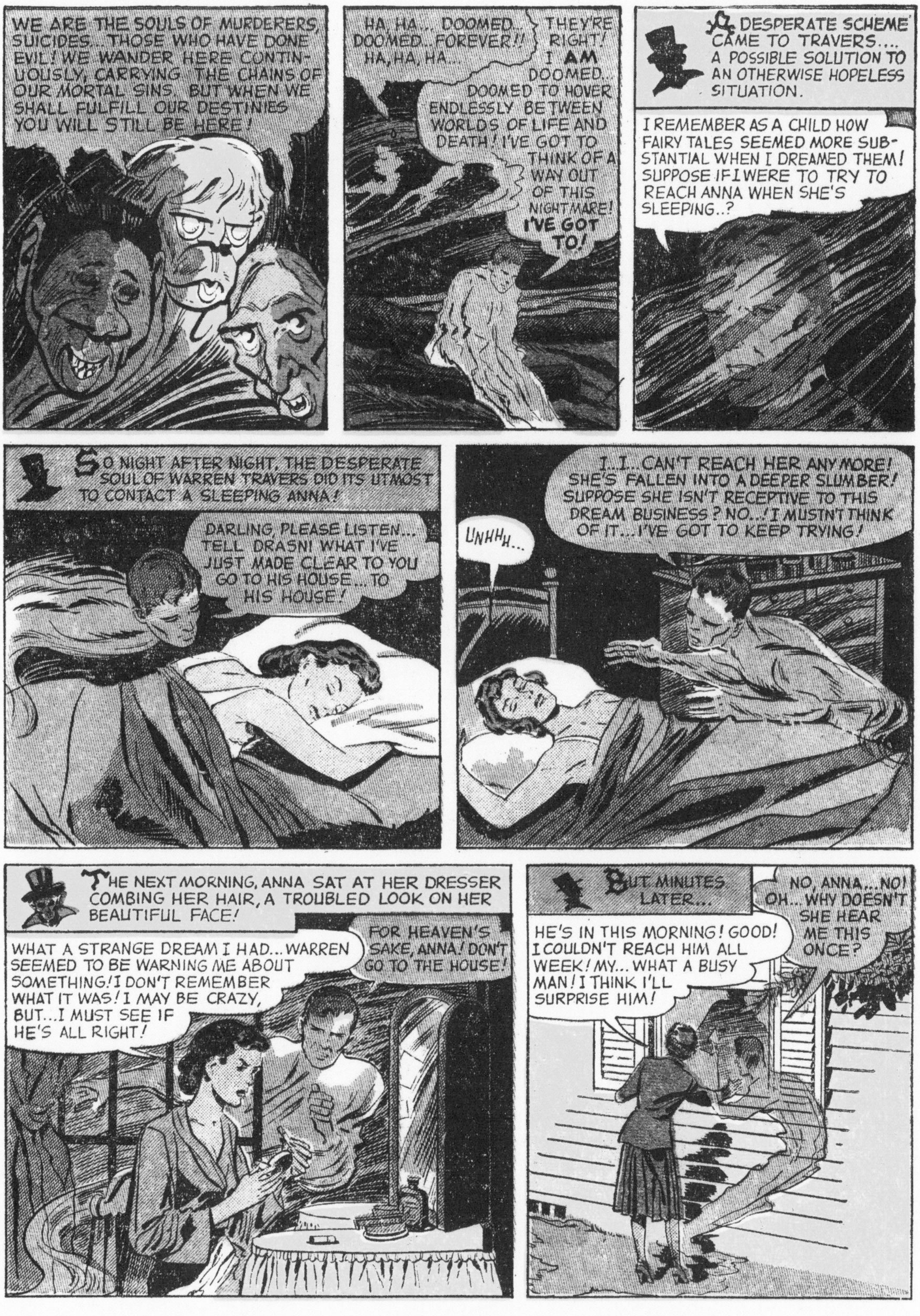
WE ARE THE SOULS OF MURDERERS, SUICIDES... THOSE WHO HAVE DONE EVIL! WE WANDER HERE CONTINUOUSLY, CARRYING THE CHAINS OF OUR MORTAL SINS. BUT WHEN WE SHALL FULFILL OUR DESTINIES YOU WILL STILL BE HERE!
HA, HA... DOOMED... DOOMED... FOREVER!! HA, HA, HA...
THEY'RE RIGHT! I AM DOOMED... DOOMED TO HOVER ENDLESSLY BETWEEN WORLDS OF LIFE AND DEATH! I'VE GOT TO THINK OF A WAY OUT OF THIS NIGHTMARE! I'VE GOT TO!
A DESPERATE SCHEME CAME TO TRAVERS.... A POSSIBLE SOLUTION TO AN OTHERWISE HOPELESS SITUATION.
I REMEMBER AS A CHILD HOW FAIRY TALES SEEMED MORE SUBSTANTIAL WHEN I DREAMED THEM! SUPPOSE IF I WERE TO TRY TO REACH ANNA WHEN SHE'S SLEEPING..?
SO NIGHT AFTER NIGHT, THE DESPERATE SOUL OF WARREN TRAVERS DID ITS UTMOST TO CONTACT A SLEEPING ANNA!
DARLING PLEASE LISTEN... TELL DRASNI WHAT I'VE JUST MADE CLEAR TO YOU GO TO HIS HOUSE... TO HIS HOUSE!
I..I... CAN'T REACH HER ANY MORE! SHE'S FALLEN INTO A DEEPER SLUMBER! SUPPOSE SHE ISN'T RECEPTIVE TO THIS DREAM BUSINESS? NO...! I MUSTN'T THINK OF IT... I'VE GOT TO KEEP TRYING!
UNHHH...
THE NEXT MORNING, ANNA SAT AT HER DRESSER COMBING HER HAIR, A TROUBLED LOOK ON HER BEAUTIFUL FACE!
WHAT A STRANGE DREAM I HAD... WARREN SEEMED TO BE WARNING ME ABOUT SOMETHING! I DON'T REMEMBER WHAT IT WAS! I MAY BE CRAZY, BUT... I MUST SEE IF HE'S ALL RIGHT!
FOR HEAVEN'S SAKE, ANNA! DON'T GO TO THE HOUSE!
BUT MINUTES LATER...
HE'S IN THIS MORNING! GOOD! I COULDN'T REACH HIM ALL WEEK! MY... WHAT A BUSY MAN! I THINK I'LL SURPRISE HIM!
NO, ANNA... NO! OH... WHY DOESN'T SHE HEAR ME THIS ONCE?

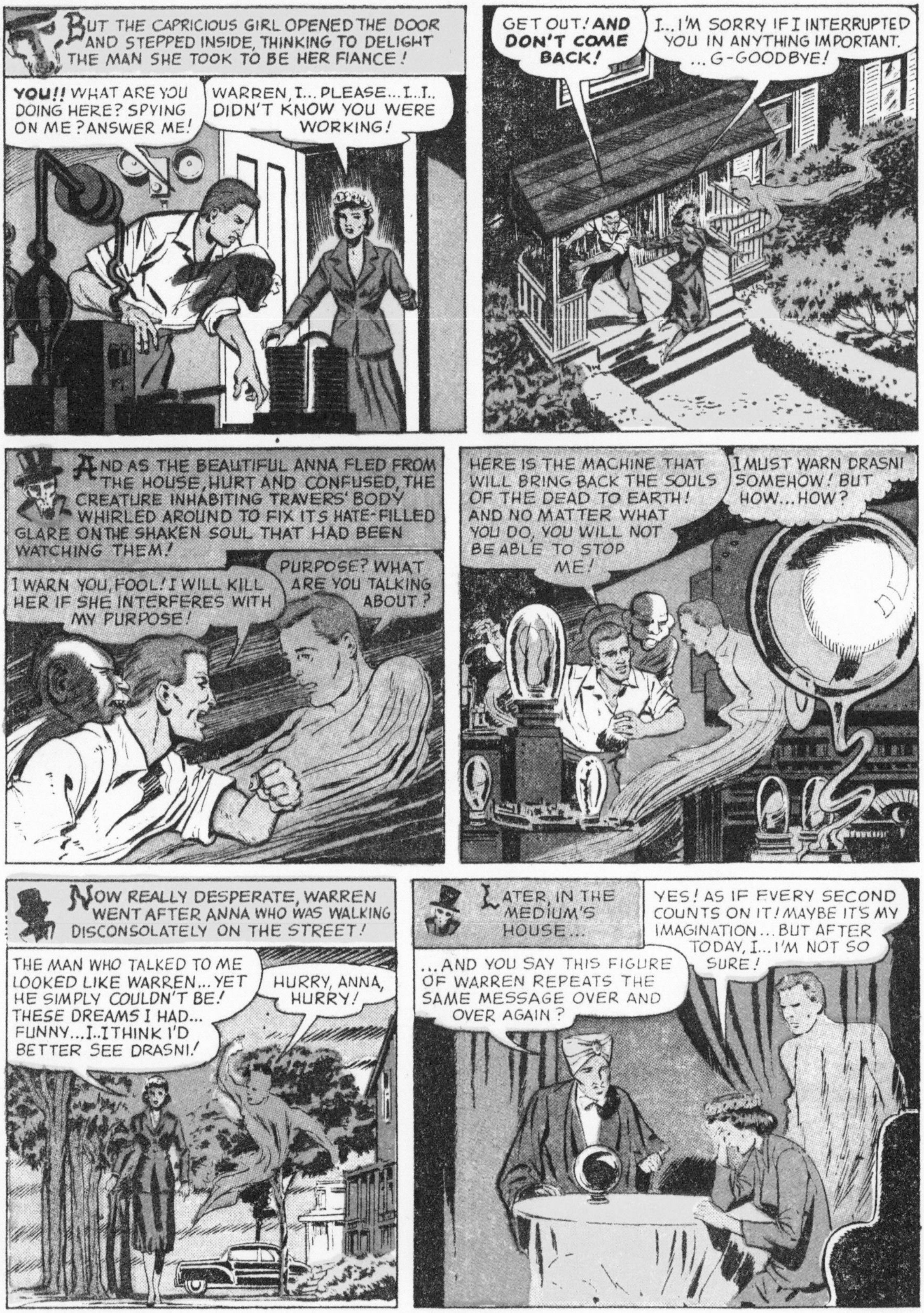
BUT THE CAPRICIOUS GIRL OPENED THE DOOR AND STEPPED INSIDE, THINKING TO DELIGHT THE MAN SHE TOOK TO BE HER FIANCE!
YOU!! WHAT ARE YOU DOING HERE? SPYING ON ME? ANSWER ME!
WARREN, I... PLEASE... I..I.. DIDN'T KNOW YOU WERE WORKING!
GET OUT! AND DON'T COME BACK!
I... I'M SORRY IF I INTERRUPTED YOU IN ANYTHING IMPORTANT. ... G-GOODBYE!
AND AS THE BEAUTIFUL ANNA FLED FROM THE HOUSE, HURT AND CONFUSED, THE CREATURE INHABITING TRAVERS' BODY WHIRLED AROUND TO FIX ITS HATE-FILLED GLARE ON THE SHAKEN SOUL THAT HAD BEEN WATCHING THEM!
I WARN YOU, FOOL! I WILL KILL HER IF SHE INTERFERES WITH MY PURPOSE!
PURPOSE? WHAT ARE YOU TALKING ABOUT?
HERE IS THE MACHINE THAT WILL BRING BACK THE SOULS OF THE DEAD TO EARTH! AND NO MATTER WHAT YOU DO, YOU WILL NOT BE ABLE TO STOP ME!
I MUST WARN DRASNI SOMEHOW! BUT HOW... HOW?
NOW REALLY DESPERATE, WARREN WENT AFTER ANNA WHO WAS WALKING DISCONSOLATELY ON THE STREET!
THE MAN WHO TALKED TO ME LOOKED LIKE WARREN... YET HE SIMPLY COULDN'T BE! THESE DREAMS I HAD... FUNNY... I..I THINK I'D BETTER SEE DRASNI!
HURRY, ANNA, HURRY!
LATER, IN THE MEDIUM'S HOUSE...
... AND YOU SAY THIS FIGURE OF WARREN REPEATS THE SAME MESSAGE OVER AND OVER AGAIN?
YES! AS IF EVERY SECOND COUNTS ON IT! MAYBE IT'S MY IMAGINATION... BUT AFTER TODAY, I... I'M NOT SO SURE!

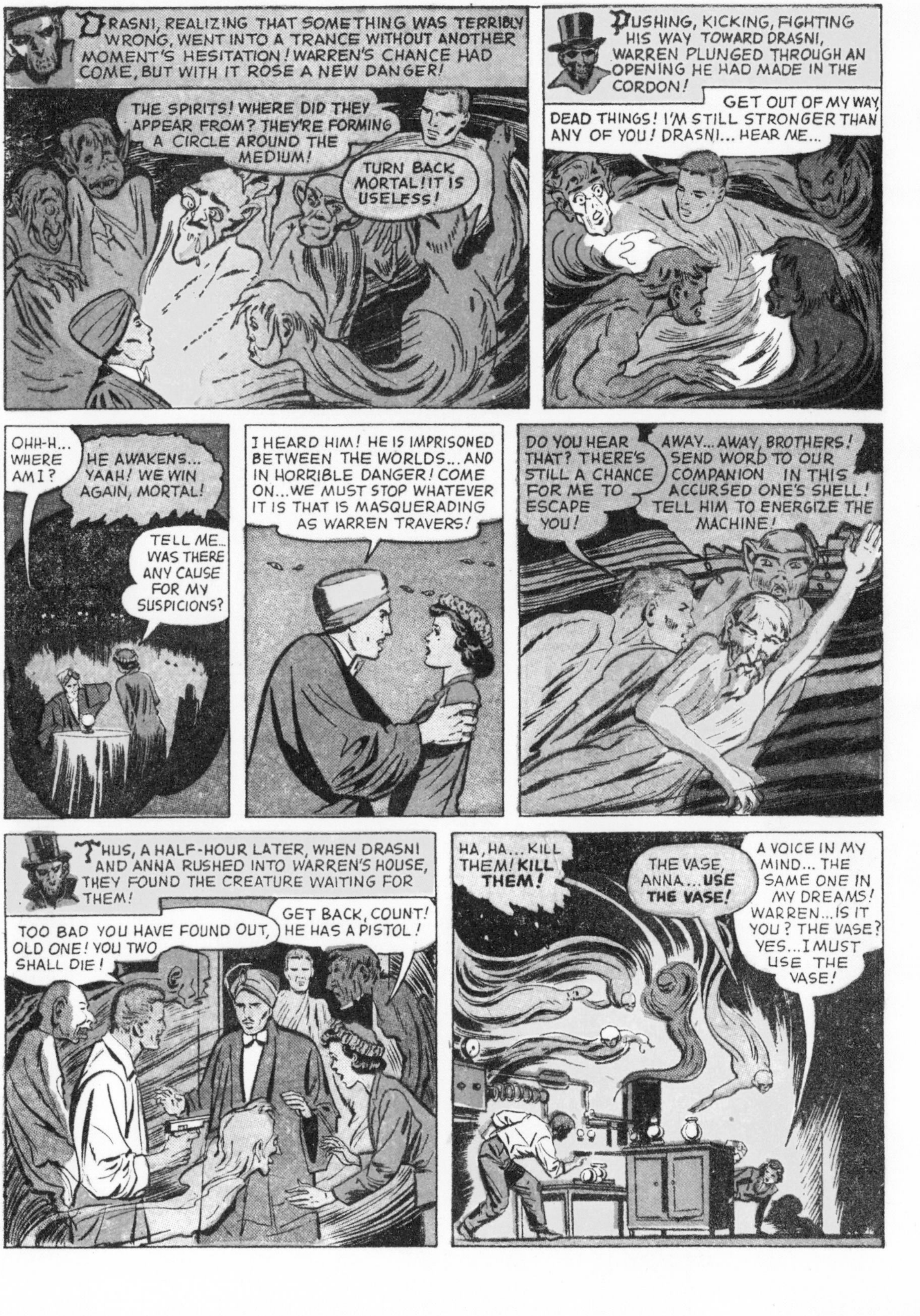
DRASNI, REALIZING THAT SOMETHING WAS TERRIBLY WRONG, WENT INTO A TRANCE WITHOUT ANOTHER MOMENT'S HESITATION! WARREN'S CHANCE HAD COME, BUT WITH IT ROSE A NEW DANGER!
THE SPIRITS! WHERE DID THEY APPEAR FROM? THEY'RE FORMING A CIRCLE AROUND THE MEDIUM!
TURN BACK MORTAL! IT IS USELESS!
PUSHING, KICKING, FIGHTING HIS WAY TOWARD DRASNI, WARREN PLUNGED THROUGH AN OPENING HE HAD MADE IN THE CORDON!
GET OUT OF MY WAY, DEAD THINGS! I'M STILL STRONGER THAN ANY OF YOU! DRASNI... HEAR ME...
OHH-H... WHERE AM I?
HE AWAKENS... YAAH! WE WIN AGAIN, MORTAL!
TELL ME... WAS THERE ANY CAUSE FOR MY SUSPICIONS?
I HEARD HIM! HE IS IMPRISONED BETWEEN THE WORLDS... AND IN HORRIBLE DANGER! COME ON... WE MUST STOP WHATEVER IT IS THAT IS MASQUERADING AS WARREN TRAVERS!
DO YOU HEAR THAT? THERE'S STILL A CHANCE FOR ME TO ESCAPE YOU!
AWAY... AWAY, BROTHERS! SEND WORD TO OUR COMPANION IN THIS ACCURSED ONE'S SHELL! TELL HIM TO ENERGIZE THE MACHINE!
THUS, A HALF-HOUR LATER, WHEN DRASNI AND ANNA RUSHED INTO WARREN'S HOUSE, THEY FOUND THE CREATURE WAITING FOR THEM!
TOO BAD YOU HAVE FOUND OUT, OLD ONE! YOU TWO SHALL DIE!
GET BACK, COUNT! HE HAS A PISTOL!
HA, HA... KILL THEM! **KILL THEM!**
THE VASE, ANNA... **USE THE VASE!**
A VOICE IN MY MIND... THE SAME ONE IN MY DREAMS! WARREN... IS IT YOU? THE VASE? YES... I MUST USE THE VASE!

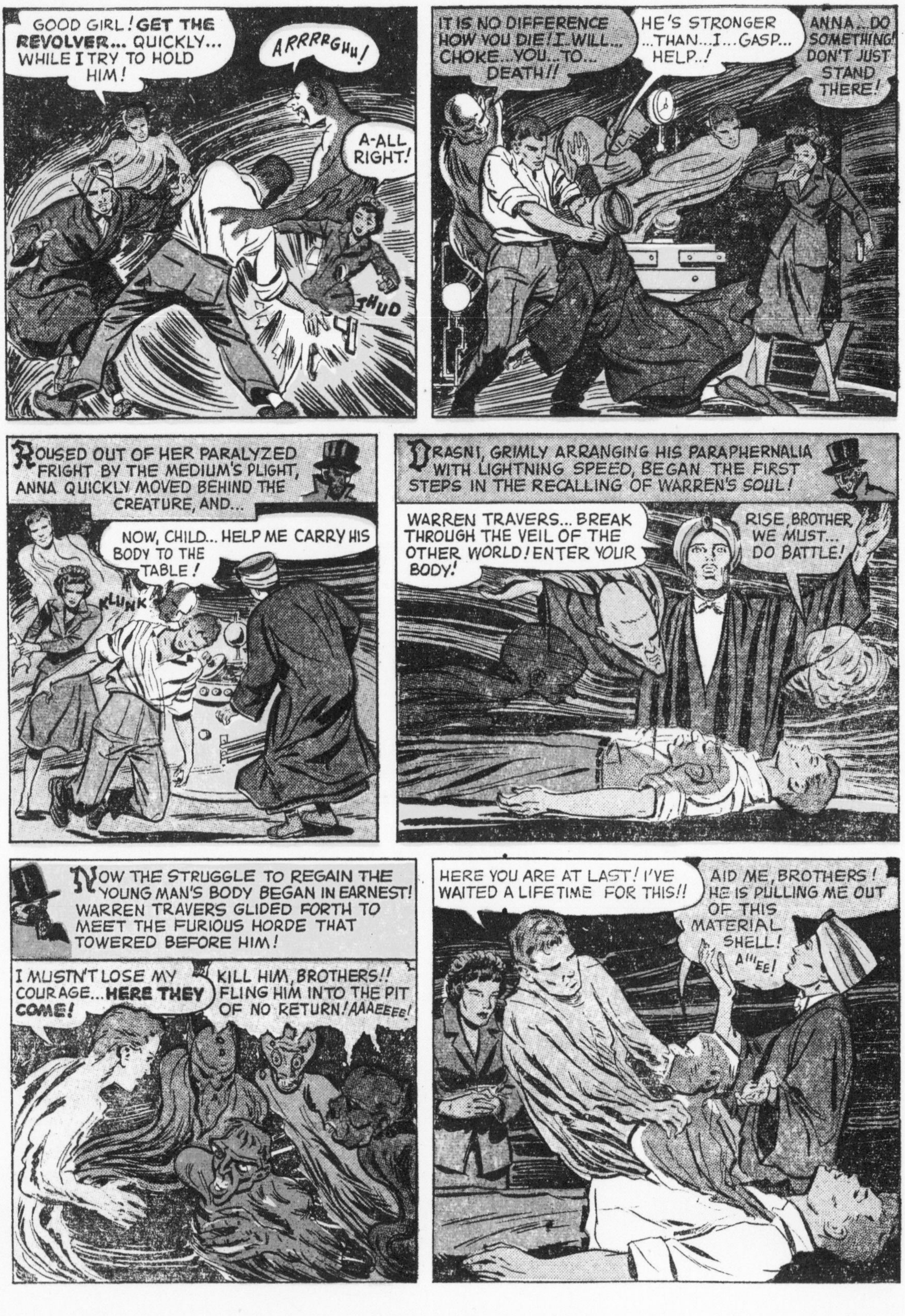
GOOD GIRL! GET THE REVOLVER... QUICKLY... WHILE I TRY TO HOLD HIM!
ARRRRGHH!
A-ALL RIGHT!
THUD
IT IS NO DIFFERENCE HOW YOU DIE! I..WILL... CHOKE...YOU...TO... DEATH!!
HE'S STRONGER ...THAN...I...GASP... HELP..!
ANNA...DO SOMETHING! DON'T JUST STAND THERE!
ROUSED OUT OF HER PARALYZED FRIGHT BY THE MEDIUM'S PLIGHT, ANNA QUICKLY MOVED BEHIND THE CREATURE, AND...
NOW, CHILD... HELP ME CARRY HIS BODY TO THE TABLE!
KLUNK
DRASNI, GRIMLY ARRANGING HIS PARAPHERNALIA WITH LIGHTNING SPEED, BEGAN THE FIRST STEPS IN THE RECALLING OF WARREN'S SOUL!
WARREN TRAVERS... BREAK THROUGH THE VEIL OF THE OTHER WORLD! ENTER YOUR BODY!
RISE, BROTHER, WE MUST... DO BATTLE!
NOW THE STRUGGLE TO REGAIN THE YOUNG MAN'S BODY BEGAN IN EARNEST! WARREN TRAVERS GLIDED FORTH TO MEET THE FURIOUS HORDE THAT TOWERED BEFORE HIM!
I MUSTN'T LOSE MY COURAGE... HERE THEY COME!
KILL HIM, BROTHERS!! FLING HIM INTO THE PIT OF NO RETURN! AAAEEEE!
HERE YOU ARE AT LAST! I'VE WAITED A LIFETIME FOR THIS!!
AID ME, BROTHERS! HE IS PULLING ME OUT OF THIS MATERIAL SHELL!
AIIEE!

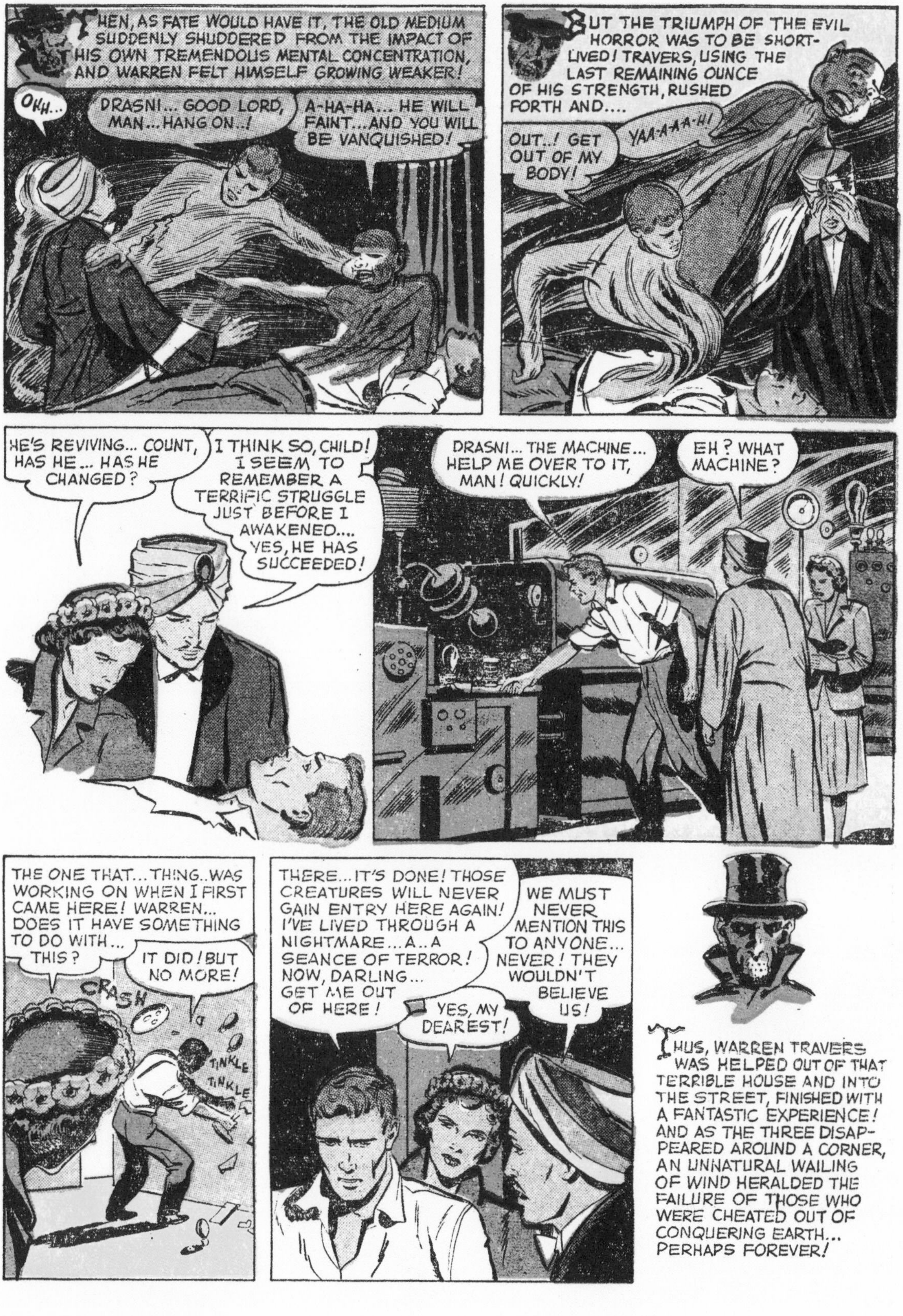
THEN, AS FATE WOULD HAVE IT, THE OLD MEDIUM SUDDENLY SHUDDERED FROM THE IMPACT OF HIS OWN TREMENDOUS MENTAL CONCENTRATION, AND WARREN FELT HIMSELF GROWING WEAKER!
OHH...
DRASNI... GOOD LORD, MAN... HANG ON..!
A-HA-HA... HE WILL FAINT... AND YOU WILL BE VANQUISHED!
BUT THE TRIUMPH OF THE EVIL HORROR WAS TO BE SHORT-LIVED! TRAVERS, USING THE LAST REMAINING OUNCE OF HIS STRENGTH, RUSHED FORTH AND....
OUT..! GET OUT OF MY BODY!
YAA-A-A-A-H!
HE'S REVIVING... COUNT, HAS HE... HAS HE CHANGED?
I THINK SO, CHILD! I SEEM TO REMEMBER A TERRIFIC STRUGGLE JUST BEFORE I AWAKENED.... YES, HE HAS SUCCEEDED!
DRASNI... THE MACHINE... HELP ME OVER TO IT, MAN! QUICKLY!
EH? WHAT MACHINE?
THE ONE THAT... THING.. WAS WORKING ON WHEN I FIRST CAME HERE! WARREN... DOES IT HAVE SOMETHING TO DO WITH... THIS?
IT DID! BUT NO MORE!
CRASH
TINKLE
TINKLE
THERE... IT'S DONE! THOSE CREATURES WILL NEVER GAIN ENTRY HERE AGAIN! I'VE LIVED THROUGH A NIGHTMARE... A.. A SEANCE OF TERROR! NOW, DARLING... GET ME OUT OF HERE!
YES, MY DEAREST!
WE MUST NEVER MENTION THIS TO ANYONE... NEVER! THEY WOULDN'T BELIEVE US!
THUS, WARREN TRAVERS WAS HELPED OUT OF THAT TERRIBLE HOUSE AND INTO THE STREET, FINISHED WITH A FANTASTIC EXPERIENCE! AND AS THE THREE DISAPPEARED AROUND A CORNER, AN UNNATURAL WAILING OF WIND HERALDED THE FAILURE OF THOSE WHO WERE CHEATED OUT OF CONQUERING EARTH... PERHAPS FOREVER!

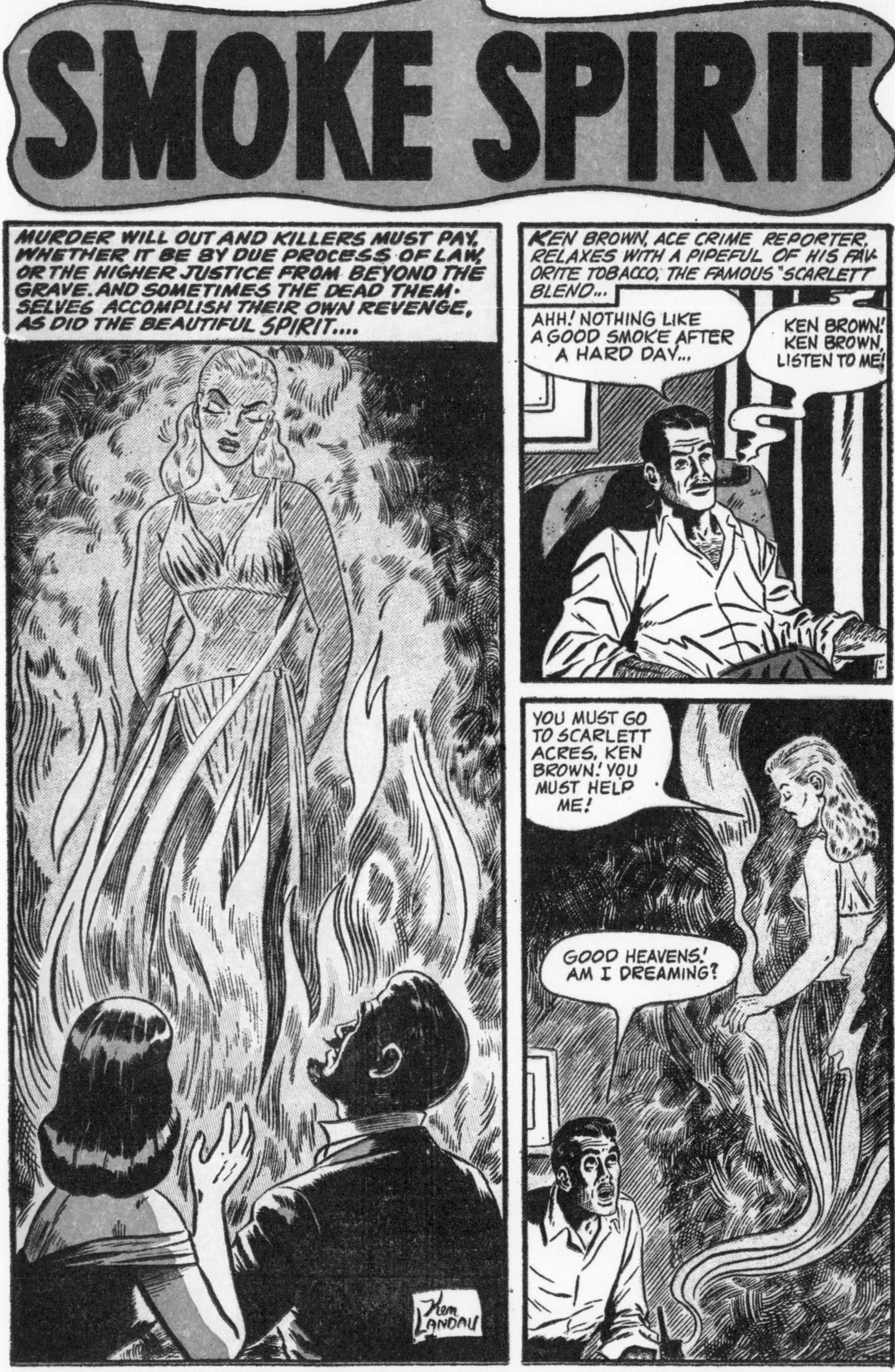
SMOKE SPIRIT
MURDER WILL OUT AND KILLERS MUST PAY, WHETHER IT BE BY DUE PROCESS OF LAW, OR THE HIGHER JUSTICE FROM BEYOND THE GRAVE. AND SOMETIMES THE DEAD THEMSELVES ACCOMPLISH THEIR OWN REVENGE, AS DID THE BEAUTIFUL SPIRIT....
Ken Landau
KEN BROWN, ACE CRIME REPORTER, RELAXES WITH A PIPEFUL OF HIS FAVORITE TOBACCO, THE FAMOUS "SCARLETT BLEND...
AHH! NOTHING LIKE A GOOD SMOKE AFTER A HARD DAY...
KEN BROWN! KEN BROWN, LISTEN TO ME!
YOU MUST GO TO SCARLETT ACRES, KEN BROWN! YOU MUST HELP ME!
GOOD HEAVENS! AM I DREAMING?

Horrific #5, May 1953. Kenneth Landau. Comic Media.

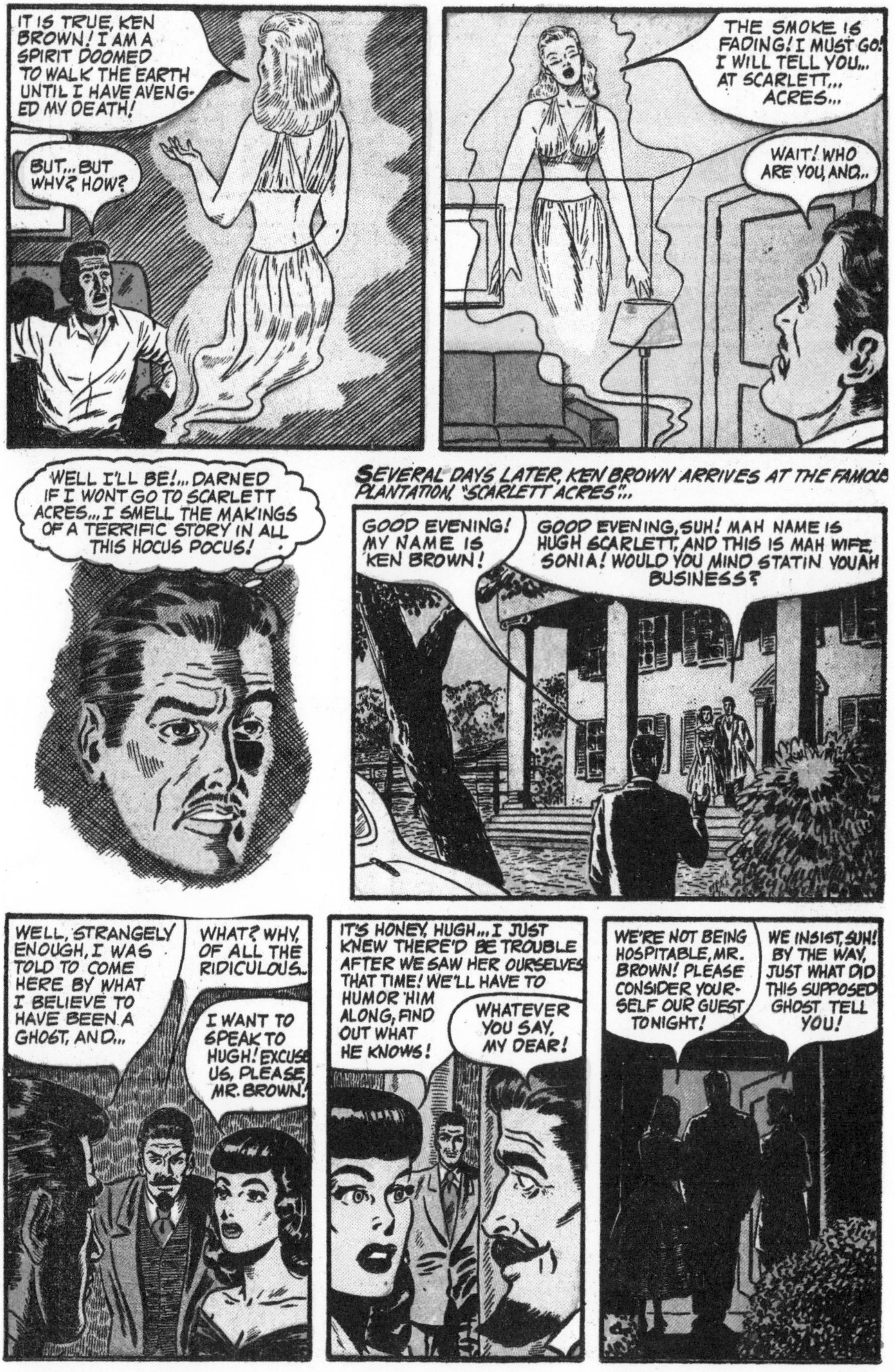
IT IS TRUE, KEN BROWN! I AM A SPIRIT DOOMED TO WALK THE EARTH UNTIL I HAVE AVENGED MY DEATH!
BUT... BUT WHY? HOW?
THE SMOKE IS FADING! I MUST GO! I WILL TELL YOU... AT SCARLETT... ACRES...
WAIT! WHO ARE YOU, AND...
WELL I'LL BE!... DARNED IF I WONT GO TO SCARLETT ACRES... I SMELL THE MAKINGS OF A TERRIFIC STORY IN ALL THIS HOCUS POCUS!
SEVERAL DAYS LATER, KEN BROWN ARRIVES AT THE FAMOUS PLANTATION, "SCARLETT ACRES"...
GOOD EVENING! MY NAME IS KEN BROWN!
GOOD EVENING, SUH! MAH NAME IS HUGH SCARLETT, AND THIS IS MAH WIFE, SONIA! WOULD YOU MIND STATIN YOUAH BUSINESS?
WELL, STRANGELY ENOUGH, I WAS TOLD TO COME HERE BY WHAT I BELIEVE TO HAVE BEEN A GHOST, AND...
WHAT? WHY, OF ALL THE RIDICULOUS...
I WANT TO SPEAK TO HUGH! EXCUSE US, PLEASE, MR. BROWN!
IT'S HONEY, HUGH... I JUST KNEW THERE'D BE TROUBLE AFTER WE SAW HER OURSELVES THAT TIME! WE'LL HAVE TO HUMOR 'HIM ALONG, FIND OUT WHAT HE KNOWS!
WHATEVER YOU SAY, MY DEAR!
WE'RE NOT BEING HOSPITABLE, MR. BROWN! PLEASE CONSIDER YOURSELF OUR GUEST TONIGHT!
WE INSIST, SUH! BY THE WAY, JUST WHAT DID THIS SUPPOSED GHOST TELL YOU!

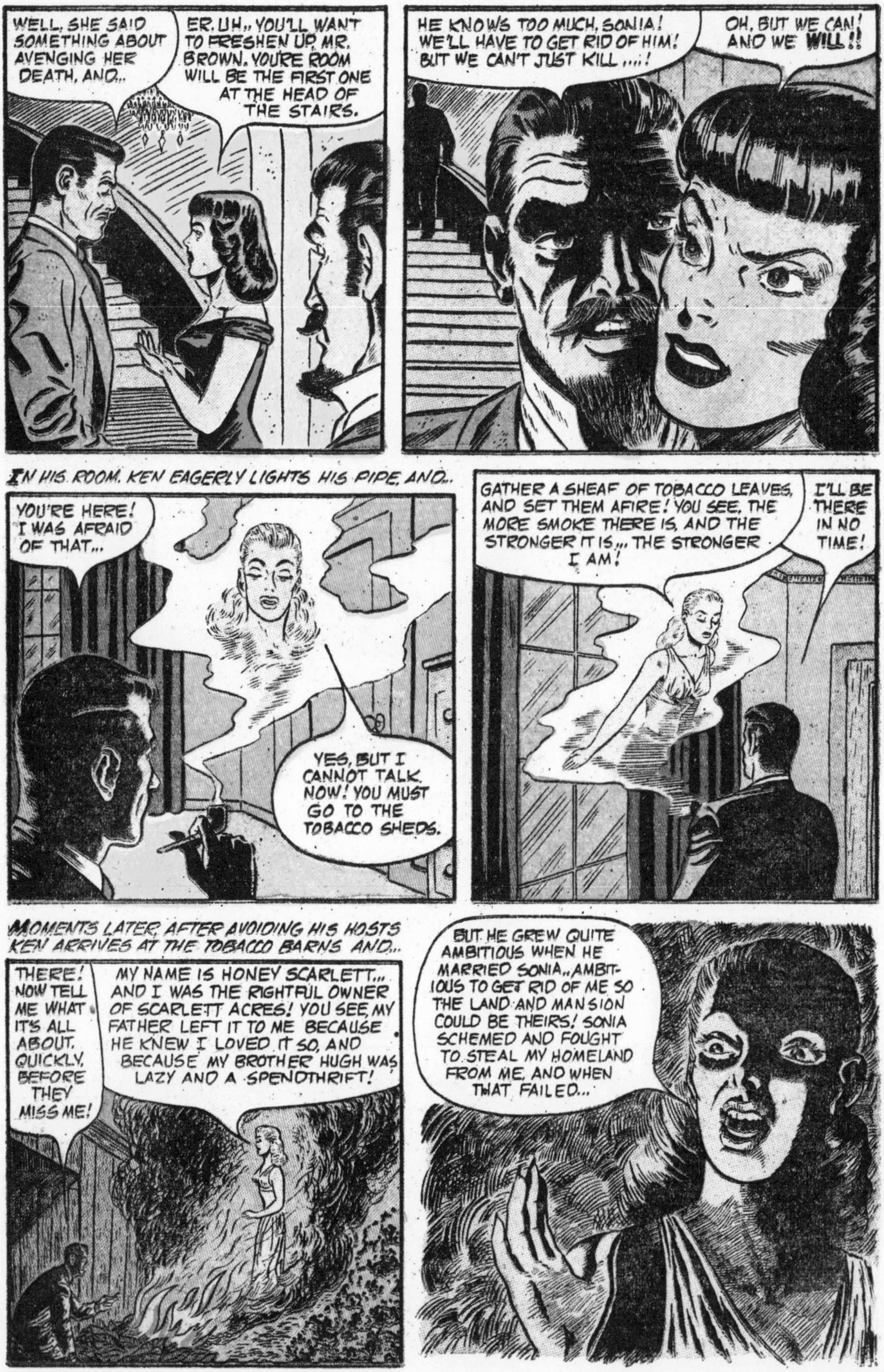

WELL, SHE SAID SOMETHING ABOUT AVENGING HER DEATH, AND...
ER, UH... YOU'LL WANT TO FRESHEN UP, MR. BROWN. YOU'RE ROOM WILL BE THE FIRST ONE AT THE HEAD OF THE STAIRS.
HE KNOWS TOO MUCH, SONIA! WE'LL HAVE TO GET RID OF HIM! BUT WE CAN'T JUST KILL ....!
OH, BUT WE CAN! AND WE WILL!!
IN HIS ROOM, KEN EAGERLY LIGHTS HIS PIPE, AND...
YOU'RE HERE! I WAS AFRAID OF THAT...
YES, BUT I CANNOT TALK NOW! YOU MUST GO TO THE TOBACCO SHEDS.
GATHER A SHEAF OF TOBACCO LEAVES, AND SET THEM AFIRE! YOU SEE, THE MORE SMOKE THERE IS, AND THE STRONGER IT IS... THE STRONGER I AM!
I'LL BE THERE IN NO TIME!
MOMENTS LATER, AFTER AVOIDING HIS HOSTS KEN ARRIVES AT THE TOBACCO BARNS AND...
THERE! NOW TELL ME WHAT IT'S ALL ABOUT. QUICKLY, BEFORE THEY MISS ME!
MY NAME IS HONEY SCARLETT... AND I WAS THE RIGHTFUL OWNER OF SCARLETT ACRES! YOU SEE, MY FATHER LEFT IT TO ME BECAUSE HE KNEW I LOVED IT SO, AND BECAUSE MY BROTHER HUGH WAS LAZY AND A SPENDTHRIFT!
BUT HE GREW QUITE AMBITIOUS WHEN HE MARRIED SONIA... AMBITIOUS TO GET RID OF ME SO THE LAND AND MANSION COULD BE THEIRS! SONIA SCHEMED AND FOUGHT TO STEAL MY HOMELAND FROM ME, AND WHEN THAT FAILED...

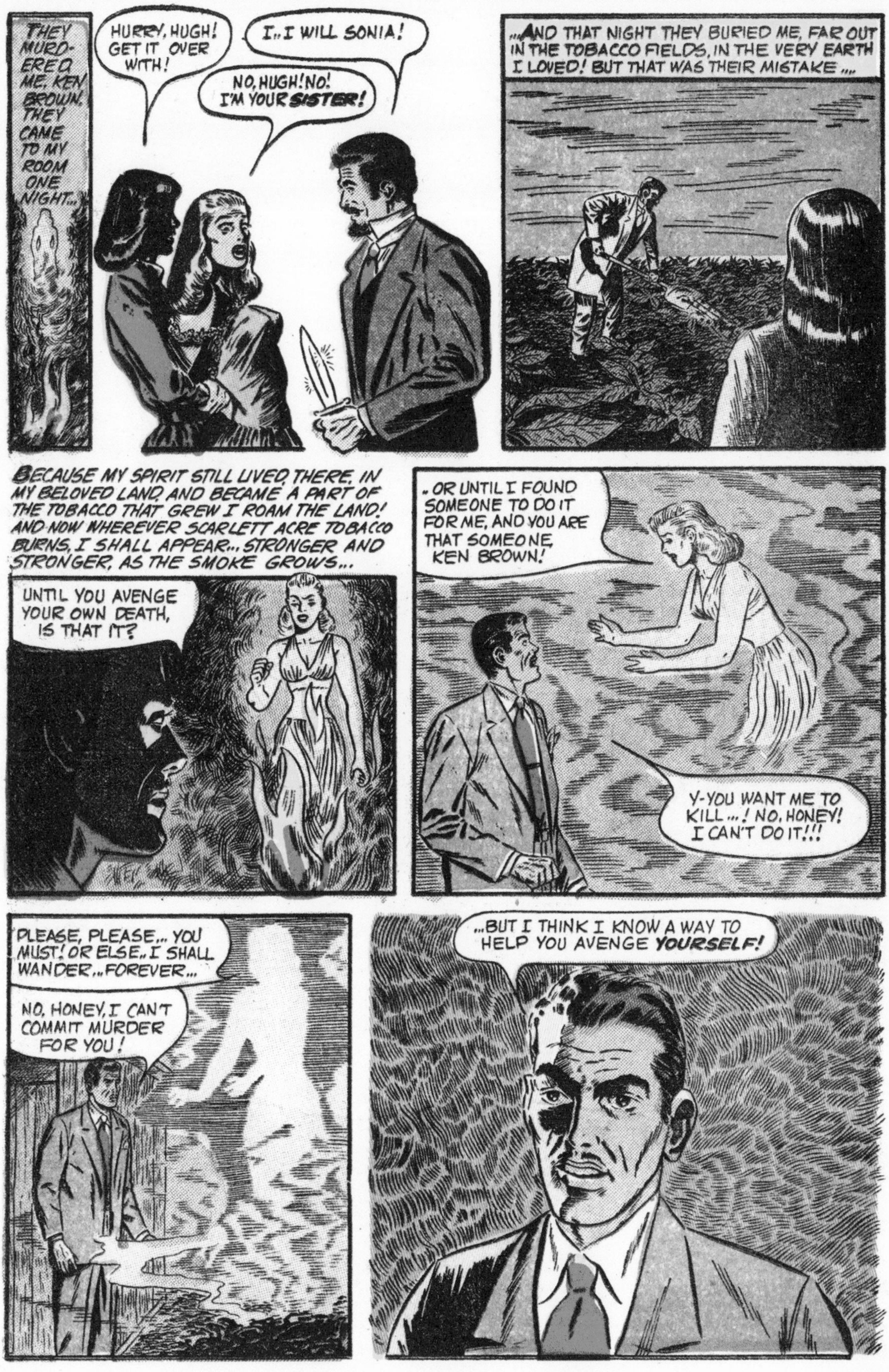

THEY MURDERED ME, KEN BROWN. THEY CAME TO MY ROOM ONE NIGHT...
HURRY, HUGH! GET IT OVER WITH!
I.. I WILL SONIA!
NO, HUGH! NO! I'M YOUR SISTER!
...AND THAT NIGHT THEY BURIED ME, FAR OUT IN THE TOBACCO FIELDS, IN THE VERY EARTH I LOVED! BUT THAT WAS THEIR MISTAKE ....
BECAUSE MY SPIRIT STILL LIVED THERE, IN MY BELOVED LAND AND BECAME A PART OF THE TOBACCO THAT GREW I ROAM THE LAND! AND NOW WHEREVER SCARLETT ACRE TOBACCO BURNS, I SHALL APPEAR... STRONGER AND STRONGER, AS THE SMOKE GROWS...
UNTIL YOU AVENGE YOUR OWN DEATH, IS THAT IT?
.. OR UNTIL I FOUND SOMEONE TO DO IT FOR ME, AND YOU ARE THAT SOMEONE, KEN BROWN!
Y-YOU WANT ME TO KILL ... ! NO, HONEY! I CAN'T DO IT!!!
PLEASE, PLEASE... YOU MUST! OR ELSE.. I SHALL WANDER... FOREVER...
NO, HONEY, I CAN'T COMMIT MURDER FOR YOU!
...BUT I THINK I KNOW A WAY TO HELP YOU AVENGE YOURSELF!

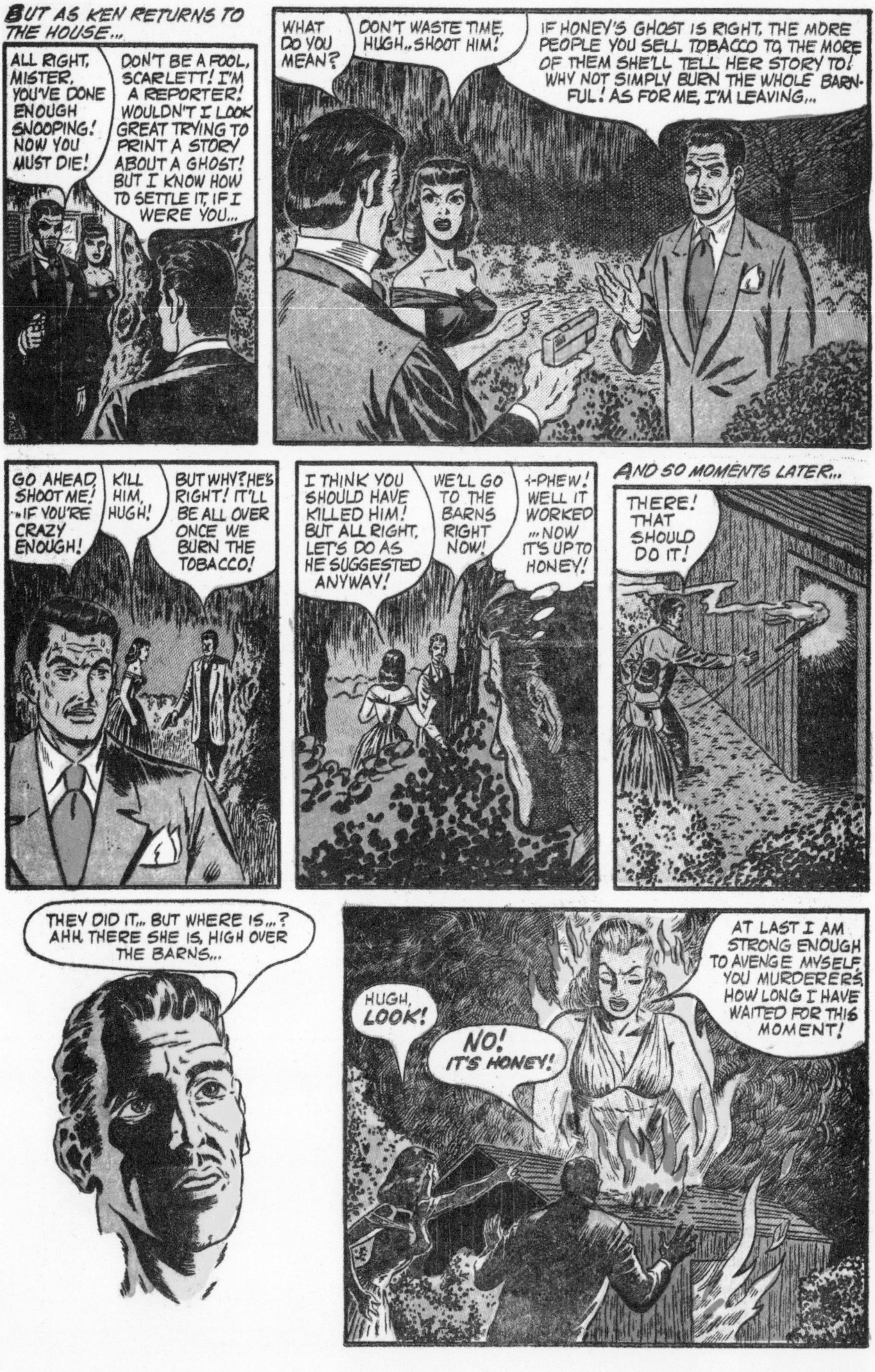
BUT AS KEN RETURNS TO THE HOUSE...
ALL RIGHT, MISTER, YOU'VE DONE ENOUGH SNOOPING! NOW YOU MUST DIE!
DON'T BE A FOOL, SCARLETT! I'M A REPORTER! WOULDN'T I LOOK GREAT TRYING TO PRINT A STORY ABOUT A GHOST! BUT I KNOW HOW TO SETTLE IT, IF I WERE YOU...
WHAT DO YOU MEAN?
DON'T WASTE TIME, HUGH.. SHOOT HIM!
IF HONEY'S GHOST IS RIGHT, THE MORE PEOPLE YOU SELL TOBACCO TO, THE MORE OF THEM SHE'LL TELL HER STORY TO! WHY NOT SIMPLY BURN THE WHOLE BARN-FUL! AS FOR ME, I'M LEAVING...
GO AHEAD, SHOOT ME! ..IF YOU'RE CRAZY ENOUGH!
KILL HIM, HUGH!
BUT WHY? HE'S RIGHT! IT'LL BE ALL OVER ONCE WE BURN THE TOBACCO!
I THINK YOU SHOULD HAVE KILLED HIM! BUT ALL RIGHT, LET'S DO AS HE SUGGESTED ANYWAY!
WE'LL GO TO THE BARNS RIGHT NOW!
--PHEW! WELL IT WORKED ...NOW IT'S UP TO HONEY!
AND SO MOMENTS LATER...
THERE! THAT SHOULD DO IT!
THEY DID IT... BUT WHERE IS...? AHH, THERE SHE IS, HIGH OVER THE BARNS...
AT LAST I AM STRONG ENOUGH TO AVENGE MYSELF, YOU MURDERERS, HOW LONG I HAVE WAITED FOR THIS MOMENT!
HUGH, LOOK!
NO! IT'S HONEY!

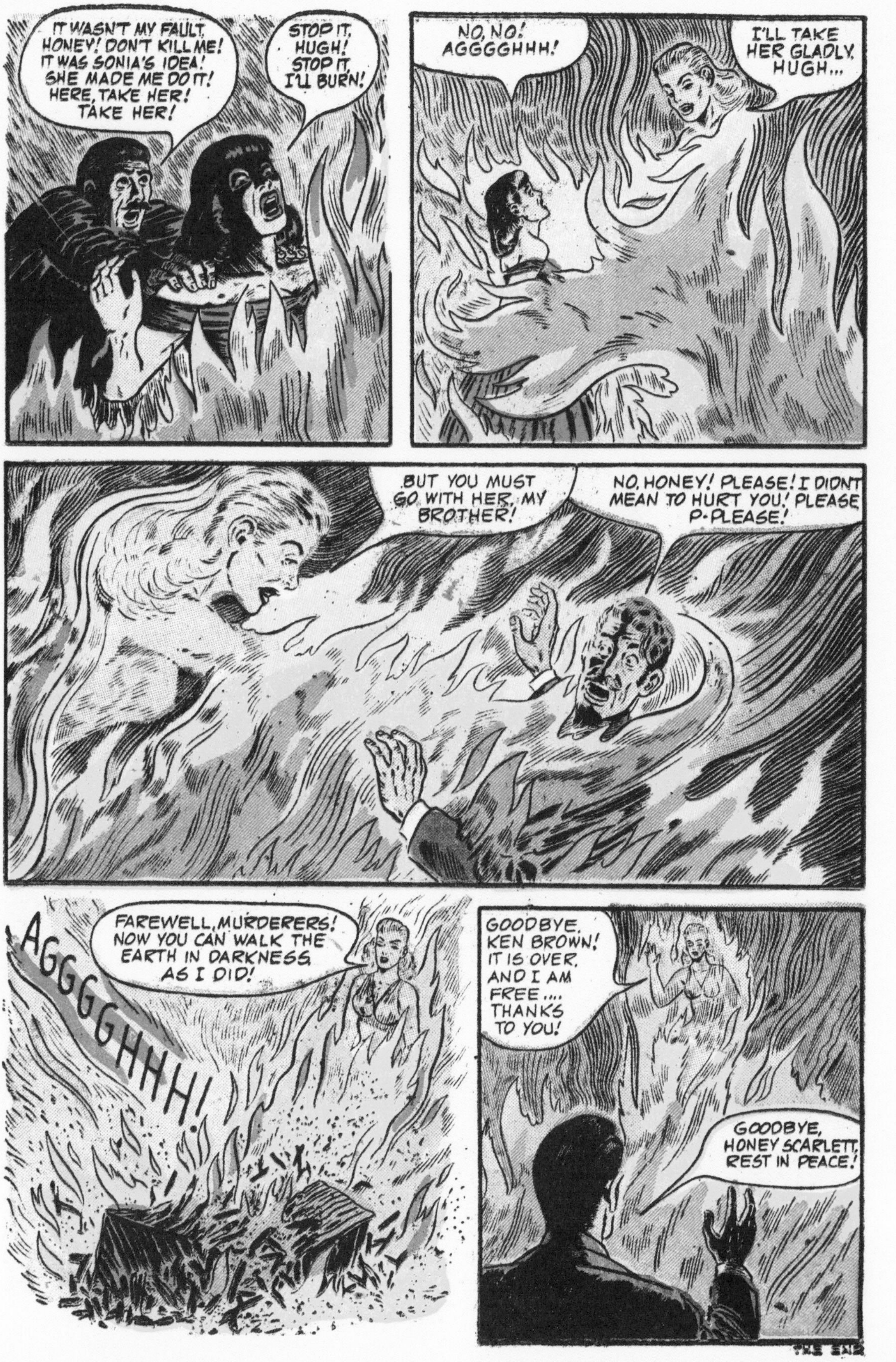
IT WASN'T MY FAULT, HONEY! DON'T KILL ME! IT WAS SONIA'S IDEA! SHE MADE ME DO IT! HERE, TAKE HER! TAKE HER!
STOP IT, HUGH! STOP IT, I'LL BURN!
NO, NO! AGGGGHHH!
I'LL TAKE HER GLADLY, HUGH...
BUT YOU MUST GO WITH HER, MY BROTHER!
NO, HONEY! PLEASE! I DIDNT MEAN TO HURT YOU! PLEASE P-PLEASE!
FAREWELL, MURDERERS! NOW YOU CAN WALK THE EARTH IN DARKNESS AS I DID!
AGGGGHHHH!
GOODBYE, KEN BROWN! IT IS OVER, AND I AM FREE.... THANKS TO YOU!
GOODBYE, HONEY SCARLETT, REST IN PEACE!
THE END

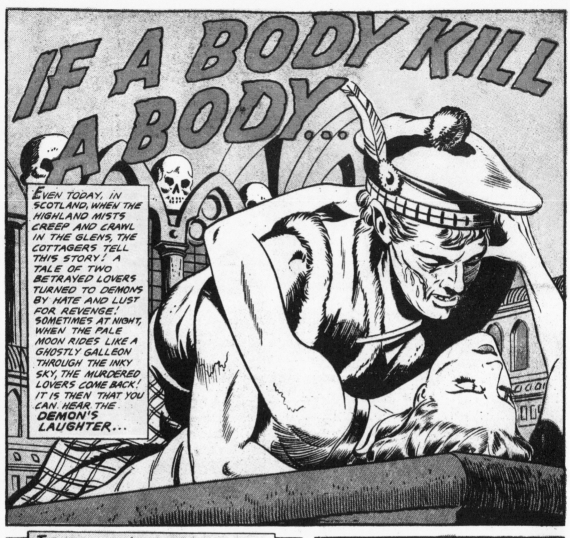

IF A BODY KILL A BODY...

EVEN TODAY, IN SCOTLAND, WHEN THE HIGHLAND MISTS CREEP AND CRAWL IN THE GLENS, THE COTTAGERS TELL THIS STORY! A TALE OF TWO BETRAYED LOVERS TURNED TO DEMONS BY HATE AND LUST FOR REVENGE! SOMETIMES AT NIGHT, WHEN THE PALE MOON RIDES LIKE A GHOSTLY GALLEON THROUGH THE INKY SKY, THE MURDERED LOVERS COME BACK! IT IS THEN THAT YOU CAN HEAR THE DEMON'S LAUGHTER...

THE YEAR IS 1560! THE LOVERS ARE ANGUS MCCANN AND MARY MCLEOD! THEIR LOVE IS A FORBIDDEN ONE...

AYE, MARY, YOU KNOW I HATE THESE SECRET MEETINGS AS MUCH AS YOU DO! BUT MY FATHER...

AND MINE, ANGUS! THE FEUD OF OUR FAMILIES HAS KEPT US APART FOR TOO LONG NOW!

BUT I CANNOT LIVE WITHOUT YOU, LASS! WE MUST DO SOMETHING AT ONCE! WE'LL RUN AWAY TOGETHER, TO THE LOWLANDS, AND BE MARRIED!

ALL RIGHT, DARLING! I'D GO TO THE ENDS OF THE EARTH WITH YOU!

Fantastic Fears #9, September – October 1954. Iger Shop. Farrell.

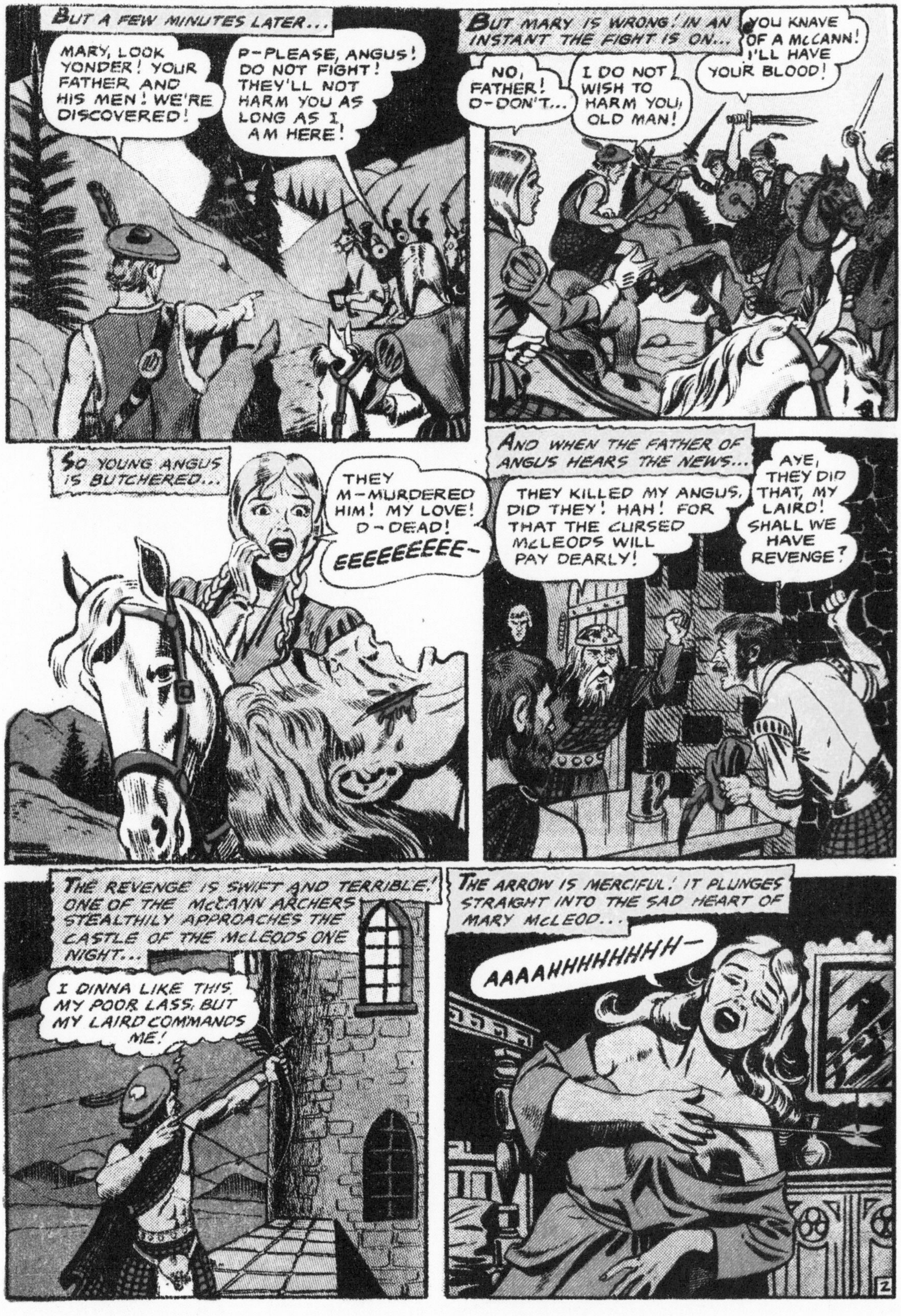
BUT A FEW MINUTES LATER...
MARY, LOOK YONDER! YOUR FATHER AND HIS MEN! WE'RE DISCOVERED!
P-PLEASE, ANGUS! DO NOT FIGHT! THEY'LL NOT HARM YOU AS LONG AS I AM HERE!
BUT MARY IS WRONG! IN AN INSTANT THE FIGHT IS ON...
YOU KNAVE OF A McCANN! I'LL HAVE YOUR BLOOD!
NO, FATHER! D-DON'T...
I DO NOT WISH TO HARM YOU, OLD MAN!
SO YOUNG ANGUS IS BUTCHERED...
THEY M-MURDERED HIM! MY LOVE! D-DEAD! EEEEEEEEE-
AND WHEN THE FATHER OF ANGUS HEARS THE NEWS...
THEY KILLED MY ANGUS, DID THEY! HAH! FOR THAT THE CURSED McLEODS WILL PAY DEARLY!
AYE, THEY DID THAT, MY LAIRD! SHALL WE HAVE REVENGE?
THE REVENGE IS SWIFT AND TERRIBLE! ONE OF THE McCANN ARCHERS STEALTHILY APPROACHES THE CASTLE OF THE McLEODS ONE NIGHT...
I DINNA LIKE THIS, MY POOR LASS, BUT MY LAIRD COMMANDS ME!
THE ARROW IS MERCIFUL! IT PLUNGES STRAIGHT INTO THE SAD HEART OF MARY McLEOD...
AAAAHHHHHHHH-
2

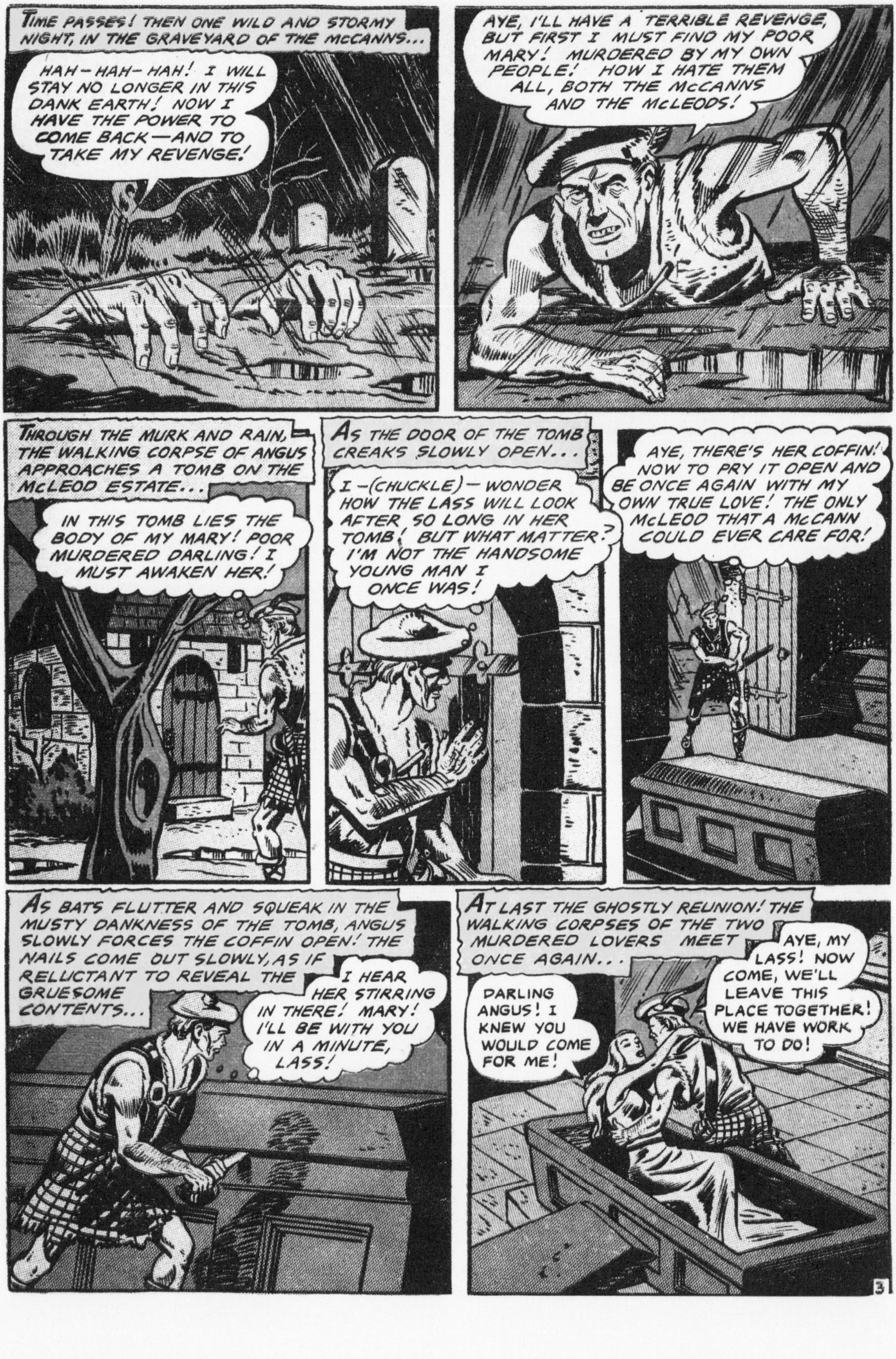

TIME PASSES! THEN ONE WILD AND STORMY NIGHT, IN THE GRAVEYARD OF THE McCANNS...
HAH-HAH-HAH! I WILL STAY NO LONGER IN THIS DANK EARTH! NOW I HAVE THE POWER TO COME BACK—AND TO TAKE MY REVENGE!
AYE, I'LL HAVE A TERRIBLE REVENGE, BUT FIRST I MUST FIND MY POOR MARY! MURDERED BY MY OWN PEOPLE! HOW I HATE THEM ALL, BOTH THE McCANNS AND THE McLEODS!
THROUGH THE MURK AND RAIN, THE WALKING CORPSE OF ANGUS APPROACHES A TOMB ON THE McLEOD ESTATE...
IN THIS TOMB LIES THE BODY OF MY MARY! POOR MURDERED DARLING! I MUST AWAKEN HER!
AS THE DOOR OF THE TOMB CREAKS SLOWLY OPEN...
I-(CHUCKLE)-WONDER HOW THE LASS WILL LOOK AFTER SO LONG IN HER TOMB! BUT WHAT MATTER? I'M NOT THE HANDSOME YOUNG MAN I ONCE WAS!
AYE, THERE'S HER COFFIN! NOW TO PRY IT OPEN AND BE ONCE AGAIN WITH MY OWN TRUE LOVE! THE ONLY McLEOD THAT A McCANN COULD EVER CARE FOR!
AS BATS FLUTTER AND SQUEAK IN THE MUSTY DANKNESS OF THE TOMB, ANGUS SLOWLY FORCES THE COFFIN OPEN! THE NAILS COME OUT SLOWLY, AS IF RELUCTANT TO REVEAL THE GRUESOME CONTENTS...
I HEAR HER STIRRING IN THERE! MARY! I'LL BE WITH YOU IN A MINUTE, LASS!
AT LAST THE GHOSTLY REUNION! THE WALKING CORPSES OF THE TWO MURDERED LOVERS MEET ONCE AGAIN...
DARLING ANGUS! I KNEW YOU WOULD COME FOR ME!
AYE, MY LASS! NOW COME, WE'LL LEAVE THIS PLACE TOGETHER! WE HAVE WORK TO DO!
3

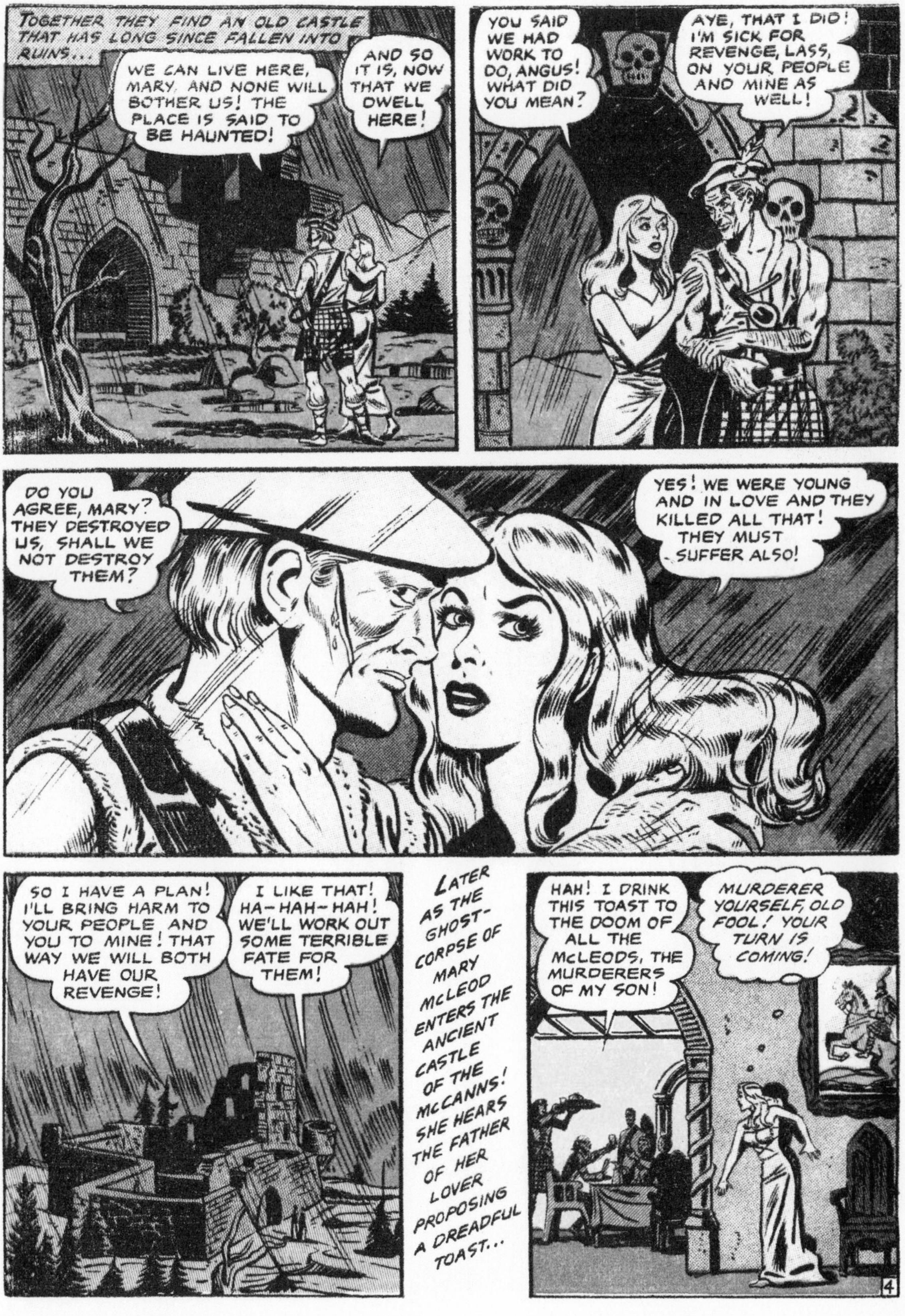
TOGETHER THEY FIND AN OLD CASTLE THAT HAS LONG SINCE FALLEN INTO RUINS...
WE CAN LIVE HERE, MARY, AND NONE WILL BOTHER US! THE PLACE IS SAID TO BE HAUNTED!
AND SO IT IS, NOW THAT WE DWELL HERE!
YOU SAID WE HAD WORK TO DO, ANGUS! WHAT DID YOU MEAN?
AYE, THAT I DID! I'M SICK FOR REVENGE, LASS, ON YOUR PEOPLE AND MINE AS WELL!
DO YOU AGREE, MARY? THEY DESTROYED US, SHALL WE NOT DESTROY THEM?
YES! WE WERE YOUNG AND IN LOVE AND THEY KILLED ALL THAT! THEY MUST SUFFER ALSO!
SO I HAVE A PLAN! I'LL BRING HARM TO YOUR PEOPLE AND YOU TO MINE! THAT WAY WE WILL BOTH HAVE OUR REVENGE!
I LIKE THAT! HA-HAH-HAH! WE'LL WORK OUT SOME TERRIBLE FATE FOR THEM!
LATER AS THE GHOST-CORPSE OF MARY McLEOD ENTERS THE ANCIENT CASTLE OF THE McCANNS! SHE HEARS THE FATHER OF HER LOVER PROPOSING A DREADFUL TOAST...
HAH! I DRINK THIS TOAST TO THE DOOM OF ALL THE McLEODS, THE MURDERERS OF MY SON!
MURDERER YOURSELF, OLD FOOL! YOUR TURN IS COMING!
4

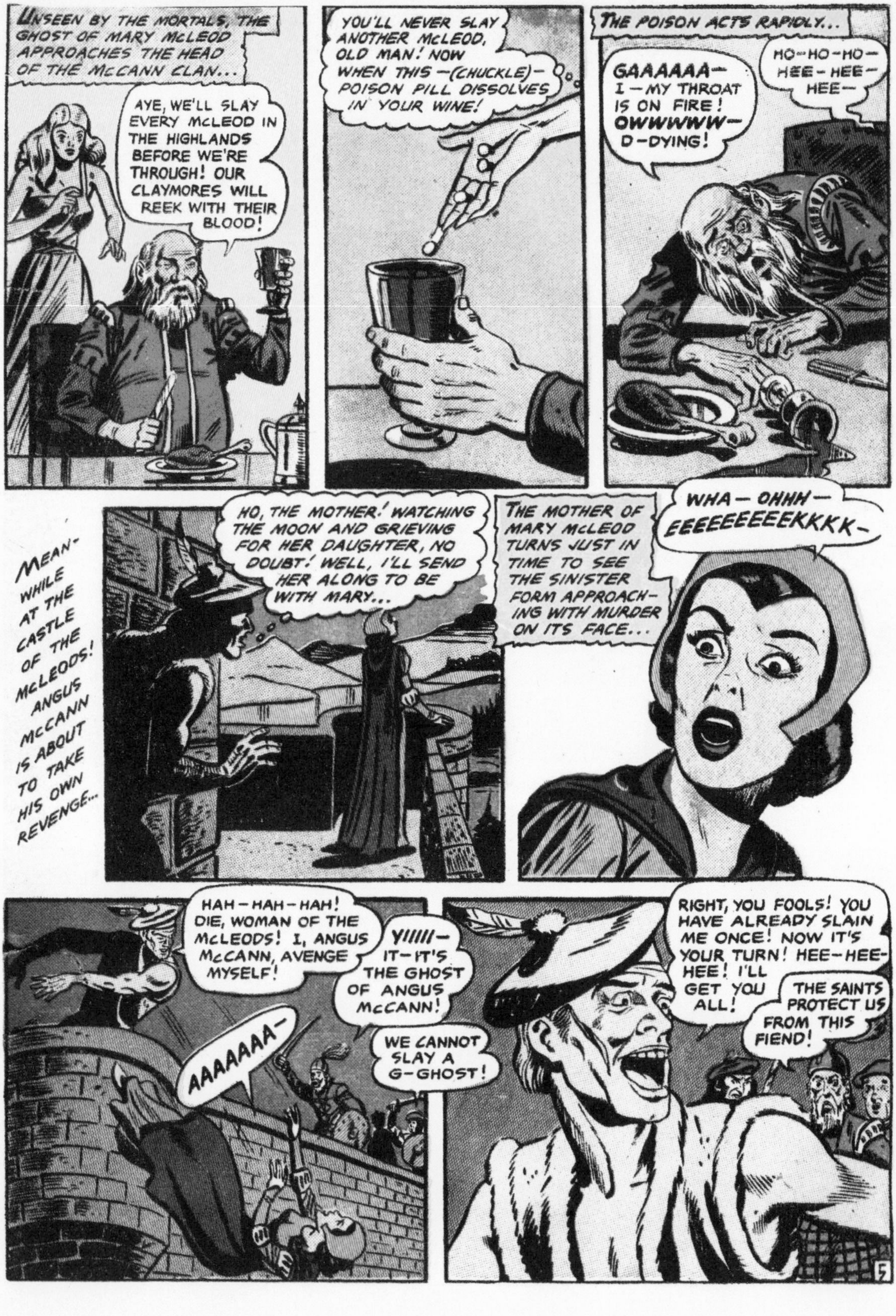
UNSEEN BY THE MORTALS, THE GHOST OF MARY McLEOD APPROACHES THE HEAD OF THE McCANN CLAN...
AYE, WE'LL SLAY EVERY McLEOD IN THE HIGHLANDS BEFORE WE'RE THROUGH! OUR CLAYMORES WILL REEK WITH THEIR BLOOD!
YOU'LL NEVER SLAY ANOTHER McLEOD, OLD MAN! NOW WHEN THIS —(CHUCKLE)— POISON PILL DISSOLVES IN YOUR WINE!
THE POISON ACTS RAPIDLY...
GAAAAAA— I — MY THROAT IS ON FIRE! OWWWWW— D-DYING!
HO-HO-HO— HEE-HEE-HEE—
MEAN-WHILE AT THE CASTLE OF THE McLEODS! ANGUS McCANN IS ABOUT TO TAKE HIS OWN REVENGE...
HO, THE MOTHER! WATCHING THE MOON AND GRIEVING FOR HER DAUGHTER, NO DOUBT! WELL, I'LL SEND HER ALONG TO BE WITH MARY...
THE MOTHER OF MARY McLEOD TURNS JUST IN TIME TO SEE THE SINISTER FORM APPROACHING WITH MURDER ON ITS FACE...
WHA— OHHH— EEEEEEEEEKKKK—
HAH-HAH-HAH! DIE, WOMAN OF THE McLEODS! I, ANGUS McCANN, AVENGE MYSELF!
AAAAAAA—
YIIIII— IT—IT'S THE GHOST OF ANGUS McCANN!
WE CANNOT SLAY A G-GHOST!
RIGHT, YOU FOOLS! YOU HAVE ALREADY SLAIN ME ONCE! NOW IT'S YOUR TURN! HEE-HEE-HEE! I'LL GET YOU ALL!
THE SAINTS PROTECT US FROM THIS FIEND!
5

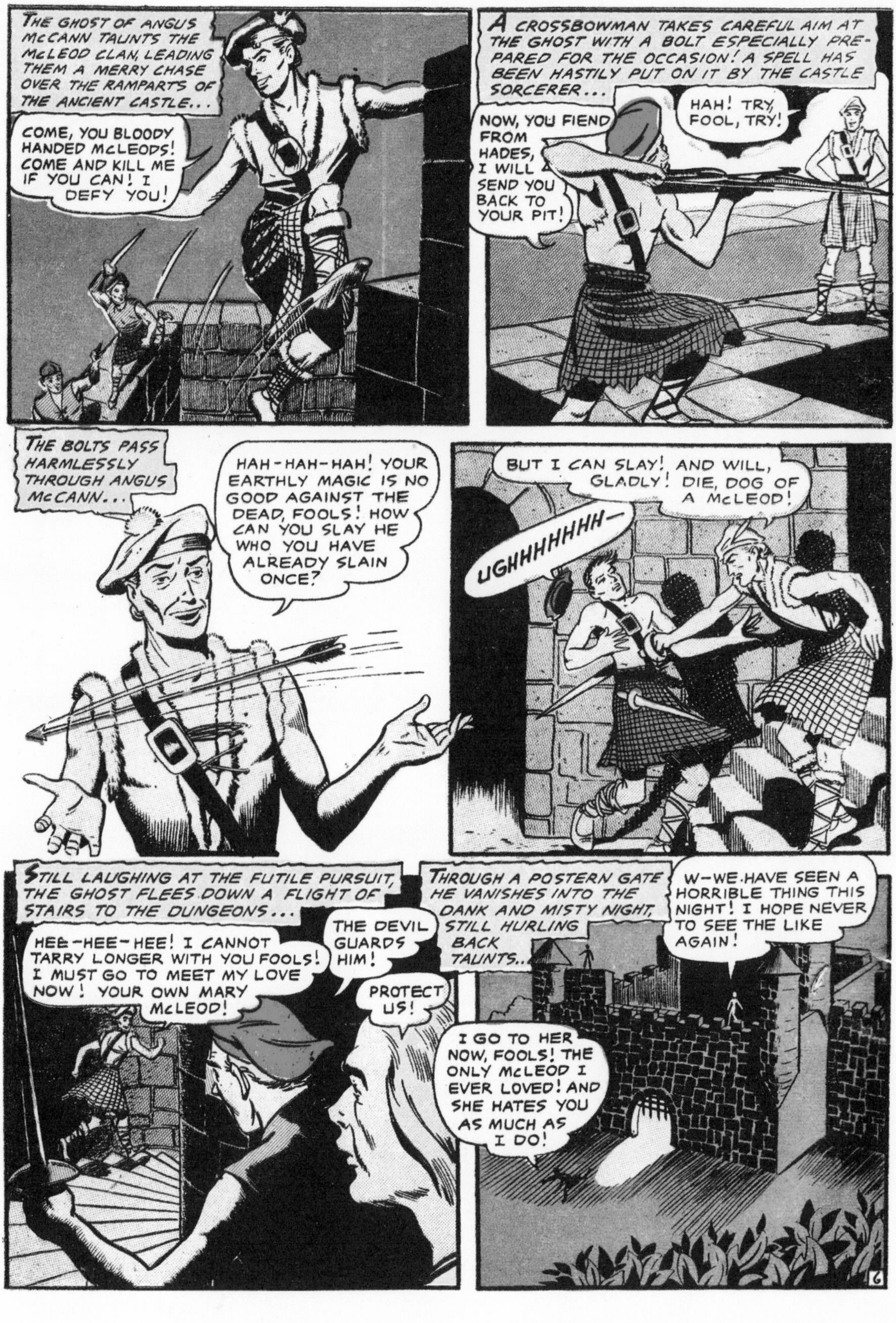
THE GHOST OF ANGUS McCANN TAUNTS THE McLEOD CLAN, LEADING THEM A MERRY CHASE OVER THE RAMPARTS OF THE ANCIENT CASTLE...
COME, YOU BLOODY HANDED McLEODS! COME AND KILL ME IF YOU CAN! I DEFY YOU!
A CROSSBOWMAN TAKES CAREFUL AIM AT THE GHOST WITH A BOLT ESPECIALLY PREPARED FOR THE OCCASION! A SPELL HAS BEEN HASTILY PUT ON IT BY THE CASTLE SORCERER...
NOW, YOU FIEND FROM HADES, I WILL SEND YOU BACK TO YOUR PIT!
HAH! TRY, FOOL, TRY!
THE BOLTS PASS HARMLESSLY THROUGH ANGUS McCANN...
HAH-HAH-HAH! YOUR EARTHLY MAGIC IS NO GOOD AGAINST THE DEAD, FOOLS! HOW CAN YOU SLAY HE WHO YOU HAVE ALREADY SLAIN ONCE?
BUT I CAN SLAY! AND WILL, GLADLY! DIE, DOG OF A McLEOD!
UGHHHHHHH—
STILL LAUGHING AT THE FUTILE PURSUIT, THE GHOST FLEES DOWN A FLIGHT OF STAIRS TO THE DUNGEONS...
HEE-HEE-HEE! I CANNOT TARRY LONGER WITH YOU FOOLS! I MUST GO TO MEET MY LOVE NOW! YOUR OWN MARY McLEOD!
THE DEVIL GUARDS HIM!
PROTECT US!
THROUGH A POSTERN GATE HE VANISHES INTO THE DANK AND MISTY NIGHT, STILL HURLING BACK TAUNTS...
W-WE HAVE SEEN A HORRIBLE THING THIS NIGHT! I HOPE NEVER TO SEE THE LIKE AGAIN!
I GO TO HER NOW, FOOLS! THE ONLY McLEOD I EVER LOVED! AND SHE HATES YOU AS MUCH AS I DO!
6

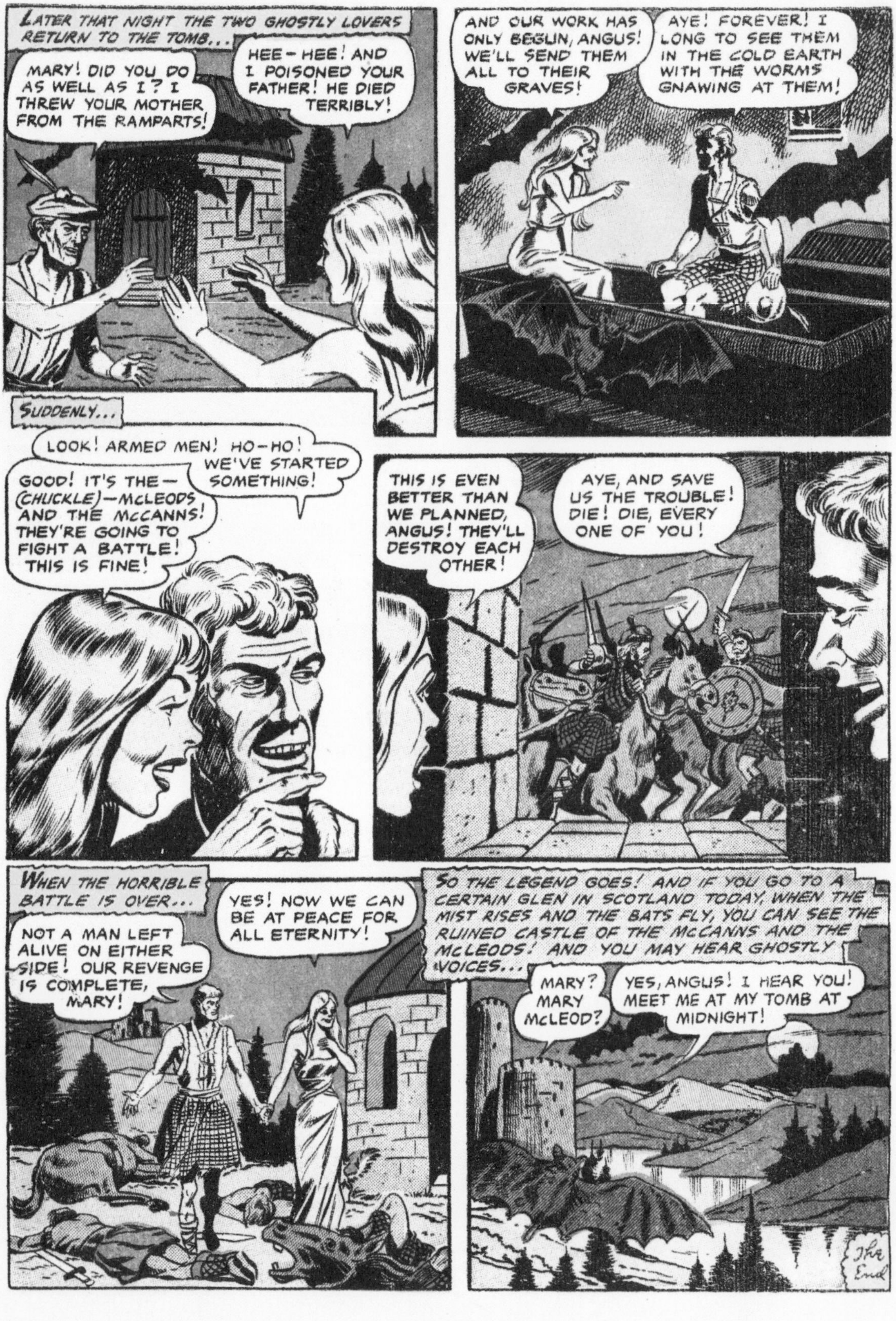

LATER THAT NIGHT THE TWO GHOSTLY LOVERS RETURN TO THE TOMB...
MARY! DID YOU DO AS WELL AS I? I THREW YOUR MOTHER FROM THE RAMPARTS!
HEE-HEE! AND I POISONED YOUR FATHER! HE DIED TERRIBLY!
AND OUR WORK HAS ONLY BEGUN, ANGUS! WE'LL SEND THEM ALL TO THEIR GRAVES!
AYE! FOREVER! I LONG TO SEE THEM IN THE COLD EARTH WITH THE WORMS GNAWING AT THEM!
SUDDENLY...
LOOK! ARMED MEN! HO-HO! WE'VE STARTED SOMETHING!
GOOD! IT'S THE—(CHUCKLE)—McLEODS AND THE McCANNS! THEY'RE GOING TO FIGHT A BATTLE! THIS IS FINE!
THIS IS EVEN BETTER THAN WE PLANNED, ANGUS! THEY'LL DESTROY EACH OTHER!
AYE, AND SAVE US THE TROUBLE! DIE! DIE, EVERY ONE OF YOU!
WHEN THE HORRIBLE BATTLE IS OVER...
NOT A MAN LEFT ALIVE ON EITHER SIDE! OUR REVENGE IS COMPLETE, MARY!
YES! NOW WE CAN BE AT PEACE FOR ALL ETERNITY!
SO THE LEGEND GOES! AND IF YOU GO TO A CERTAIN GLEN IN SCOTLAND TODAY, WHEN THE MIST RISES AND THE BATS FLY, YOU CAN SEE THE RUINED CASTLE OF THE McCANNS AND THE McLEODS! AND YOU MAY HEAR GHOSTLY VOICES...
MARY? MARY McLEOD?
YES, ANGUS! I HEAR YOU! MEET ME AT MY TOMB AT MIDNIGHT!
The End

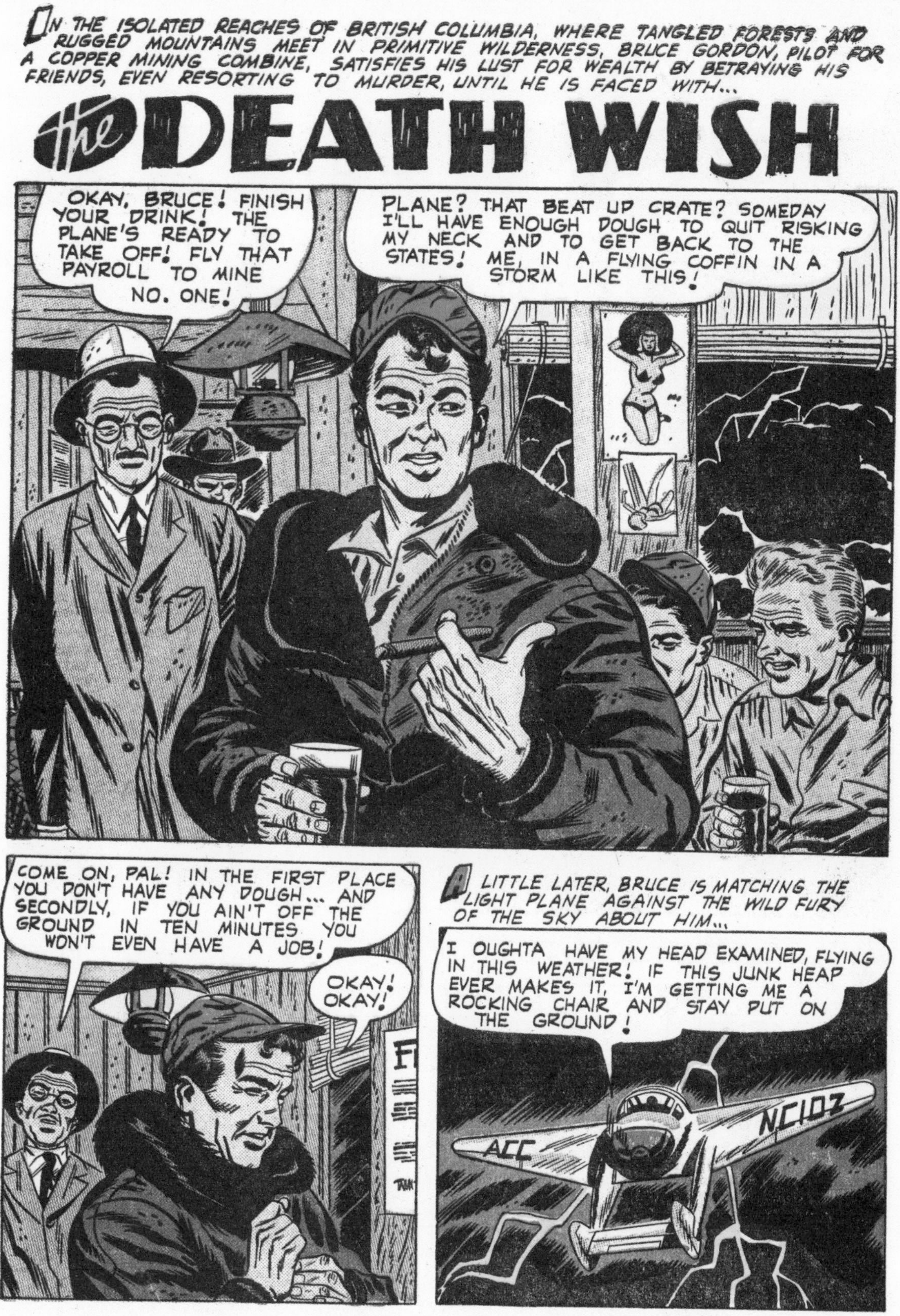
ON THE ISOLATED REACHES OF BRITISH COLUMBIA, WHERE TANGLED FORESTS AND RUGGED MOUNTAINS MEET IN PRIMITIVE WILDERNESS, BRUCE GORDON, PILOT FOR A COPPER MINING COMBINE, SATISFIES HIS LUST FOR WEALTH BY BETRAYING HIS FRIENDS, EVEN RESORTING TO MURDER, UNTIL HE IS FACED WITH...
THE DEATH WISH
OKAY, BRUCE! FINISH YOUR DRINK! THE PLANE'S READY TO TAKE OFF! FLY THAT PAYROLL TO MINE NO. ONE!
PLANE? THAT BEAT UP CRATE? SOMEDAY I'LL HAVE ENOUGH DOUGH TO QUIT RISKING MY NECK AND TO GET BACK TO THE STATES! ME, IN A FLYING COFFIN IN A STORM LIKE THIS!
COME ON, PAL! IN THE FIRST PLACE YOU DON'T HAVE ANY DOUGH... AND SECONDLY, IF YOU AIN'T OFF THE GROUND IN TEN MINUTES YOU WON'T EVEN HAVE A JOB!
OKAY! OKAY!
A LITTLE LATER, BRUCE IS MATCHING THE LIGHT PLANE AGAINST THE WILD FURY OF THE SKY ABOUT HIM...
I OUGHTA HAVE MY HEAD EXAMINED, FLYING IN THIS WEATHER! IF THIS JUNK HEAP EVER MAKES IT, I'M GETTING ME A ROCKING CHAIR AND STAY PUT ON THE GROUND!
NC107
ACC

The Unseen #13, February 1954. Mike Sekowsky. Pines.

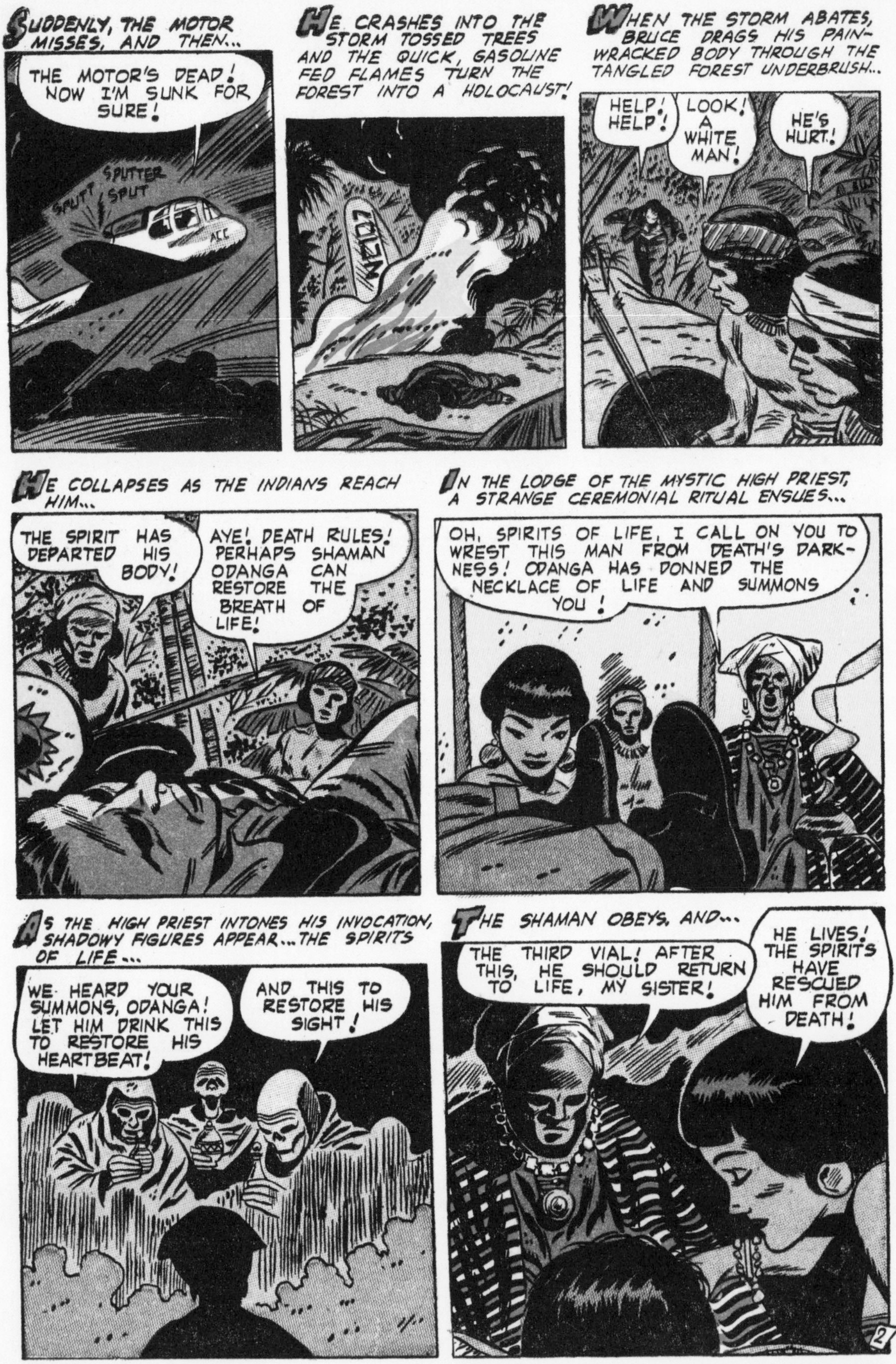
SUDDENLY, THE MOTOR MISSES, AND THEN...
THE MOTOR'S DEAD! NOW I'M SUNK FOR SURE!
SPUTT SPUTTER SPUT
ACC
HE CRASHES INTO THE STORM TOSSED TREES AND THE QUICK, GASOLINE FED FLAMES TURN THE FOREST INTO A HOLOCAUST!
WHEN THE STORM ABATES, BRUCE DRAGS HIS PAIN-WRACKED BODY THROUGH THE TANGLED FOREST UNDERBRUSH...
HELP! HELP!
LOOK! A WHITE MAN!
HE'S HURT!
HE COLLAPSES AS THE INDIANS REACH HIM...
THE SPIRIT HAS DEPARTED HIS BODY!
AYE! DEATH RULES! PERHAPS SHAMAN ODANGA CAN RESTORE THE BREATH OF LIFE!
IN THE LODGE OF THE MYSTIC HIGH PRIEST, A STRANGE CEREMONIAL RITUAL ENSUES...
OH, SPIRITS OF LIFE, I CALL ON YOU TO WREST THIS MAN FROM DEATH'S DARKNESS! ODANGA HAS DONNED THE NECKLACE OF LIFE AND SUMMONS YOU!
AS THE HIGH PRIEST INTONES HIS INVOCATION, SHADOWY FIGURES APPEAR...THE SPIRITS OF LIFE...
WE HEARD YOUR SUMMONS, ODANGA! LET HIM DRINK THIS TO RESTORE HIS HEARTBEAT!
AND THIS TO RESTORE HIS SIGHT!
THE SHAMAN OBEYS, AND...
THE THIRD VIAL! AFTER THIS, HE SHOULD RETURN TO LIFE, MY SISTER!
HE LIVES! THE SPIRITS HAVE RESCUED HIM FROM DEATH!
2

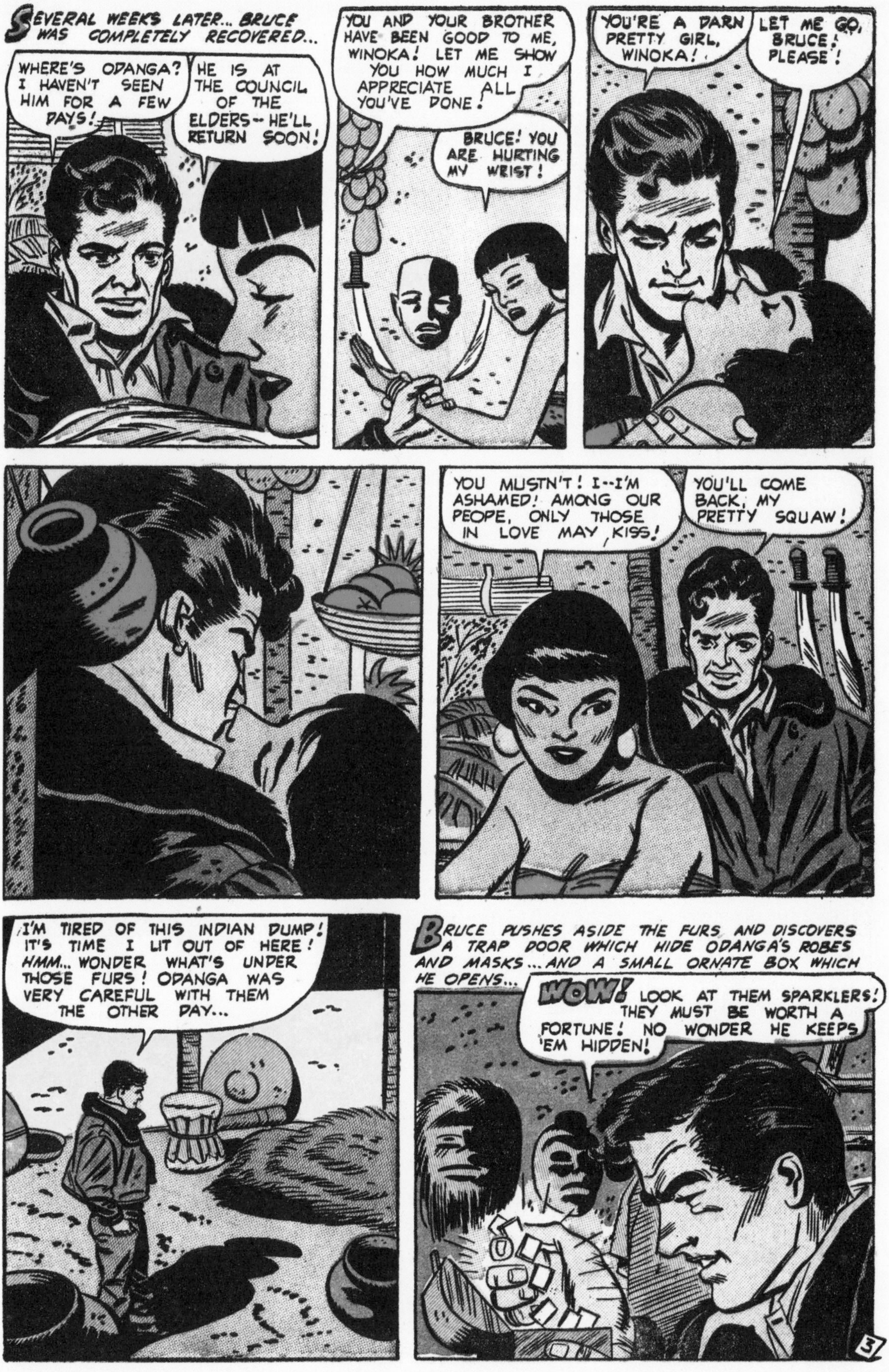
SEVERAL WEEKS LATER... BRUCE WAS COMPLETELY RECOVERED...
WHERE'S ODANGA? I HAVEN'T SEEN HIM FOR A FEW DAYS!
HE IS AT THE COUNCIL OF THE ELDERS -- HE'LL RETURN SOON!
YOU AND YOUR BROTHER HAVE BEEN GOOD TO ME, WINOKA! LET ME SHOW YOU HOW MUCH I APPRECIATE ALL YOU'VE DONE!
BRUCE! YOU ARE HURTING MY WRIST!
YOU'RE A DARN PRETTY GIRL, WINOKA!
LET ME GO, BRUCE! PLEASE!
YOU MUSTN'T! I--I'M ASHAMED! AMONG OUR PEOPE, ONLY THOSE IN LOVE MAY KISS!
YOU'LL COME BACK, MY PRETTY SQUAW!
I'M TIRED OF THIS INDIAN DUMP! IT'S TIME I LIT OUT OF HERE! HMM... WONDER WHAT'S UNDER THOSE FURS! ODANGA WAS VERY CAREFUL WITH THEM THE OTHER DAY...
BRUCE PUSHES ASIDE THE FURS AND DISCOVERS A TRAP DOOR WHICH HIDE ODANGA'S ROBES AND MASKS... AND A SMALL ORNATE BOX WHICH HE OPENS...
WOW! LOOK AT THEM SPARKLERS! THEY MUST BE WORTH A FORTUNE! NO WONDER HE KEEPS 'EM HIDDEN!
3

SUDDENLY... "DROP THAT! YOU'VE BROKEN OUR MOST SACRED TABOO BY TOUCHING THE NECKLACE OF LIFE! DROP IT, I SAY!"

"ODANGA! I I-- I WAS JUST NOSING AROUND!"

"SEIZE HIM AND TAKE HIM TO THE LEDGE OF DARKNESS! HE MUST PAY THE FULL PENALTY FOR HIS EVIL ACTION!"

"WAIT! WAIT A MINUTE! I CAN EXPLAIN!"

"SILENCE!"

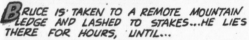

BRUCE IS TAKEN TO A REMOTE MOUNTAIN LEDGE AND LASHED TO STAKES...HE LIES THERE FOR HOURS, UNTIL...

"SOMEBODY'S COMING WITH A KNIFE! DON'T KILL ME! DON'T KILL ME, PLEASE! HELP! HELP!"

"HAVE NO FEAR, BRUCE... I'M YOUR FRIEND!"

"WINOKA! IT WAS BAD OUT HERE ALL ALONE!"

"YOUR TROUBLES ARE NOT OVER! THE COUNCIL OF ELDERS NOW SITS TO DETERMINE YOUR FATE! THERE CAN BE BUT ONE DECISION-- YOU MUST DIE! I COULDN'T BEAR THAT FOR I REMEMBER YOUR KISS--YOU BELONG TO ME!"

"WHY DO THEY WANT TO KILL ME?"

"YOU DEFILED THE NECKLACE! BRUCE, GO NOW WHILE THERE IS STILL TIME!"

"WAIT A MINUTE! ALL THE WARRIORS ARE AT THE COUNCIL MEETING! NO ONE IS GUARDING THE NECKLACE! I'LL GO... BUT I'LL TAKE IT WITH ME!"

"NO, YOU MUST NOT! I WILL NOT LET YOU, BRUCE!"

"YOU CAN'T STOP ME WHEN THERE'S A WAD OF DOUGH AT STAKE! SORRY, BUT THIS IS HOW IT HAS TO BE! I WANT THAT NECKLACE ... BAD!"

"AGGH!"

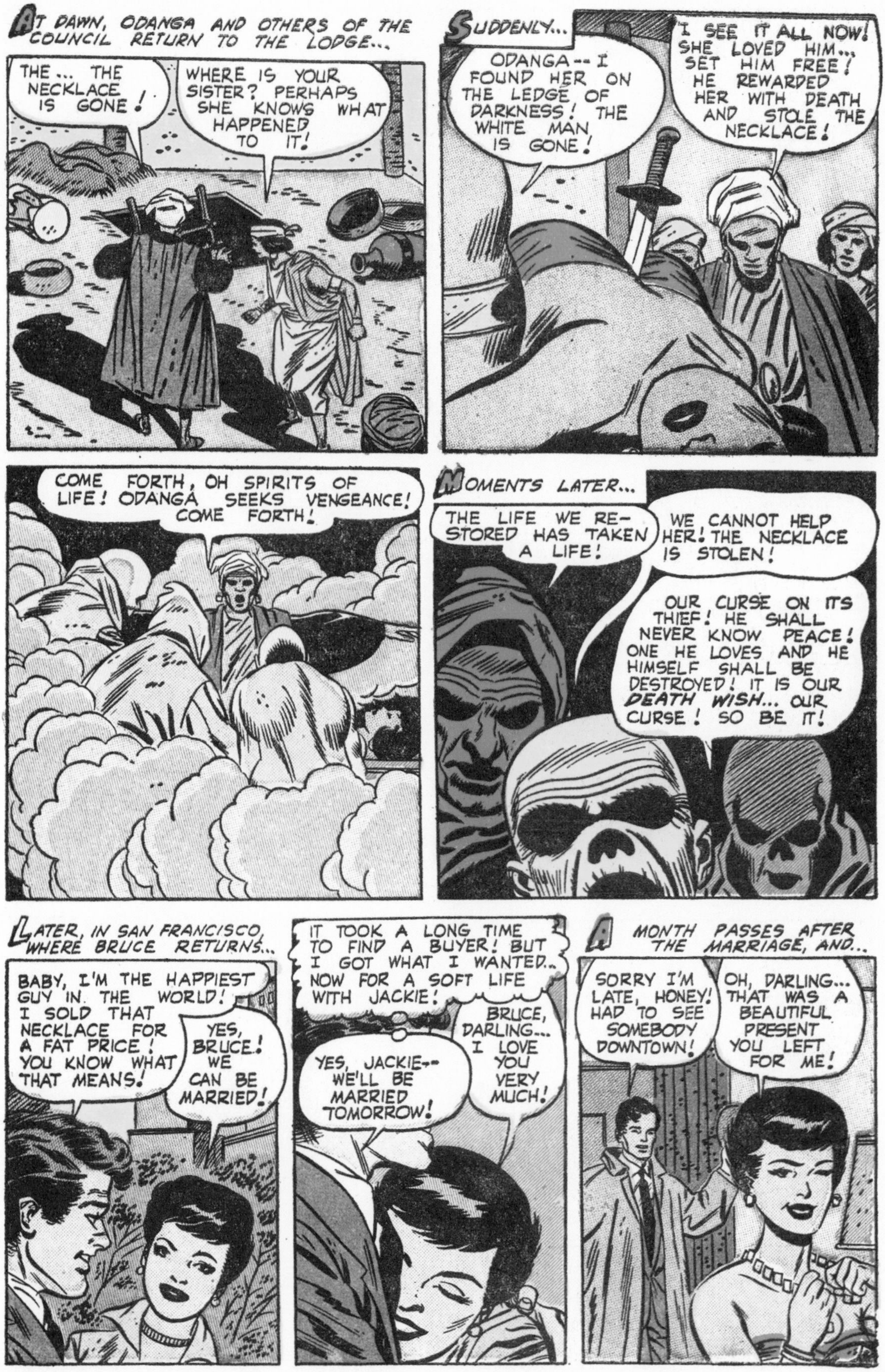

AT DAWN, ODANGA AND OTHERS OF THE COUNCIL RETURN TO THE LODGE...
THE... THE NECKLACE IS GONE!
WHERE IS YOUR SISTER? PERHAPS SHE KNOWS WHAT HAPPENED TO IT!
SUDDENLY...
ODANGA-- I FOUND HER ON THE LEDGE OF DARKNESS! THE WHITE MAN IS GONE!
I SEE IT ALL NOW! SHE LOVED HIM... SET HIM FREE! HE REWARDED HER WITH DEATH AND STOLE THE NECKLACE!
COME FORTH, OH SPIRITS OF LIFE! ODANGA SEEKS VENGEANCE! COME FORTH!
MOMENTS LATER...
THE LIFE WE RESTORED HAS TAKEN A LIFE!
WE CANNOT HELP HER! THE NECKLACE IS STOLEN!
OUR CURSE ON ITS THIEF! HE SHALL NEVER KNOW PEACE! ONE HE LOVES AND HE HIMSELF SHALL BE DESTROYED! IT IS OUR DEATH WISH... OUR CURSE! SO BE IT!
LATER, IN SAN FRANCISCO, WHERE BRUCE RETURNS...
BABY, I'M THE HAPPIEST GUY IN THE WORLD! I SOLD THAT NECKLACE FOR A FAT PRICE! YOU KNOW WHAT THAT MEANS!
YES, BRUCE! WE CAN BE MARRIED!
IT TOOK A LONG TIME TO FIND A BUYER! BUT I GOT WHAT I WANTED.. NOW FOR A SOFT LIFE WITH JACKIE!
BRUCE, DARLING... I LOVE YOU VERY MUCH!
YES, JACKIE-- WE'LL BE MARRIED TOMORROW!
A MONTH PASSES AFTER THE MARRIAGE, AND...
SORRY I'M LATE, HONEY! HAD TO SEE SOMEBODY DOWNTOWN!
OH, DARLING... THAT WAS A BEAUTIFUL PRESENT YOU LEFT FOR ME!

WHAT PRESENT ARE YOU TALKING ABOUT?

STOP KIDDING! I FOUND THIS NECKLACE IN ITS LOVELY BOX ON MY DRESSER THIS MORNING! YOU SHOULDN'T BE SO EXTRAVAGANT!

IT LOOKS SO WELL ON ME TOO! WHAT'S THE MATTER?

TAKE THAT THING OFF!

BRUCE! BRUCE! I'M CHOKING! THE NECKLACE... AAAHHHH!

JACKIE! JACKIE!

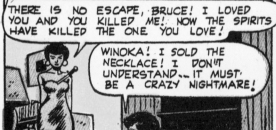

WITH A WILD CRY, JACKIE FALLS DEAD, STRANGLED BY THE NECKLACE! AS BRUCE TURNS TO FLEE IN TERROR...

THERE IS NO ESCAPE, BRUCE! I LOVED YOU AND YOU KILLED ME! NOW THE SPIRITS HAVE KILLED THE ONE YOU LOVE!

WINOKA! I SOLD THE NECKLACE! I DON'T UNDERSTAND... IT MUST BE A CRAZY NIGHTMARE!

IT'S NO DREAM! THE SPIRITS SENT ME TO RECLAIM THE NECKLACE FOR MY PEOPLE! NOW YOUR PUNISHMENT CAN BE COMPLETED!

MY PUNISHMENT? WHAT DO YOU MEAN?

AS LONG AS YOU LIVE, THIS KNIFE REMAINS IN MY HEART! WHEN YOU DIE, I CAN REMOVE IT AND LIVE AGAIN!

NO! NO! NO!

JACKIE! JACKIE! HELP ME!

OPEN UP! IT'S THE POLICE!

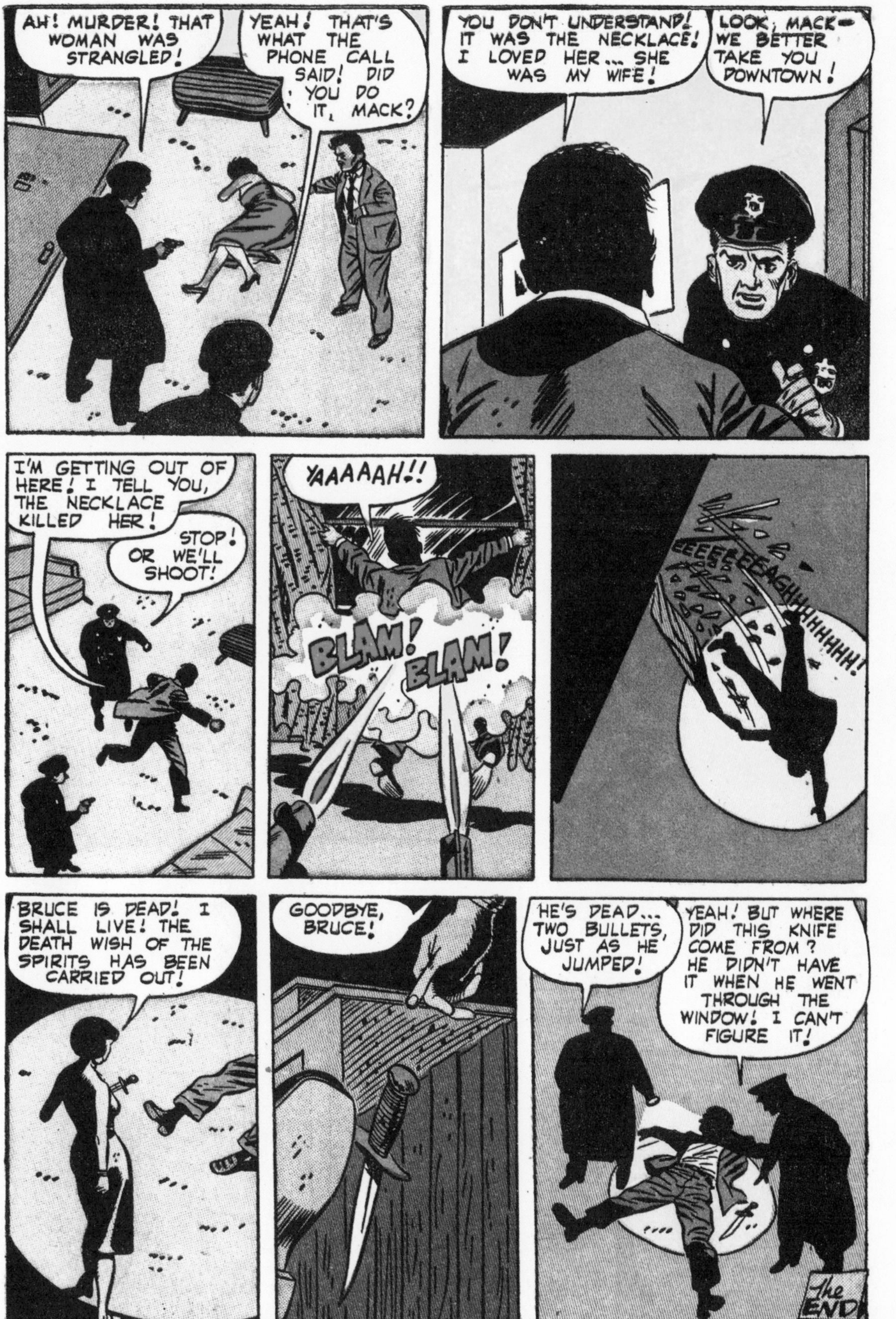
AH! MURDER! THAT WOMAN WAS STRANGLED!
YEAH! THAT'S WHAT THE PHONE CALL SAID! DID YOU DO IT, MACK?
YOU DON'T UNDERSTAND! IT WAS THE NECKLACE! I LOVED HER... SHE WAS MY WIFE!
LOOK, MACK— WE BETTER TAKE YOU DOWNTOWN!
I'M GETTING OUT OF HERE! I TELL YOU, THE NECKLACE KILLED HER!
STOP! OR WE'LL SHOOT!
YAAAAAH!!
BLAM! BLAM!
EEEEEEEEAGHHHHHHHHHH!
BRUCE IS DEAD! I SHALL LIVE! THE DEATH WISH OF THE SPIRITS HAS BEEN CARRIED OUT!
GOODBYE, BRUCE!
HE'S DEAD... TWO BULLETS, JUST AS HE JUMPED!
YEAH! BUT WHERE DID THIS KNIFE COME FROM? HE DIDN'T HAVE IT WHEN HE WENT THROUGH THE WINDOW! I CAN'T FIGURE IT!
The END

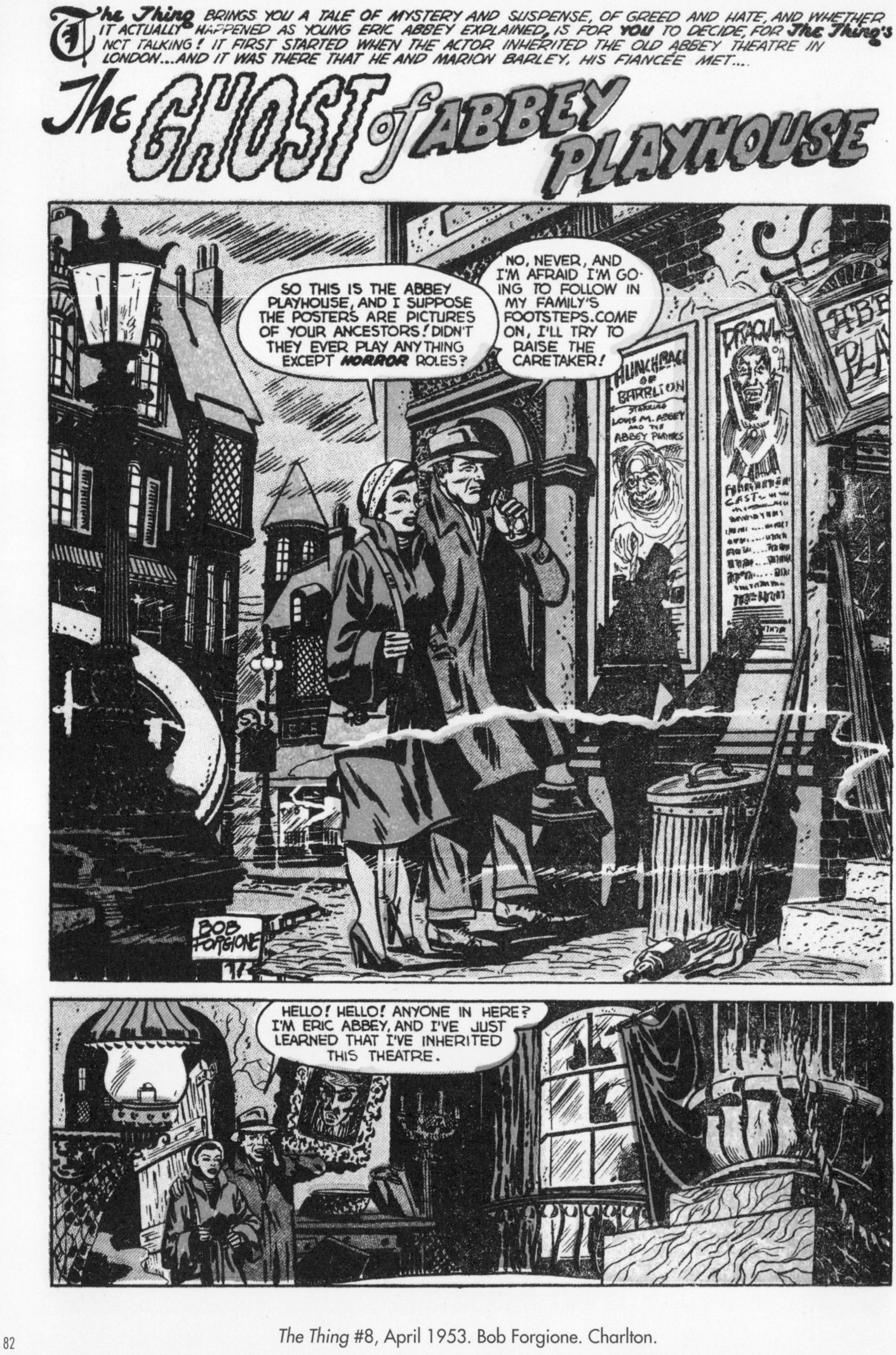
The Thing BRINGS YOU A TALE OF MYSTERY AND SUSPENSE, OF GREED AND HATE, AND WHETHER IT ACTUALLY HAPPENED AS YOUNG ERIC ABBEY EXPLAINED, IS FOR YOU TO DECIDE, FOR The Thing's NOT TALKING! IT FIRST STARTED WHEN THE ACTOR INHERITED THE OLD ABBEY THEATRE IN LONDON...AND IT WAS THERE THAT HE AND MARION BARLEY, HIS FIANCÉE MET...
The GHOST of ABBEY PLAYHOUSE
SO THIS IS THE ABBEY PLAYHOUSE, AND I SUPPOSE THE POSTERS ARE PICTURES OF YOUR ANCESTORS! DIDN'T THEY EVER PLAY ANYTHING EXCEPT HORROR ROLES?
NO, NEVER, AND I'M AFRAID I'M GOING TO FOLLOW IN MY FAMILY'S FOOTSTEPS. COME ON, I'LL TRY TO RAISE THE CARETAKER!
HUNCHBACK OF BARRLTON
STARRING LOUIS M. ABBEY AND THE ABBEY PLAYERS
BOB FORGIONE
HELLO! HELLO! ANYONE IN HERE? I'M ERIC ABBEY, AND I'VE JUST LEARNED THAT I'VE INHERITED THIS THEATRE.

The Thing #8, April 1953. Bob Forgione. Charlton.

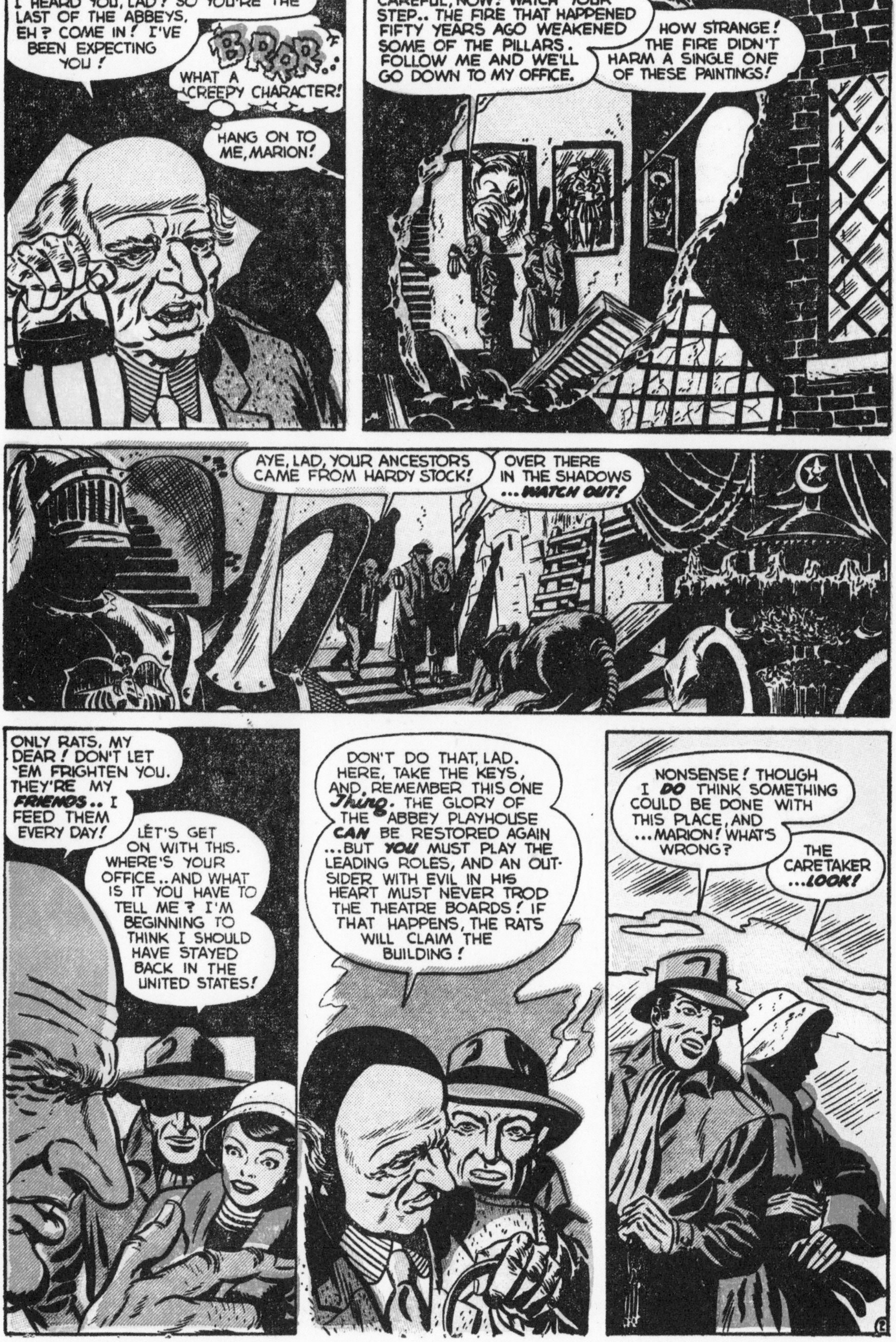
I HEARD YOU, LAD! SO YOU'RE THE LAST OF THE ABBEYS, EH? COME IN! I'VE BEEN EXPECTING YOU!
BRRR..
WHAT A CREEPY CHARACTER!
HANG ON TO ME, MARION!
CAREFUL, NOW! WATCH YOUR STEP.. THE FIRE THAT HAPPENED FIFTY YEARS AGO WEAKENED SOME OF THE PILLARS. FOLLOW ME AND WE'LL GO DOWN TO MY OFFICE.
HOW STRANGE! THE FIRE DIDN'T HARM A SINGLE ONE OF THESE PAINTINGS!
AYE, LAD, YOUR ANCESTORS CAME FROM HARDY STOCK!
OVER THERE IN THE SHADOWS ...WATCH OUT!
ONLY RATS, MY DEAR! DON'T LET 'EM FRIGHTEN YOU. THEY'RE MY FRIENDS.. I FEED THEM EVERY DAY!
LET'S GET ON WITH THIS. WHERE'S YOUR OFFICE..AND WHAT IS IT YOU HAVE TO TELL ME? I'M BEGINNING TO THINK I SHOULD HAVE STAYED BACK IN THE UNITED STATES!
DON'T DO THAT, LAD. HERE, TAKE THE KEYS, AND, REMEMBER THIS ONE THING. THE GLORY OF THE ABBEY PLAYHOUSE CAN BE RESTORED AGAIN ...BUT YOU MUST PLAY THE LEADING ROLES, AND AN OUTSIDER WITH EVIL IN HIS HEART MUST NEVER TROD THE THEATRE BOARDS! IF THAT HAPPENS, THE RATS WILL CLAIM THE BUILDING!
NONSENSE! THOUGH I DO THINK SOMETHING COULD BE DONE WITH THIS PLACE, AND ...MARION! WHAT'S WRONG?
THE CARETAKER ...LOOK!

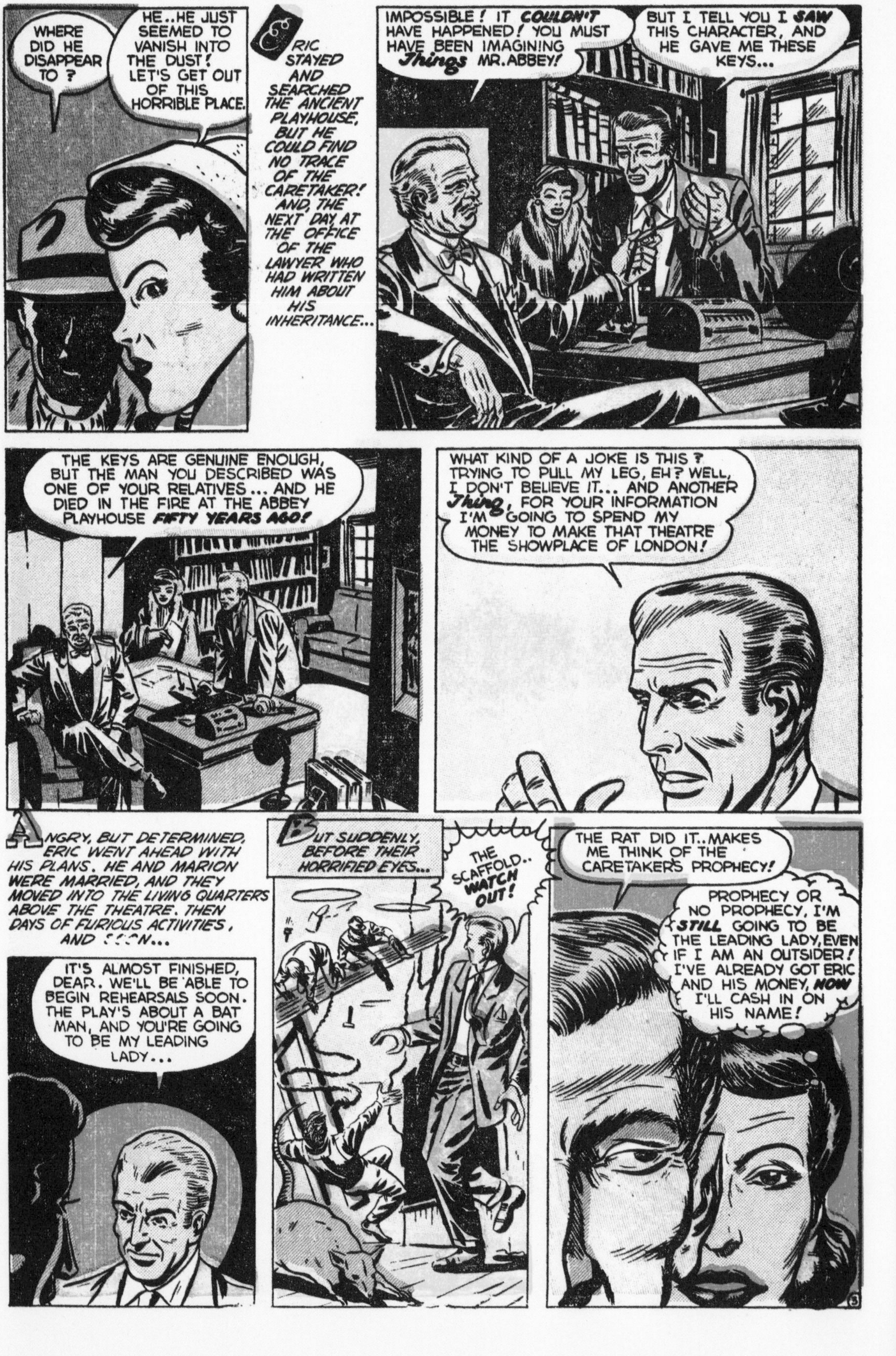

WHERE DID HE DISAPPEAR TO ?
HE..HE JUST SEEMED TO VANISH INTO THE DUST! LET'S GET OUT OF THIS HORRIBLE PLACE.
ERIC STAYED AND SEARCHED THE ANCIENT PLAYHOUSE, BUT HE COULD FIND NO TRACE OF THE CARETAKER! AND, THE NEXT DAY AT THE OFFICE OF THE LAWYER WHO HAD WRITTEN HIM ABOUT HIS INHERITANCE...
IMPOSSIBLE! IT COULDN'T HAVE HAPPENED! YOU MUST HAVE BEEN IMAGINING THINGS MR. ABBEY!
BUT I TELL YOU I SAW THIS CHARACTER, AND HE GAVE ME THESE KEYS...
THE KEYS ARE GENUINE ENOUGH, BUT THE MAN YOU DESCRIBED WAS ONE OF YOUR RELATIVES... AND HE DIED IN THE FIRE AT THE ABBEY PLAYHOUSE FIFTY YEARS AGO!
WHAT KIND OF A JOKE IS THIS? TRYING TO PULL MY LEG, EH? WELL, I DON'T BELIEVE IT... AND ANOTHER THING, FOR YOUR INFORMATION I'M GOING TO SPEND MY MONEY TO MAKE THAT THEATRE THE SHOWPLACE OF LONDON!
ANGRY, BUT DETERMINED, ERIC WENT AHEAD WITH HIS PLANS. HE AND MARION WERE MARRIED, AND THEY MOVED INTO THE LIVING QUARTERS ABOVE THE THEATRE. THEN DAYS OF FURIOUS ACTIVITIES, AND
IT'S ALMOST FINISHED, DEAR. WE'LL BE ABLE TO BEGIN REHEARSALS SOON. THE PLAY'S ABOUT A BAT MAN, AND YOU'RE GOING TO BE MY LEADING LADY...
BUT SUDDENLY, BEFORE THEIR HORRIFIED EYES...
THE SCAFFOLD.. WATCH OUT!
THE RAT DID IT..MAKES ME THINK OF THE CARETAKER'S PROPHECY!
PROPHECY OR NO PROPHECY, I'M STILL GOING TO BE THE LEADING LADY, EVEN IF I AM AN OUTSIDER! I'VE ALREADY GOT ERIC AND HIS MONEY, NOW I'LL CASH IN ON HIS NAME!
3

ACCIDENTS CONTINUED, BUT IN SPITE OF THE DIFFICULTIES ERIC WENT AHEAD WITH HIS PLANS, AND EVENTUALLY OPENING NIGHT DREW NEAR. UNABLE TO SLEEP, ERIC WANDERED DOWN TO THE DESERTED STAGE LATE ONE NIGHT...

HE STOOD THERE ALONE, THINKING OF THE GLORY THAT WOULD SOON COME...

ERIC ABBEY LAST NIGHT RECREATED ONE OF THE HORROR ROLES FOR WHICH HIS FAMILY HAS BECOME FAMOUS.. I CAN JUST SEE THE HEADLINES! OR IS THIS WISHFUL THINKING? SAY WHAT'S THAT? I THOUGHT I SAW SOME SHADOWS MOVING IN THE WINGS!

ACT III

SHADOWS OF THE PAST, ERIC ABBEY! WE ARE YOUR ANCESTORS...LISTEN TO OUR WARNING!

VOICES.. NOW I KNOW I NEED A REST!

IT WAS MORE THAN FIFTY YEARS AGO THAT IT FIRST HAPPENED! THE ABBEYS WERE GATHERED TOGETHER IN THE DRESSING ROOM, WHEN SUDDENLY TOM ABBEY ENTERED WITH VIOLET HASTINGS, A RANK OUTSIDER.. A SCHEMER!

HERE SHE IS, FOLKS. THE NEW BRIDE, AND MY FUTURE LEADING LADY! I'M GOING TO PLAY DRACULA!

TOM WAS AS GOOD AS HIS WORD. BUT THE SAME COULDN'T BE SAID FOR HIS WIFE. THE CRITICS HAD A WAY OF DESCRIBING IT..."

THAT WOMAN IS TERRIBLE.. SHE'LL RUIN THE REPUTATION OF THE ABBEY PLAYERS!

DISGUSTING..SHE'S NOTHING BUT A TRAMP!

HOW TRUE! VIOLET TOOK HIS MONEY, HIS PRIDE, AND FOR THE FINAL INSULT...

KICK ME OUT O' THE PLAY, WILL THEY? I'LL SHOW 'EM UP PROPER, THAT'S WOT!

SHE DESTROYED US, ALL RIGHT. BUT BEFORE WE DIED WE VOWED THAT THE THEATRE WOULD BE RETURNED TO THE RATS IF EVER AGAIN SUCH AN OUTSIDER TROD THE BOARDS! YOUR WIFE DOESN'T LOVE YOU, ERIC ABBEY, SHE WANTS ONLY YOUR MONEY AND NAME! THE PLAY MUST NOT GO ON!"

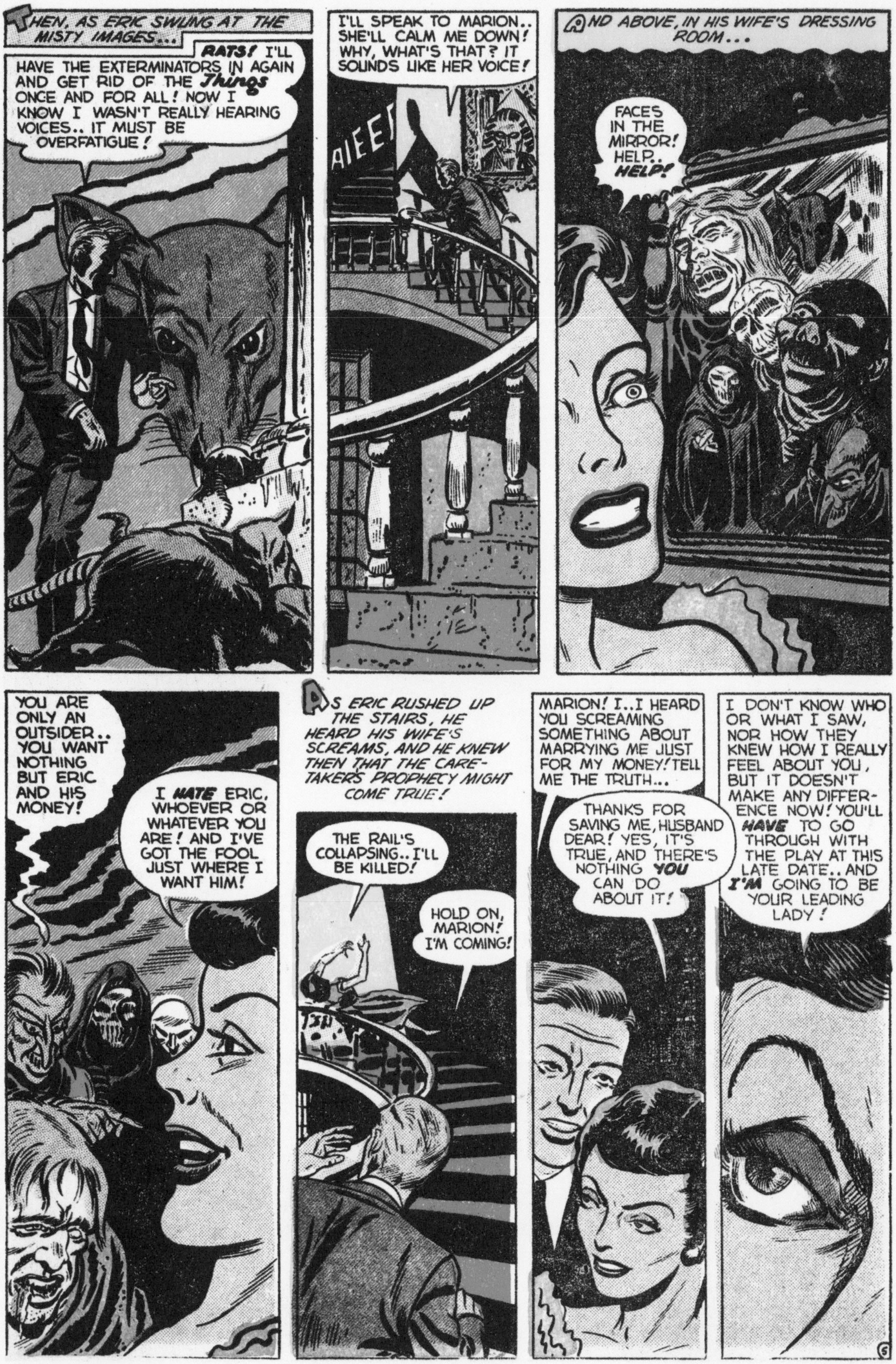
THEN, AS ERIC SWUNG AT THE MISTY IMAGES...
RATS! I'LL HAVE THE EXTERMINATORS IN AGAIN AND GET RID OF THE *Things* ONCE AND FOR ALL! NOW I KNOW I WASN'T REALLY HEARING VOICES.. IT MUST BE OVERFATIGUE!
I'LL SPEAK TO MARION.. SHE'LL CALM ME DOWN! WHY, WHAT'S THAT? IT SOUNDS LIKE HER VOICE!
AIEEE
AND ABOVE, IN HIS WIFE'S DRESSING ROOM...
FACES IN THE MIRROR! HELP.. **HELP!**
YOU ARE ONLY AN OUTSIDER.. YOU WANT NOTHING BUT ERIC AND HIS MONEY!
I **HATE** ERIC, WHOEVER OR WHATEVER YOU ARE! AND I'VE GOT THE FOOL JUST WHERE I WANT HIM!
AS ERIC RUSHED UP THE STAIRS, HE HEARD HIS WIFE'S SCREAMS, AND HE KNEW THEN THAT THE CARETAKER'S PROPHECY MIGHT COME TRUE!
THE RAIL'S COLLAPSING.. I'LL BE KILLED!
HOLD ON, MARION! I'M COMING!
MARION! I..I HEARD YOU SCREAMING SOMETHING ABOUT MARRYING ME JUST FOR MY MONEY! TELL ME THE TRUTH...
THANKS FOR SAVING ME, HUSBAND DEAR! YES, IT'S TRUE, AND THERE'S NOTHING **YOU** CAN DO ABOUT IT!
I DON'T KNOW WHO OR WHAT I SAW, NOR HOW THEY KNEW HOW I REALLY FEEL ABOUT YOU, BUT IT DOESN'T MAKE ANY DIFFERENCE NOW! YOU'LL **HAVE** TO GO THROUGH WITH THE PLAY AT THIS LATE DATE.. AND **I'M** GOING TO BE YOUR LEADING LADY!
5

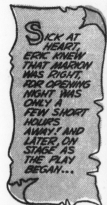

Sick at heart, Eric knew that Marion was right. For opening night was only a few short hours away! And later, on stage as the play began...

DRINK THIS, WOMAN!

ERIC'S HAND! IT ..IT'S CHANGING!

YOUR HAND... YOU'RE A *RAT!* GET AWAY FROM ME... OWW!

SOMETHING'S WRONG.. SHE'S FAINTING!

RING DOWN THE CURTAIN... *HURRY!* I'LL TAKE HER TO THE DRESSING ROOM AND CALL A DOCTOR!

YES, SIR!

EVERYTHING'S LOST NOW.. THE PLAY.. MY LIFE WITH MARION! AND THAT LOCKET SHE'S WEARING USED TO SYMBOLIZE SO MUCH... WHERE THE DEVIL IS THAT DOCTOR?

OH, THERE YOU ARE! I THOUGHT YOU'D NEVER GET HERE! MY WIFE.. SHE COLLAPSED ON THE STAGE. I PUT HER RIGHT TO BED...

YOUR WIFE? *LOOK!*

NO! *NO!* IT'S SOME KIND OF A TRICK! BUT THAT LOCKET.. IT'S THE *SAME* ONE I GAVE MY WIFE!

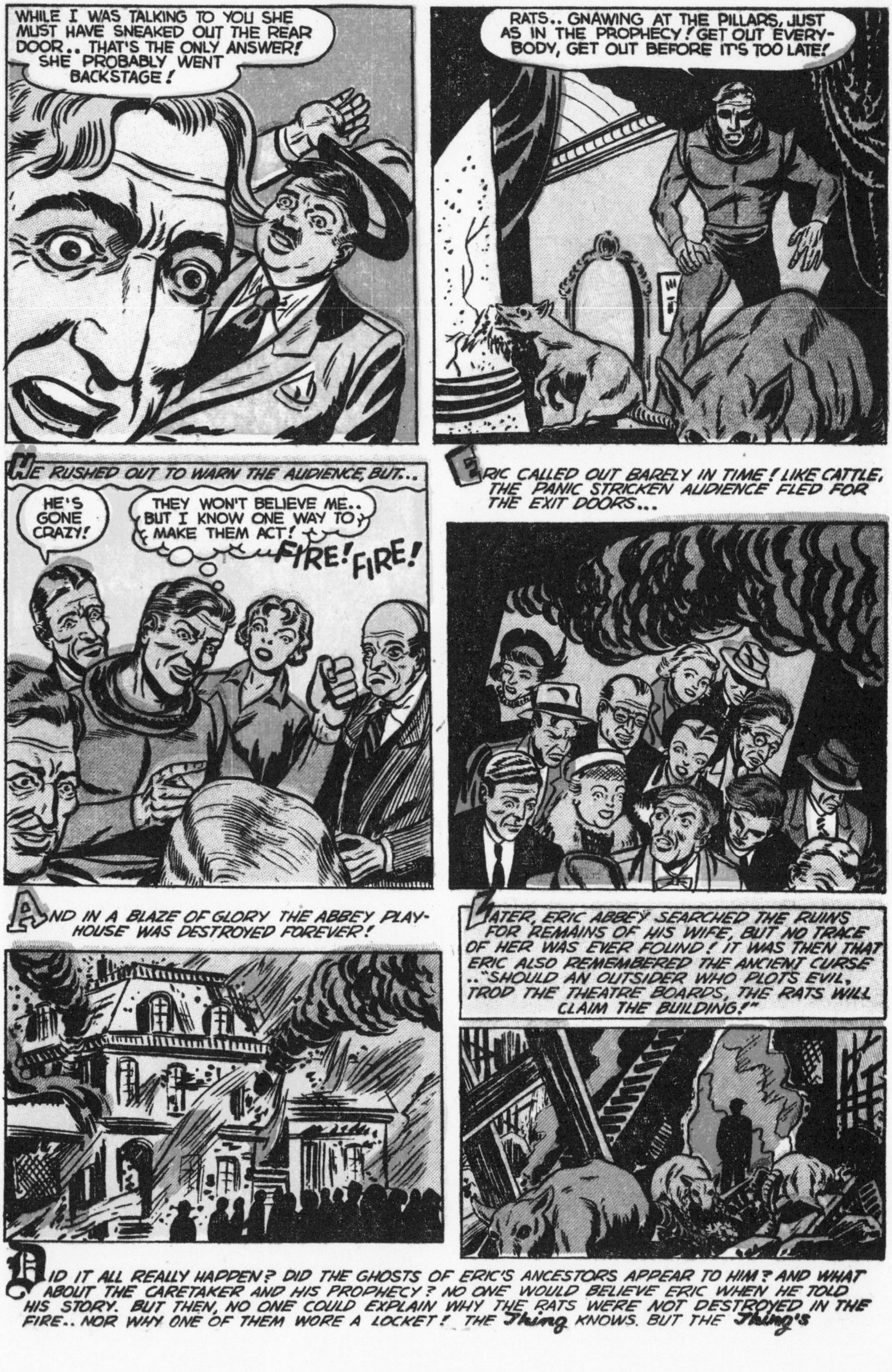

WHILE I WAS TALKING TO YOU SHE MUST HAVE SNEAKED OUT THE REAR DOOR.. THAT'S THE ONLY ANSWER! SHE PROBABLY WENT BACKSTAGE!
RATS.. GNAWING AT THE PILLARS, JUST AS IN THE PROPHECY! GET OUT EVERYBODY, GET OUT BEFORE IT'S TOO LATE!
HE RUSHED OUT TO WARN THE AUDIENCE, BUT...
HE'S GONE CRAZY!
THEY WON'T BELIEVE ME.. BUT I KNOW ONE WAY TO MAKE THEM ACT!
FIRE! FIRE!
ERIC CALLED OUT BARELY IN TIME! LIKE CATTLE, THE PANIC STRICKEN AUDIENCE FLED FOR THE EXIT DOORS...
AND IN A BLAZE OF GLORY THE ABBEY PLAYHOUSE WAS DESTROYED FOREVER!
LATER, ERIC ABBEY SEARCHED THE RUINS FOR REMAINS OF HIS WIFE, BUT NO TRACE OF HER WAS EVER FOUND! IT WAS THEN THAT ERIC ALSO REMEMBERED THE ANCIENT CURSE .."SHOULD AN OUTSIDER WHO PLOTS EVIL, TROD THE THEATRE BOARDS, THE RATS WILL CLAIM THE BUILDING!"
DID IT ALL REALLY HAPPEN? DID THE GHOSTS OF ERIC'S ANCESTORS APPEAR TO HIM? AND WHAT ABOUT THE CARETAKER AND HIS PROPHECY? NO ONE WOULD BELIEVE ERIC WHEN HE TOLD HIS STORY. BUT THEN, NO ONE COULD EXPLAIN WHY THE RATS WERE NOT DESTROYED IN THE FIRE.. NOR WHY ONE OF THEM WORE A LOCKET! THE Thing KNOWS. BUT THE Thing's

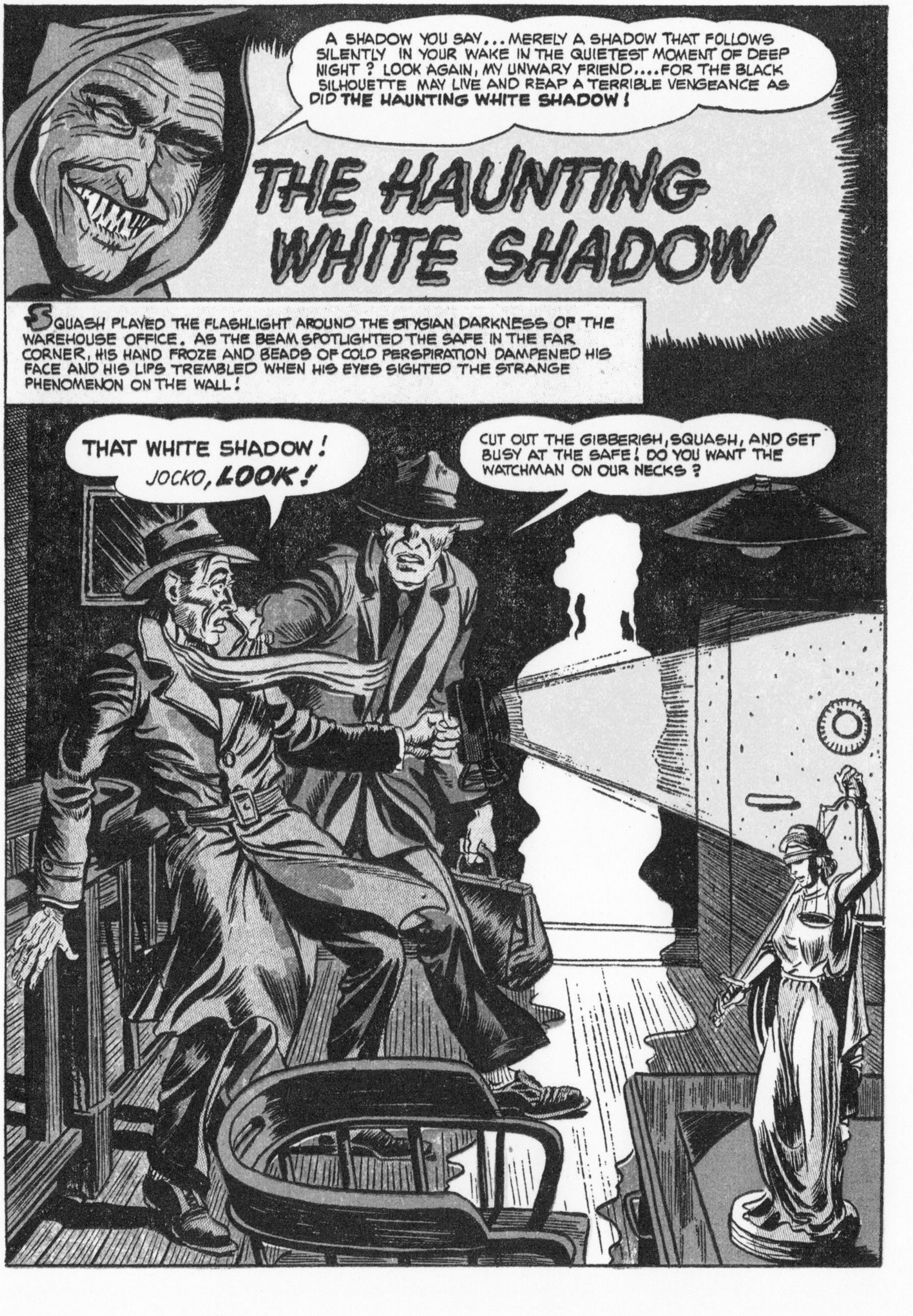

A SHADOW YOU SAY... MERELY A SHADOW THAT FOLLOWS SILENTLY IN YOUR WAKE IN THE QUIETEST MOMENT OF DEEP NIGHT ? LOOK AGAIN, MY UNWARY FRIEND.... FOR THE BLACK SILHOUETTE MAY LIVE AND REAP A TERRIBLE VENGEANCE AS DID THE HAUNTING WHITE SHADOW !
THE HAUNTING WHITE SHADOW
SQUASH PLAYED THE FLASHLIGHT AROUND THE STYGIAN DARKNESS OF THE WAREHOUSE OFFICE. AS THE BEAM SPOTLIGHTED THE SAFE IN THE FAR CORNER, HIS HAND FROZE AND BEADS OF COLD PERSPIRATION DAMPENED HIS FACE AND HIS LIPS TREMBLED WHEN HIS EYES SIGHTED THE STRANGE PHENOMENON ON THE WALL !
THAT WHITE SHADOW ! JOCKO, LOOK !
CUT OUT THE GIBBERISH, SQUASH, AND GET BUSY AT THE SAFE ! DO YOU WANT THE WATCHMAN ON OUR NECKS ?

Beware! Terror Tales #3, September 1952. Bob McCarty. Fawcett.

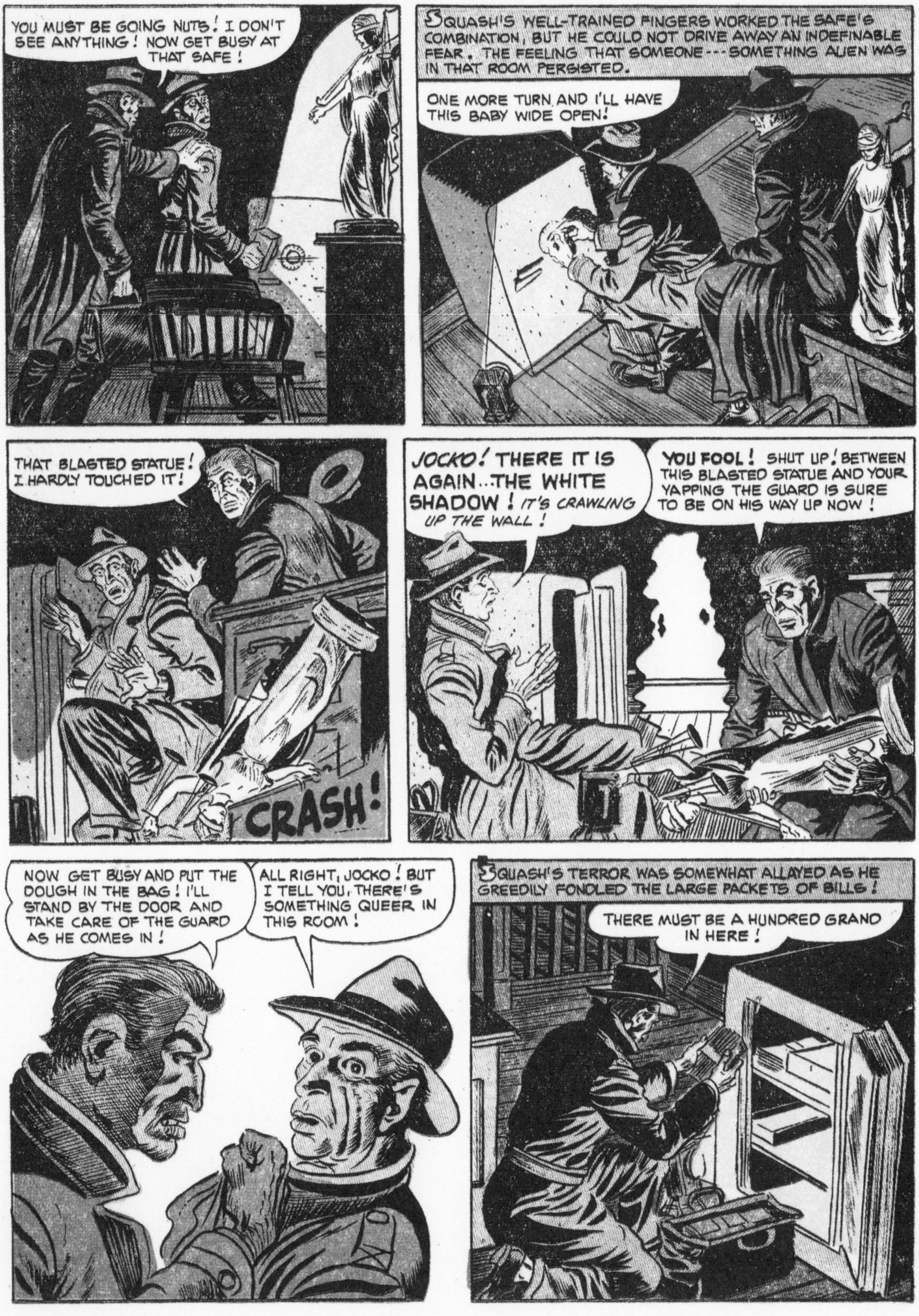

YOU MUST BE GOING NUTS! I DON'T SEE ANYTHING!
NOW GET BUSY AT THAT SAFE!
SQUASH'S WELL-TRAINED FINGERS WORKED THE SAFE'S COMBINATION, BUT HE COULD NOT DRIVE AWAY AN INDEFINABLE FEAR. THE FEELING THAT SOMEONE --- SOMETHING ALIEN WAS IN THAT ROOM PERSISTED.
ONE MORE TURN AND I'LL HAVE THIS BABY WIDE OPEN!
THAT BLASTED STATUE! I HARDLY TOUCHED IT!
CRASH!
JOCKO! THERE IT IS AGAIN...THE WHITE SHADOW! IT'S CRAWLING UP THE WALL!
YOU FOOL! SHUT UP! BETWEEN THIS BLASTED STATUE AND YOUR YAPPING THE GUARD IS SURE TO BE ON HIS WAY UP NOW!
NOW GET BUSY AND PUT THE DOUGH IN THE BAG! I'LL STAND BY THE DOOR AND TAKE CARE OF THE GUARD AS HE COMES IN!
ALL RIGHT, JOCKO! BUT I TELL YOU, THERE'S SOMETHING QUEER IN THIS ROOM!
SQUASH'S TERROR WAS SOMEWHAT ALLAYED AS HE GREEDILY FONDLED THE LARGE PACKETS OF BILLS!
THERE MUST BE A HUNDRED GRAND IN HERE!

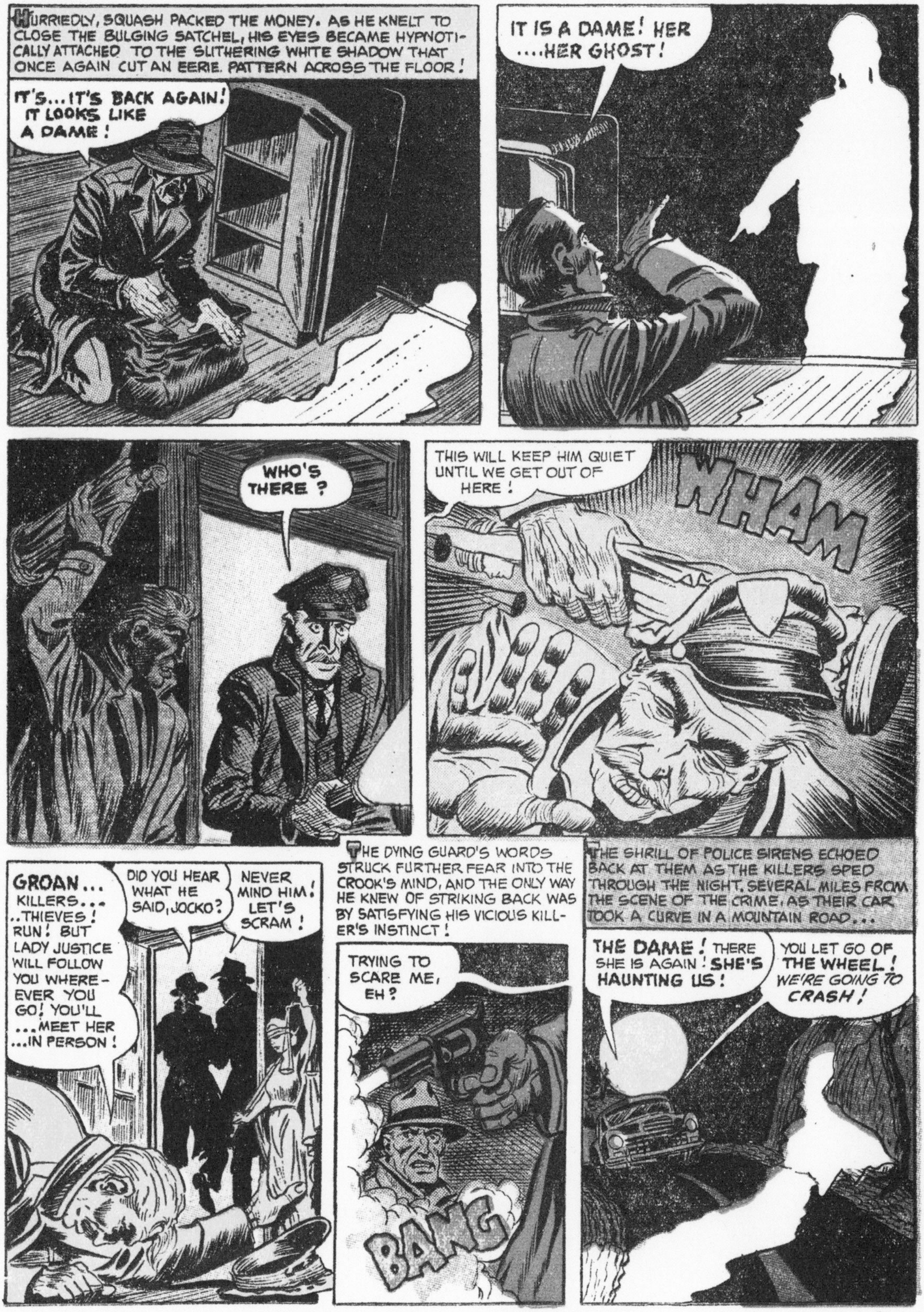
HURRIEDLY, SQUASH PACKED THE MONEY. AS HE KNELT TO CLOSE THE BULGING SATCHEL, HIS EYES BECAME HYPNOTICALLY ATTACHED TO THE SLITHERING WHITE SHADOW THAT ONCE AGAIN CUT AN EERIE PATTERN ACROSS THE FLOOR!
IT'S... IT'S BACK AGAIN! IT LOOKS LIKE A DAME!
IT IS A DAME! HER ....HER GHOST!
WHO'S THERE?
THIS WILL KEEP HIM QUIET UNTIL WE GET OUT OF HERE!
WHAM
GROAN... KILLERS... ..THIEVES! RUN! BUT LADY JUSTICE WILL FOLLOW YOU WHEREEVER YOU GO! YOU'LL ...MEET HER ...IN PERSON!
DID YOU HEAR WHAT HE SAID, JOCKO?
NEVER MIND HIM! LET'S SCRAM!
THE DYING GUARD'S WORDS STRUCK FURTHER FEAR INTO THE CROOK'S MIND, AND THE ONLY WAY HE KNEW OF STRIKING BACK WAS BY SATISFYING HIS VICIOUS KILLER'S INSTINCT!
TRYING TO SCARE ME, EH?
BANG
THE SHRILL OF POLICE SIRENS ECHOED BACK AT THEM AS THE KILLERS SPED THROUGH THE NIGHT. SEVERAL MILES FROM THE SCENE OF THE CRIME, AS THEIR CAR TOOK A CURVE IN A MOUNTAIN ROAD...
THE DAME! THERE SHE IS AGAIN! SHE'S HAUNTING US!
YOU LET GO OF THE WHEEL! WE'RE GOING TO CRASH!

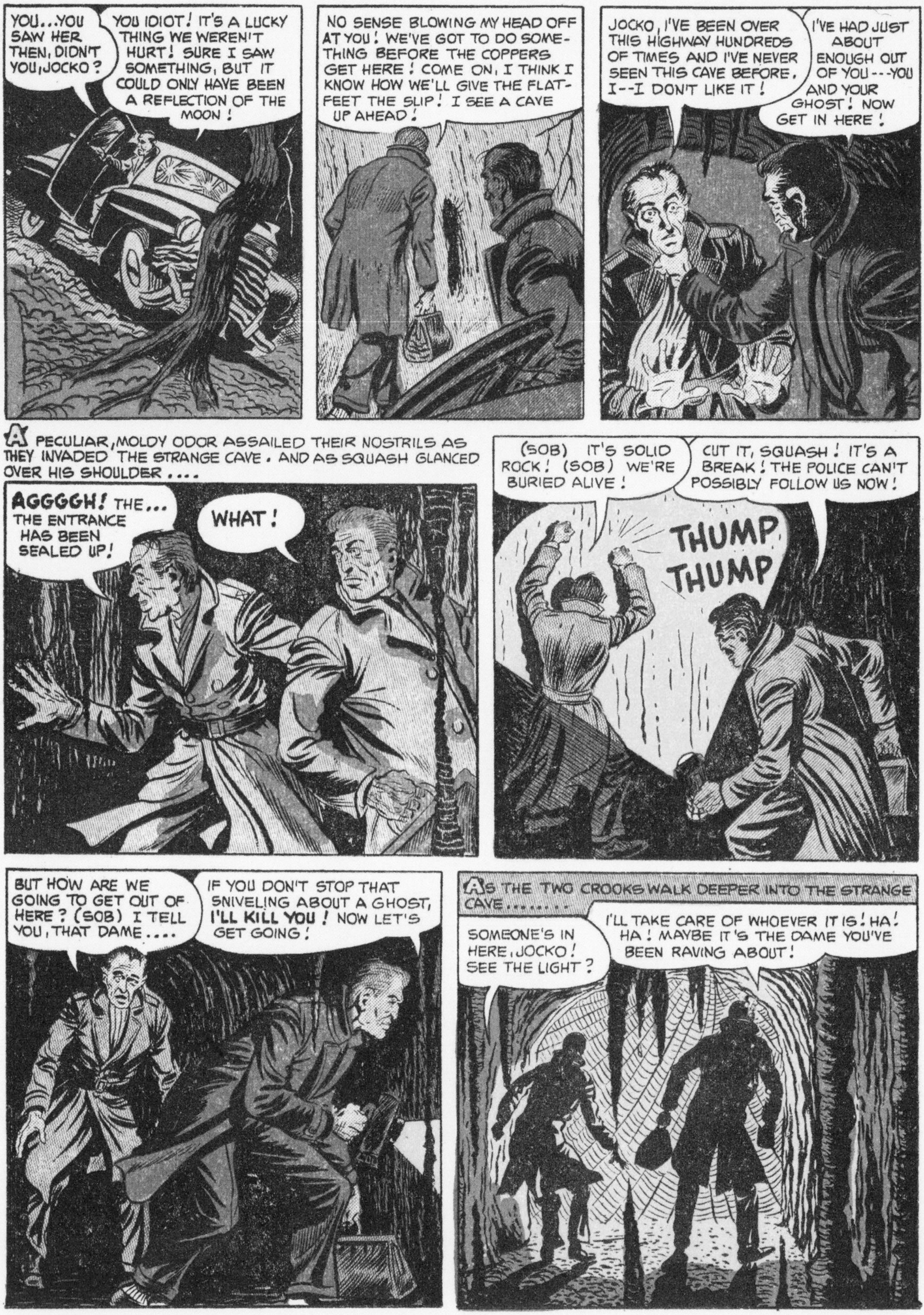
YOU...YOU SAW HER THEN, DIDN'T YOU, JOCKO?
YOU IDIOT! IT'S A LUCKY THING WE WEREN'T HURT! SURE I SAW SOMETHING, BUT IT COULD ONLY HAVE BEEN A REFLECTION OF THE MOON!
NO SENSE BLOWING MY HEAD OFF AT YOU! WE'VE GOT TO DO SOMETHING BEFORE THE COPPERS GET HERE! COME ON, I THINK I KNOW HOW WE'LL GIVE THE FLATFEET THE SLIP! I SEE A CAVE UP AHEAD!
JOCKO, I'VE BEEN OVER THIS HIGHWAY HUNDREDS OF TIMES AND I'VE NEVER SEEN THIS CAVE BEFORE. I--I DON'T LIKE IT!
I'VE HAD JUST ABOUT ENOUGH OUT OF YOU---YOU AND YOUR GHOST! NOW GET IN HERE!
A PECULIAR, MOLDY ODOR ASSAILED THEIR NOSTRILS AS THEY INVADED THE STRANGE CAVE. AND AS SQUASH GLANCED OVER HIS SHOULDER....
AGGGGH! THE... THE ENTRANCE HAS BEEN SEALED UP!
WHAT!
(SOB) IT'S SOLID ROCK! (SOB) WE'RE BURIED ALIVE!
CUT IT, SQUASH! IT'S A BREAK! THE POLICE CAN'T POSSIBLY FOLLOW US NOW!
THUMP THUMP
BUT HOW ARE WE GOING TO GET OUT OF HERE? (SOB) I TELL YOU, THAT DAME....
IF YOU DON'T STOP THAT SNIVELING ABOUT A GHOST, I'LL KILL YOU! NOW LET'S GET GOING!
AS THE TWO CROOKS WALK DEEPER INTO THE STRANGE CAVE.......
SOMEONE'S IN HERE, JOCKO! SEE THE LIGHT?
I'LL TAKE CARE OF WHOEVER IT IS! HA! HA! MAYBE IT'S THE DAME YOU'VE BEEN RAVING ABOUT!

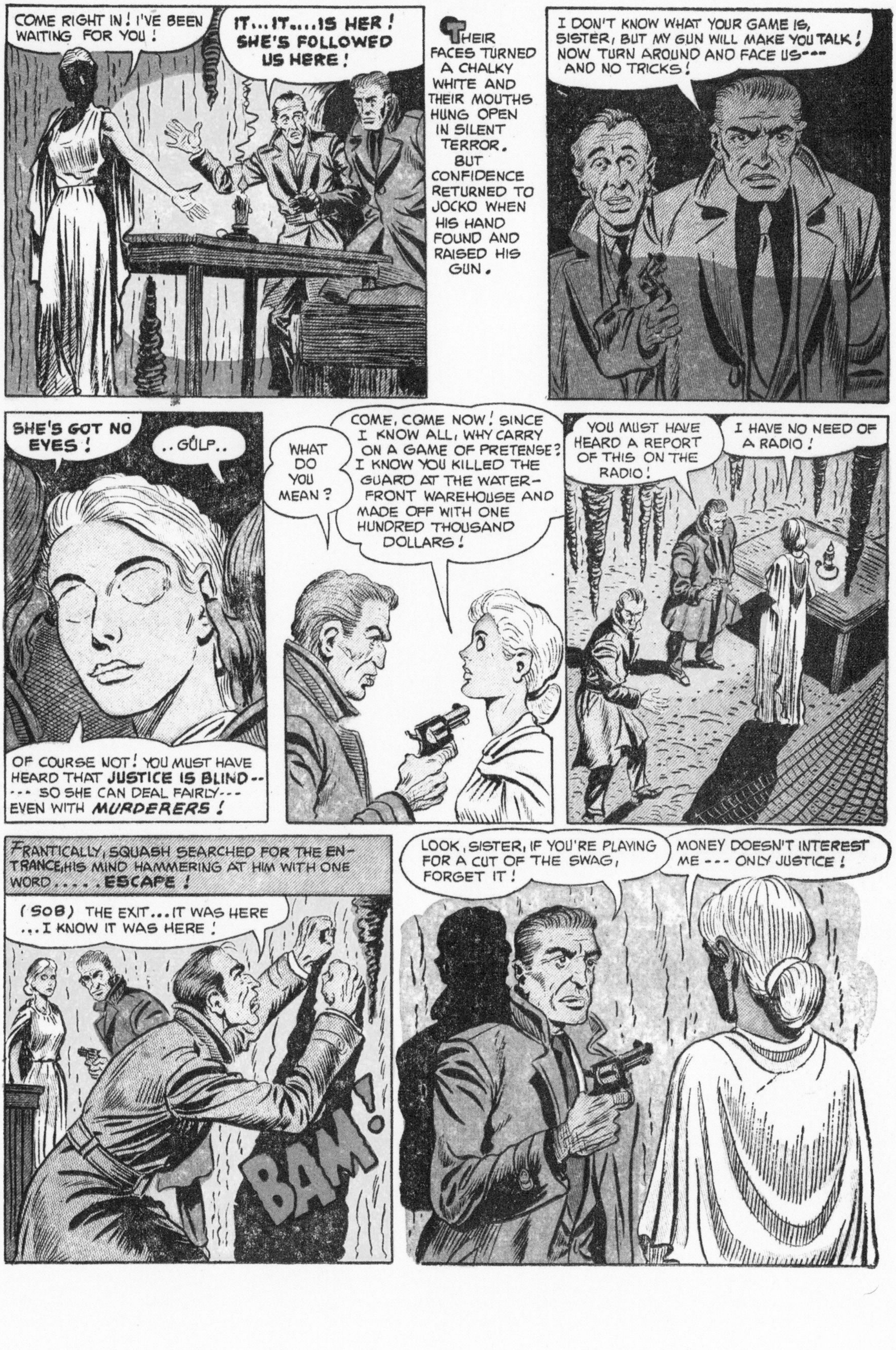

COME RIGHT IN! I'VE BEEN WAITING FOR YOU!
IT... IT.... IS HER! SHE'S FOLLOWED US HERE!
THEIR FACES TURNED A CHALKY WHITE AND THEIR MOUTHS HUNG OPEN IN SILENT TERROR. BUT CONFIDENCE RETURNED TO JOCKO WHEN HIS HAND FOUND AND RAISED HIS GUN.
I DON'T KNOW WHAT YOUR GAME IS, SISTER, BUT MY GUN WILL MAKE YOU TALK! NOW TURN AROUND AND FACE US--- AND NO TRICKS!
SHE'S GOT NO EYES!
..GULP..
OF COURSE NOT! YOU MUST HAVE HEARD THAT JUSTICE IS BLIND-- --- SO SHE CAN DEAL FAIRLY--- EVEN WITH MURDERERS!
WHAT DO YOU MEAN?
COME, COME NOW! SINCE I KNOW ALL, WHY CARRY ON A GAME OF PRETENSE? I KNOW YOU KILLED THE GUARD AT THE WATER-FRONT WAREHOUSE AND MADE OFF WITH ONE HUNDRED THOUSAND DOLLARS!
YOU MUST HAVE HEARD A REPORT OF THIS ON THE RADIO!
I HAVE NO NEED OF A RADIO!
FRANTICALLY, SQUASH SEARCHED FOR THE EN-TRANCE, HIS MIND HAMMERING AT HIM WITH ONE WORD.... ESCAPE!
(SOB) THE EXIT... IT WAS HERE ...I KNOW IT WAS HERE!
BAM!
LOOK, SISTER, IF YOU'RE PLAYING FOR A CUT OF THE SWAG, FORGET IT!
MONEY DOESN'T INTEREST ME --- ONLY JUSTICE!

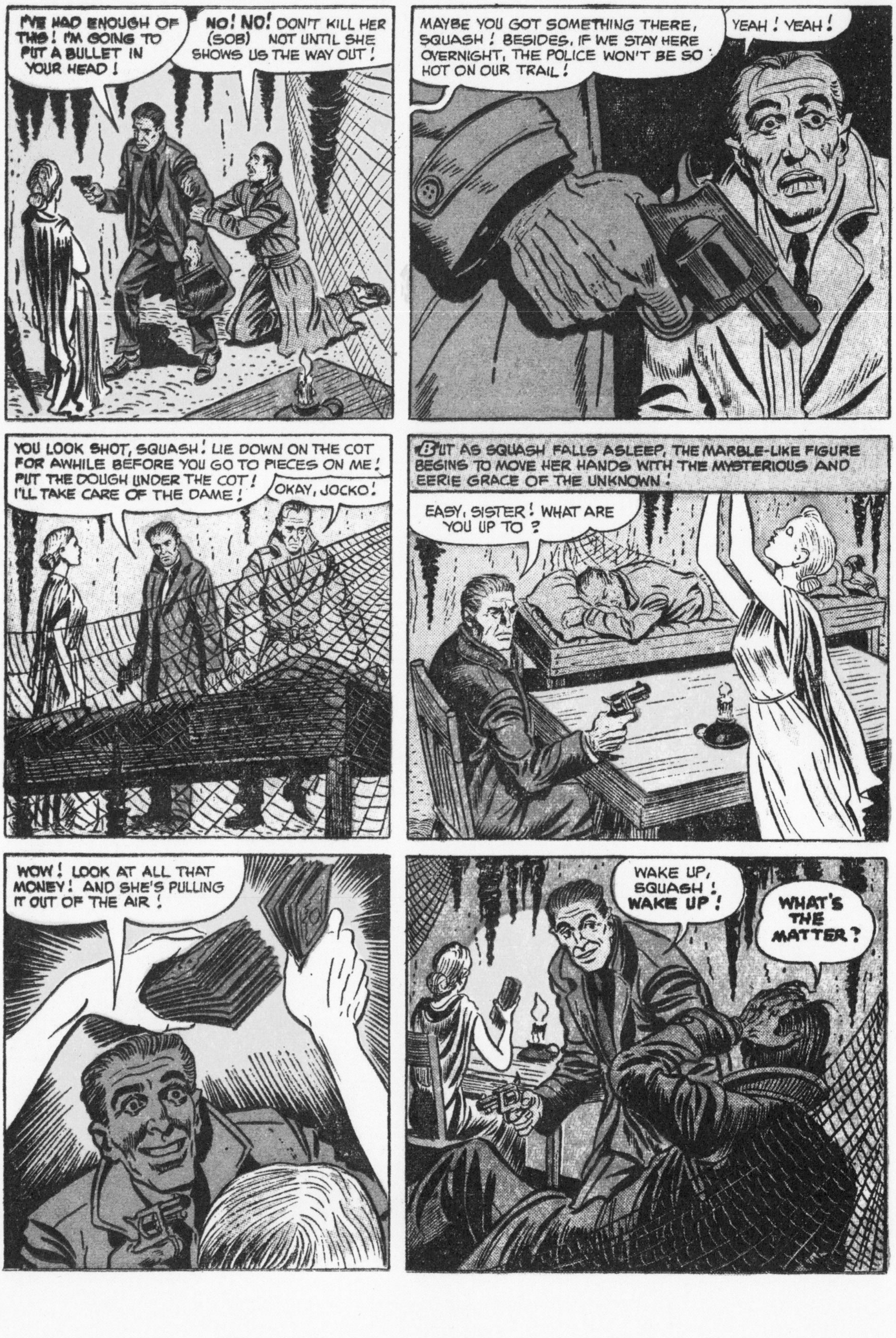

I'VE HAD ENOUGH OF THIS! I'M GOING TO PUT A BULLET IN YOUR HEAD!
NO! NO! DON'T KILL HER (SOB) NOT UNTIL SHE SHOWS US THE WAY OUT!
MAYBE YOU GOT SOMETHING THERE, SQUASH! BESIDES, IF WE STAY HERE OVERNIGHT, THE POLICE WON'T BE SO HOT ON OUR TRAIL!
YEAH! YEAH!
YOU LOOK SHOT, SQUASH! LIE DOWN ON THE COT FOR AWHILE BEFORE YOU GO TO PIECES ON ME! PUT THE DOUGH UNDER THE COT! I'LL TAKE CARE OF THE DAME!
OKAY, JOCKO!
BUT AS SQUASH FALLS ASLEEP, THE MARBLE-LIKE FIGURE BEGINS TO MOVE HER HANDS WITH THE MYSTERIOUS AND EERIE GRACE OF THE UNKNOWN!
EASY, SISTER! WHAT ARE YOU UP TO?
WOW! LOOK AT ALL THAT MONEY! AND SHE'S PULLING IT OUT OF THE AIR!
WAKE UP, SQUASH! WAKE UP!
WHAT'S THE MATTER?

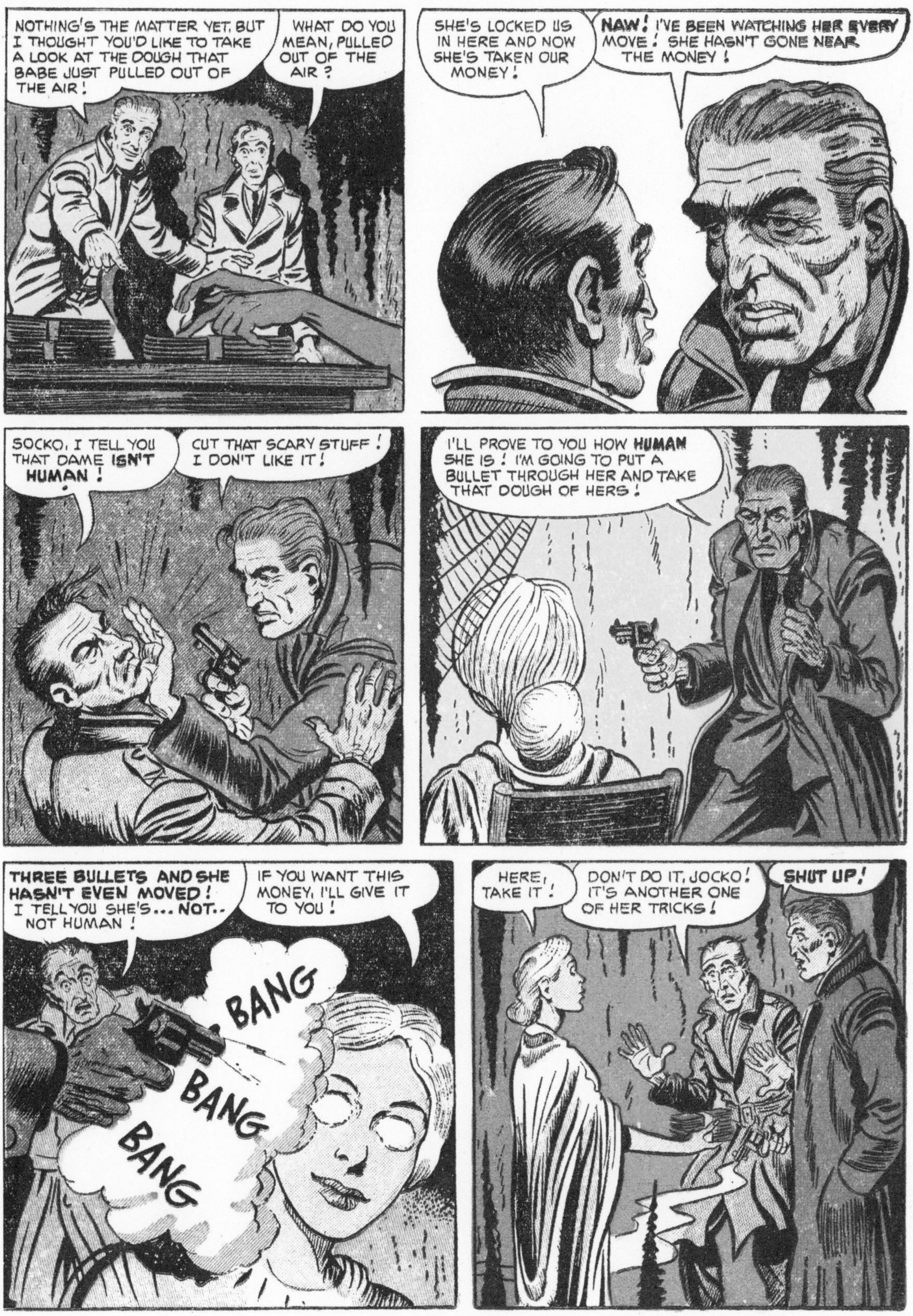
NOTHING'S THE MATTER YET, BUT I THOUGHT YOU'D LIKE TO TAKE A LOOK AT THE DOUGH THAT BABE JUST PULLED OUT OF THE AIR!
WHAT DO YOU MEAN, PULLED OUT OF THE AIR?
SHE'S LOCKED US IN HERE AND NOW SHE'S TAKEN OUR MONEY!
NAW! I'VE BEEN WATCHING HER EVERY MOVE! SHE HASN'T GONE NEAR THE MONEY!
SOCKO, I TELL YOU THAT DAME ISN'T HUMAN!
CUT THAT SCARY STUFF! I DON'T LIKE IT!
I'LL PROVE TO YOU HOW HUMAN SHE IS! I'M GOING TO PUT A BULLET THROUGH HER AND TAKE THAT DOUGH OF HERS!
THREE BULLETS AND SHE HASN'T EVEN MOVED! I TELL YOU SHE'S... NOT.. NOT HUMAN!
IF YOU WANT THIS MONEY, I'LL GIVE IT TO YOU!
BANG
BANG
BANG
HERE, TAKE IT!
DON'T DO IT, JOCKO! IT'S ANOTHER ONE OF HER TRICKS!
SHUT UP!

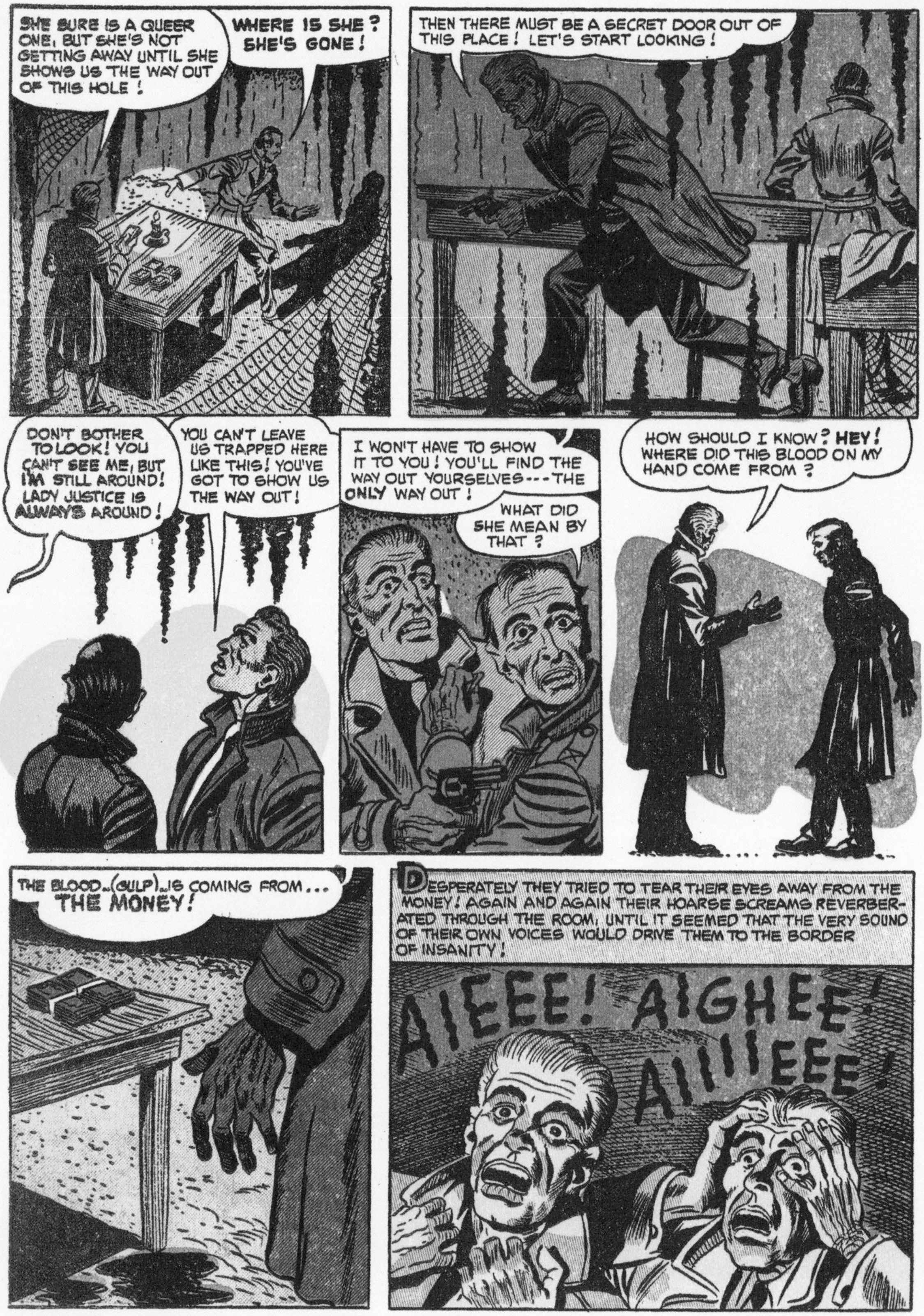
SHE SURE IS A QUEER ONE, BUT SHE'S NOT GETTING AWAY UNTIL SHE SHOWS US THE WAY OUT OF THIS HOLE!
WHERE IS SHE? SHE'S GONE!
THEN THERE MUST BE A SECRET DOOR OUT OF THIS PLACE! LET'S START LOOKING!
DON'T BOTHER TO LOOK! YOU CAN'T SEE ME, BUT I'M STILL AROUND! LADY JUSTICE IS ALWAYS AROUND!
YOU CAN'T LEAVE US TRAPPED HERE LIKE THIS! YOU'VE GOT TO SHOW US THE WAY OUT!
I WON'T HAVE TO SHOW IT TO YOU! YOU'LL FIND THE WAY OUT YOURSELVES---THE ONLY WAY OUT!
WHAT DID SHE MEAN BY THAT?
HOW SHOULD I KNOW? HEY! WHERE DID THIS BLOOD ON MY HAND COME FROM?
THE BLOOD..(GULP)..IS COMING FROM... THE MONEY!
DESPERATELY THEY TRIED TO TEAR THEIR EYES AWAY FROM THE MONEY! AGAIN AND AGAIN THEIR HOARSE SCREAMS REVERBERATED THROUGH THE ROOM, UNTIL IT SEEMED THAT THE VERY SOUND OF THEIR OWN VOICES WOULD DRIVE THEM TO THE BORDER OF INSANITY!
AIEEE! AIGHEE! AIIIIEEE!

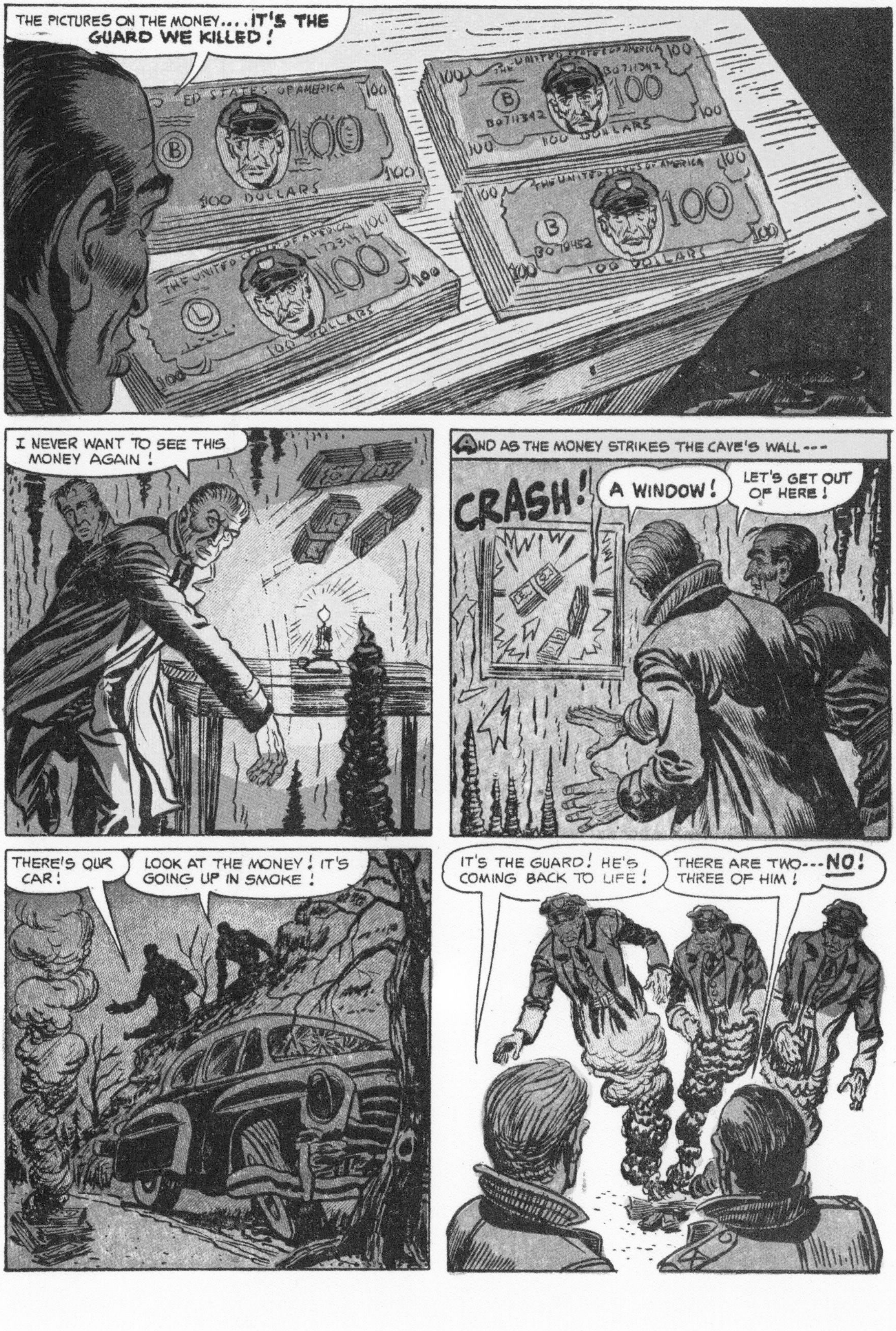
THE PICTURES ON THE MONEY....IT'S THE GUARD WE KILLED!
I NEVER WANT TO SEE THIS MONEY AGAIN!
AND AS THE MONEY STRIKES THE CAVE'S WALL---
CRASH!
A WINDOW!
LET'S GET OUT OF HERE!
THERE'S OUR CAR!
LOOK AT THE MONEY! IT'S GOING UP IN SMOKE!
IT'S THE GUARD! HE'S COMING BACK TO LIFE!
THERE ARE TWO---NO! THREE OF HIM!

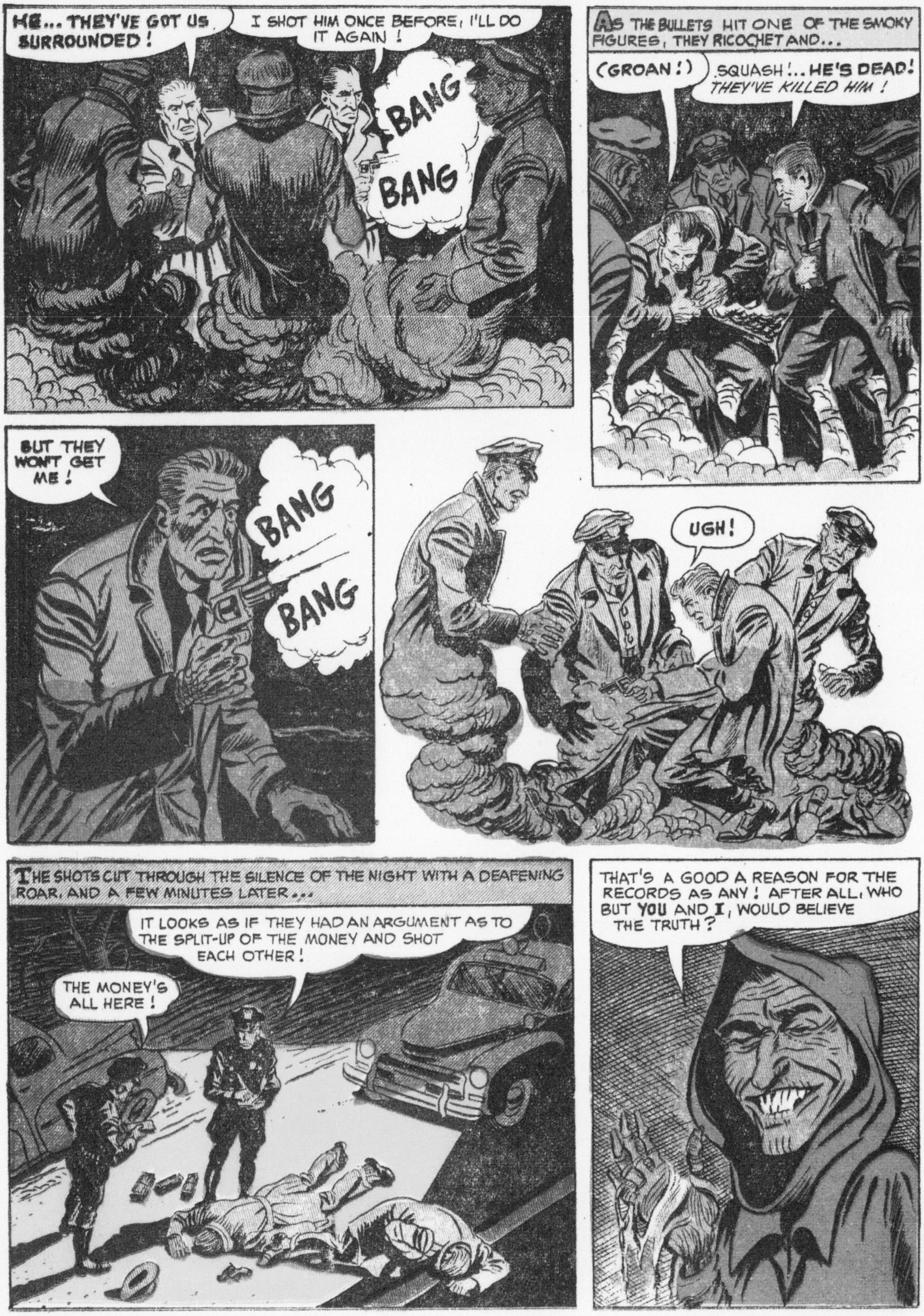

HE... THEY'VE GOT US SURROUNDED!
I SHOT HIM ONCE BEFORE; I'LL DO IT AGAIN!
BANG
BANG
AS THE BULLETS HIT ONE OF THE SMOKY FIGURES, THEY RICOCHET AND...
(GROAN!)
SQUASH!.. HE'S DEAD! THEY'VE KILLED HIM!
BUT THEY WON'T GET ME!
BANG
BANG
UGH!
THE SHOTS CUT THROUGH THE SILENCE OF THE NIGHT WITH A DEAFENING ROAR, AND A FEW MINUTES LATER...
IT LOOKS AS IF THEY HAD AN ARGUMENT AS TO THE SPLIT-UP OF THE MONEY AND SHOT EACH OTHER!
THE MONEY'S ALL HERE!
THAT'S A GOOD A REASON FOR THE RECORDS AS ANY! AFTER ALL, WHO BUT YOU AND I, WOULD BELIEVE THE TRUTH?

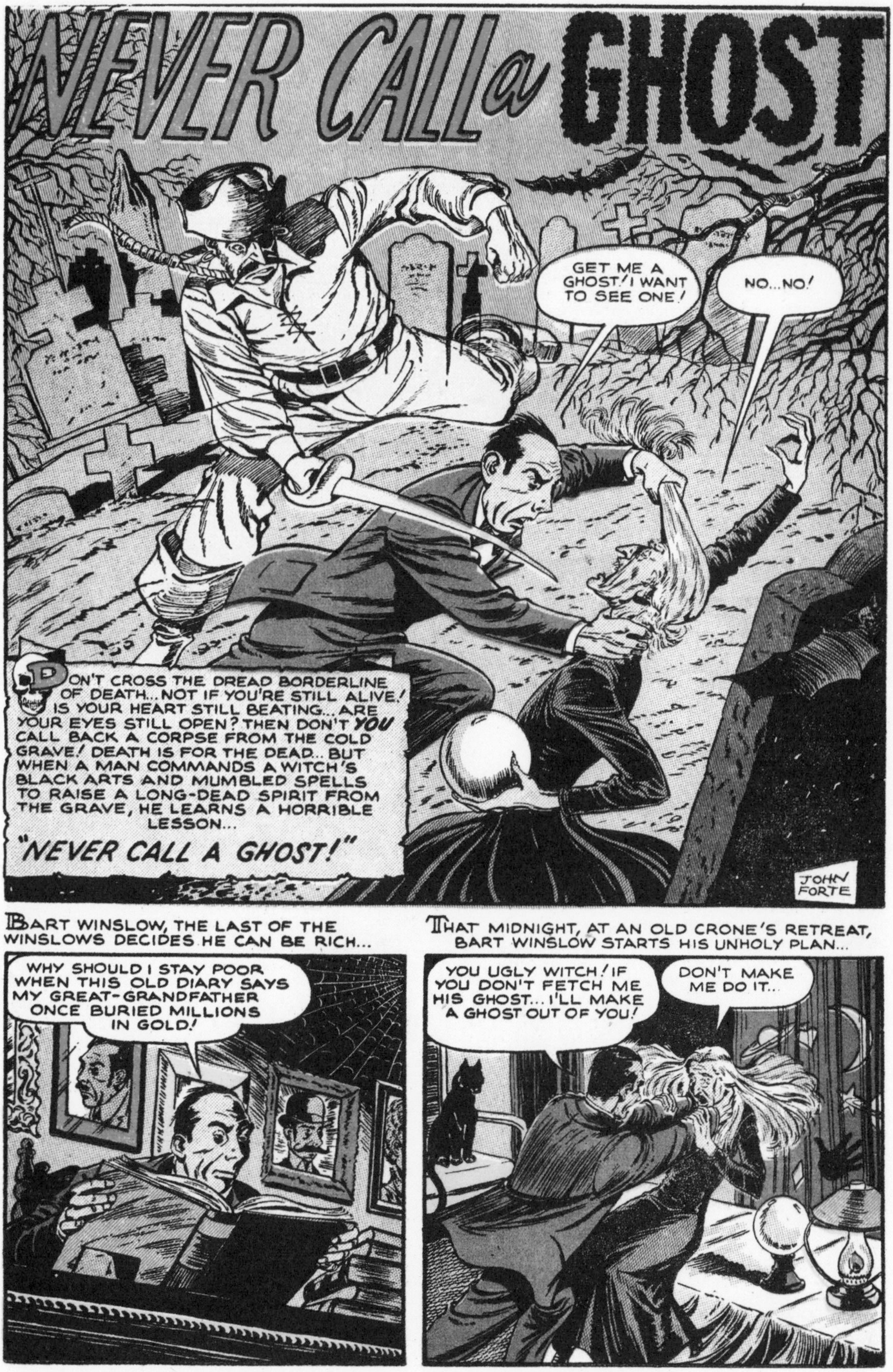
NEVER CALL a GHOST
GET ME A GHOST! I WANT TO SEE ONE!
NO...NO!
DON'T CROSS THE DREAD BORDERLINE OF DEATH... NOT IF YOU'RE STILL ALIVE! IS YOUR HEART STILL BEATING... ARE YOUR EYES STILL OPEN? THEN DON'T YOU CALL BACK A CORPSE FROM THE COLD GRAVE! DEATH IS FOR THE DEAD... BUT WHEN A MAN COMMANDS A WITCH'S BLACK ARTS AND MUMBLED SPELLS TO RAISE A LONG-DEAD SPIRIT FROM THE GRAVE, HE LEARNS A HORRIBLE LESSON...
"NEVER CALL A GHOST!"
JOHN FORTE
BART WINSLOW, THE LAST OF THE WINSLOWS DECIDES HE CAN BE RICH...
WHY SHOULD I STAY POOR WHEN THIS OLD DIARY SAYS MY GREAT-GRANDFATHER ONCE BURIED MILLIONS IN GOLD!
THAT MIDNIGHT, AT AN OLD CRONE'S RETREAT, BART WINSLOW STARTS HIS UNHOLY PLAN...
YOU UGLY WITCH! IF YOU DON'T FETCH ME HIS GHOST... I'LL MAKE A GHOST OUT OF YOU!
DON'T MAKE ME DO IT...

Beware #15, May 1953. John Forte. Trojan Magazines.

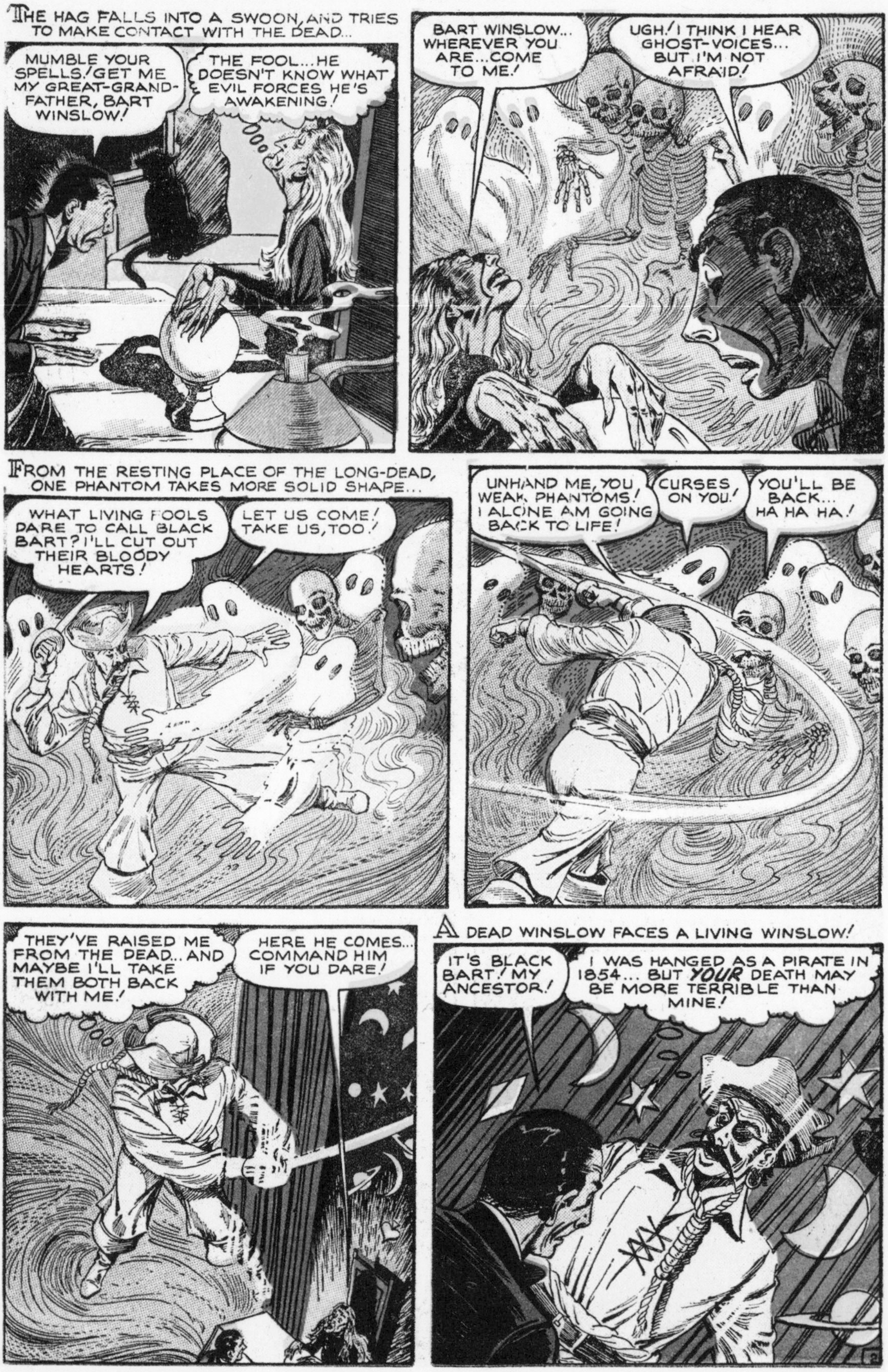

THE HAG FALLS INTO A SWOON, AND TRIES TO MAKE CONTACT WITH THE DEAD...
MUMBLE YOUR SPELLS! GET ME MY GREAT-GRAND-FATHER, BART WINSLOW!
THE FOOL...HE DOESN'T KNOW WHAT EVIL FORCES HE'S AWAKENING!
BART WINSLOW... WHEREVER YOU ARE...COME TO ME!
UGH! I THINK I HEAR GHOST-VOICES... BUT I'M NOT AFRAID!
FROM THE RESTING PLACE OF THE LONG-DEAD, ONE PHANTOM TAKES MORE SOLID SHAPE...
WHAT LIVING FOOLS DARE TO CALL BLACK BART? I'LL CUT OUT THEIR BLOODY HEARTS!
LET US COME! TAKE US, TOO!
UNHAND ME, YOU WEAK PHANTOMS! I ALONE AM GOING BACK TO LIFE!
CURSES ON YOU!
YOU'LL BE BACK... HA HA HA!
THEY'VE RAISED ME FROM THE DEAD... AND MAYBE I'LL TAKE THEM BOTH BACK WITH ME!
HERE HE COMES... COMMAND HIM IF YOU DARE!
A DEAD WINSLOW FACES A LIVING WINSLOW!
IT'S BLACK BART! MY ANCESTOR!
I WAS HANGED AS A PIRATE IN 1854... BUT YOUR DEATH MAY BE MORE TERRIBLE THAN MINE!

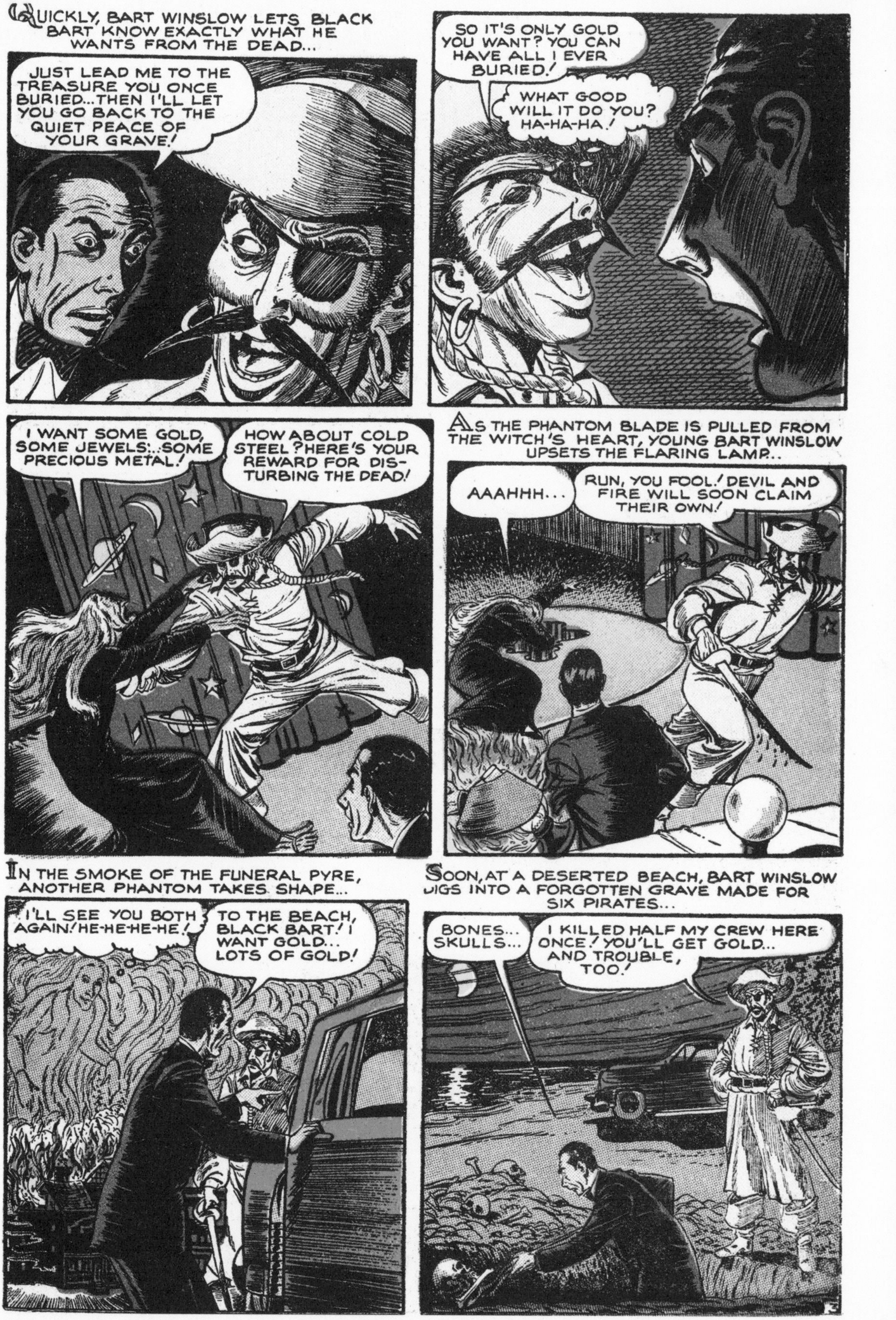
QUICKLY, BART WINSLOW LETS BLACK BART KNOW EXACTLY WHAT HE WANTS FROM THE DEAD...
JUST LEAD ME TO THE TREASURE YOU ONCE BURIED...THEN I'LL LET YOU GO BACK TO THE QUIET PEACE OF YOUR GRAVE!
SO IT'S ONLY GOLD YOU WANT? YOU CAN HAVE ALL I EVER BURIED!
WHAT GOOD WILL IT DO YOU? HA-HA-HA!
I WANT SOME GOLD, SOME JEWELS...SOME PRECIOUS METAL!
HOW ABOUT COLD STEEL? HERE'S YOUR REWARD FOR DISTURBING THE DEAD!
AS THE PHANTOM BLADE IS PULLED FROM THE WITCH'S HEART, YOUNG BART WINSLOW UPSETS THE FLARING LAMP...
AAAHHH...
RUN, YOU FOOL! DEVIL AND FIRE WILL SOON CLAIM THEIR OWN!
IN THE SMOKE OF THE FUNERAL PYRE, ANOTHER PHANTOM TAKES SHAPE...
I'LL SEE YOU BOTH AGAIN! HE-HE-HE-HE!
TO THE BEACH, BLACK BART! I WANT GOLD... LOTS OF GOLD!
SOON, AT A DESERTED BEACH, BART WINSLOW DIGS INTO A FORGOTTEN GRAVE MADE FOR SIX PIRATES...
BONES... SKULLS...
I KILLED HALF MY CREW HERE ONCE! YOU'LL GET GOLD... AND TROUBLE, TOO!

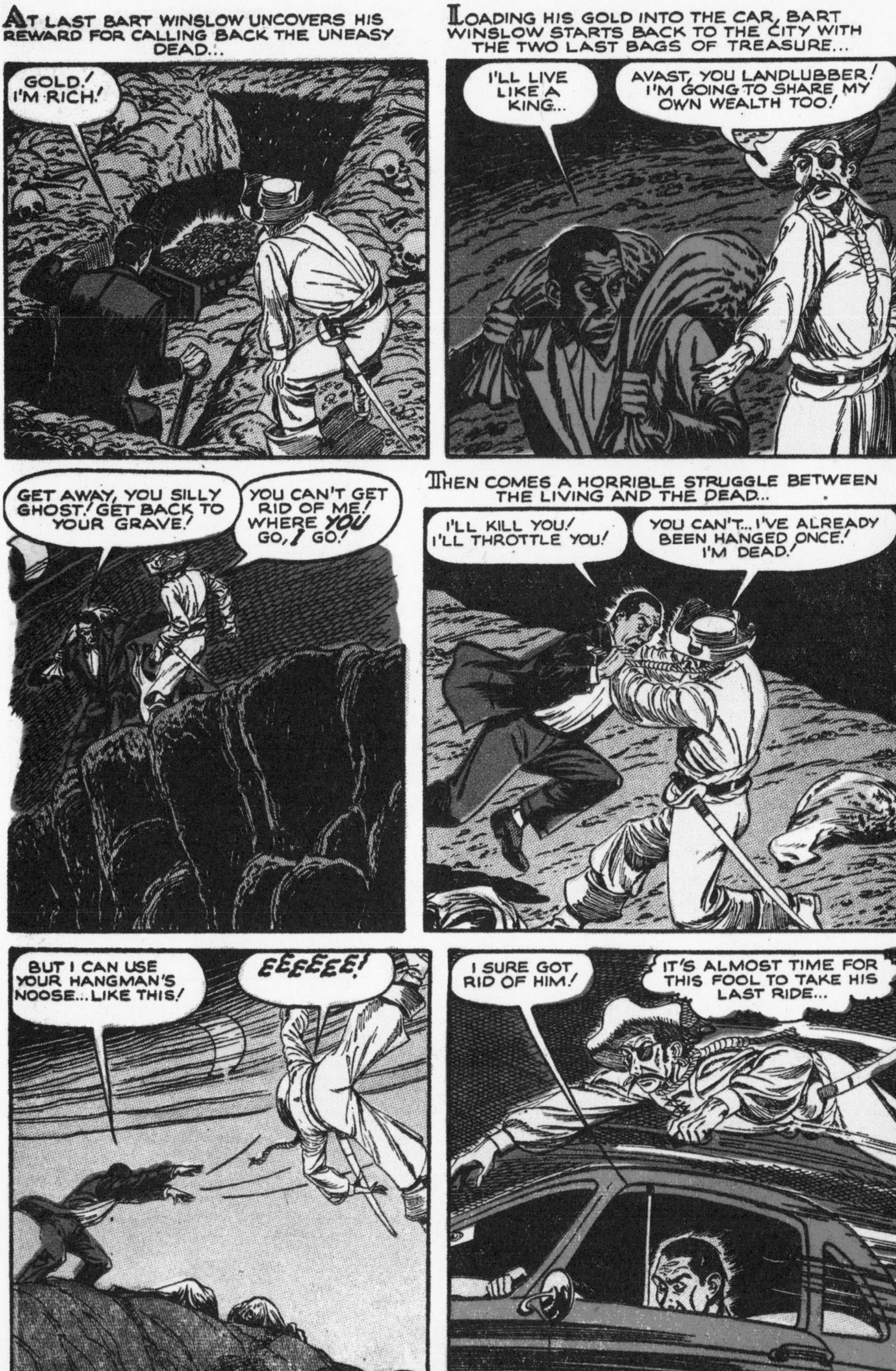
AT LAST BART WINSLOW UNCOVERS HIS REWARD FOR CALLING BACK THE UNEASY DEAD...
GOLD! I'M RICH!
LOADING HIS GOLD INTO THE CAR, BART WINSLOW STARTS BACK TO THE CITY WITH THE TWO LAST BAGS OF TREASURE...
I'LL LIVE LIKE A KING...
AVAST, YOU LANDLUBBER! I'M GOING TO SHARE MY OWN WEALTH TOO!
GET AWAY, YOU SILLY GHOST! GET BACK TO YOUR GRAVE!
YOU CAN'T GET RID OF ME! WHERE YOU GO, I GO!
THEN COMES A HORRIBLE STRUGGLE BETWEEN THE LIVING AND THE DEAD...
I'LL KILL YOU! I'LL THROTTLE YOU!
YOU CAN'T... I'VE ALREADY BEEN HANGED ONCE! I'M DEAD!
BUT I CAN USE YOUR HANGMAN'S NOOSE... LIKE THIS!
EEEEEE!
I SURE GOT RID OF HIM!
IT'S ALMOST TIME FOR THIS FOOL TO TAKE HIS LAST RIDE...
4

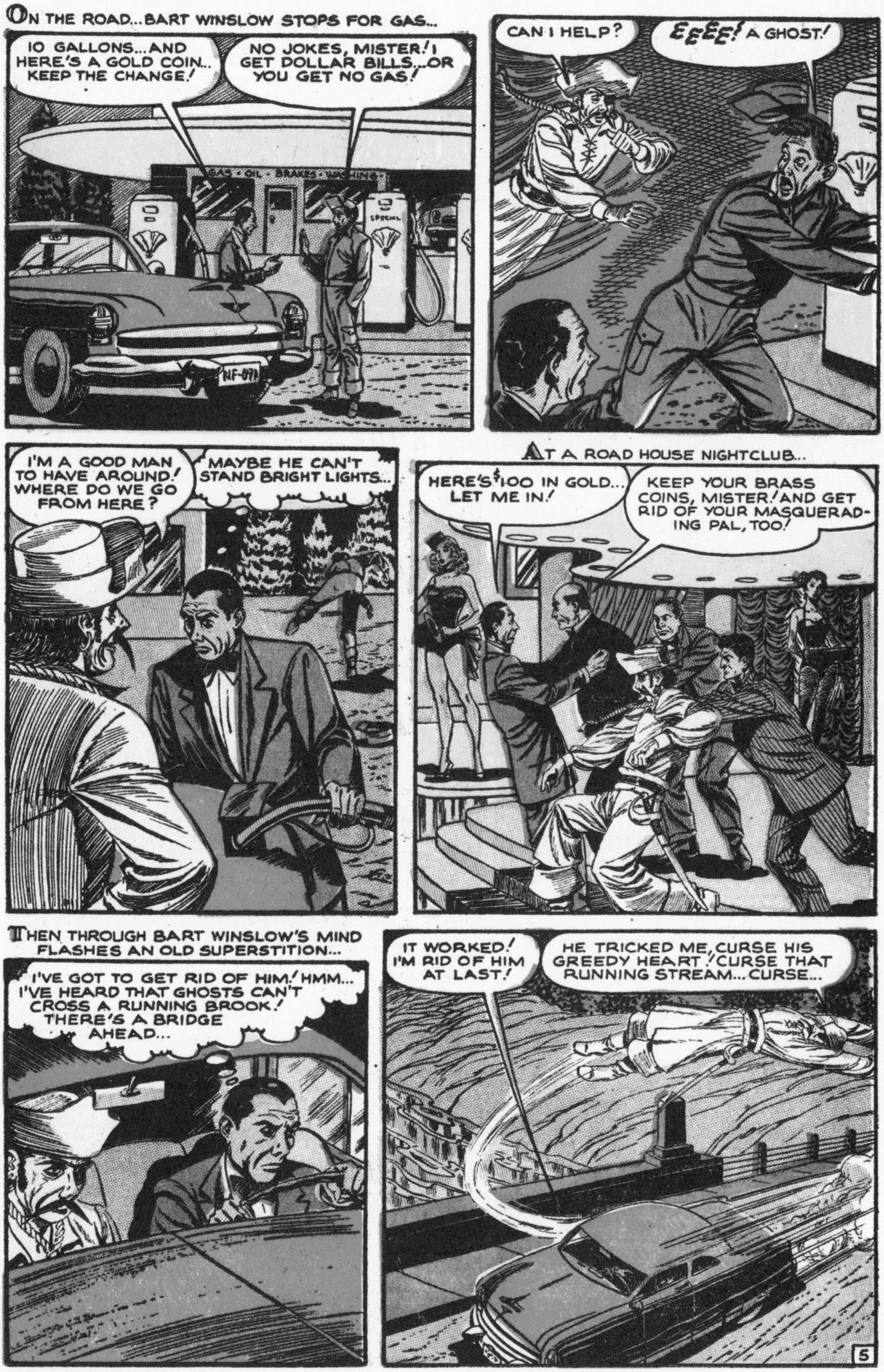
ON THE ROAD...BART WINSLOW STOPS FOR GAS...
10 GALLONS...AND HERE'S A GOLD COIN... KEEP THE CHANGE!
NO JOKES, MISTER! I GET DOLLAR BILLS...OR YOU GET NO GAS!
GAS · OIL · BRAKES · WASHING
SPECIAL
NF-071
CAN I HELP?
EEEE! A GHOST!
I'M A GOOD MAN TO HAVE AROUND! WHERE DO WE GO FROM HERE?
MAYBE HE CAN'T STAND BRIGHT LIGHTS...
AT A ROAD HOUSE NIGHTCLUB...
HERE'S $100 IN GOLD... LET ME IN!
KEEP YOUR BRASS COINS, MISTER! AND GET RID OF YOUR MASQUERADING PAL, TOO!
THEN THROUGH BART WINSLOW'S MIND FLASHES AN OLD SUPERSTITION...
I'VE GOT TO GET RID OF HIM! HMM... I'VE HEARD THAT GHOSTS CAN'T CROSS A RUNNING BROOK! THERE'S A BRIDGE AHEAD...
IT WORKED! I'M RID OF HIM AT LAST!
HE TRICKED ME, CURSE HIS GREEDY HEART! CURSE THAT RUNNING STREAM...CURSE...
5

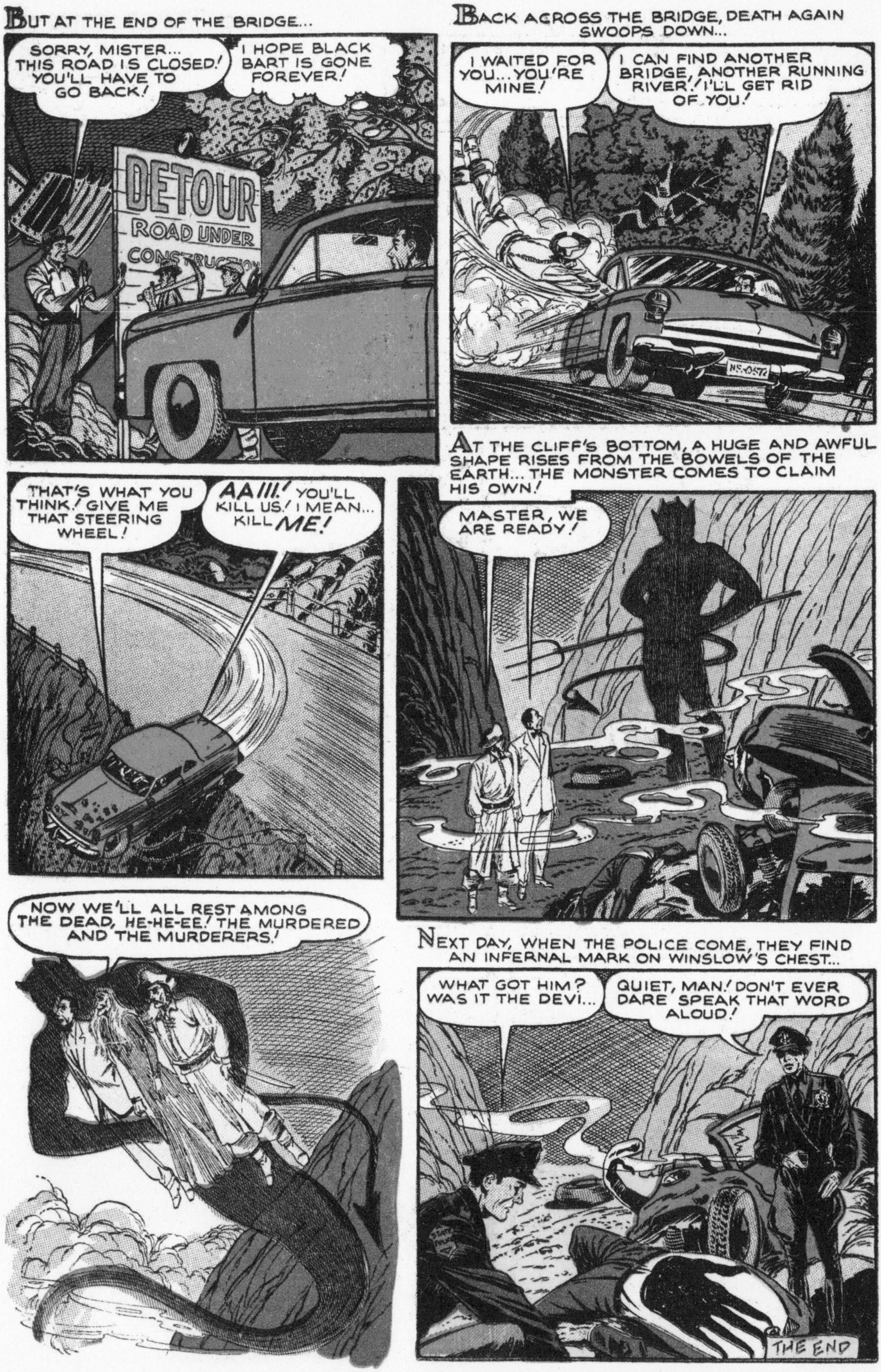
BUT AT THE END OF THE BRIDGE...
SORRY, MISTER... THIS ROAD IS CLOSED! YOU'LL HAVE TO GO BACK!
I HOPE BLACK BART IS GONE FOREVER!
DETOUR
ROAD UNDER CONSTRUCTION
BACK ACROSS THE BRIDGE, DEATH AGAIN SWOOPS DOWN...
I WAITED FOR YOU... YOU'RE MINE!
I CAN FIND ANOTHER BRIDGE, ANOTHER RUNNING RIVER! I'LL GET RID OF YOU!
THAT'S WHAT YOU THINK! GIVE ME THAT STEERING WHEEL!
AAIII! YOU'LL KILL US! I MEAN... KILL ME!
AT THE CLIFF'S BOTTOM, A HUGE AND AWFUL SHAPE RISES FROM THE BOWELS OF THE EARTH... THE MONSTER COMES TO CLAIM HIS OWN!
MASTER, WE ARE READY!
NOW WE'LL ALL REST AMONG THE DEAD, HE-HE-EE! THE MURDERED AND THE MURDERERS!
NEXT DAY, WHEN THE POLICE COME, THEY FIND AN INFERNAL MARK ON WINSLOW'S CHEST...
WHAT GOT HIM? WAS IT THE DEVI...
QUIET, MAN! DON'T EVER DARE SPEAK THAT WORD ALOUD!
THE END

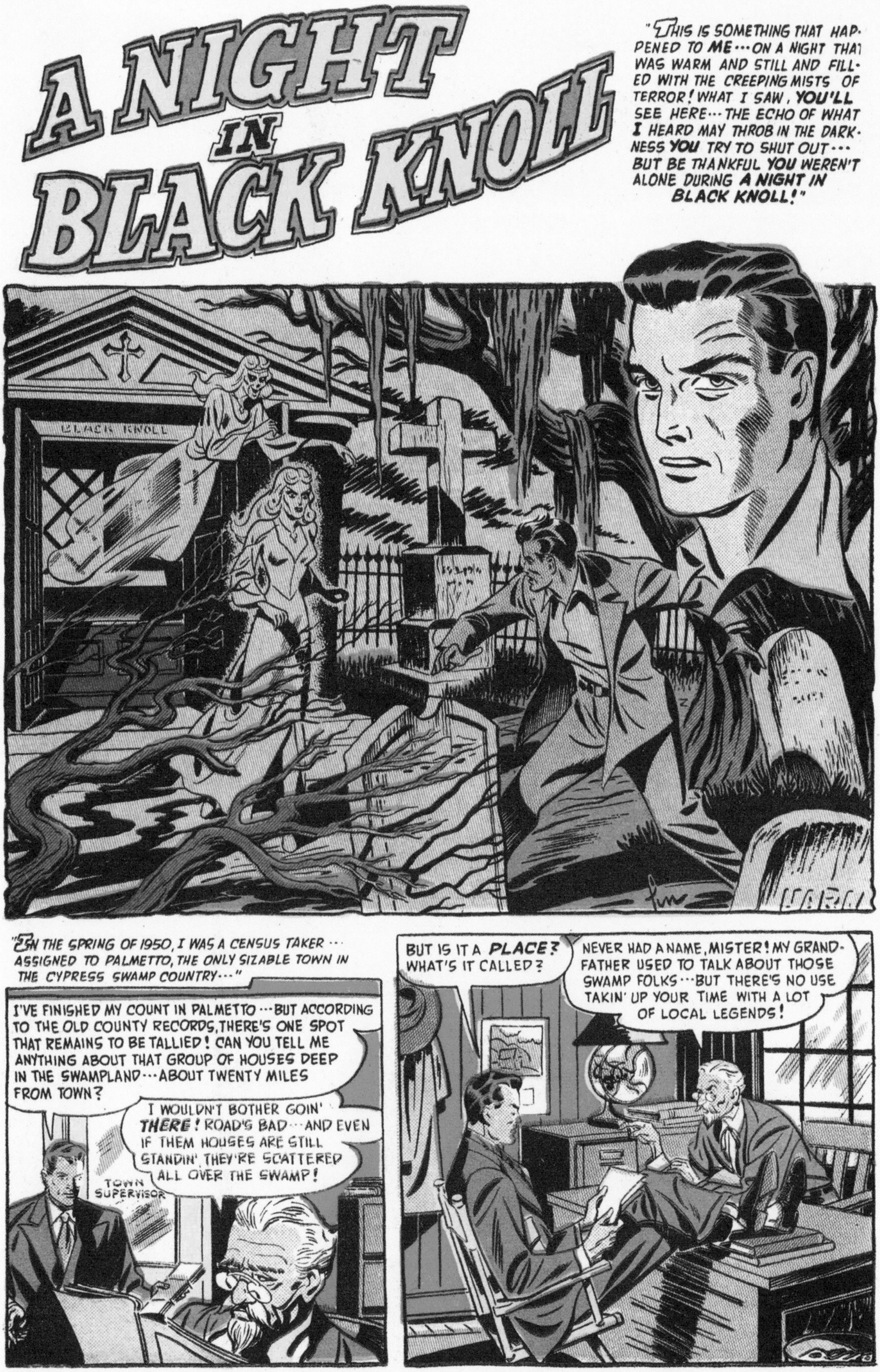

A NIGHT IN BLACK KNOLL
"THIS IS SOMETHING THAT HAPPENED TO ME···ON A NIGHT THAT WAS WARM AND STILL AND FILLED WITH THE CREEPING MISTS OF TERROR! WHAT I SAW, YOU'LL SEE HERE···THE ECHO OF WHAT I HEARD MAY THROB IN THE DARKNESS YOU TRY TO SHUT OUT···BUT BE THANKFUL YOU WEREN'T ALONE DURING A NIGHT IN BLACK KNOLL!"
BLACK KNOLL
"IN THE SPRING OF 1950, I WAS A CENSUS TAKER···ASSIGNED TO PALMETTO, THE ONLY SIZABLE TOWN IN THE CYPRESS SWAMP COUNTRY···"
I'VE FINISHED MY COUNT IN PALMETTO···BUT ACCORDING TO THE OLD COUNTY RECORDS, THERE'S ONE SPOT THAT REMAINS TO BE TALLIED! CAN YOU TELL ME ANYTHING ABOUT THAT GROUP OF HOUSES DEEP IN THE SWAMPLAND···ABOUT TWENTY MILES FROM TOWN?
I WOULDN'T BOTHER GOIN' THERE! ROAD'S BAD···AND EVEN IF THEM HOUSES ARE STILL STANDIN' THEY'RE SCATTERED ALL OVER THE SWAMP!
TOWN SUPERVISOR
BUT IS IT A PLACE? WHAT'S IT CALLED?
NEVER HAD A NAME, MISTER! MY GRANDFATHER USED TO TALK ABOUT THOSE SWAMP FOLKS···BUT THERE'S NO USE TAKIN' UP YOUR TIME WITH A LOT OF LOCAL LEGENDS!

Adventures into The Unknown #13, October – November 1950. Lin Streeter. ACG.

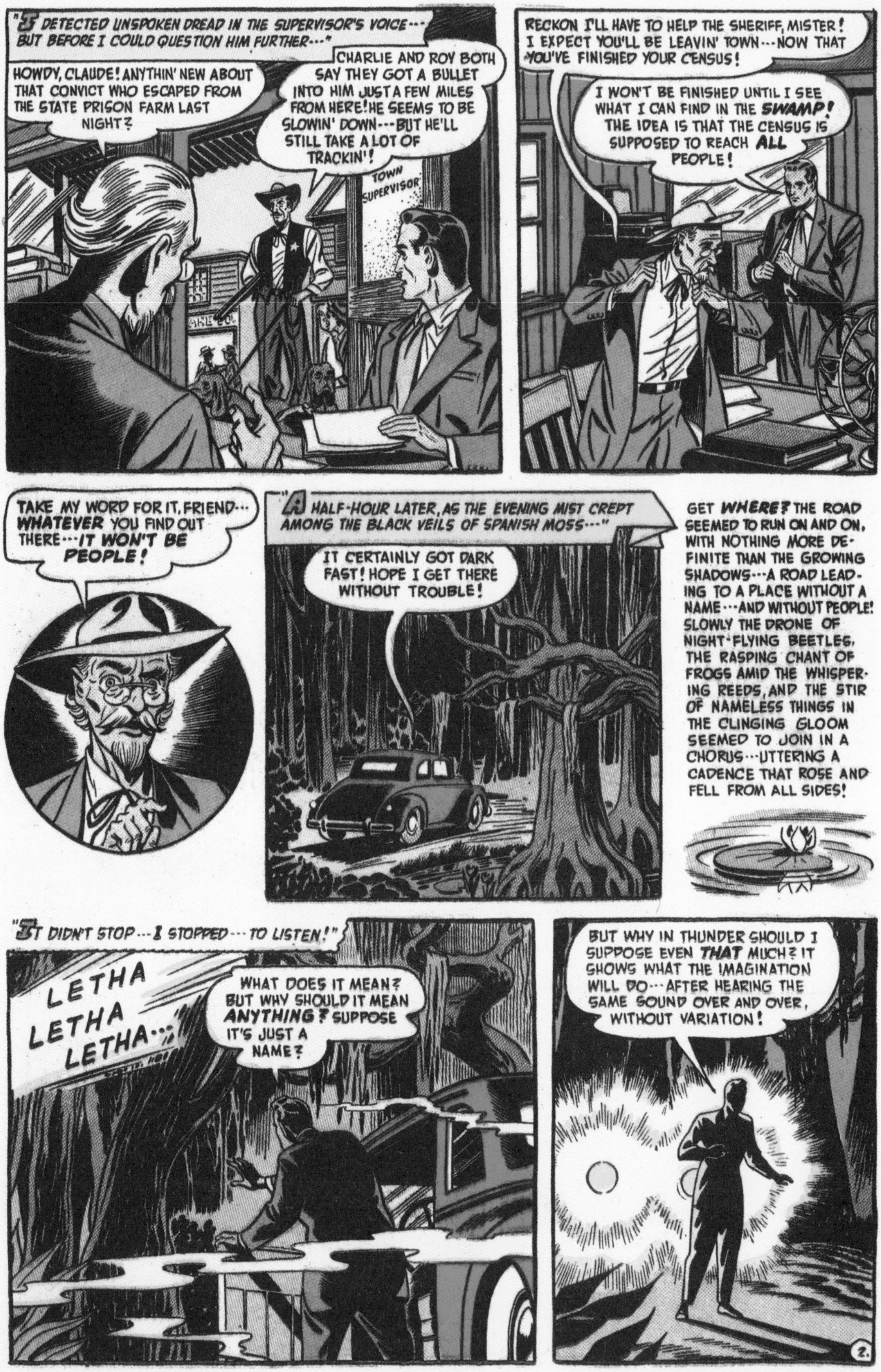
"I DETECTED UNSPOKEN DREAD IN THE SUPERVISOR'S VOICE--- BUT BEFORE I COULD QUESTION HIM FURTHER---"
HOWDY, CLAUDE! ANYTHIN' NEW ABOUT THAT CONVICT WHO ESCAPED FROM THE STATE PRISON FARM LAST NIGHT?
CHARLIE AND ROY BOTH SAY THEY GOT A BULLET INTO HIM JUST A FEW MILES FROM HERE! HE SEEMS TO BE SLOWIN' DOWN---BUT HE'LL STILL TAKE A LOT OF TRACKIN'!
TOWN SUPERVISOR
RECKON I'LL HAVE TO HELP THE SHERIFF, MISTER! I EXPECT YOU'LL BE LEAVIN' TOWN---NOW THAT YOU'VE FINISHED YOUR CENSUS!
I WON'T BE FINISHED UNTIL I SEE WHAT I CAN FIND IN THE SWAMP! THE IDEA IS THAT THE CENSUS IS SUPPOSED TO REACH ALL PEOPLE!
TAKE MY WORD FOR IT, FRIEND--- WHATEVER YOU FIND OUT THERE---IT WON'T BE PEOPLE!
"A HALF-HOUR LATER, AS THE EVENING MIST CREPT AMONG THE BLACK VEILS OF SPANISH MOSS---"
IT CERTAINLY GOT DARK FAST! HOPE I GET THERE WITHOUT TROUBLE!
GET WHERE? THE ROAD SEEMED TO RUN ON AND ON, WITH NOTHING MORE DEFINITE THAN THE GROWING SHADOWS---A ROAD LEADING TO A PLACE WITHOUT A NAME---AND WITHOUT PEOPLE! SLOWLY THE DRONE OF NIGHT-FLYING BEETLES, THE RASPING CHANT OF FROGS AMID THE WHISPERING REEDS, AND THE STIR OF NAMELESS THINGS IN THE CLINGING GLOOM SEEMED TO JOIN IN A CHORUS---UTTERING A CADENCE THAT ROSE AND FELL FROM ALL SIDES!
"IT DIDN'T STOP---I STOPPED---TO LISTEN!"
LETHA LETHA LETHA...
WHAT DOES IT MEAN? BUT WHY SHOULD IT MEAN ANYTHING? SUPPOSE IT'S JUST A NAME?
BUT WHY IN THUNDER SHOULD I SUPPOSE EVEN THAT MUCH? IT SHOWS WHAT THE IMAGINATION WILL DO---AFTER HEARING THE SAME SOUND OVER AND OVER, WITHOUT VARIATION!
2.

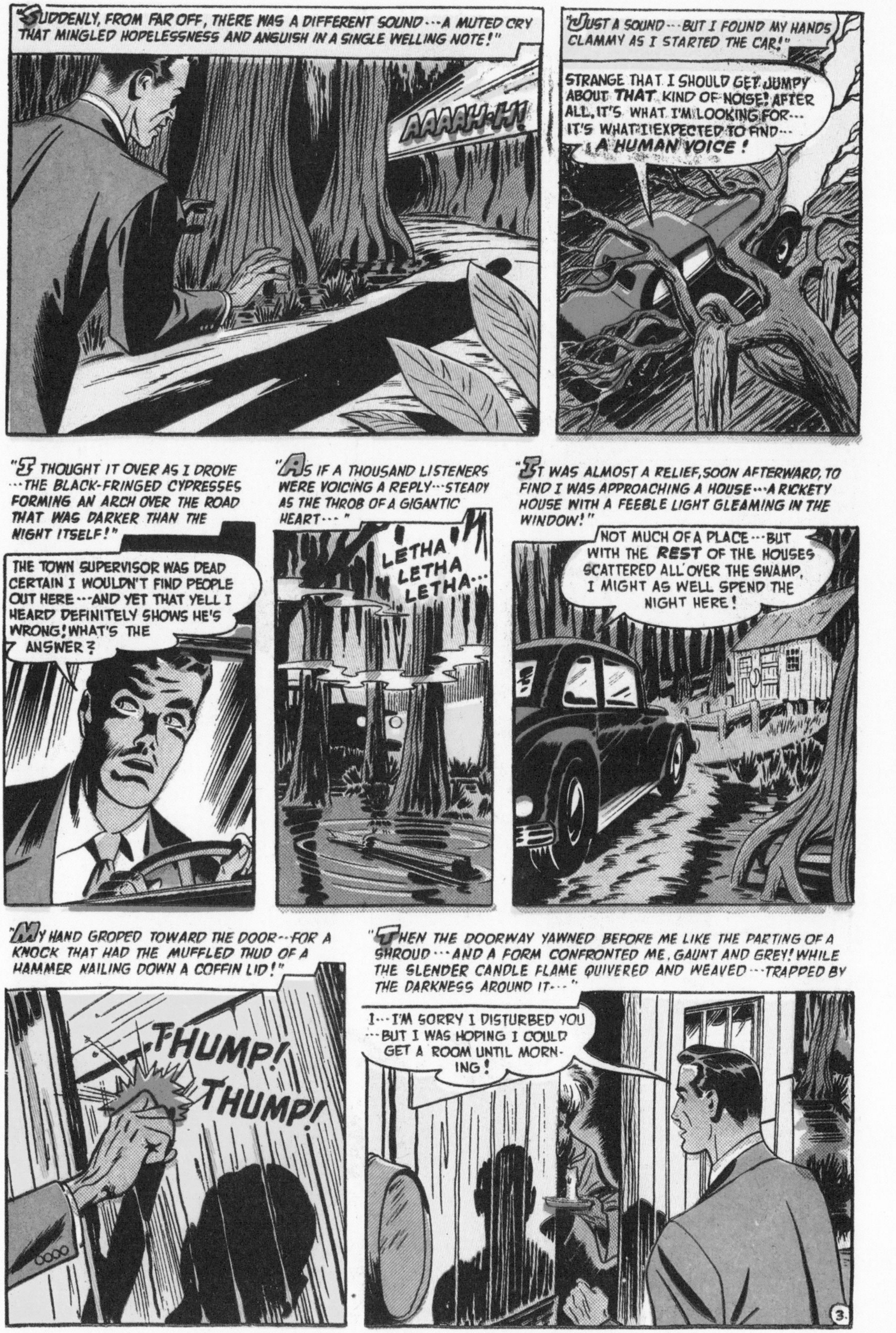
"SUDDENLY, FROM FAR OFF, THERE WAS A DIFFERENT SOUND... A MUTED CRY THAT MINGLED HOPELESSNESS AND ANGUISH IN A SINGLE WELLING NOTE!"
AAAAH-H!
"JUST A SOUND... BUT I FOUND MY HANDS CLAMMY AS I STARTED THE CAR!"
STRANGE THAT I SHOULD GET JUMPY ABOUT THAT KIND OF NOISE! AFTER ALL, IT'S WHAT I'M LOOKING FOR... IT'S WHAT I EXPECTED TO FIND... A HUMAN VOICE!
"I THOUGHT IT OVER AS I DROVE ...THE BLACK-FRINGED CYPRESSES FORMING AN ARCH OVER THE ROAD THAT WAS DARKER THAN THE NIGHT ITSELF!"
THE TOWN SUPERVISOR WAS DEAD CERTAIN I WOULDN'T FIND PEOPLE OUT HERE... AND YET THAT YELL I HEARD DEFINITELY SHOWS HE'S WRONG! WHAT'S THE ANSWER?
"AS IF A THOUSAND LISTENERS WERE VOICING A REPLY... STEADY AS THE THROB OF A GIGANTIC HEART..."
LETHA LETHA LETHA...
"IT WAS ALMOST A RELIEF, SOON AFTERWARD, TO FIND I WAS APPROACHING A HOUSE... A RICKETY HOUSE WITH A FEEBLE LIGHT GLEAMING IN THE WINDOW!"
NOT MUCH OF A PLACE... BUT WITH THE REST OF THE HOUSES SCATTERED ALL OVER THE SWAMP, I MIGHT AS WELL SPEND THE NIGHT HERE!
"MY HAND GROPED TOWARD THE DOOR... FOR A KNOCK THAT HAD THE MUFFLED THUD OF A HAMMER NAILING DOWN A COFFIN LID!"
THUMP! THUMP!
"THEN THE DOORWAY YAWNED BEFORE ME LIKE THE PARTING OF A SHROUD... AND A FORM CONFRONTED ME, GAUNT AND GREY! WHILE THE SLENDER CANDLE FLAME QUIVERED AND WEAVED... TRAPPED BY THE DARKNESS AROUND IT..."
I... I'M SORRY I DISTURBED YOU ...BUT I WAS HOPING I COULD GET A ROOM UNTIL MORNING!
3.

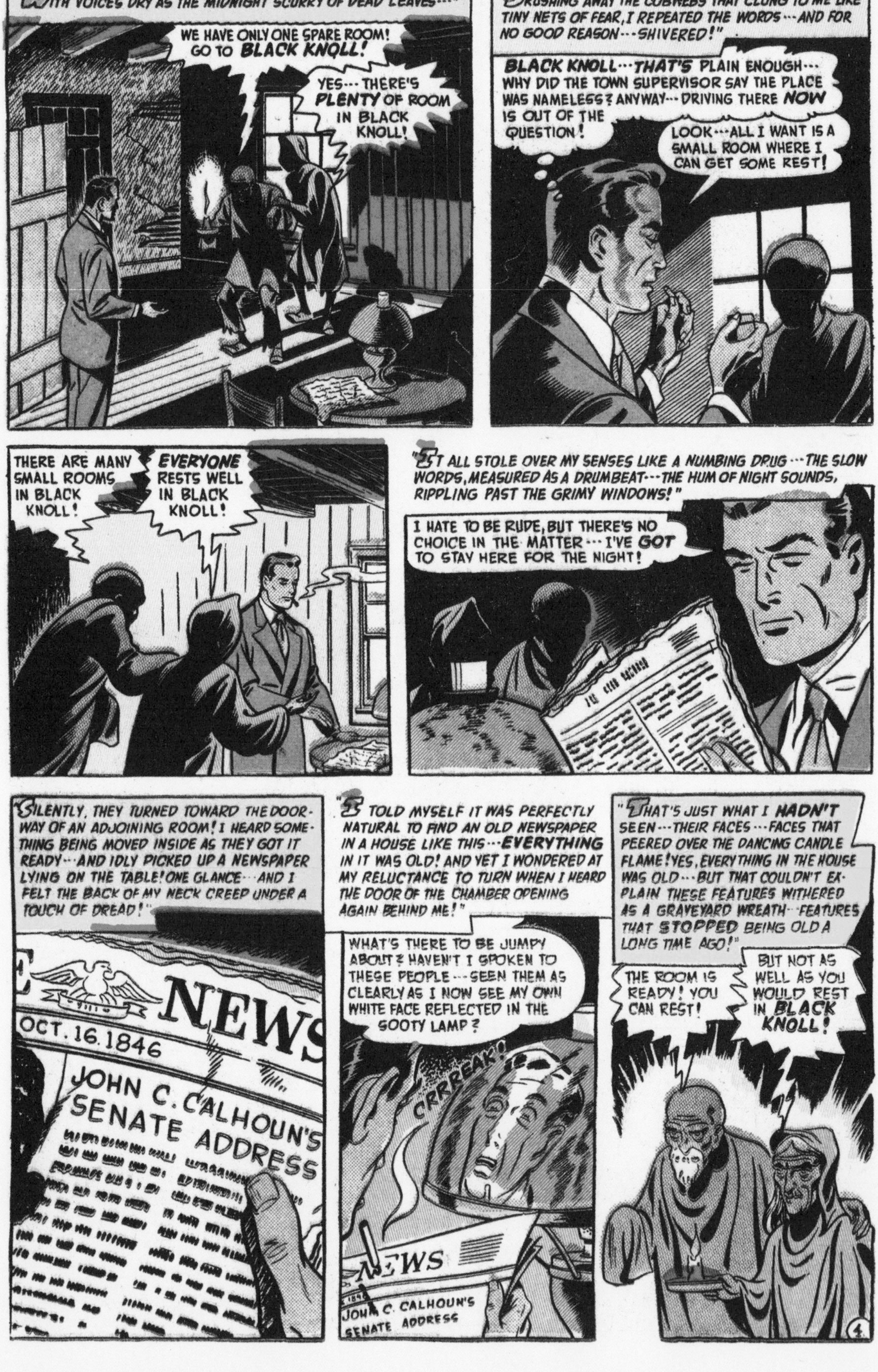
"WITH VOICES DRY AS THE MIDNIGHT SCURRY OF DEAD LEAVES---"
WE HAVE ONLY ONE SPARE ROOM! GO TO BLACK KNOLL!
YES--- THERE'S PLENTY OF ROOM IN BLACK KNOLL!
"BRUSHING AWAY THE COBWEBS THAT CLUNG TO ME LIKE TINY NETS OF FEAR, I REPEATED THE WORDS --- AND FOR NO GOOD REASON --- SHIVERED!"
BLACK KNOLL --- THAT'S PLAIN ENOUGH--- WHY DID THE TOWN SUPERVISOR SAY THE PLACE WAS NAMELESS? ANYWAY--- DRIVING THERE NOW IS OUT OF THE QUESTION!
LOOK --- ALL I WANT IS A SMALL ROOM WHERE I CAN GET SOME REST!
THERE ARE MANY SMALL ROOMS IN BLACK KNOLL!
EVERYONE RESTS WELL IN BLACK KNOLL!
"IT ALL STOLE OVER MY SENSES LIKE A NUMBING DRUG --- THE SLOW WORDS, MEASURED AS A DRUMBEAT--- THE HUM OF NIGHT SOUNDS, RIPPLING PAST THE GRIMY WINDOWS!"
I HATE TO BE RUDE, BUT THERE'S NO CHOICE IN THE MATTER --- I'VE GOT TO STAY HERE FOR THE NIGHT!
"SILENTLY, THEY TURNED TOWARD THE DOORWAY OF AN ADJOINING ROOM! I HEARD SOMETHING BEING MOVED INSIDE AS THEY GOT IT READY --- AND IDLY PICKED UP A NEWSPAPER LYING ON THE TABLE! ONE GLANCE --- AND I FELT THE BACK OF MY NECK CREEP UNDER A TOUCH OF DREAD!"
NEWS
OCT. 16.1846
JOHN C. CALHOUN'S SENATE ADDRESS
"I TOLD MYSELF IT WAS PERFECTLY NATURAL TO FIND AN OLD NEWSPAPER IN A HOUSE LIKE THIS --- EVERYTHING IN IT WAS OLD! AND YET I WONDERED AT MY RELUCTANCE TO TURN WHEN I HEARD THE DOOR OF THE CHAMBER OPENING AGAIN BEHIND ME!"
WHAT'S THERE TO BE JUMPY ABOUT? HAVEN'T I SPOKEN TO THESE PEOPLE --- SEEN THEM AS CLEARLY AS I NOW SEE MY OWN WHITE FACE REFLECTED IN THE SOOTY LAMP?
CRRREAK!
NEWS
JOHN C. CALHOUN'S SENATE ADDRESS
"THAT'S JUST WHAT I HADN'T SEEN --- THEIR FACES --- FACES THAT PEERED OVER THE DANCING CANDLE FLAME! YES, EVERYTHING IN THE HOUSE WAS OLD --- BUT THAT COULDN'T EXPLAIN THESE FEATURES WITHERED AS A GRAVEYARD WREATH --- FEATURES THAT STOPPED BEING OLD A LONG TIME AGO!"
THE ROOM IS READY! YOU CAN REST!
BUT NOT AS WELL AS YOU WOULD REST IN BLACK KNOLL!

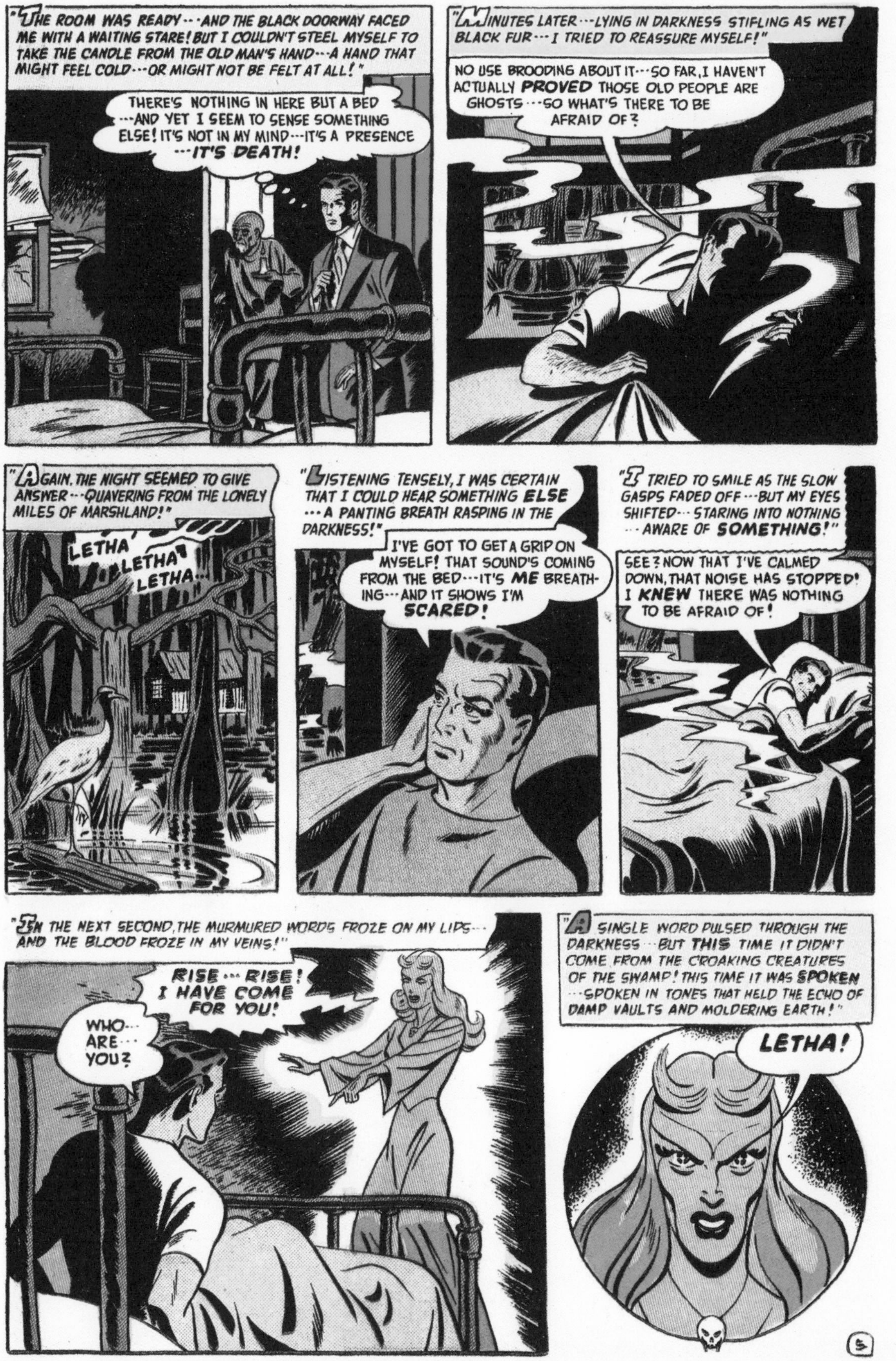
"THE ROOM WAS READY... AND THE BLACK DOORWAY FACED ME WITH A WAITING STARE! BUT I COULDN'T STEEL MYSELF TO TAKE THE CANDLE FROM THE OLD MAN'S HAND... A HAND THAT MIGHT FEEL COLD... OR MIGHT NOT BE FELT AT ALL!"
THERE'S NOTHING IN HERE BUT A BED ... AND YET I SEEM TO SENSE SOMETHING ELSE! IT'S NOT IN MY MIND... IT'S A PRESENCE ... IT'S DEATH!
"MINUTES LATER... LYING IN DARKNESS STIFLING AS WET BLACK FUR... I TRIED TO REASSURE MYSELF!"
NO USE BROODING ABOUT IT... SO FAR, I HAVEN'T ACTUALLY PROVED THOSE OLD PEOPLE ARE GHOSTS... SO WHAT'S THERE TO BE AFRAID OF?
"AGAIN, THE NIGHT SEEMED TO GIVE ANSWER... QUAVERING FROM THE LONELY MILES OF MARSHLAND!"
LETHA
LETHA
LETHA...
"LISTENING TENSELY, I WAS CERTAIN THAT I COULD HEAR SOMETHING ELSE ... A PANTING BREATH RASPING IN THE DARKNESS!"
I'VE GOT TO GET A GRIP ON MYSELF! THAT SOUND'S COMING FROM THE BED... IT'S ME BREATHING... AND IT SHOWS I'M SCARED!
"I TRIED TO SMILE AS THE SLOW GASPS FADED OFF... BUT MY EYES SHIFTED... STARING INTO NOTHING ... AWARE OF SOMETHING!"
SEE? NOW THAT I'VE CALMED DOWN, THAT NOISE HAS STOPPED! I KNEW THERE WAS NOTHING TO BE AFRAID OF!
"IN THE NEXT SECOND, THE MURMURED WORDS FROZE ON MY LIPS... AND THE BLOOD FROZE IN MY VEINS!"
RISE... RISE! I HAVE COME FOR YOU!
WHO... ARE YOU?
"A SINGLE WORD PULSED THROUGH THE DARKNESS... BUT THIS TIME IT DIDN'T COME FROM THE CROAKING CREATURES OF THE SWAMP! THIS TIME IT WAS SPOKEN ... SPOKEN IN TONES THAT HELD THE ECHO OF DAMP VAULTS AND MOLDERING EARTH!"
LETHA!
5

IS SHE TALKING TO *ME*? SHE SEEMS TO BE LOOKING AT SOMETHING ON THE FLOOR, NEAR THE BED---OR IS IT *UNDER* THE BED?

RISE---*RISE!* LETHA KNOWS THE WAY UNDER THE BLACK SKY---PAST THE BLACK POOLS---*TO BLACK KNOLL!*

"*S*OMETHING MOVED LIKE A SLEEPER STIRRING---SOMETHING CLUMPED AGAINST THE FLOOR LIKE A LIFELESS LIMB---"

UNDER--- THE BED!

"*O*NE LOOK AT THE PALE EYEBALLS STARING OUT FROM BEHIND THE CLOSED, TRANSPARENT LIDS, AND I *KNEW* ---KNEW THAT THE HEAVY BREATHING I HAD HEARD WERE THE LAST GASPS OF A DYING MAN---AND THAT *THIS*, WHICH WOULD NEVER BREATHE AGAIN, NO LONGER LIVED!"

FOLLOW--- *FOLLOW!* YOU CAME HERE AS A LAST REFUGE---YOU *DIED* HERE---AND YOU WILL STAY HERE FOREVER WITH THE LIVING DEAD OF BLACK KNOLL!

"*I* WATCHED FROM THE WINDOW AS THEY MOVED AMONG THE BROODING CYPRESSES---THE MORTALLY WOUNDED CONVICT WHO HAD FLED TO THE SWAMPS LIKE A HUNTED ANIMAL---AND *LETHA,* WHO HAD SOUGHT HIM OUT LIKE A HUNTING FIEND!"

THERE'S NO USE WONDERING NOW ABOUT THE WORD I HEARD CHANTED FROM THE INKY SWAMP WATER---THE WORD I KNEW WAS A *NAME!* LETHA MEANS *DEATH*---THE KIND OF DEATH THAT CAN SOMETIMES PROWL THE NIGHT IN A GRISLY IMITATION OF LIFE!

"*M*Y FIRST IMPULSE WAS TO GET INTO MY CAR AND DRIVE AWAY---FORGETTING ALL I KNEW ABOUT BLACK KNOLL! BUT AFTER ALL---"

"*I* FELT THEIR DULL, GLAZED EYES UPON ME AS I ENTERED THE OUTER ROOM---WRAPPED IN THE HUSH OF ITS SPECTRAL SECRETS!"

"*A* MOMENT LATER---I FOUND WHAT I WAS LOOKING FOR!"

WHAT *DO* I KNOW ABOUT IT? HOW MANY QUESTIONS WILL PLAGUE MY MIDNIGHT THOUGHTS LIKE PHANTOMS FOR THE REST OF MY LIFE---UNLESS THEY'RE ANSWERED? *INSIDE* IS WHERE I MAY FIND THOSE ANSWERS---FROM THE CRINKLED PAGES OF A NEWSPAPER OVER A HUNDRED YEARS OLD---FROM THE CRINKLED LIPS OF PEOPLE WHO READ THAT PAPER *THE DAY IT WAS PRINTED!*

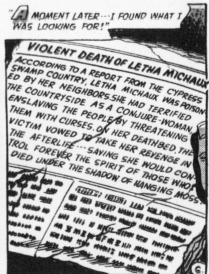

VIOLENT DEATH OF LETHA MICHAUX

ACCORDING TO A REPORT FROM THE CYPRESS SWAMP COUNTRY, LETHA MICHAUX WAS POISONED BY HER NEIGHBORS. SHE HAD TERRIFIED THE COUNTRYSIDE AS A CONJURE-WOMAN ENSLAVING THE PEOPLE BY THREATENING THEM WITH CURSES. ON HER DEATHBED, THE VICTIM VOWED TO TAKE HER REVENGE IN THE AFTERLIFE---SAYING SHE WOULD CONTROL FOREVER THE SPIRIT OF THOSE WHO DIED UNDER THE SHADOW OF HANGING MOSS.

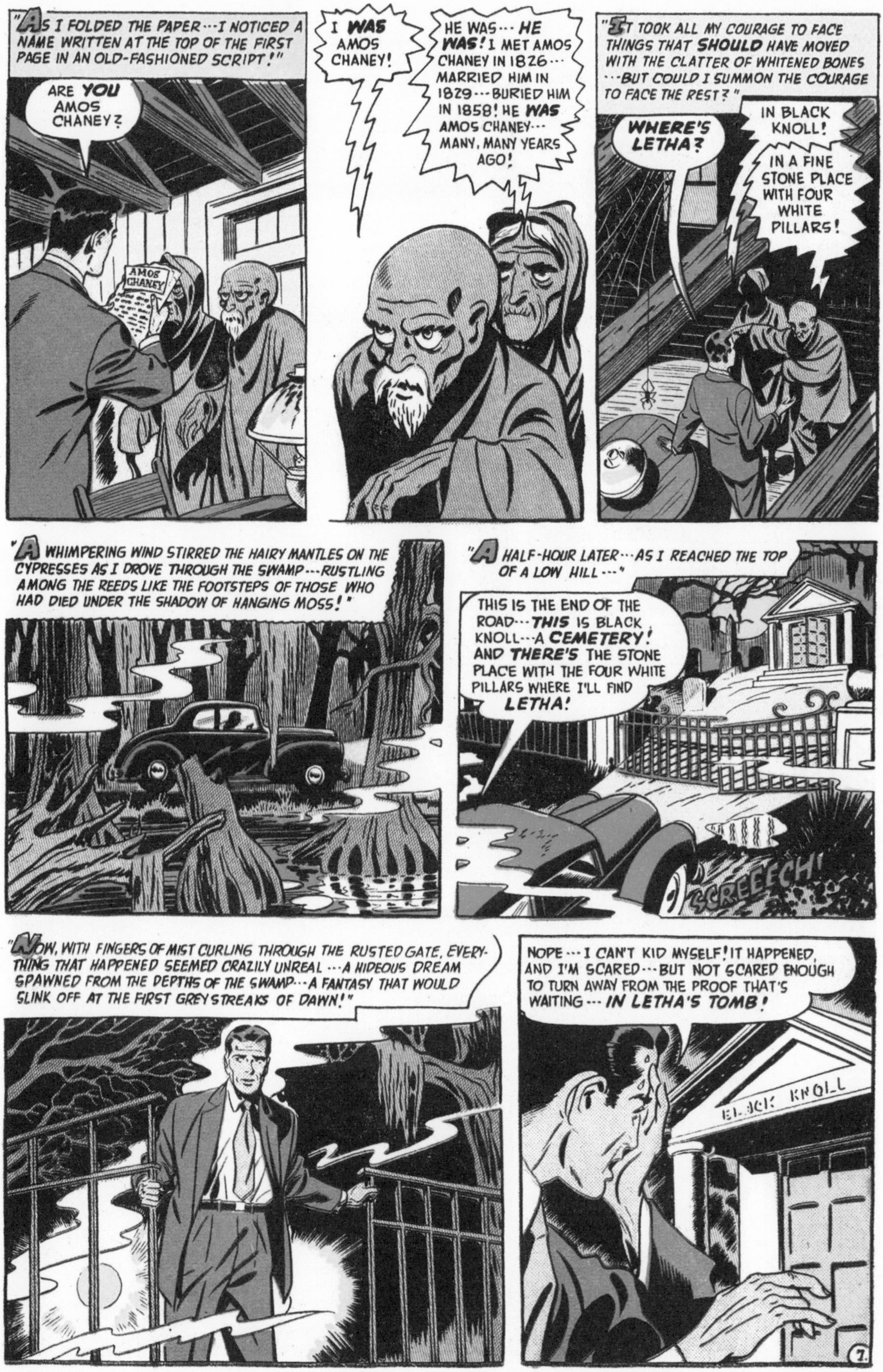
"AS I FOLDED THE PAPER --- I NOTICED A NAME WRITTEN AT THE TOP OF THE FIRST PAGE IN AN OLD-FASHIONED SCRIPT!"
ARE YOU AMOS CHANEY?
AMOS CHANEY
I WAS AMOS CHANEY!
HE WAS --- HE WAS! I MET AMOS CHANEY IN 1826 --- MARRIED HIM IN 1829 --- BURIED HIM IN 1858! HE WAS AMOS CHANEY --- MANY, MANY YEARS AGO!
"IT TOOK ALL MY COURAGE TO FACE THINGS THAT SHOULD HAVE MOVED WITH THE CLATTER OF WHITENED BONES --- BUT COULD I SUMMON THE COURAGE TO FACE THE REST?"
WHERE'S LETHA?
IN BLACK KNOLL!
IN A FINE STONE PLACE WITH FOUR WHITE PILLARS!
"A WHIMPERING WIND STIRRED THE HAIRY MANTLES ON THE CYPRESSES AS I DROVE THROUGH THE SWAMP --- RUSTLING AMONG THE REEDS LIKE THE FOOTSTEPS OF THOSE WHO HAD DIED UNDER THE SHADOW OF HANGING MOSS!"
"A HALF-HOUR LATER --- AS I REACHED THE TOP OF A LOW HILL ---"
THIS IS THE END OF THE ROAD --- THIS IS BLACK KNOLL --- A CEMETERY! AND THERE'S THE STONE PLACE WITH THE FOUR WHITE PILLARS WHERE I'LL FIND LETHA!
SCREEECH!
"NOW, WITH FINGERS OF MIST CURLING THROUGH THE RUSTED GATE, EVERYTHING THAT HAPPENED SEEMED CRAZILY UNREAL --- A HIDEOUS DREAM SPAWNED FROM THE DEPTHS OF THE SWAMP --- A FANTASY THAT WOULD SLINK OFF AT THE FIRST GREY STREAKS OF DAWN!"
NOPE --- I CAN'T KID MYSELF! IT HAPPENED, AND I'M SCARED --- BUT NOT SCARED ENOUGH TO TURN AWAY FROM THE PROOF THAT'S WAITING --- IN LETHA'S TOMB!
7.

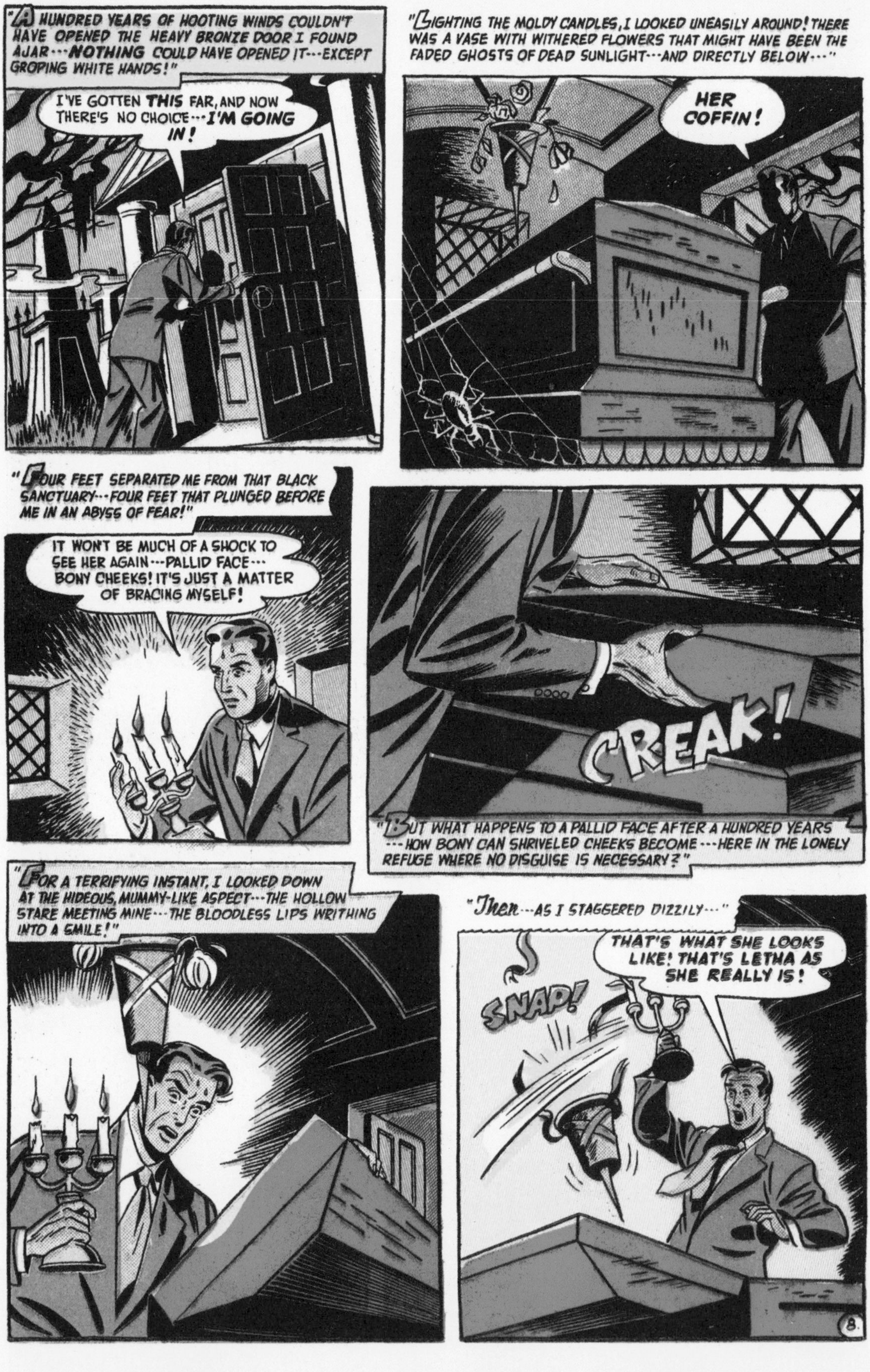
"A HUNDRED YEARS OF HOOTING WINDS COULDN'T HAVE OPENED THE HEAVY BRONZE DOOR I FOUND AJAR---NOTHING COULD HAVE OPENED IT---EXCEPT GROPING WHITE HANDS!"
I'VE GOTTEN THIS FAR, AND NOW THERE'S NO CHOICE---I'M GOING IN!
"LIGHTING THE MOLDY CANDLES, I LOOKED UNEASILY AROUND! THERE WAS A VASE WITH WITHERED FLOWERS THAT MIGHT HAVE BEEN THE FADED GHOSTS OF DEAD SUNLIGHT---AND DIRECTLY BELOW---"
HER COFFIN!
"FOUR FEET SEPARATED ME FROM THAT BLACK SANCTUARY---FOUR FEET THAT PLUNGED BEFORE ME IN AN ABYSS OF FEAR!"
IT WON'T BE MUCH OF A SHOCK TO SEE HER AGAIN---PALLID FACE---BONY CHEEKS! IT'S JUST A MATTER OF BRACING MYSELF!
CREAK!
"BUT WHAT HAPPENS TO A PALLID FACE AFTER A HUNDRED YEARS---HOW BONY CAN SHRIVELED CHEEKS BECOME---HERE IN THE LONELY REFUGE WHERE NO DISGUISE IS NECESSARY?"
"FOR A TERRIFYING INSTANT, I LOOKED DOWN AT THE HIDEOUS, MUMMY-LIKE ASPECT---THE HOLLOW STARE MEETING MINE---THE BLOODLESS LIPS WRITHING INTO A SMILE!"
"Then---AS I STAGGERED DIZZILY---"
SNAP!
THAT'S WHAT SHE LOOKS LIKE! THAT'S LETHA AS SHE REALLY IS!
8

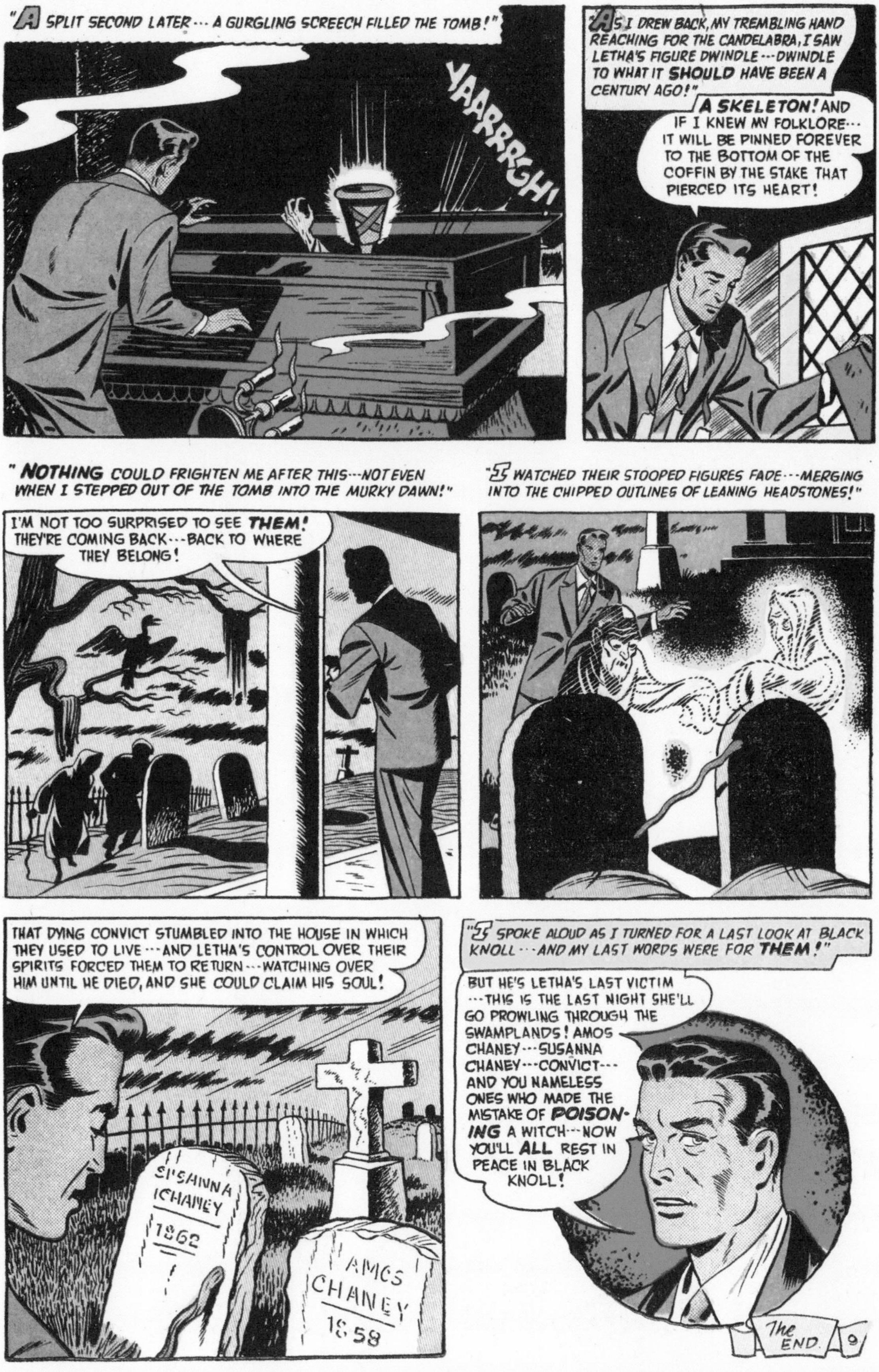
"A SPLIT SECOND LATER... A GURGLING SCREECH FILLED THE TOMB!"
YAARRRGH!
"AS I DREW BACK, MY TREMBLING HAND REACHING FOR THE CANDELABRA, I SAW LETHA'S FIGURE DWINDLE---DWINDLE TO WHAT IT SHOULD HAVE BEEN A CENTURY AGO!"
A SKELETON! AND IF I KNEW MY FOLKLORE... IT WILL BE PINNED FOREVER TO THE BOTTOM OF THE COFFIN BY THE STAKE THAT PIERCED ITS HEART!
"NOTHING COULD FRIGHTEN ME AFTER THIS---NOT EVEN WHEN I STEPPED OUT OF THE TOMB INTO THE MURKY DAWN!"
I'M NOT TOO SURPRISED TO SEE THEM! THEY'RE COMING BACK---BACK TO WHERE THEY BELONG!
"I WATCHED THEIR STOOPED FIGURES FADE---MERGING INTO THE CHIPPED OUTLINES OF LEANING HEADSTONES!"
THAT DYING CONVICT STUMBLED INTO THE HOUSE IN WHICH THEY USED TO LIVE---AND LETHA'S CONTROL OVER THEIR SPIRITS FORCED THEM TO RETURN---WATCHING OVER HIM UNTIL HE DIED, AND SHE COULD CLAIM HIS SOUL!
SUSANNA CHANEY 1862
AMOS CHANEY 1858
"I SPOKE ALOUD AS I TURNED FOR A LAST LOOK AT BLACK KNOLL---AND MY LAST WORDS WERE FOR THEM!"
BUT HE'S LETHA'S LAST VICTIM ---THIS IS THE LAST NIGHT SHE'LL GO PROWLING THROUGH THE SWAMPLANDS! AMOS CHANEY---SUSANNA CHANEY---CONVICT--- AND YOU NAMELESS ONES WHO MADE THE MISTAKE OF POISONING A WITCH---NOW YOU'LL ALL REST IN PEACE IN BLACK KNOLL!
The END.
9

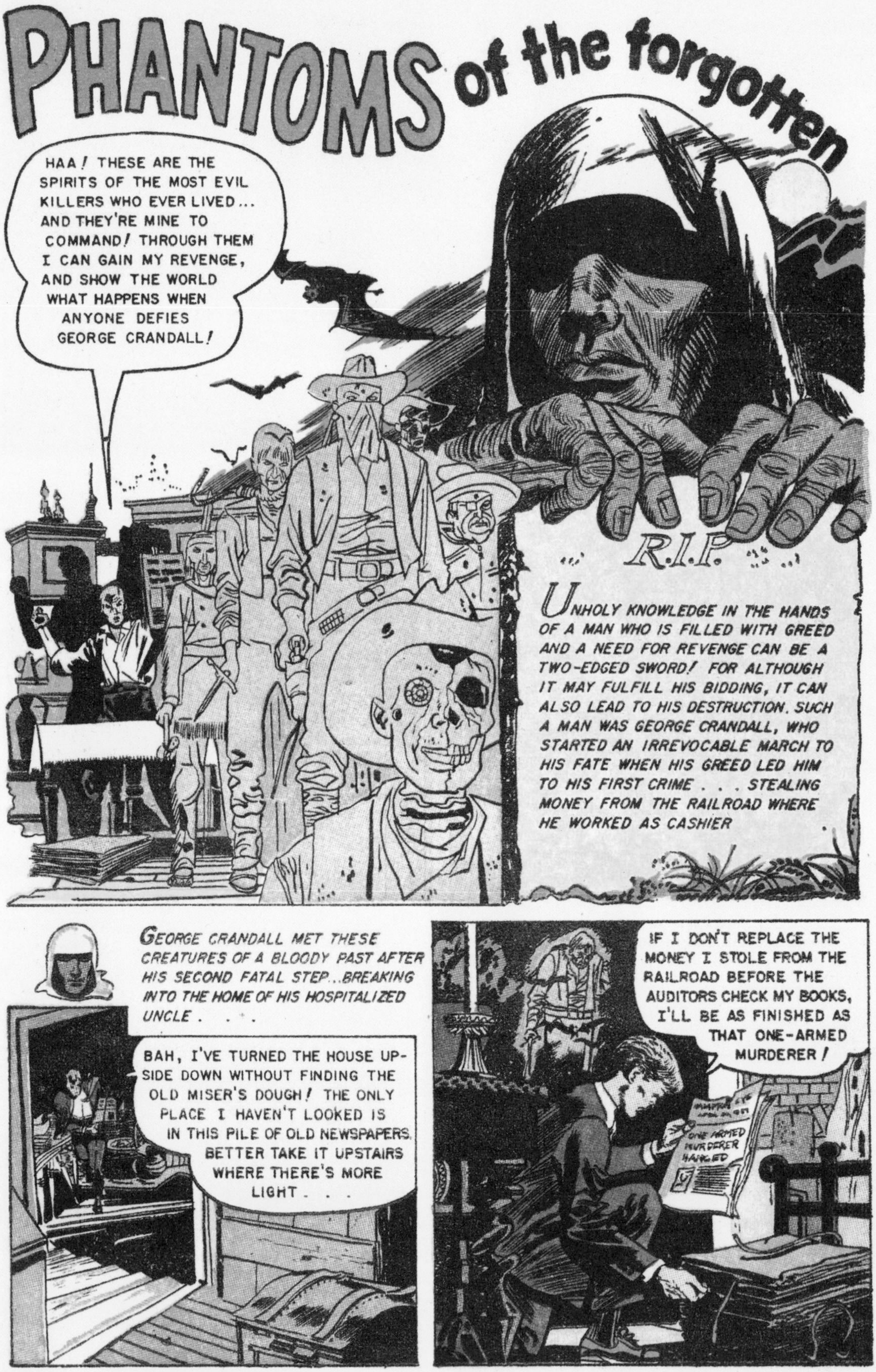
PHANTOMS of the forgotten
HAA! THESE ARE THE SPIRITS OF THE MOST EVIL KILLERS WHO EVER LIVED... AND THEY'RE MINE TO COMMAND! THROUGH THEM I CAN GAIN MY REVENGE, AND SHOW THE WORLD WHAT HAPPENS WHEN ANYONE DEFIES GEORGE CRANDALL!
R.I.P.
UNHOLY KNOWLEDGE IN THE HANDS OF A MAN WHO IS FILLED WITH GREED AND A NEED FOR REVENGE CAN BE A TWO-EDGED SWORD! FOR ALTHOUGH IT MAY FULFILL HIS BIDDING, IT CAN ALSO LEAD TO HIS DESTRUCTION. SUCH A MAN WAS GEORGE CRANDALL, WHO STARTED AN IRREVOCABLE MARCH TO HIS FATE WHEN HIS GREED LED HIM TO HIS FIRST CRIME . . . STEALING MONEY FROM THE RAILROAD WHERE HE WORKED AS CASHIER
GEORGE CRANDALL MET THESE CREATURES OF A BLOODY PAST AFTER HIS SECOND FATAL STEP...BREAKING INTO THE HOME OF HIS HOSPITALIZED UNCLE . . .
BAH, I'VE TURNED THE HOUSE UPSIDE DOWN WITHOUT FINDING THE OLD MISER'S DOUGH! THE ONLY PLACE I HAVEN'T LOOKED IS IN THIS PILE OF OLD NEWSPAPERS. BETTER TAKE IT UPSTAIRS WHERE THERE'S MORE LIGHT . . .
IF I DON'T REPLACE THE MONEY I STOLE FROM THE RAILROAD BEFORE THE AUDITORS CHECK MY BOOKS, I'LL BE AS FINISHED AS THAT ONE-ARMED MURDERER!
ONE ARMED MURDERER HANGED

Hand of Fate #21, December 1953. Louis Zansky. Ace Magazines.

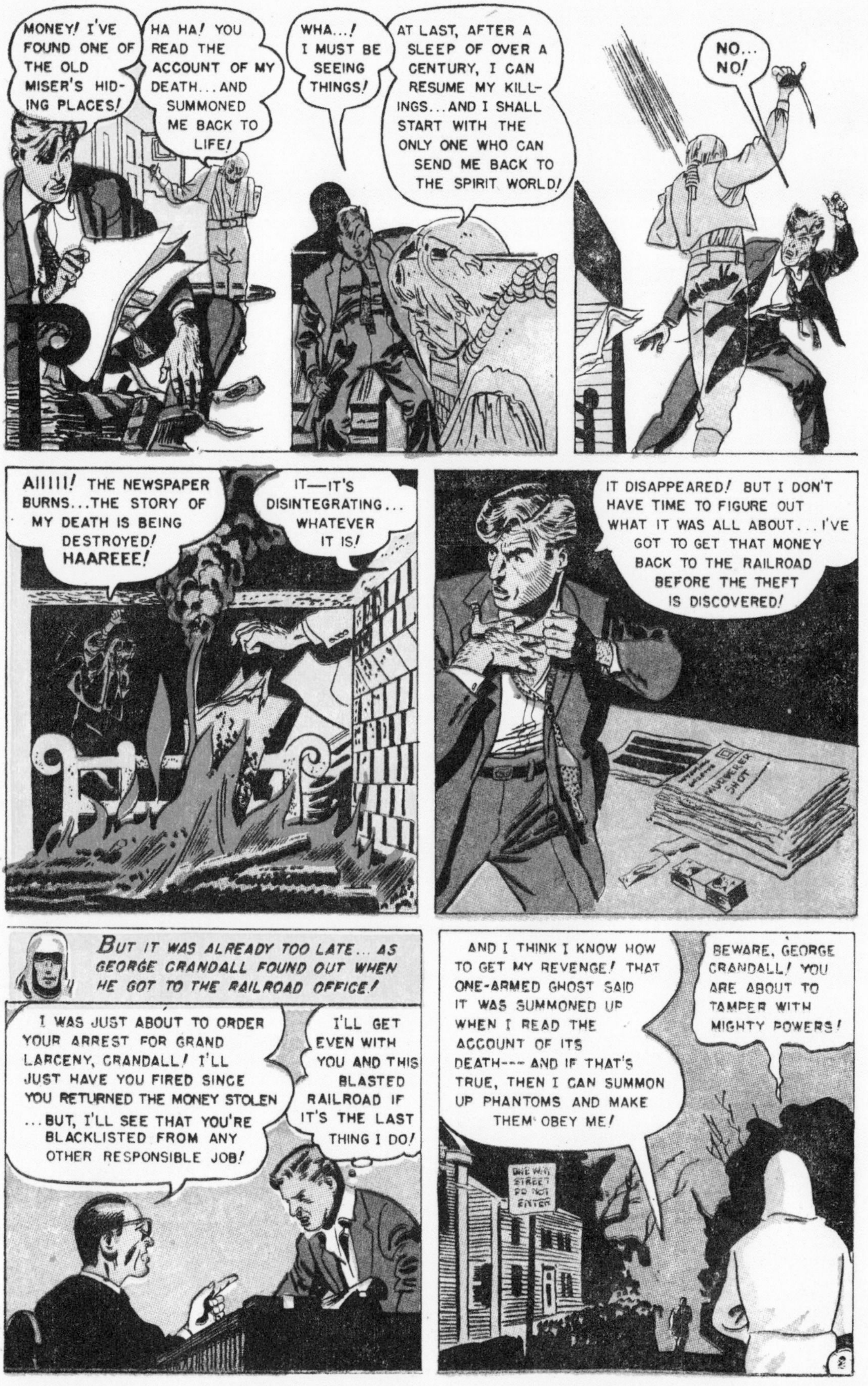

MONEY! I'VE FOUND ONE OF THE OLD MISER'S HID-ING PLACES!
HA HA! YOU READ THE ACCOUNT OF MY DEATH... AND SUMMONED ME BACK TO LIFE!
WHA...! I MUST BE SEEING THINGS!
AT LAST, AFTER A SLEEP OF OVER A CENTURY, I CAN RESUME MY KILL-INGS... AND I SHALL START WITH THE ONLY ONE WHO CAN SEND ME BACK TO THE SPIRIT WORLD!
NO... NO!
AIIIII! THE NEWSPAPER BURNS... THE STORY OF MY DEATH IS BEING DESTROYED! HAAREEE!
IT—IT'S DISINTEGRATING... WHATEVER IT IS!
IT DISAPPEARED! BUT I DON'T HAVE TIME TO FIGURE OUT WHAT IT WAS ALL ABOUT... I'VE GOT TO GET THAT MONEY BACK TO THE RAILROAD BEFORE THE THEFT IS DISCOVERED!
BUT IT WAS ALREADY TOO LATE... AS GEORGE CRANDALL FOUND OUT WHEN HE GOT TO THE RAILROAD OFFICE!
I WAS JUST ABOUT TO ORDER YOUR ARREST FOR GRAND LARCENY, CRANDALL! I'LL JUST HAVE YOU FIRED SINCE YOU RETURNED THE MONEY STOLEN ... BUT, I'LL SEE THAT YOU'RE BLACKLISTED FROM ANY OTHER RESPONSIBLE JOB!
I'LL GET EVEN WITH YOU AND THIS BLASTED RAILROAD IF IT'S THE LAST THING I DO!
AND I THINK I KNOW HOW TO GET MY REVENGE! THAT ONE-ARMED GHOST SAID IT WAS SUMMONED UP WHEN I READ THE ACCOUNT OF ITS DEATH--- AND IF THAT'S TRUE, THEN I CAN SUMMON UP PHANTOMS AND MAKE THEM OBEY ME!
BEWARE, GEORGE CRANDALL! YOU ARE ABOUT TO TAMPER WITH MIGHTY POWERS!
ONE WAY STREET DO NOT ENTER

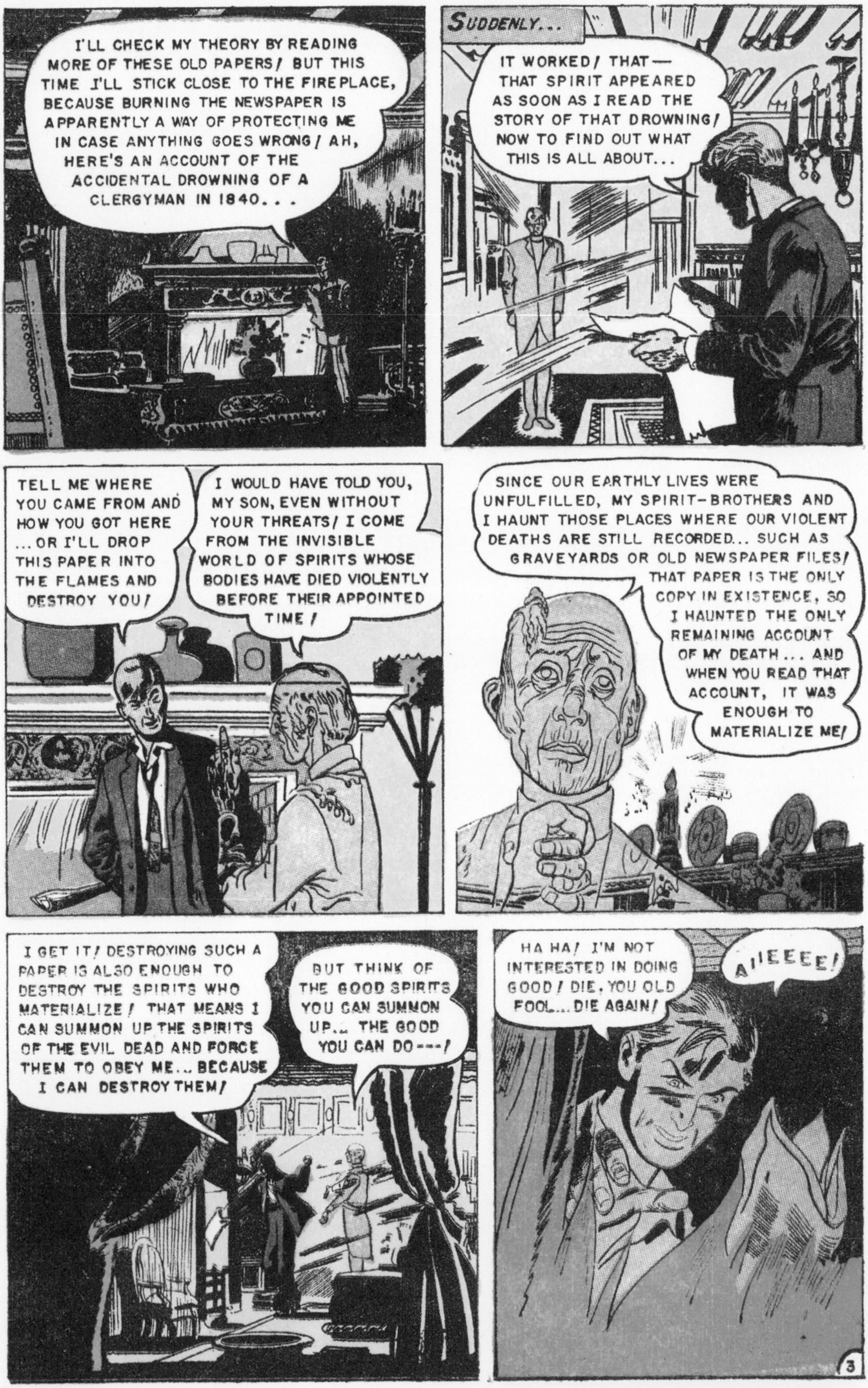
I'LL CHECK MY THEORY BY READING MORE OF THESE OLD PAPERS! BUT THIS TIME I'LL STICK CLOSE TO THE FIREPLACE, BECAUSE BURNING THE NEWSPAPER IS APPARENTLY A WAY OF PROTECTING ME IN CASE ANYTHING GOES WRONG! AH, HERE'S AN ACCOUNT OF THE ACCIDENTAL DROWNING OF A CLERGYMAN IN 1840. . .
SUDDENLY...
IT WORKED! THAT— THAT SPIRIT APPEARED AS SOON AS I READ THE STORY OF THAT DROWNING! NOW TO FIND OUT WHAT THIS IS ALL ABOUT...
TELL ME WHERE YOU CAME FROM AND HOW YOU GOT HERE ...OR I'LL DROP THIS PAPER INTO THE FLAMES AND DESTROY YOU!
I WOULD HAVE TOLD YOU, MY SON, EVEN WITHOUT YOUR THREATS! I COME FROM THE INVISIBLE WORLD OF SPIRITS WHOSE BODIES HAVE DIED VIOLENTLY BEFORE THEIR APPOINTED TIME!
SINCE OUR EARTHLY LIVES WERE UNFULFILLED, MY SPIRIT-BROTHERS AND I HAUNT THOSE PLACES WHERE OUR VIOLENT DEATHS ARE STILL RECORDED... SUCH AS GRAVEYARDS OR OLD NEWSPAPER FILES! THAT PAPER IS THE ONLY COPY IN EXISTENCE, SO I HAUNTED THE ONLY REMAINING ACCOUNT OF MY DEATH ... AND WHEN YOU READ THAT ACCOUNT, IT WAS ENOUGH TO MATERIALIZE ME!
I GET IT! DESTROYING SUCH A PAPER IS ALSO ENOUGH TO DESTROY THE SPIRITS WHO MATERIALIZE! THAT MEANS I CAN SUMMON UP THE SPIRITS OF THE EVIL DEAD AND FORCE THEM TO OBEY ME... BECAUSE I CAN DESTROY THEM!
BUT THINK OF THE GOOD SPIRITS YOU CAN SUMMON UP... THE GOOD YOU CAN DO---!
HA HA! I'M NOT INTERESTED IN DOING GOOD! DIE, YOU OLD FOOL... DIE AGAIN!
AIIEEEE!
3

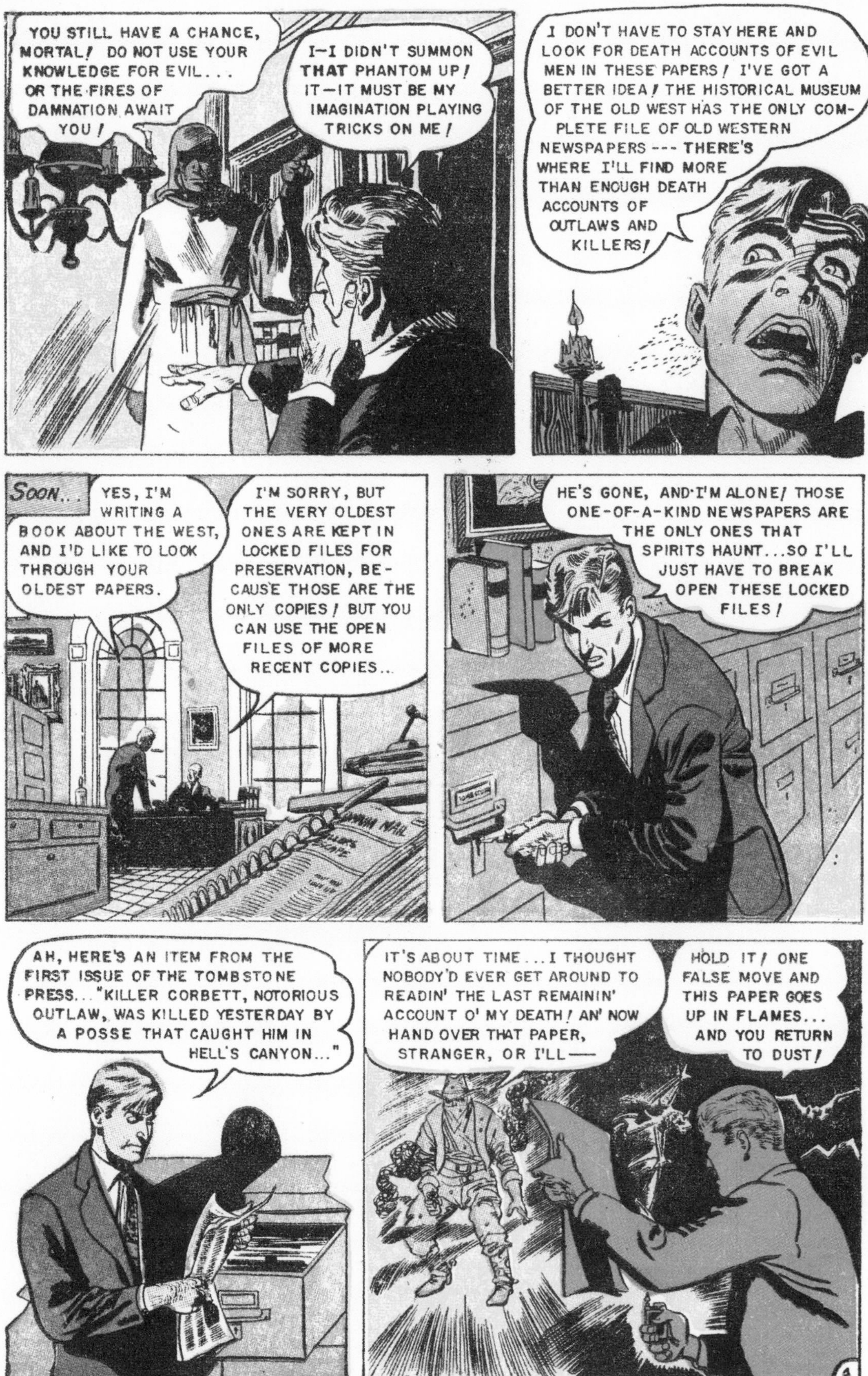
YOU STILL HAVE A CHANCE, MORTAL! DO NOT USE YOUR KNOWLEDGE FOR EVIL... OR THE FIRES OF DAMNATION AWAIT YOU!
I—I DIDN'T SUMMON THAT PHANTOM UP! IT—IT MUST BE MY IMAGINATION PLAYING TRICKS ON ME!
I DON'T HAVE TO STAY HERE AND LOOK FOR DEATH ACCOUNTS OF EVIL MEN IN THESE PAPERS! I'VE GOT A BETTER IDEA! THE HISTORICAL MUSEUM OF THE OLD WEST HAS THE ONLY COMPLETE FILE OF OLD WESTERN NEWSPAPERS --- THERE'S WHERE I'LL FIND MORE THAN ENOUGH DEATH ACCOUNTS OF OUTLAWS AND KILLERS!
SOON...
YES, I'M WRITING A BOOK ABOUT THE WEST, AND I'D LIKE TO LOOK THROUGH YOUR OLDEST PAPERS.
I'M SORRY, BUT THE VERY OLDEST ONES ARE KEPT IN LOCKED FILES FOR PRESERVATION, BECAUSE THOSE ARE THE ONLY COPIES! BUT YOU CAN USE THE OPEN FILES OF MORE RECENT COPIES...
HE'S GONE, AND I'M ALONE! THOSE ONE-OF-A-KIND NEWSPAPERS ARE THE ONLY ONES THAT SPIRITS HAUNT...SO I'LL JUST HAVE TO BREAK OPEN THESE LOCKED FILES!
AH, HERE'S AN ITEM FROM THE FIRST ISSUE OF THE TOMBSTONE PRESS..."KILLER CORBETT, NOTORIOUS OUTLAW, WAS KILLED YESTERDAY BY A POSSE THAT CAUGHT HIM IN HELL'S CANYON..."
IT'S ABOUT TIME...I THOUGHT NOBODY'D EVER GET AROUND TO READIN' THE LAST REMAININ' ACCOUNT O' MY DEATH! AN' NOW HAND OVER THAT PAPER, STRANGER, OR I'LL—
HOLD IT! ONE FALSE MOVE AND THIS PAPER GOES UP IN FLAMES... AND YOU RETURN TO DUST!
4

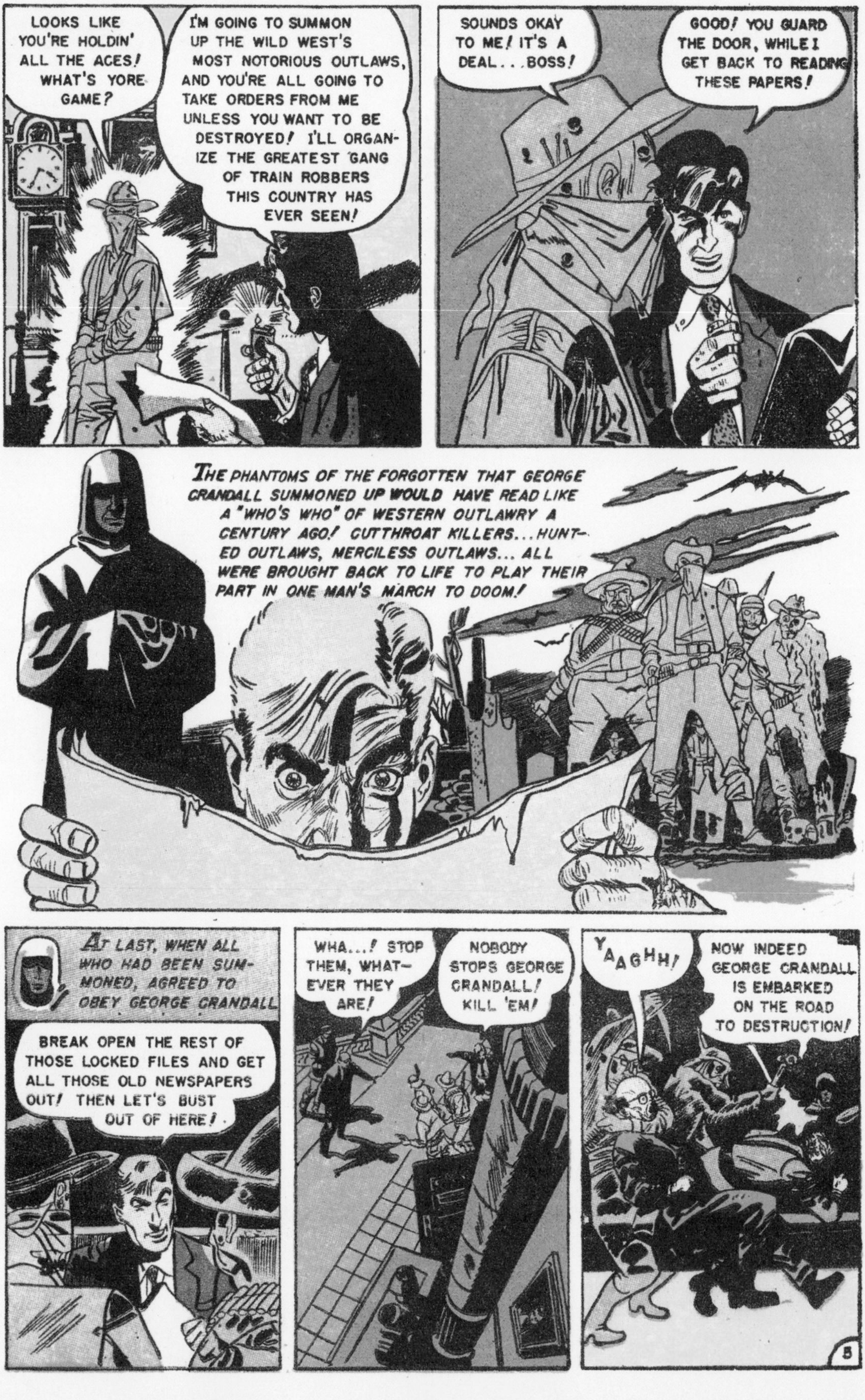

LOOKS LIKE YOU'RE HOLDIN' ALL THE ACES! WHAT'S YORE GAME?
I'M GOING TO SUMMON UP THE WILD WEST'S MOST NOTORIOUS OUTLAWS, AND YOU'RE ALL GOING TO TAKE ORDERS FROM ME UNLESS YOU WANT TO BE DESTROYED! I'LL ORGANIZE THE GREATEST GANG OF TRAIN ROBBERS THIS COUNTRY HAS EVER SEEN!
SOUNDS OKAY TO ME! IT'S A DEAL...BOSS!
GOOD! YOU GUARD THE DOOR, WHILE I GET BACK TO READING THESE PAPERS!
THE PHANTOMS OF THE FORGOTTEN THAT GEORGE CRANDALL SUMMONED UP WOULD HAVE READ LIKE A "WHO'S WHO" OF WESTERN OUTLAWRY A CENTURY AGO! CUTTHROAT KILLERS...HUNTED OUTLAWS, MERCILESS OUTLAWS... ALL WERE BROUGHT BACK TO LIFE TO PLAY THEIR PART IN ONE MAN'S MARCH TO DOOM!
AT LAST, WHEN ALL WHO HAD BEEN SUMMONED, AGREED TO OBEY GEORGE CRANDALL
BREAK OPEN THE REST OF THOSE LOCKED FILES AND GET ALL THOSE OLD NEWSPAPERS OUT! THEN LET'S BUST OUT OF HERE!
WHA...! STOP THEM, WHATEVER THEY ARE!
NOBODY STOPS GEORGE CRANDALL! KILL 'EM!
YAAGHH!
NOW INDEED GEORGE CRANDALL IS EMBARKED ON THE ROAD TO DESTRUCTION!
5

LATER, IN A RENTED HOUSE IN A SECLUDED NEIGHBORHOOD...

OKAY, YOU'VE ALL GOT YOUR ORDERS! HIT THAT RAILROAD... AND KEEP HITTING IT UNTIL IT'S SMASHED!

WE'VE GOT PLENTY OF EXPERIENCE, BOSS! JEST LEAVE IT TO US!

SOON...

OUR BULLETS GO RIGHT THROUGH THOSE DEVILS--- AARGHH!

BANG!

BANG!?

BANG!

U.S. MAIL

U.S. MAIL

AGAIN AND AGAIN THE PHANTOMS FROM THE PAST STRUCK... IN A FIENDISH ORGY OF MURDER AND MAYHEM!

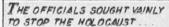
THE OFFICIALS SOUGHT VAINLY TO STOP THE HOLOCAUST...

GENTLEMEN, IF THESE RAIDS AGAINST OUR RAILROAD DON'T STOP, WE'LL BE RUINED!

BUT WHAT CAN WE DO AGAINST THOSE FIENDS FROM THE GRAVE? HOW CAN YOU KILL THE DEAD!

BUT GEORGE CRANDALL'S EVIL KNEW NO BOUNDS...

I'VE GOT A FORTUNE IN LOOT FROM THE RAIDS, BUT I WANT TO SEE THAT RAILROAD BANKRUPT BEFORE I TURN MY ATTENTION ELSEWHERE! THINK I'LL SUMMON UP SOME MORE SPIRITS...

I WARN YOU, MORTAL---DO NOT READ THAT NEWSPAPER!

YOU AGAIN! I DON'T KNOW WHO OR WHAT YOU ARE... BUT THERE MUST BE SOMETHING MIGHTY USEFUL TO ME IN THIS PAPER IF YOU DON'T WANT ME TO READ IT!

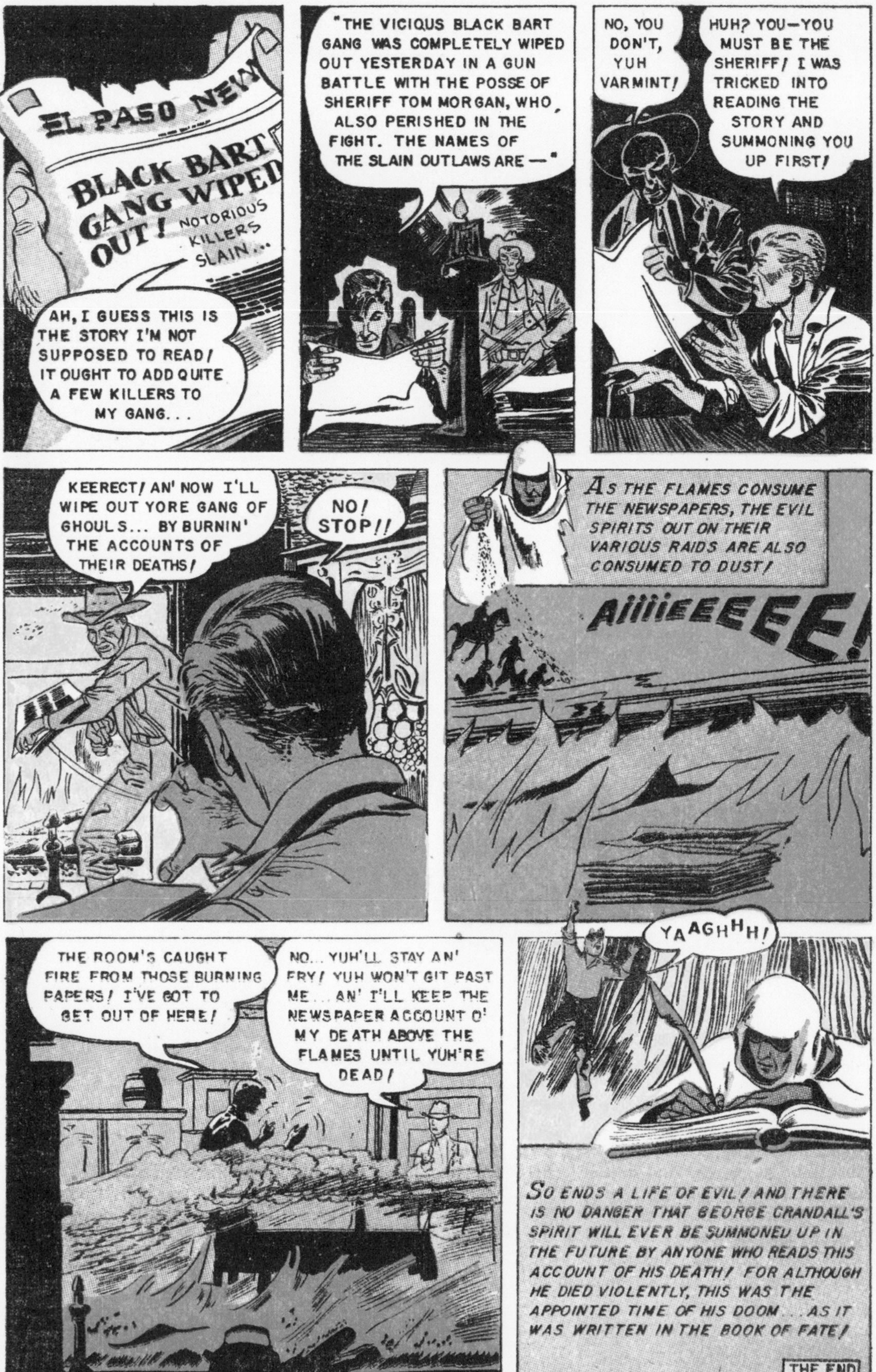
EL PASO NEWS
BLACK BART GANG WIPED OUT! NOTORIOUS KILLERS SLAIN...
AH, I GUESS THIS IS THE STORY I'M NOT SUPPOSED TO READ! IT OUGHT TO ADD QUITE A FEW KILLERS TO MY GANG...
"THE VICIOUS BLACK BART GANG WAS COMPLETELY WIPED OUT YESTERDAY IN A GUN BATTLE WITH THE POSSE OF SHERIFF TOM MORGAN, WHO ALSO PERISHED IN THE FIGHT. THE NAMES OF THE SLAIN OUTLAWS ARE —"
NO, YOU DON'T, YUH VARMINT!
HUH? YOU—YOU MUST BE THE SHERIFF! I WAS TRICKED INTO READING THE STORY AND SUMMONING YOU UP FIRST!
KEERECT! AN' NOW I'LL WIPE OUT YORE GANG OF GHOULS... BY BURNIN' THE ACCOUNTS OF THEIR DEATHS!
NO! STOP!!
AS THE FLAMES CONSUME THE NEWSPAPERS, THE EVIL SPIRITS OUT ON THEIR VARIOUS RAIDS ARE ALSO CONSUMED TO DUST!
AIIIIEEEEEE!
THE ROOM'S CAUGHT FIRE FROM THOSE BURNING PAPERS! I'VE GOT TO GET OUT OF HERE!
NO... YUH'LL STAY AN' FRY! YUH WON'T GIT PAST ME... AN' I'LL KEEP THE NEWSPAPER ACCOUNT O' MY DEATH ABOVE THE FLAMES UNTIL YUH'RE DEAD!
YAAGHHH!
SO ENDS A LIFE OF EVIL! AND THERE IS NO DANGER THAT GEORGE CRANDALL'S SPIRIT WILL EVER BE SUMMONED UP IN THE FUTURE BY ANYONE WHO READS THIS ACCOUNT OF HIS DEATH! FOR ALTHOUGH HE DIED VIOLENTLY, THIS WAS THE APPOINTED TIME OF HIS DOOM... AS IT WAS WRITTEN IN THE BOOK OF FATE!
THE END

JAROD PARKS KILLED THE BEAUTIFUL DANCER, MONA TRAVIS! HE LAUGHED WHEN THE PHANTOM OF THE DEAD GIRL TRIED TO HAUNT HIM, THREATENING HIM WITH A FATE MOST HORRIBLE! ONLY AFTER JAROD PARKS HIMSELF HAD DIED, DID HE REALIZE THAT AHEAD OF HIM LAY...

THE GHOST'S CURSE!

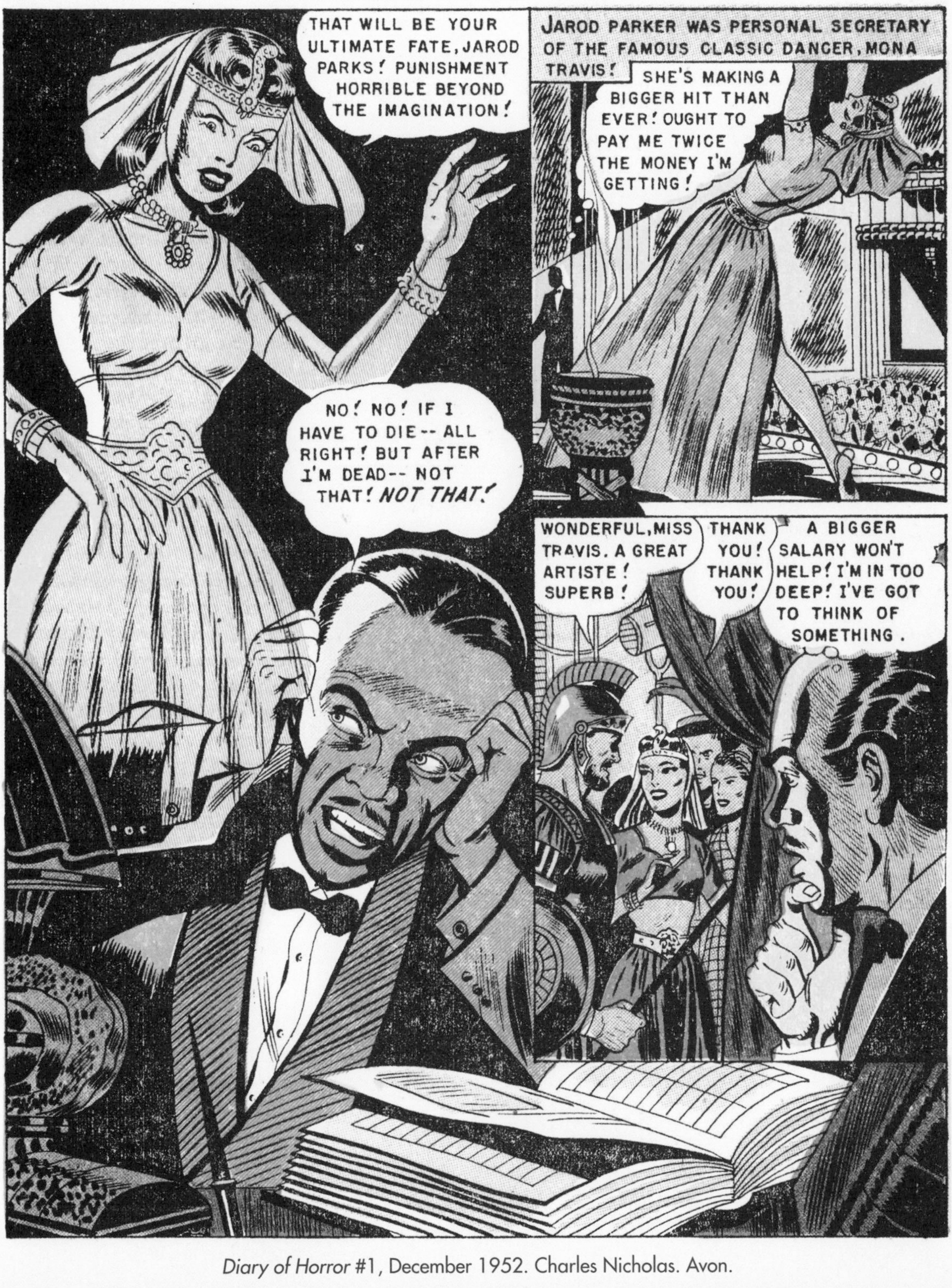

THAT WILL BE YOUR ULTIMATE FATE, JAROD PARKS! PUNISHMENT HORRIBLE BEYOND THE IMAGINATION!
NO! NO! IF I HAVE TO DIE -- ALL RIGHT! BUT AFTER I'M DEAD -- NOT THAT! NOT THAT!
JAROD PARKER WAS PERSONAL SECRETARY OF THE FAMOUS CLASSIC DANCER, MONA TRAVIS!
SHE'S MAKING A BIGGER HIT THAN EVER! OUGHT TO PAY ME TWICE THE MONEY I'M GETTING!
WONDERFUL, MISS TRAVIS. A GREAT ARTISTE! SUPERB!
THANK YOU! THANK YOU!
A BIGGER SALARY WON'T HELP! I'M IN TOO DEEP! I'VE GOT TO THINK OF SOMETHING.

Diary of Horror #1, December 1952. Charles Nicholas. Avon.

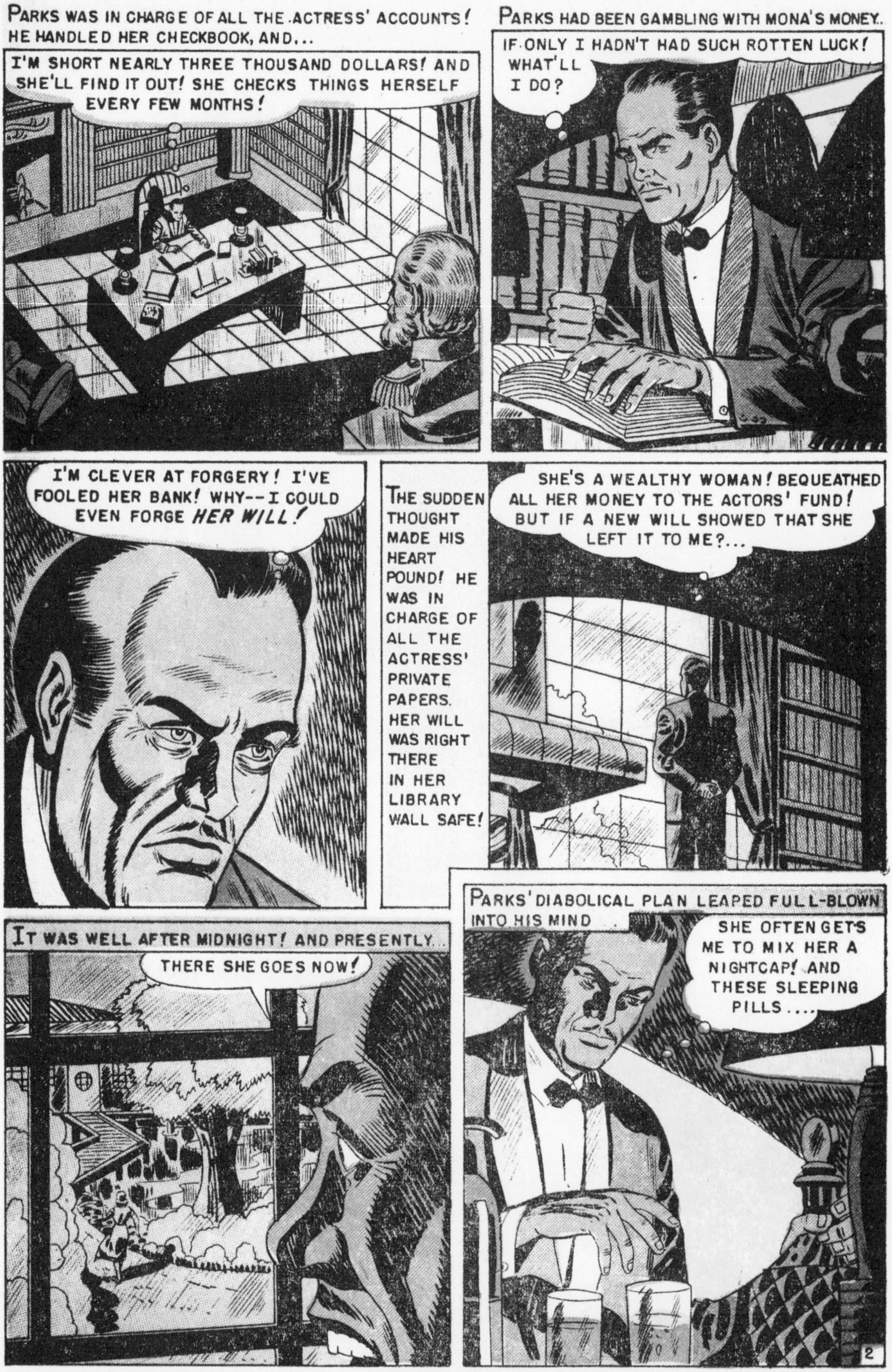

PARKS WAS IN CHARGE OF ALL THE ACTRESS' ACCOUNTS! HE HANDLED HER CHECKBOOK, AND...
I'M SHORT NEARLY THREE THOUSAND DOLLARS! AND SHE'LL FIND IT OUT! SHE CHECKS THINGS HERSELF EVERY FEW MONTHS!
PARKS HAD BEEN GAMBLING WITH MONA'S MONEY..
IF ONLY I HADN'T HAD SUCH ROTTEN LUCK! WHAT'LL I DO?
I'M CLEVER AT FORGERY! I'VE FOOLED HER BANK! WHY--I COULD EVEN FORGE HER WILL!
THE SUDDEN THOUGHT MADE HIS HEART POUND! HE WAS IN CHARGE OF ALL THE ACTRESS' PRIVATE PAPERS. HER WILL WAS RIGHT THERE IN HER LIBRARY WALL SAFE!
SHE'S A WEALTHY WOMAN! BEQUEATHED ALL HER MONEY TO THE ACTORS' FUND! BUT IF A NEW WILL SHOWED THAT SHE LEFT IT TO ME?...
IT WAS WELL AFTER MIDNIGHT! AND PRESENTLY..
THERE SHE GOES NOW!
PARKS' DIABOLICAL PLAN LEAPED FULL-BLOWN INTO HIS MIND
SHE OFTEN GETS ME TO MIX HER A NIGHTCAP! AND THESE SLEEPING PILLS....
2

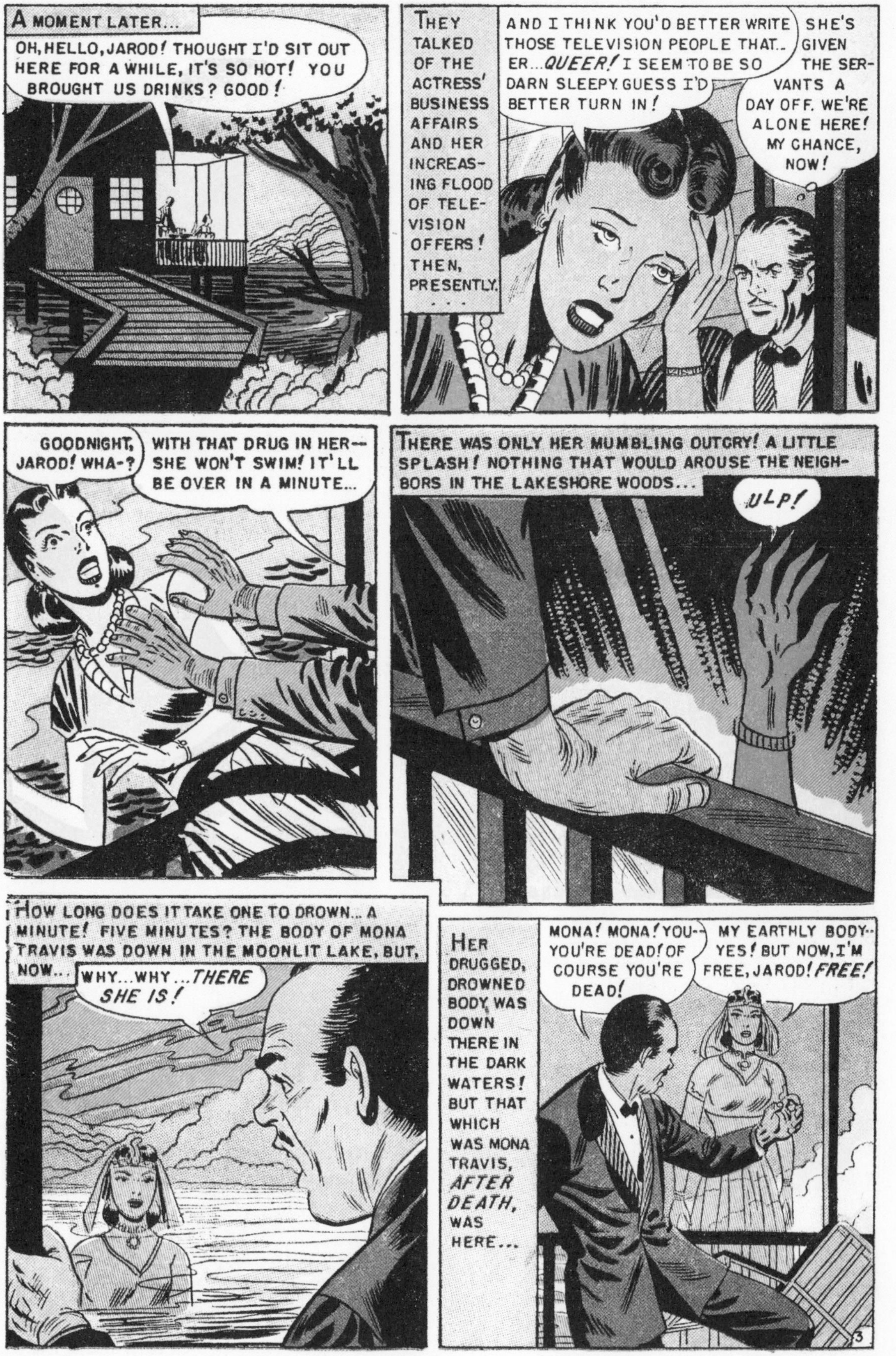

A MOMENT LATER...
OH, HELLO, JAROD! THOUGHT I'D SIT OUT HERE FOR A WHILE, IT'S SO HOT! YOU BROUGHT US DRINKS? GOOD!
THEY TALKED OF THE ACTRESS' BUSINESS AFFAIRS AND HER INCREASING FLOOD OF TELEVISION OFFERS! THEN, PRESENTLY...
AND I THINK YOU'D BETTER WRITE THOSE TELEVISION PEOPLE THAT.. ER... QUEER! I SEEM TO BE SO DARN SLEEPY. GUESS I'D BETTER TURN IN!
SHE'S GIVEN THE SERVANTS A DAY OFF. WE'RE ALONE HERE! MY CHANCE, NOW!
GOODNIGHT, JAROD! WHA-?
WITH THAT DRUG IN HER-- SHE WON'T SWIM! IT'LL BE OVER IN A MINUTE...
THERE WAS ONLY HER MUMBLING OUTCRY! A LITTLE SPLASH! NOTHING THAT WOULD AROUSE THE NEIGHBORS IN THE LAKESHORE WOODS...
ULP!
HOW LONG DOES IT TAKE ONE TO DROWN... A MINUTE! FIVE MINUTES? THE BODY OF MONA TRAVIS WAS DOWN IN THE MOONLIT LAKE, BUT, NOW...
WHY... WHY... THERE SHE IS!
HER DRUGGED, DROWNED BODY WAS DOWN THERE IN THE DARK WATERS! BUT THAT WHICH WAS MONA TRAVIS, AFTER DEATH, WAS HERE...
MONA! MONA! YOU-- YOU'RE DEAD! OF COURSE YOU'RE DEAD!
MY EARTHLY BODY-- YES! BUT NOW, I'M FREE, JAROD! FREE!
3

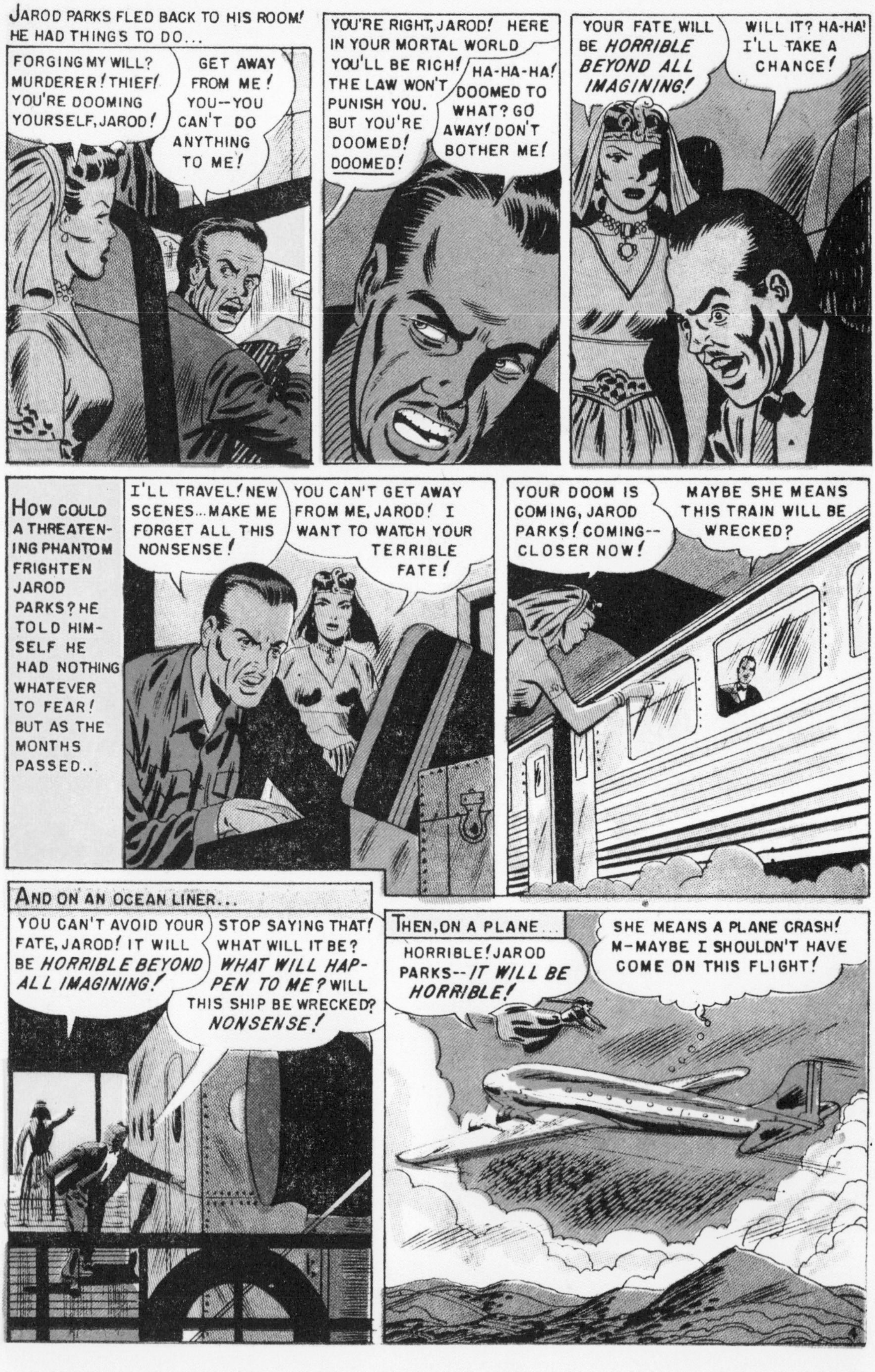
JAROD PARKS FLED BACK TO HIS ROOM! HE HAD THINGS TO DO...
FORGING MY WILL? MURDERER! THIEF! YOU'RE DOOMING YOURSELF, JAROD!
GET AWAY FROM ME! YOU--YOU CAN'T DO ANYTHING TO ME!
YOU'RE RIGHT, JAROD! HERE IN YOUR MORTAL WORLD YOU'LL BE RICH! THE LAW WON'T PUNISH YOU. BUT YOU'RE DOOMED! DOOMED!
HA-HA-HA! DOOMED TO WHAT? GO AWAY! DON'T BOTHER ME!
YOUR FATE WILL BE HORRIBLE BEYOND ALL IMAGINING!
WILL IT? HA-HA! I'LL TAKE A CHANCE!
HOW COULD A THREATENING PHANTOM FRIGHTEN JAROD PARKS? HE TOLD HIMSELF HE HAD NOTHING WHATEVER TO FEAR! BUT AS THE MONTHS PASSED..
I'LL TRAVEL! NEW SCENES...MAKE ME FORGET ALL THIS NONSENSE!
YOU CAN'T GET AWAY FROM ME, JAROD! I WANT TO WATCH YOUR TERRIBLE FATE!
YOUR DOOM IS COMING, JAROD PARKS! COMING--CLOSER NOW!
MAYBE SHE MEANS THIS TRAIN WILL BE WRECKED?
AND ON AN OCEAN LINER...
YOU CAN'T AVOID YOUR FATE, JAROD! IT WILL BE HORRIBLE BEYOND ALL IMAGINING!
STOP SAYING THAT! WHAT WILL IT BE? WHAT WILL HAPPEN TO ME? WILL THIS SHIP BE WRECKED? NONSENSE!
THEN, ON A PLANE...
HORRIBLE! JAROD PARKS--IT WILL BE HORRIBLE!
SHE MEANS A PLANE CRASH! M-MAYBE I SHOULDN'T HAVE COME ON THIS FLIGHT!

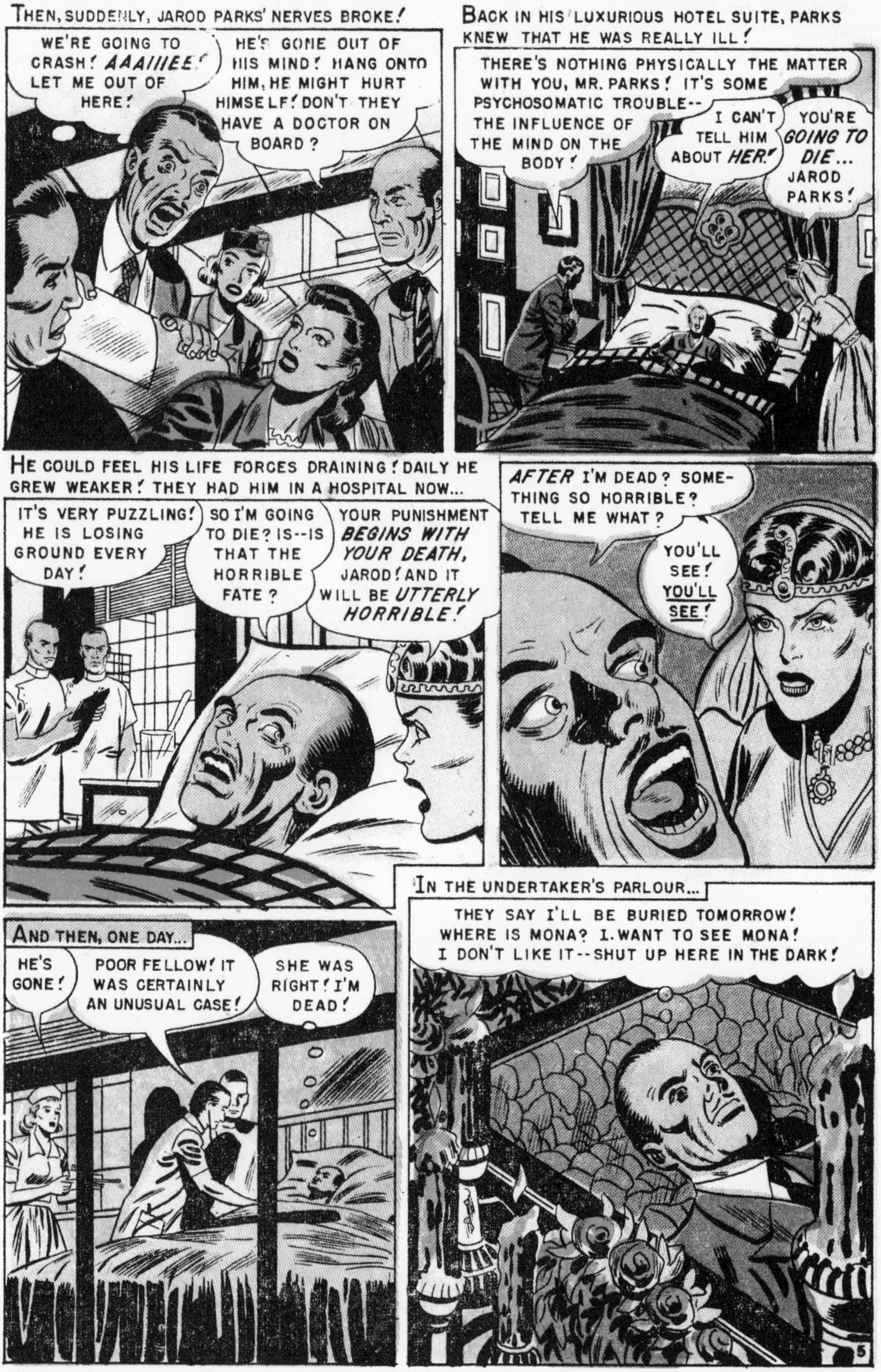
THEN, SUDDENLY, JAROD PARKS' NERVES BROKE!
WE'RE GOING TO CRASH! AAAIIIEE! LET ME OUT OF HERE!
HE'S GONE OUT OF HIS MIND! HANG ONTO HIM, HE MIGHT HURT HIMSELF! DON'T THEY HAVE A DOCTOR ON BOARD?
BACK IN HIS LUXURIOUS HOTEL SUITE, PARKS KNEW THAT HE WAS REALLY ILL!
THERE'S NOTHING PHYSICALLY THE MATTER WITH YOU, MR. PARKS! IT'S SOME PSYCHOSOMATIC TROUBLE-- THE INFLUENCE OF THE MIND ON THE BODY!
I CAN'T TELL HIM ABOUT HER!
YOU'RE GOING TO DIE... JAROD PARKS!
HE COULD FEEL HIS LIFE FORCES DRAINING! DAILY HE GREW WEAKER! THEY HAD HIM IN A HOSPITAL NOW...
IT'S VERY PUZZLING! HE IS LOSING GROUND EVERY DAY!
SO I'M GOING TO DIE? IS--IS THAT THE HORRIBLE FATE?
YOUR PUNISHMENT BEGINS WITH YOUR DEATH, JAROD! AND IT WILL BE UTTERLY HORRIBLE!
AFTER I'M DEAD? SOMETHING SO HORRIBLE? TELL ME WHAT?
YOU'LL SEE! YOU'LL SEE!
AND THEN, ONE DAY...
HE'S GONE!
POOR FELLOW! IT WAS CERTAINLY AN UNUSUAL CASE!
SHE WAS RIGHT! I'M DEAD!
IN THE UNDERTAKER'S PARLOUR...
THEY SAY I'LL BE BURIED TOMORROW! WHERE IS MONA? I WANT TO SEE MONA! I DON'T LIKE IT--SHUT UP HERE IN THE DARK!
5

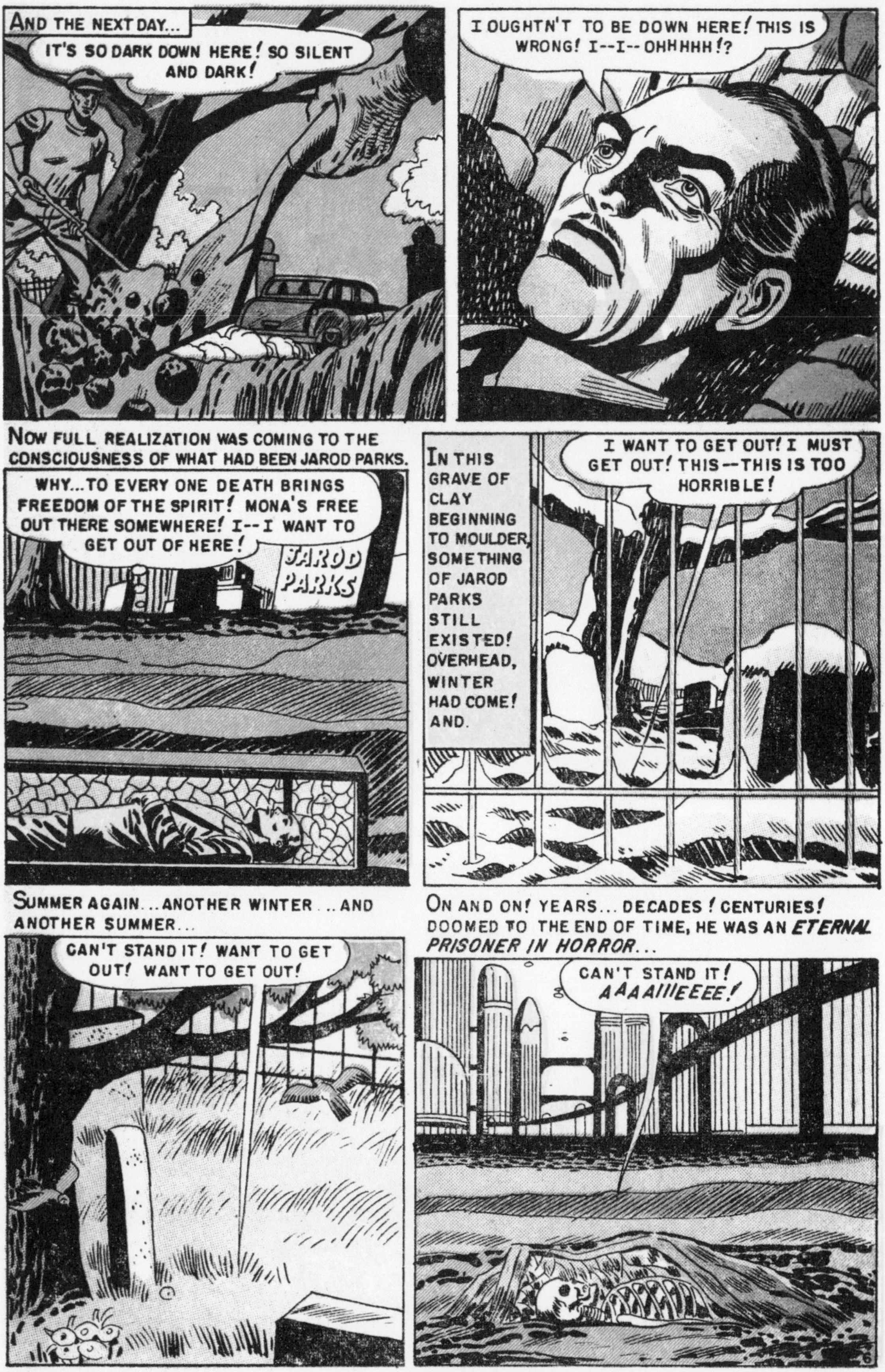

AND THE NEXT DAY...
IT'S SO DARK DOWN HERE! SO SILENT AND DARK!
I OUGHTN'T TO BE DOWN HERE! THIS IS WRONG! I--I--OHHHHH!?
NOW FULL REALIZATION WAS COMING TO THE CONSCIOUSNESS OF WHAT HAD BEEN JAROD PARKS.
WHY...TO EVERY ONE DEATH BRINGS FREEDOM OF THE SPIRIT! MONA'S FREE OUT THERE SOMEWHERE! I-- I WANT TO GET OUT OF HERE!
JAROD PARKS
IN THIS GRAVE OF CLAY BEGINNING TO MOULDER, SOMETHING OF JAROD PARKS STILL EXISTED! OVERHEAD, WINTER HAD COME! AND.
I WANT TO GET OUT! I MUST GET OUT! THIS--THIS IS TOO HORRIBLE!
SUMMER AGAIN...ANOTHER WINTER...AND ANOTHER SUMMER...
CAN'T STAND IT! WANT TO GET OUT! WANT TO GET OUT!
ON AND ON! YEARS... DECADES! CENTURIES! DOOMED TO THE END OF TIME, HE WAS AN *ETERNAL PRISONER IN HORROR*...
CAN'T STAND IT! AAAAIIIEEEE!
6